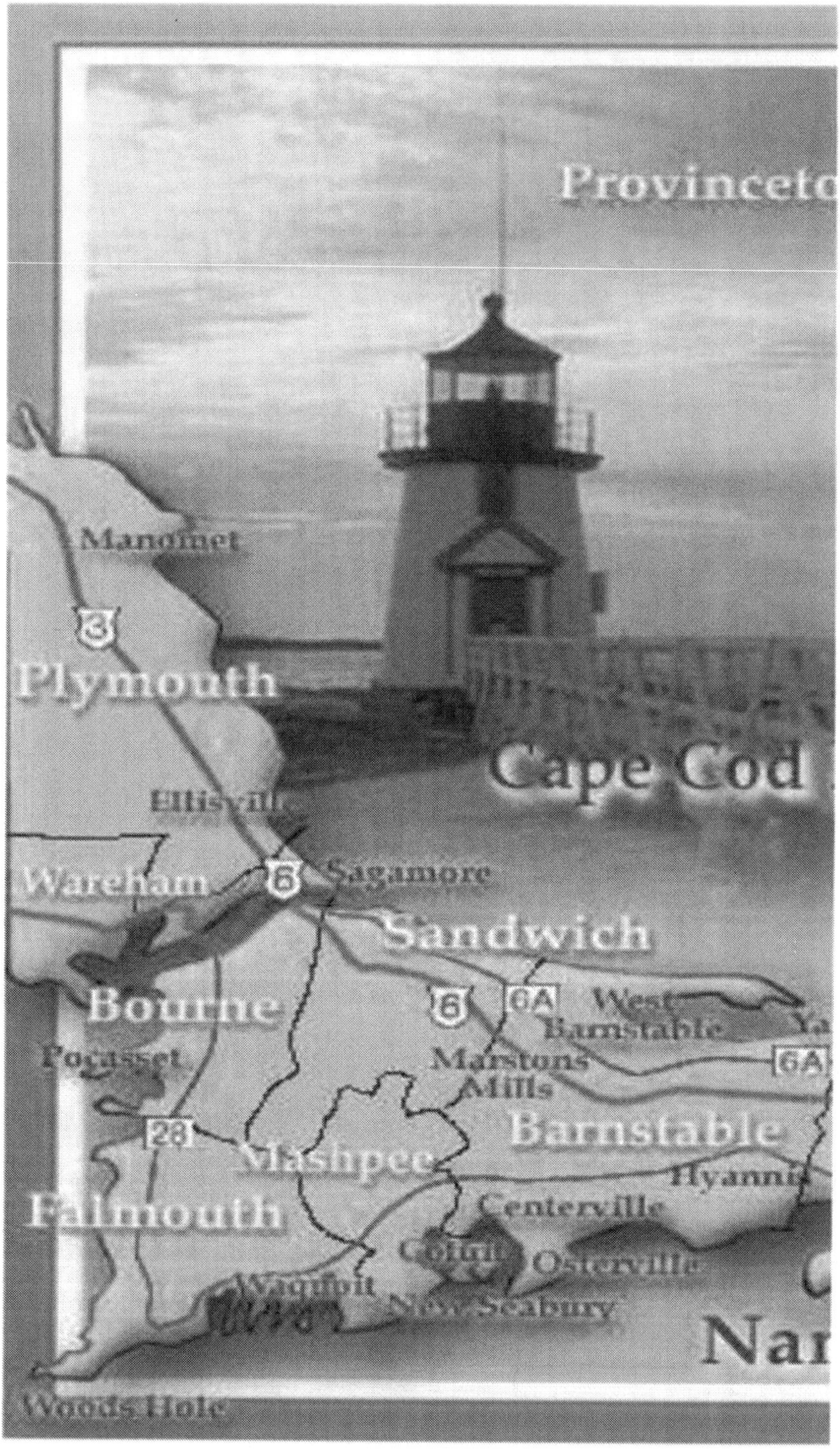

Manomet
Plymouth
Cape Cod
Ellisville
Wareham
Sagamore
Sandwich
Bourne
West
Barnstable
Pocasset
Marstons
Mills
Barnstable
Mashpee
Falmouth
Centerville
Osterville
New Seabury
Woods Hole

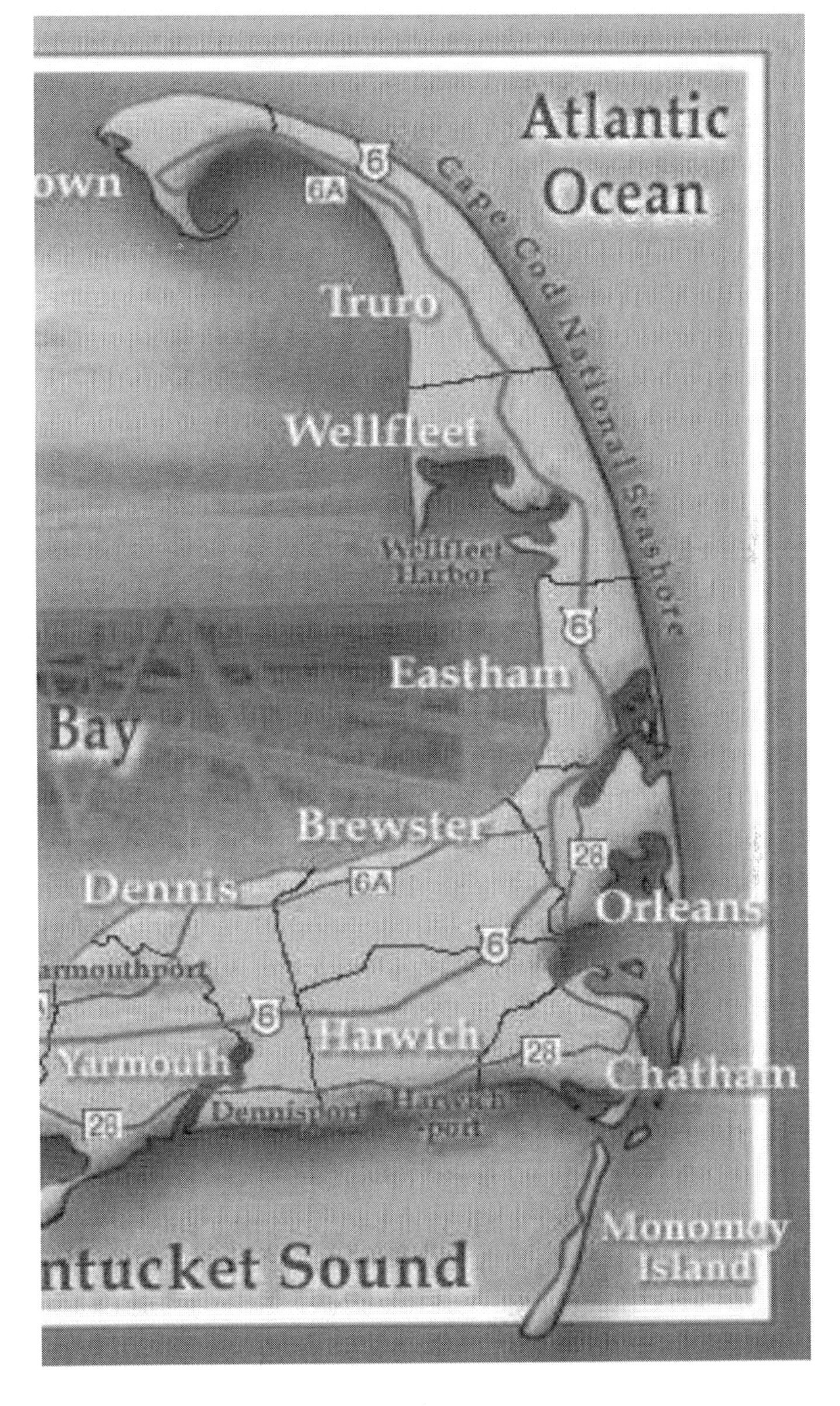
Atlantic
Ocean
Cape Cod National Seashore
own
6A
6
Truro
Wellfleet
Wellfleet
Harbor
6
Eastham
Bay
Brewster
28
Dennis
6A
Orleans
6
armouthport
6
Harwich
28
Yarmouth
Chatham
28
Dennisport
Harwich
port
Monomoy
Island
ntucket Sound

Paint Her Dead

A Casey Quinby Novel

By

Judi Ciance

To Barb —
Casey's on the move... again!
Judi Ciance
February 21, 2015

Paint Her Dead
By Judi Ciance
judiciance@gmail.com
Published: October, 2013

ISBN-13: 978-1492134121
ISBN—10: 1492134120

This is a work of fiction. Although some of the locations
Mentioned throughout the book are real, the characters, events
and situations are a product of the author's
Imagination

Also in the
Casey Quinby series:

Empty Rocker (November 2012)

Dedication

To my husband
Paul Ciance

*Without his patience, placidity,
perseverance and love of
Boston sports,
Casey Quinby
wouldn't be on the
move again.*

Acknowledgements

*This author wishes to thank
Beverly Blackwell and Diana Washburn.
It was through their
expertise and inspiration
that Casey found herself
involved in another
suspenseful and intriguing escapade.*

PAINT HER DEAD

CHAPTER ONE

Watson scurried across the back yard, running relay races with the squirrels who were trying to gather their winter stash.

I sat back in my rocking chair and sipped my French vanilla. It was nine o'clock, Saturday morning.

I live in paradise, lazing out on the deck taking in all the smells and sounds nature is dishing out. Cape Cod sure has its moments and this was definitely one of them. Summer is beautiful, but the fall is the best. I enjoy these rare days of relaxation.

My cell phone rang.

"Casey Quinby, you up?" was the question from the other end.

"If I wasn't, I am now—only kidding. What's happening?"

It was Marnie. She sounded far too chipper for nine o'clock, but something would be wrong if she was any other way.

"How did you do on the exams? Or should I say, how do you think you did? Do I have to call you Attorney Levine?" I knew she'd have to wait at least three weeks before she'd get formal notification.

"I don't want to jinx myself, but I think I did all right. I don't ever want to take them again though. Hey, listen, I was wondering if you and Annie would like to take a ride to Provincetown. I haven't talked to her yet, but Thursday when I left the office, she said she was just hanging around this weekend."

"I'm actually busy. As we speak, I can hear my laundry basket, vacuum cleaner, dust rag, and iron all calling my name in perfect harmony—like a barbershop quartet." I looked at the open back door and held my cell out for Marnie to listen. "Did you hear them?" I laughed. "They must have forgotten who they were singing to and how easily I can tune them out."

"Know what, I think you better tighten that screw that's loose in your head."

I pictured Marnie rolling her eyes and turning her hand mimicking a screwdriver in motion.

"Of course, I'd like to go. What time do you want to start this adventure?" I glanced at my Minnie Mouse watch.

"If we leave early, we can get the whole day in. How's ten-thirty sound?" Without skipping a beat she continued, "Let me call Annie and I'll call you right back."

Before I had a chance to answer, the phone went silent. If I didn't know better, I'd say the girl is on drugs.

I finished my coffee and figured I'd let Watson play some more while I decided what to wear. The part about the laundry basket calling me wasn't that far from reality. I'd slacked off for almost two weeks. *Oh well*, I thought, *what's another day*?

When Marnie refers to a whole day, she means it. For that reason, I think I'll wear a pair of jeans and a long sleeve jersey. I was searching for my white hoodie when my cell rang again.

"Just me," said Marnie. "Annie's in. She said, no problem, she could be ready by ten-thirty. In fact, she said she'd drive."

"Why don't I meet you guys at your house, then she won't have to backtrack to pick me up," I said.

"Sounds like a plan. I'll call her to let her know. See you in a little while." And again she was gone.

I still had plenty of time after I finished my shower and got dressed. Watson was lying down outside the back door. I guess the squirrels gave him a good workout. Normally on a day like today, I'd hook him to his run and let him stay outside with his food and water in a shady spot on the deck and his blanket beside them. Today, since I'm not sure what time I'll be home, I figure I'll leave him and all his stuff inside.

Sometimes during the week, if Sam has the day off, he stops by while I'm at work and checks up on the little guy. When I talked to him Thursday, he planned on being at the station most of the day today preparing testimony in the case that almost did me in last summer. Usually he doesn't work on Saturdays, but this was an exception.

Sam and I make a perfect pair—the chief detective in the Bourne Police Department and the head investigative reporter for the Cape Cod Tribune. Sometimes this perfect pair takes separate 'vacations', but not for long. And, it's always fun making up.

Since we're not ready to make a permanent commitment, Sam thought it wise I have some live-in company. Hence, he presented me with Watson. At first, I wasn't thrilled. There are days I don't take care of myself very well. Now, I have a furry little guy to feed and care for on a daily basis—not to mention, giving him a bath, at least once a week.

It didn't take long, though. He won my heart. Sometimes when Sam comes over, he just sits and watches me and the pup play.

Last summer I had a brush with death—one I hope will never be repeated. I had a hard time sleeping, and accepting what almost happened to me. At work, I put on a good show, but my close friends—Sam, Annie and Marnie—know I'm hurting inside. And now with the trial coming up, I may have to re-live everything all over again. The worst part is, the person on trial is, or should I say was, a friend of mine.

So, my little Watson is my therapy, my buddy, my whatever you want to call him. He's helping me and I'm helping him. He was a rescue dog. He's a beautiful six month old golden retriever who was neglected and abused. Fortunately, Sam's partner at the Bourne PD, Bill Martin, was involved with the rescue program and the rest is history.

I was in such deep thought, that I jumped a mile when my house phone rang emitting an irritating chirping noise. One day last month when Sam was here, he found it amusing to change my perfectly normal ring tone to the sound of a flock of birds flying directly overhead. Since I don't get many calls on my land line, the sound rattles me when it plays. Sam usually calls it just to annoy me.

"What do you want," I said sharply.

The voice on the other end was quiet.

"Sam, is that you?"

"No, and what's up with you?" It was Marnie.

"Sorry. Sam put this damn ring tone on my land line and I haven't changed it back yet. He thinks it's funny. That's his weird sense of humor. Anyway, has something changed?"

"I have an idea. If you can get Sam to check in on Watson or maybe stay at your house, you and Annie can come back here and stay the night. You know, like a sleep-over. I've finished the guest room. There are two twin beds. What do you say?"

"I don't know. If I had time to plan, it would work, but I haven't talked to Sam since Thursday."

"Can you at least try?"

I felt a little emptiness in her voice. "Let me make a phone call and I'll get right back to you."

"Okay, I'll wait to call Annie." Then Marnie added, "Don't just try, give it a good try."

"Yes, *Mother*."

I pushed the button down until I got a dial tone then punched in Sam's cell.

He answered on the second ring, "Hey, hi. You okay?"

"I will be when I change that stupid ring tone you put on my phone."

He laughed, "Aw, come on, it's not all that bad. Just because it reminds you of Alfred Hitchcock …"

I didn't let him finish. "Well, anyway, that's not why I called. I have a favor to ask." I waited for a second, then continued, "Marnie wants Annie and me to go to P-town for the day. Watson would be fine with that, but she's asked us if we'd like to end up back at her place and stay the night."

"So, you want me to check in on the little guy?" He continued, "Why don't I just stay the night. I have lots of reading and organizing to do for the case and your kitchen table makes a great desk."

"I've got some lemon-pepper chicken from last night and there's stuff for salad in the fridge." I couldn't believe I was saying that, the fast-food and peanut butter junkie I am.

"You sure have come a long way, Sherlock. I'll probably just pick up a pizza and some beer. You go ahead and have a good time. Maybe tomorrow night we'll go get some clams and rings. I'll need a break by then, and you can tell me all about your girl-party."

"I like it. Thanks, Buddy. Clams and rings sound good," I said. "I'll call you during the day on Sunday and let you know what time I'll be back."

"Have fun. Say 'hi' to the girls for me."

"Will do," I said. I disconnected Sam and pushed number three on speed dial for Marnie. "It's a go. Sam is going to stay at my house and dog-sit. I'm going to put some things in a bag and be on my way. See you in a few."

It was just an overnight, but I needed something like this, where I could just let go. My life had been turned upside down. It's about time I took back control. I didn't have to pretend with Annie and Marnie. Actually, I felt bad for Marnie.

She left New York City last July to visit her cousin Barry Binder, a Court Officer for Barnstable Superior Court. In the back of her mind, she was on a mission. She had just graduated from law school and wanted to pursue her career anywhere but the City. She'd heard Barry talk about Cape Cod so much that she decided to check it out as a possible place to hang a shingle.

She fell into a relationship for which nobody could have predicted the outcome. James Keaton worked with Barry at the Court House as the Chief Court Officer. He swept her off her feet. He sure had us buffaloed. Who'd have thought he was capable of murder.

Over the last eight years, I've dealt with lots of deaths—some were homicides and others were tragic accidents. This was, however, the first time I was the intended victim. I'll still continue my investigations, and probably in the same manner I've always done. Next time, though, I'll watch over my shoulder and leave word with somebody before I run off rogue. At least, I think I will.

The ride down 6A to Marnie's house is breath-taking. The color change isn't as striking as New Hampshire's, but it is beautiful. Just the ride down Route 6A is beautiful, no matter what time of year.

When I pulled into the driveway, I could see Annie was already there. She only lives in Cummaquid, the next town over. Annie Kane is the right hand for District Attorney Michael Sullivan. She's been with him going on twelve years. She landed a job in the DA's office right out of high school and has worked her way up to the top of the ladder. We became friends when I moved from central Massachusetts to Cape Cod some eight years ago.

I was about fifteen minutes early. I grabbed my duffle bag and headed for the door. They must have seen me pull in. Before I could knock, the door opened.

"Come on in," said Annie. "I just got here myself. I thought I was going to have a ho-hum weekend until Marnie called."

"I can't wait. I've heard so much about P-town, but never made it down there."

"It's colorful—like a rainbow." I turned and looked at Annie who was sitting on the couch, giggling.

"Yeah, a rainbow without a pot of gold, but they've got great little shops and wonderful restaurants. Maybe we could go to the Lobster Pot. You remember that place don't you Casey?"

"How could I forget. It was Sam and me and you and I can't remember who. But I do remember we ended up with eight lobsters between us. And the bill—it was over $200. I think that's why he won't take me back to P-town."

"Marnie, if you like silver, bring your credit card. There are a couple of little shops that sell hand-crafted silver jewelry to die for.

It’s really unique. I have a ring in the shape of a dolphin. It wraps partway around my finger. I had a small diamond put on the top of it. It’s wicked cool.” Annie was salivating. She loved her jewelry.

“Well, let’s get going,” I said.

CHAPTER TWO

With the tourists gone, the traffic was minimal. In the summer, the ride to P-town can take up to two hours. Today, we should make it in an hour and a half, maybe sooner.

No matter where I go, I always take my camera, whether for business or pleasure. And in my line of work, I never know when I might come across something newsworthy. Another reason I always carry my camera is, I used to paint from photographs. I'd take pictures of things I thought would pop on a canvas. In my eyes, my originals were beautiful. But, as an artist, I would have starved. Who knows, maybe I'll see some of those eye-popping scenes again and pull out the old paint brushes. Wouldn't Sam be surprised—a side of me he's never seen.

Marnie was like a little kid on her way to an amusement park. She kept looking from one side of the road to the other. "I never made it past the furniture store in Dennisport. This is amazing. I'm glad I suggested we make our little trip today."

"Imagine this—Sam and I bought bikes with the idea of riding them to P-town."

Before I could finish, Marnie asked, "Did you do it?"

"Nope. In fact, until last July, before I rode across the cranberry bogs in Bourne, I think we only rode them twice. And that was maybe two miles each time. I thought I'd ask him if we could truck them down to P-town, use them to ride around, and then truck them home. He may go for that."

"About a mile up the road, on the left hand side, is a breakfast place called Grumpys. I think they're open for lunch too, but their breakfasts are yummy. They make the best pancakes and the toppings for the waffles are beyond good. Why don't we do breakfast there tomorrow?" Anne slowed down as we passed the restaurant.

“I can handle that,” I said. “Also, if I remember correctly, just up the street is a kitchen gadget store. Marnie, let me tell you, if you’re looking for a designer melon baller, this is the place.” I pointed in the direction of the store.

“A what?” Marnie asked

I laughed. “Never mind.”

The traffic picked up a little when we got to Wellfleet. “Wonder what’s going on up ahead?” asked Marnie as she strained her neck trying to see around the cars.

“Don’t get neck spasms. It’s Saturday, nice weather, and the flea market—a perfect combination for traffic congestion. This is the only part of the ride I hate,” Annie sighed.

“A flea market?” Marnie shrugged her shoulders. “What in the world is that?” She hesitated. “I’m afraid you’ll tell me they sell trained fleas or something just as weird.”

I looked at her. I could have fun with this, but I won’t be cruel. “A flea market is a place where vendors go to sell stuff—and I mean stuff. Half of the field is for new things—mostly from China—and the other half is divided up between junk dealers, veggie and fruit vendors and, sometimes, there are puppies or kittens for sale.” I guess New York, at least the City, is really different than Cape Cod. *This must be a culture shock for our Miss Marnie*, I thought.

Marnie had her head tilted back, looking up at the sign at the entrance. “If this is called a flea market, then why does the sign say ‘Drive-In’ and have a couple of movies listed on the marquee?”

“Tell me you’ve never heard of a Drive-In movie theater either,” I said.

“Nope.”

“Well, looks like we’re about to have a brief educational moment. The main function of a Drive-In is, of course, to see the movie they’re showing on that giant screen over there. It’s usually frequented either by families who watch the movie or by couples making mad passionate love behind steamed-up windows.” For a moment I drifted back to when I was a kid and it was a big night out for Mom, Dad and me to go to the Drive-In. I'd wait till intermission so I could get popcorn and a soda, then I'd miss the second flick 'cause I was curled up in the back seat like a sleeping puppy dog. Dad always had to carry me to my room when we got home.

Our car came to a quick stop. The jolt snapped me back to reality. "Hey, Annie, we got our work cut out for us. It's high time we make this city girl into a country bumpkin."

"Don't think we have enough time. There's a Dunkin's just around the next corner. Does anybody want an iced coffee?"

I knew Annie must or she wouldn't have asked. "Fine with me," I said. "Let's go inside to get it though, 'cause if they've got k-cups on sale, I want to pick up a couple of boxes."

"Yeah, I'll get something too," said Marnie. "My treat."

The place was empty except for one person who was busying himself on his laptop. He had papers and a couple of books spread over the entire table. His stare was so intense, he could have burned a permanent image onto the screen.

I leaned over and whispered, "Doesn't that guy know its Saturday—time to play, not work."

Marnie shrugged her shoulders. "All work and no play makes Jack a dull boy."

"Certainly not the guy for us," added Annie. "Don't you agree Casey? Oh, wait a minute, I forgot you have Sam and I'll bet he's anything but dull."

"That's enough you two. Let's get going." Once on the road, I asked, "Annie, remember those little cottages along the shore, just as you start into P-town?"

"Yeah, there's about twelve of them in a row, aren't there?"

"Those are the ones. Could you pull over in their parking lot?"

"I can," said Annie. "What do you have in mind?"

"Well, first, Marnie should see the view from in front of them. The panorama of P-town is absolutely beautiful. Then, when we get into Town, she can look back in their direction and see how quaint the surroundings are. I think she'd like that. It's like looking at living postcards."

"I agree—it's quite amazing."

"I'm enjoying the peace and tranquility. This is like heaven on earth," Marnie said as she closed her eyes and drew in a deep breath.

"We haven't gotten into Town yet. It's not quite as quiet there. You'll see," said Annie.

"Second, I'd like to take some pictures of the cottages," I said. "My artistic side is trying to escape, so this might be my new project. When I was cleaning out my closet a few weeks ago, I came across my paints and brushes."

Less than a mile up the road, Annie made a left turn into the parking lot for Seaside Cottages.

"Wow, look at these little places. They all look alike except for the numbers. If you've had too much to drink, you better remember what number you're at or a stranger could be in for a surprise. Have you ever stayed in one?" Marnie's head pivoted back and forth taking in every detail.

"I haven't. How about you, Annie?" I asked.

"I've always wanted to, but like lots of other things, I just haven't done it. I know they're pretty expensive and they book up quickly. Maybe next summer we could try it for a few days—even a week. If we split the cost, it wouldn't be so bad. That'd be fun."

Marnie's head stopped moving at number three. "That's the one. We should rent number three. You know, for the three of us."

If I didn't know better, I'd say she's trying to relive her childhood, only in a different setting. It didn't sound like a bad idea, though.

"They close the cottages up right after Labor Day and don't open them until Memorial Day, so I'm sure there's nobody around. I've never seen the inside. Let's take a look in number three." I started to walk toward the cottage, then remembered I forgot to take my camera. "You guys go on up. I'm going to get my camera. I'll be right there."

Marnie ran ahead and scurried up the stairs onto the front porch. Before I could get my camera, close the door, and start back to the cottage, Marnie and Annie had their hands cupped against the window, looking in. In that split second, Marnie jumped back and let out an ear piercing scream. Annie just froze.

I slammed the car door and ran toward the cottage. "What's going on with you two?" I yelled.

Marnie had one hand over her mouth and the other pointed at the window. Annie had backed up against the railing—her mouth open wide and her eyes even wider.

"You guys look like you just saw a ghost—or worse." I leaned against the pane and tried to survey the inside. There was a dried film of salt air spray covering the entire window giving a fuzzy outline to everything beyond the pane. "I don't see anything unusual or out of place. Are you two trying to spook me?"

"Move down here and look in," said Annie. The porch was small, so we switched places. "Look at the floor, on the window side of the second twin bed."

My heart raced. There was a pair of feet visible only to the ankles. They appeared to be small, not child small, but female small. They were pointing straight up. So, if there was a body attached, and I assumed there was, the person was beside the bed, facing the ceiling. I knocked on the window—nothing. I knocked again—no movement at all.

"What are you doing?" whispered Marnie.

"Whoever that is can't hear you and there's nobody else around, so you can speak up," I said.

Annie stared out over the water, her arms crossed. "Casey, what should we do?"

"Don't touch anything," I said. "Stay up here on the porch. This way I can tell the officers exactly where we walked and what we touched. I've got the numbers for all the Cape Police Departments on my cell. Bear with me for a few."

I backed away from the window and proceeded to call Provincetown PD.

"Good morning, Provincetown Police Department, Sgt. Costa speaking. How may I help you?"

"Hi Bubba. It's Casey Quinby."

Before I could continue, he said, "Hey, 'hi' Case. How're things going?"

"Not so good, I'm afraid. I stopped with two of my friends at Seaside Cottages on our way into Town. We peeked in the window of number three and I think there's a problem."

"Did somebody break in?"

"No, worse, I think somebody was brought in. It appears that there's a body beside the bed. I can only see from the ankles down, but my guess is that it's a female."

"Number three you said? I'll send a cruiser out immediately. Do me a favor and wait for them to get there."

"No problem Sarge. I'll talk to you later."

Marnie and Annie started to speak at the same time. You could tell this whole scenario had them rattled. What a way to start, and presumably end, a day on the Town. Maybe I can talk them into at least having lunch at the Lobster Pot. I doubt it. This stuff was all new to them, but old hat to me. Not that I liked it, but I guess I was used to it. Come to think of it, neither one of them has probably ever seen an up-close and personal crime scene.

"Whoa, get a grip on, you two," I said.

We stood in silence, just looking out over the water. I leaned forward, rested my elbows on the deck rail, and molded my hands around my chin. "Here we go again," I said.

Only five minutes had passed when the first black and white pulled into the parking lot. Officer Fortuna radioed in his position, got out of the car, and walked up the stairs to where the girls were standing. "Hi Casey, I was in the area and got the call. There are a couple more cars on the way. What's going on? Sarge said something about a body?"

"Marco, take a look in that window." I pointed to the furthest one from where we were standing. "The sun has baked the sea mist on the glass pretty good. If nosey people, like us, hadn't passed by, this person would have probably gone undiscovered until the cottages were open again in the spring."

The officer cupped his hands and pressed his face against the window. "Where am I supposed to be looking?" he asked.

"To the left, then down on the floor, between the bed and the side window," I said.

"There certainly is what appears to be a body lying there. I'm going to wait for the other two guys to get here before I go in. But, in the meantime, let me start taking your statements. Casey, why don't you start."

"Sure—first let me introduce you to my friends, Annie Kane and Marnie Levine. They both work in the DA's office."

Marco held out his hand, "Hi, I'm Officer Fortuna with the Provincetown Police Department."

"Since Marnie just moved to the Cape four months ago and has never been to P-town, we decided to do a day trip. I've always thought the view of the Town from the front of Seaside Cottages was spectacular, so I wanted her to see it before we continued on. Then, we kidded about renting one of them next summer. We decided on number three because of the three of us. I won't go into details, but we've kinda bonded and formed a close friendship." I looked at Marco's face. "You know, like girlfriends—friends—no more."

"I got ya," he said.

"Anyway, I left my camera in the car and when I went back to get it, I heard Marnie scream. That's when they looked in the window and saw the feet looking back at them."

He turned to Annie and Marnie, "Do either of you have anything else to add?"

"No," they answered in unison.

"There may be some more questions later."

Another black and white, with its strobe lights flashing, and an unmarked pulled into the lot beside Officer Fortuna's car.

I didn't recognize the young officer from the black and white, but Sgt. Costa got out of the unmarked.

"I got someone to cover the phone, so I could come out myself. We had a quiet summer, but looks like things are going to heat up."

I introduced the girls, as he reached out to shake their hands.

"Casey, you know Officer Fortuna. I assume you introduced him to the girls," Sgt. Costa said as he turned to face the third responding officer. "This guy here is Officer Rusty Maloney, our newest addition."

I put my hands on my hips and swung around to face Officer Maloney. "Now how did an Irish boy end up with a bunch of Portuguese? Have they got you eating kale and bean soup yet or has Sarge's wife made you some bacalhau?" I looked at the girls. "The soups good, but bacalhau is salted cod. I never did acquire a taste for it."

"Casey, you're bad. You have to know how to cook it and Mary makes it so that it melts in your mouth." Sgt. Costa made a lip-smacking noise, then went back to the business at hand. "He transferred down to us from Boston last June and we're glad to have him."

He sure looked young—reminded me of myself. For a minute my mind wondered back to the Academy and my dream of becoming a member of a police department and eventually a detective.

I snapped back to realty when Sgt. Costa said, "I heard you had a close call in July."

"I'm trying to forget."

Sarge turned to Officer Maloney. "Casey had extensive training at an off Cape police academy, but because of an accident, she wasn't able to finish. She's now the head investigative reporter for the Cape Cod Tribune. We're very lucky to have her expertise and skills to complement our detective bureau. We call her our 'Kelly Girl' detective. She's helped not only us, but most of the Cape PDs, at one time or another, solve a difficult case."

"And because of my job, I'd like to ask permission to take some job related pictures."

Sarge walked over to the window and looked in. "Let's get inside and see what we're up against. We've been very fortunate in the crime department. The last real newsworthy crime involving our department was a few of years ago. The daughter of a prominent Provincetown family was found murdered in her home. Sad, things like that have to happen, but then again, maybe this one isn't foul play." Sgt. Costa took a pair of gloves from his side pocket and put them on.

He reached forward to try the door knob—nothing. It was locked. "These old locks can be opened by anyone." He pulled a plastic card from his pocket and slid it down the slit in the door jamb. "I told you." He motioned the two officers in. "You girls stay out here for now. I'll be right back."

Marnie looked at me, "And he thought we were going to race right in? I don't think so. In fact, even if he gives us the clear sign, I'm not interested."

"Counselor, a first-hand viewing of a crime scene and you don't want to know."

"It's not my case. I'm going to the car to get my iced coffee. Anybody else want theirs?" Marnie asked and without hesitation started down the stairs.

"I'll go with you," said Annie.

I stuck my head in the door. "Is it okay if I come in? I know the drill—don't touch anything."

"Yeah, Casey, come take a look."

I walked over beside Sgt. Costa and looked down at the girl lying beside the bed. She appeared to be in her early twenties, maybe twenty-three or four. Her curly, long brown hair was arranged carefully around her face. Her eyes were closed, either because she was asleep when she died or somebody shut them after the fact. A small, chocolate-brown teddy bear with one eye missing, a tattered green and pink scarf around its neck, and a red heart sewed on its paw was cradled in her arms.

"Sarge, can I take some pictures of the girl? And, also a couple of the inside of the cottage? I promise I won't use any in the paper, unless I get permission from your department."

By the look on Officer Maloney's face, I surmised this was his first encounter with a dead body. At this point, nobody knew if she died of natural causes or if it was a homicide. Either way, it shouldn't have happened.

Sgt. Costa gave me the go ahead to take my pictures. He stepped outside to call the medical examiner while I snapped ten pictures from various angles.

"Marco, you got an extra pair of gloves on you?"

He fumbled in his pocket, then handed me a pair of disposable latex ones. "I've got an extra issue pair in the car, but these should do for now."

Officer Maloney walked over to Marco and me. "I don't know which would be a more disturbing crime scene for me—a young girl looking so peaceful and content, as our Jane Doe, or somebody who's been hacked up and lying in a pool of blood."

All went quiet.

The squawk of a lone seagull, outside on the beach, broke the silence.

"You'll remember this one the rest of your life. You'll see many others, but this one will stay with you forever. It will be a constant reminder of how precious life is and how fast it can be taken away." I patted him on the back and headed for the open door. "Now, it's up to your department to come up with the 'who, when, where, and why's' behind this tragedy."

The medical examiner was just backing in when I rounded the corner of the cottage. Sgt. Costa met him in the lot. "We've got a young one," Sarge said to Bernie Montalvo.

Bernie's seen them all. He's from a third or fourth generation Provincetown fishing family. When he graduated from P-town high school, he had big dreams of being an orthopedic surgeon. He did his stint in med school, but changed his major to pathology. The former ME for the lower Cape was about ready to retire, so Bernie worked with him for two years, then took over the office. That was thirty-five or so years ago.

He's still very much involved in the family business even though he doesn't go out in the boats anymore. But his number one love is his medical world.

Annie and Marnie were nowhere to be found. I knew they didn't desert me because Annie's car was still there.

"Casey, nice to see you. I know, not under these circumstances, but none the less, you're looking great."

"Thanks," I said. "It has been a while."

At a guess, he stood five-feet-ten, medium build, with a little pot belly. He had married his childhood sweetheart before finishing medical school. She stayed in P-town and he came home a couple times a month to be with her. Four years ago, she was diagnosed with breast cancer and died less than six months later. They were married for thirty-seven years. It was just the two of them. They had no children. But everybody loved Bernie and came together as one big family to support him.

"Let's go inside and check out the situation." Bernie walked in first and we followed.

It was a sight I had witnessed before. There were certain procedures every ME performs at a crime scene. First and foremost, the gloves go on. Rule number one, never touch anything without putting on your gloves.

"Casey, please do me a favor."

"Sure, what do you need?"

"There's a black notebook and a pen in my bag. This area beside the bed has limited space for me to work. Would you please take notes for me while I examine Jane Doe?"

This was right up my alley. What more could I ask for? First-hand information from the ME to an investigative reporter and at the scene of the crime to boot. "No problem," I said. "I'm ready whenever you are."

For the next fifteen minutes, I basically took dictation.

"From the temperature and the stiffness of the body, it appears she's been dead twelve to fifteen hours, maybe a tad longer. I'll run more tests back at the lab to get a more exact time. There doesn't appear to be any obvious trauma to the body. I don't see any blood or bruises. Again, once I can perform a thorough examination, I can narrow down the cause of death."

I watched intently as Bernie examined the girl.

He continued, "I find no puncture marks or anything that would indicate strangulation. Everything is very clean." He stood up and moved away from the side of the bed.

"Sgt. Costa, as soon as you're finished taking pictures and securing the scene, we'll get her into the wagon and move her to my lab."

"Marco, here's the camera. Take the necessary pictures so we can transport her and get this place closed up. Detective Adams is away until next Sunday, so as soon as I get back to the station, I'm going to give the Sheriff's Department a call. They'll send a couple guys out from BCI to dust for prints and whatever else those crime scene investigators do. It may be tomorrow morning before they can come. We'll tape off the area and I'll station a black and white around the clock until they give us the all clear."

I gave Bernie back his notebook and headed for the door. Once outside, I looked around for the girls. They weren't in the car. When I turned back, I saw them walking along the beach toward the cottage.

Sgt. Costa came out and joined me on the porch. "Casey, let me get this all together and I'll give you a call." He looked at Annie and Marnie as they approached the porch. "I'm sorry you girls had to come across this whole mess. We're not sure what happened here."

He continued, "It's still early, and P-town awaits. Please continue and, without sounding insensitive, try to enjoy what we have to offer. In fact, I know that Casey likes the Lobster Pot. Dinner's on me. Do you remember Shawn McNulty?" Sgt. Costa asked.

"Actually, I do," I said. "Sam introduced me to him the last time we were here. I'm not sure how he knows him, but he does."

"Good, I'll call Shawn and make reservations for three at five o'clock. What do you say?"

I stepped down and gave them each a hug. "Are we going to salvage some of the day?"

They both managed a smile.

"We were hoping you'd want to," said Annie. "It took a little bit for the initial shock to wear off, but we're okay."

"Thanks, Bubba. I'll talk to you Monday morning before I write the story. If you need me before then, don't hesitate to call." I leaned over and gave him a hug and a kiss. "Please pass these to the Mrs. for me."

Officers Fortuna and Maloney were still inside with Bernie. "Bye guys," I called out and with that we were on our way.

CHAPTER THREE

The next mile into town was quiet.

Just before we pulled into the MacMillan Pier parking lot, Marnie said, “Wow, I never expected our day to get stuck in a pothole for a couple of hours. Casey, you really handled that like a pro. Now I see why you’re so respected in the field. Once I composed myself and we took a long walk on the beach, I realized how much I want to get involved. With you as my teacher, how could I go wrong?”

We got out of the car and without saying a word, engaged in a group hug. Here we are again—the terrific trio—reporting for duty.

“Let’s take a left on Commercial Street,” Annie said while using her free hand to point out the direction. “About three blocks up, there’s a little jewelry store that has silver to die for. Usually the guy who owns the store is behind the counter. Of course, I haven’t been here since last spring, but things don’t change that fast in P-town.”

“Here we go, Annie and her jewelry. Careful, Marnie, she’ll drag you into every store and tell you it’s her favorite. Remember, I’ve done this route with her many times.” I turned to Annie and laughed. “Lead the way, lady.”

We joined hands and swung our arms like ten-year-old schoolgirls off on a treasure hunting mission.

“I suppose you want to look in that little ‘sex toy’ store over there,” said Annie pointing across the street.

Marnie giggled, “Isn’t Sam sex toy enough for you?”

“I’ll never tell. But yes, on the way back, we’ve got to show Marnie that place. You won’t believe what they have on display.

Shops around them have come and gone but they've managed to stay for years, so it must say something about what they sell. You know the old adage about supply and demand."

"You're a sick puppy, Quinby. But we'll stop," Annie said, "as soon as I get my fill of silver."

Marnie had already started to window shop. "I want to check out some of these art galleries along the way. I might be able to find a couple of pictures for the living room." She turned to face me. "Unless, of course, you want to paint a couple for me."

Annie answered quickly, "Fat chance of that. I've never seen Casey pick up a paint brush unless it was to paint a wall."

"Very funny," I said.

Annie found some starfish earrings with a bracelet to match. They were really neat, but I knew I could put the ninety-eight dollars she spent on them to better use.

Marnie, though, found a couple of eight by ten watercolors of P-town landmarks. There actually was one of the Seaside Cottages, but she decided to wait on that one. "I totally love my new art work. I'll take them to Michaels for frames next week."

I stopped in front of the sex toy store. "It's good for a laugh. Besides, we don't have much time before dinner so we won't be here long."

Annie wrinkled her face and squinted her eyes. "You're really going in there?" she asked disgustedly.

"Yeah, Miss Prude, in fact, why don't you lead the way?" I laughed and motioned Marnie to follow.

It wasn't twenty minutes later when we emerged from the store, giggling. I did a quick scan of the street to make sure we didn't see anyone we knew.

Marnie leaned on the side of the building and reached down to adjust her sandal. "I never knew things like that existed. I can't even imagine that people actually use some of them."

"Told you it was disgusting, but no, you wouldn't listen." Annie gave me another one of her looks.

“Enough of that—I’m hungry. I’m sure the restaurant won’t mind if we’re ten minutes early,” I said.

I half expected to see Bubba and his wife waiting for us at the Lobster Pot. I didn’t recognize the young girl behind the desk inside the door. If I had to guess, I’d bet the hostess was only about eighteen or nineteen, if that. She was tiny and very reserved.

That’s P-town. There are lots of young people who come down here to lose themselves in a culture far from the city. Some stay and call it home. Others think they’ll become famous artists, musicians, or authors overnight and then find their little fantasy cloud dissipates, so they move on. Then there’s the last group. I suppose you could slip them into the run-away category. That might be a little heavy, but they don’t want to be found. My mind flashed back to the dead girl beside the bed. Where did she fit in?

My thoughts were interrupted by a tap on the shoulder. It was Shawn McNulty, one of the owners. He reached out to shake my hand. “Casey, how are you? Long time no see. Bubba gave me a call and asked me to take good care of you and your friends. It’s a beautiful night so I thought you’d like to eat in the Top of the Pot.”

“Good call,” I said and turned to Marnie. “Annie’s been upstairs before so she knows what Shawn is talking about. You’re going to love it. During season, it’s almost impossible to sit up there without waiting an hour or more.”

“Well, if you ladies are ready, your table awaits. Please follow me.” Shawn picked up three menus and headed down the corridor, past the lobster tanks and raw bar, to the stairs leading to the Top of the Pot.

Shawn looked at Marnie, “Since you haven’t been here before, I recommend the pan roasted lobster. It’s very popular with our diners. And, if you check out the appetizers, the oysters rockefeller are the best.” He smiled. “I’ll give you girls some time to decide. Katie will be your waitress. Can I give her your drink order?”

“I’ll have a white zin with a side of ice,” I said.

Annie ordered the same and Marnie asked for a pinot noir. After

Katie delivered them and took our appetizer order for some clams casino and oysters rockefeller, we clicked glasses and chanted our toast. . . .

"Here's to it
Those who get to it
And don't do it
May never get to it
To do it again."

CHAPTER FOUR

Officers Maloney and Fortuna finished securing cottage number three at Seaside and went back to Fortuna's car to wait for the black and white that Sgt. Costa was sending to relieve them.

"I've been on the job for fifteen years and have seen six murders. The last one was brutal. It was three years ago." Fortuna shook his head. "We usually get a lot of young people who come to P-town to get away from city life. Well, this was kind of a reverse situation. The person who was murdered spent her early life between here and Cambridge. I understand every summer and school vacation, she and her mother stayed at the family's house in P-town and her father would travel back and forth. I think he was a lawyer. After high school she attended some highfalutin' college in Boston and decided to stay and live the city life. I heard she studied fashion design and marketing, and was very successful.

"How old was she when she died?" asked Maloney.

"She was in her early forties."

"Was she married or have a family?"

"No, and I understand that's why she decided to come back to the Cape. She was getting burned out in the industry and wanted to settle down and start a family. She moved back into a house near the water—pretty remote. I think her family owned it or she bought it from her family's estate. Anyway, it was a typical Cape Cod house: three bedrooms, two up and one down, a living room, dining room and kitchen. To me, it was a pretty drastic change."

"Did you know her?"

"I'd see her in town, but she was usually by herself. If you ask me, the whole thing was a little strange."

"How so?" asked Maloney.

"Well, she just up and left her fancy Boston digs and her upscale life style, and did a hundred and eighty degree turn about when she decided to live here full time. Personally, I always thought she was hiding something."

"Maybe she was, but given her financial status and the opportunity to acquire property familiar to her, it might have given her the peace of mind she was looking for." Maloney said wondering where she had lived in Boston. After all, he had done something similar to that himself, but had no intentions of moving back.

Fortuna rubbed his chin in deep thought. "She lived in Boston for almost eighteen years, not including college."

"Do you know what part of Boston she lived in?"

"I think it was Beacon Hill," said Fortuna.

"Talk about nice digs and right in the middle of the 'society' action hub." Officer Maloney folded his arms and leaned back in his seat. "I'd ride by those places and wonder what the insides looked like. Never did find out. That's okay, I'm perfectly happy right here in my little one bedroom condo."

"I wonder who the Sarge is sending out to relieve us?" asked Fortuna.

"He's probably waiting for the three-thirty shift to clock in. So back to the murder—you said she didn't get married after she moved back?" Maloney was curious.

"No, but it was said she had many male friends—if you know what I mean."

"Yeah, I get your drift. How was she murdered?"

"She was stabbed to death. It was a single stab wound to the heart. Then, the son of a bitch raped her."

"Was it one of her lovers?" Maloney was intrigued.

"That's what we thought. That's where the investigation started. It sure brought out a lot of shit that was going on in and around town. I'm sure there were lots of quiet dinner tables. I know for a fact, several people have divorced since. Now, I'm not saying she was the reason, but who knows."

"So, you figured out which guy it was?"

"It wasn't any one of them."

"Now I'm really confused." Maloney looked at Fortuna. "Don't stop now. The suspense is killing me."

"It came down to the DNA. The State Police made a very unusual request of the local male residents. The department asked all the local guys to take a DNA test."

"You've got to be kidding me." Maloney threw his arms up. "This isn't even stuff you'd see on television. Sounds like it came from a c-rated crime novel. I suppose if a person had nothing to hide, there'd be no reason not to take the test. On the other hand, it's bordering on a violation of constitutional rights. I don't know what I'd do. So did they find a match?"

"Yeah, they did, but not from this random testing of guys who may or may not have played 'hide the wiener'. It seems that right after the murder, DNA samples had been taken from a handful of people who may have had contact with the victim around the time she was killed." Fortuna tilted his head and turned to look at Maloney. "The results of those tests hadn't come in when the group DNA was taken because the crime lab in Boston was so behind. Our District Attorney pushed for answers on both sets of tests. Believe it or not, it took almost a year before they got them—and bingo, a match."

"Well, who dun it?"

"The butler, with a carving knife, in the kitchen," said Fortuna with a smirk.

"You've played Clue too many times. Are you going to leave me hanging?"

"It turned out to be a driver for Speedy Air and Land Delivery out of Hyannis. Guess he'd been scoping her out for quite some time. Apparently, she ordered lots of stuff on the internet and the Hyannis Company delivered it. Nobody will ever know exactly what transpired, but she's gone and he'll never see a day of freedom again. Now he can play leap frog at Walpole with the big boys."

"Let's get back to the business at hand," Fortuna said as he turned to see a black and white pull into the lot beside them.

"Thanks for the memories," said Maloney, as he got out of the car. "See you back at the station."

CHAPTER FIVE

"It's no wonder you like it here. Shawn was right, the pan roasted lobster is outstanding. One of these babies isn't enough," Marnie said, untying the plastic lobster bib from her neck. "I definitely know what I'm having the next time we come here." She looked around. "I saw a cappuccino machine when we passed the bar. Anybody, besides me, want one?"

"The only thing better than cappuccino would be a bag of gourmet jelly beans." I said.

"I know you had wine for dinner, but jelly beans? Are you drunk?" Marnie had a dumbfounded look on her face.

"Nope. I saw them in the little candy store next door before we came in and I can't get them out of my head." I laughed, "See what crazy people you're hanging out with."

"Speak for yourself," Annie said.

I raised my arm to get the waitress' attention. "We'd like to order three cappuccinos and a piece of your five layer chocolate cake with vanilla ice cream and three forks."

"I'm on it," she said and off she went.

I could hear the whish. . .sh. . .sh of the cappuccino machine coming from behind the bar. "Good idea, Marnie. I haven't had one of those for a while and I love them."

"Remember the first girls' night out we had?" Annie asked.

"I do. It was the first time I met you, Casey. You were involved in the Becky Morgan hit and run and I was intrigued by the mystery you were carefully trying to unravel. Who would have thought that whole tragic incident and what followed would bind us together in such a strong friendship."

The waitress returned with our cappuccinos and the biggest piece of cake I'd ever seen. "There's a gentleman at the bar who'd like to buy you girls an after-dinner drink."

All at the same time, we turned to see Officer Maloney smiling back.

"Please tell the gentleman at the bar, we'd love to accept, only if he'll grab a fork and join us." I gave the waitress a nod and off she went to relay the message.

"I hope you don't mind, but I took the liberty to decide the drink of choice—my favorite, Bailey's Irish Cream." Maloney put his fork on the table, pulled up a chair from the next table and sat down.

"Good evening, Officer Maloney," I said. "You remember my friends, Annie and Marnie?"

"I do. How could I not remember such lovely ladies."

"Young, handsome, and with manners. How did the P-town Police Department lure you down from Boston?" I took a sip of my drink. "And I might add, good taste, too."

"I was ready for a change from city life. Don't get me wrong, I love Boston and always will. My father is a cop, my uncle is a cop, my cousin was a cop, and my grandfather was a cop. The business is in my blood. We were all assigned to the South Boston precinct. My grandfather retired five years ago, just when I was coming on the job. My cousin, Tommy, was shot when he responded to a domestic abuse call. He died three days later. His one year anniversary was last week. I almost got off the job." Maloney took a deep breath and continued, "After a lot of soul searching, I decided that Tommy would have wanted me to stay. So, here I am."

"South Boston, huh, home of the notorious Whitey Bulger," I said, trying to change the subject. "I understand there are mixed emotions about his capture."

"Powerful dude," said Maloney. "My grandfather knew him. They grew up on the same block. Have you girls ever been to Southie?"

Marnie wrinkled her nose and smiled. "Do they all talk like you there?"

"If you mean—do we paak the kaa in Haavad Yaad and say kawfee instead of kauwfee—yeah, I guess they do."

Annie and I looked at each other and burst out laughing.

I shifted in my chair and turned to Marnie. "Let me interpret what Maloney just said. Using the queen's English—we park the car in Harvard Yard and drink coffee."

Marnie squinted and looked at me over her eyebrows, "I know what he was saying. I didn't just fall off the turnip truck."

"A war of words between fans—Red Sox vs. Yankees." Annie said. "This ought to be good."

"I went to Southie once with my friend, Sam. He's a detective with the Bourne PD. The Boston PD hosted a seminar on some state-of-the-art safety equipment being tested by several of their divisions. Sam represented Bourne and I went along to keep him company. Actually, it was very interesting. After the seminar was over, one of his buddies, who was from Southie, asked us if we wanted to grab a burger and a beer before we headed back to the Cape. We ended up at a place called the L Street Tavern."

"Know it well. Did you see the movie *Good Will Hunting* with Ben Affleck and Matt Damon? They filmed a scene at the L Street Tavern. My cousin, Tommy, was one of the extras. Imagine, he got paid to sit on a barstool and pretend he was drinking. In Southie, you never pretend."

Annie looked at her watch, "I don't want to be a party pooper, but we'd better start thinking about heading back to Marnie's place. It's almost 7:30 and we've got about an hour and a half ride."

I took the last sip of Bailey's and stood up. "Thanks for the drink and conversation. I enjoyed them both."

"I hope it's not the last time. Maybe you can venture up around Hyannis one of these days and we can continue our tour of Boston with a cup of kawfee." Marnie chuckled. "Did I get it right?"

Maloney laughed, "Close enough for me."

"I'll be talking to Sgt. Costa sometime Monday. Depending on what he tells me, I may be back down here sooner than later."

Annie led the way to the door.

Maloney reached forward to open it. “A good night with new friends—can’t beat that.”

Maloney went right and we took a left and headed to the MacMillan Pier parking lot.

CHAPTER SIX

"Whew, what a day. I need another glass of wine. Anybody want to join me?" asked Marnie as she opened her front door.

Annie threw her arms up, "Does a cat have an ass? Of course we want a glass."

"I'm going to put on my jammies and call Sam. Give me a couple of minutes. Don't say anything good until I get back." I picked up my overnight bag and headed toward the guest bedroom. It had been a long day, but I wasn't ready to call it a night. It was time to unwind.

Sam's cell phone went right to voice mail. *Typical Sam,* I thought, *he never checks his messages*. He probably shut the ringer off and decided to call it an early night. He's been burning the midnight oil reviewing his notes for the trial. I'll call my home phone in the morning. No need to think about that now—tomorrow's another day.

"Okay, I'm ready." I scuffed my way into the kitchen and picked up my glass. "Fill her up, barkeep." I mimicked a drunk, slurring words and swaying slightly from side to side.

"What are those things on your feet?" Marnie asked. "They look like something Watson killed in the backyard."

"They're my Porky Possum hush puppies," I said, looking down and smiling. "Sam gave them to me last Christmas. He said my feet were always cold and these little guys would help warm up my tootsies." I gave them a loving pat.

Annie was already in the living room, curled up in a chair, sipping her wine. "Are you girls going to join me?"

I left the kitchen with glass in one hand and the bottle of white zin in the other.

Marnie stopped to insert a Carrie Underwood, a Jennifer Nettles and a Trace Adkins CD into her Bose, then joined me on the couch. "Soft country music always sets the mood for a soul-searching conversation. And I think we're about to enter that zone."

"Welcome to my world," I said to the girls as I lifted my glass for a toast.

Annie turned to me and scowled, "Do you think our Jane Doe committed suicide? You saw her. Was she messed up?"

"By messed up, do you mean beat up or bloody?" I asked.

"Well, I'm not really sure what I mean. I've never been greeted by a dead person before. Doesn't that stuff bother you? You were so calm and collected. I freaked. I've read ump-t-nine cases regarding murder over the last twelve years, but I guess I never really painted a visual," said Annie. "Marnie, what about you? Your father is a lawyer. Didn't you run into this when you worked for him?"

"My father isn't a criminal lawyer, so I was in the same boat as you."

I took a sip of my wine. "We don't know how she died. The ME will make that determination. I may get a call tomorrow, and then again, Sgt. Costa might wait until Monday. One way or another, I told him I'd wait till I heard from him before I wrote a story for the paper."

I really wanted Bernie to call me as soon as he had an answer. My gut feeling was our Jane Doe was the victim of murder. She was too posed. And the teddy bear—there had to be some significance to that teddy bear. She was holding it close, the same way a young child would have. She wasn't beaten—there wasn't any blood. It was way too staged for me to believe it was anything but murder.

"Casey, there's a thought bubble forming over your head. Do you care to share its contents with us?" Marnie asked.

"There's really nothing to share right now, but as soon as I hear something, I'll let you both in on it." I hoped that satisfied their need to know.

"I've got some Orville in the pantry. How about I pop it into the microwave and we watch Saturday Night Live. I looked it up earlier and Justin Timberlake is hosting." Marnie didn't wait for an answer and was already through the kitchen door when we both said, "Okay."

CHAPTER SEVEN

We were just leaving Grumpy's when my cell rang. It was Sgt. Costa.

"Morning, Casey," came the voice from the other end. "I thought I'd try to reach you early."

I knew this wasn't a good thing. "What's up, Bubba? Did you hear back from Bernie already?"

"I have, and your suspicions were right. Our Jane Doe case is now officially a homicide."

I took a deep breath. My next words had a hard time coming out. "Do you want me to venture down to P-town today?"

"I'd appreciate it. Remember I told you that Detective Adams is away. Well, he's really away. He's on a cruise ship somewhere in the Caribbean, so there's no chance he can cut his vacation short. I'm hoping you can give us a hand."

"No problem. We went out to breakfast and are just leaving. Let me get back to Marnie's and pick up my car, then I'll head on down. Let's see, it's 10:00 now. I should be there by noon. Do you want me to meet you at the station?"

"That would be great. I'll see you then."

I turned to the girls, who were waiting intently to hear the other side of my phone conversation. "Here I go again. I'm sure you're aware that was Sgt. Costa. He got some news from the ME and would like me to give them some help in the investigation, so I'm going to drive down as soon as I get my car."

"So it is a homicide?" Annie asked.

"That's what he said."

Marnie looked at Annie, then back to me, "Do you want us to ride down with you? We can hang around and then when you're ready, we'll leave. It's a long ride alone, especially since it's a two-way trip and you'll have a lot on your mind."

"It's up to you. If you drop me at the station, I can call you when I'm done." I was glad Marnie offered. It was a long ride and the company would be welcomed.

"I'm not doing anything, so let's go." Anne was already on her way to her car. "Besides, the DA's office will be getting a report from P-town PD sometime tomorrow and this way I'll have a head's up as to what's going on. Marnie, you'll probably be involved in this one too."

CHAPTER EIGHT

Boston – Two weeks earlier

"Katherine, are you having breakfast this morning?" Peter called from the kitchen. "I've got to be at the office early, so I don't have much time."

"I'll be right out. Please pour me a cup of coffee." Katherine O'Ryan wrapped her robe around her naked body and headed for the kitchen. "What's so important at work that you have to go in early?" she asked as she reached into the pantry for a box of Cherrios. "Want some?"

"No, I'm fine. My boss has an important presentation on Wednesday. It could mean a new client." Peter sighed. "With the economy in the gutter, we need all the business we can get."

"I suppose advertising isn't a priority in some business budgets right now." Katherine said between spoonfuls of cereal. "But if anybody can muster up a successful campaign, it's my honey. Your boss knows what you're capable of and that's why he relies on you."

"The phones are usually pretty quiet on Monday, so I should be able to work without interruption. What do you say that we take in dinner and a movie tonight?"

Katherine stood up and made her way to Peter's side. She leaned over and gave him a kiss on the head. "Looks like you're getting a little thin on top." She giggled and quickly moved back.

He hated to be reminded of his apparently inherited, impending bald spot.

"In another couple of years, I'll be able to use it as a mirror."

"Subject over," he said. "What are you doing today?"

She turned away from him, not wanting to see his reaction to her answer. "I want to do some more research on my family. I thought I was making some headway, but as you know, I hit a cement wall." She wanted so desperately to know who she really was. Her father, or the man she knew to be her father, Buddy O'Ryan, died ten years ago in an automobile accident. Last February, her mother, Mary Latham O'Ryan, caught pneumonia and the last thing she did before she died, was to tell Katherine she was adopted.

It was a tough time for Katherine. She was left with the job of emptying the apartment she'd shared with her parents for her nineteen years until she moved out on her own. She was cleaning out her mother's bureau when she found a box neatly tucked away in the bottom drawer. It was beautiful—bright and cheery, with blue and white hydrangeas painted on the lid and tied shut with a pale yellow ribbon that was beginning to show wear around the edges. She'd never seen it before and was almost afraid to open it—scared that it might hold more secrets about her life as it existed before becoming an O'Ryan.

She loved the mom and dad who raised her, but her desire to know her true identity began to consume her.

"Katherine, can't you be happy knowing you were raised by two people who loved you very much?" Peter and Katherine had been over and over this subject so many times. No matter what he said to her, she insisted on finding her birth mother.

Peter folded his hands and rested them on the table. He watched as her mind drifted far from their, actually his, condo in South Boston. She leaned on the counter and stared out the window. He was losing her.

Peter had done some research on his own. He had a friend at City Hall who bent—no, broke—all the rules about sealed adoption birth certificates. A few months ago, Peter was presented with a copy of Katherine's. Of course the recorded name was not that of Katherine O'Ryan, but rather Emily Mae Latham. The birth dates were the same. But that didn't mean anything—a lot of people were born on August 10, 1988. The last name was the same as her adopted mother's middle name, but Latham was a common name. He wasn't even sure she was born in Boston. For all he knew, she was born in San Francisco or Chicago or New York. And maybe it wasn't in a big city at all. Maybe she was born in Shelbourne Falls just outside of Boston, or somewhere in the Berkshires. Maybe this wasn't Katherine's birth certificate at all. Who knows—and who cares. He was her family now. He was all she needed. Why couldn't she understand that? Last week he took it out and read it again, then folded it, slid it back in the envelope and tucked it back in the shoebox he kept on the top shelf of his closet.

"I've got to get going. Don't forget we've got a dinner and movie date tonight. I'll call you somewhere around two-ish. Meanwhile, decide where you want to eat and what you want to see. Sound okay to you?" There was no response. "Katherine, did you hear me?"

"Of course I did."

He took a deep breath, "Then why didn't you answer me? Sometimes I feel like I'm talking to the wall."

She spun around and snapped at him, "Enough! I heard every word you said and I'll be ready. Now get going so you can finish up and we can enjoy our evening."

Peter stood up and walked over to Katherine. "I'm sorry. I didn't mean to upset you. How about this weekend we start over. We'll get out all your family notes, re-read them and try to find something we missed." He raised his eyebrows at her, trying to induce a response.

His embrace was warm and comforting. It always was. "Scoot—or I'll have the fife of St. Patrick lure you back into the bedroom."

CHAPTER NINE

Boston

She knew Peter had, what he thought, were her best interests at heart, but she wasn't sure if they were really her best interests. Sometimes she thought, actually she knew, she caused her own confusion by trying to recreate her family tree. He told her it would be almost impossible to find a family tree if she didn't know who her family was. What he didn't know was that she was researching the family tree of her adoptive parents. She had to start somewhere.

Katherine worked at a small art gallery on the south end of Newbury Street. It was her dream to someday have a place of her own to display and, hopefully, sell some of her paintings. But for now, they were bubble-wrapped and stored in a closet off the hallway in Peter's condo. She had attended The School of The Museum of Fine Arts in Boston for two years, but because of the increase in tuition, she had to withdraw. Even as a working artist, she wasn't able to meet the additional demands.

The Gallery didn't open until twelve o'clock on Mondays, giving her enough time to shower, dress and head to the Public Library to get in a couple hours of research. This, pretty much, was her Monday ritual ever since the news of her adoption had pierced her ear drums some seven and a half months ago.

It was nine o'clock when she finished filling her lunch bag with an apple, a package of peanut butter crackers and a couple bottles of water, grabbed her backpack, and headed out the door. It was a beautiful day. The sun smiled down through the narrow walkways that separated the rows of newly renovated three-family houses.

Years ago, every floor was occupied by some branch of the same family—grandparents on the first, perhaps a daughter and her family on the second, and maybe another child or a cousin on the third. Now most of them were converted to condos and half the time the person on the third floor had no idea who lived on the first.

The bus stop was only a two-block walk from the condo. Since the bus dropped her off at the MTA entrance, she had little time to gather her thoughts before departing down the two sets of stairs and positioning herself on the platform to wait for the train. This repetitive five-day-a-week routine was so monotonous that an untrained monkey could do it.

She could have stayed home and used Peter's computer, except for the fact that she didn't want to leave any search trails for him to discover. Not that she was doing anything wrong, but for the time being, she wanted to keep this a personal journey. Besides, the computers at the library had Ancestry.com, city directories, marriage records and death records—and Peter's didn't. She wasn't sure how these research methods were going to help her. She needed a name to punch in to get information and for the moment, the only one she had was O'Ryan.

This weekend she was going to get everything she'd worked on together and arrange it in chronological order. Peter told her he'd help. She wanted to put her trust in him. She had no reason not to. After all, it wasn't he who kept her true identity a secret for almost twenty-one years. It was just the fear of trusting anybody. In time, she was sure that feeling would go away.

"Approaching Boylston Street," came the low, raspy voice of the driver over the loud-speaker as the train started to slow. The brakes squealed and those standing up, holding onto the belt loops hanging down from the ceiling, were jolted forward, then back, before the train came to a complete stop. The doors opened and, like a herd of cattle, a rush of people pushed their way out.

"Someday I'll live far from this maddening crowd or maybe in a loft over my gallery," she whispered.

She chose the main branch of the Public Library on Boylston Street, instead of the branch in South Boston, because it was just one block away from the Newbury Street gallery where she worked. The main branch also had more resources for her to explore.

"Good day, my friend," she said looking up at the majestic pink granite building glistening in the morning sun. "What surprises do you hold for me today?"

"Did he answer you?" asked a voice from behind.

Katherine jumped forward and turned to see her friend, Raji, standing in front of her. "You nearly scared me to death. You usually don't start work until eleven. Why so early?"

"I'm filling in for Lilly. She had some appointment to go to, and I had nothing else going on, so here I am." He smiled, reached his arm out and, without hesitation, said, "Give me your backpack."

She slid the straps down her arms and handed it to him.

"Wow, what's up with this? You carrying the weight of the world on your shoulders?"

"I had no problem handling it all the way from Southie. If it's too heavy for you, I'm sure I can ...."

"Got the message," said Raji. "Where you gonna sit?"

"I figure it's early enough that I can get on a computer. There's some stuff I'd like to check out on Ancestry. I've got about an hour before I've got to be at work."

"I'm going to log in. I'll stop on by in a little bit to see if there's anything I can help you with."

"Sounds good to me, thanks." Katherine was already digging in her bag for a pad of paper and some pencils. Her hands instinctively embraced the packet of letters she'd found hidden in the box in her mother's bureau drawer. She carefully lifted them out and, without looking at them, clutched them close to her chest.

She closed her eyes and tried to imagine the person who wrote them. The only thing Katherine knew was they had passed through the Dorchester Post Office and the author's name was Emma. And that Emma and her mother shared lots of close personal thoughts. Thoughts without names. But after reading them over and over again, the thoughts and words seemed to be about her. The last letter was dated April 16, 1990. Katherine was only one and a half years old. It appeared that Emma was sick and had been for some time. Katherine couldn't imagine this Emma person had just abruptly stopped writing to her mother. She must have died. But who was she?

CHAPTER TEN

I walked through the set of heavy glass doors at the entrance to the Provincetown Police Department. Sgt. Costa was standing at the duty desk talking to an officer I didn't recognize.

"Casey," he said, waving me to join him, "Meet Officer Lambert."

I reached out to shake his hand. "You've added some new guys since the last case I worked with you."

"Well, you know, some of us do get old. I figure I'll only work another five years, then I'm gone. It'll be fishing and eating, maybe some golfing—and eating—and who knows, maybe a trip here and there." Sgt. Costa patted his belly.

"The eating part is dead on, but Bubba, you'll never retire." I looked at the new guy. "He's a permanent fixture around here. They'll have to carry him out in a box."

"We've got lots to go over, so let's head for my office. It'll be quiet there." He rolled his eyes and motioned me to walk in front of him, since I knew where his office was. Without turning around, he called to Officer Lambert, "I just made a fresh pot of coffee. Could you please bring us each a cup—one black and one with cream. Get yourself one, too."

I was about eight steps ahead of the Sarge on my way to his office, when my cell rang. It was Sam. I turned to Sgt. Costa, "I have to take this. I'll be right back." I walked back to the front of the station. "Hi …"

Before I could say anything else, Sam's voice came from the other end, "You were supposed to call me this morning. Where are you?"

"Well, it's a long story and I don't have time right now. We're back in P-town."

"What's going on or should I be afraid to ask?"

"In a nutshell, Annie, Marnie and I stumbled on what I now know was a murder. Yesterday we weren't sure if it was a natural death or a homicide. Detective Adams from the P-town PD is on vacation and Sgt. Costa asked for my help." There, I got it out and in only three sentences.

"I don't believe this. I don't know if I want you to get involved. Casey, you've just been through a life-threatening situation. Are you sure you're doing the right thing?"

"Sam, you know me better than that. Anyway, I've got to go. Are we still on for tonight?"

I sensed Sam's frustration and concern. "Of course we are. Just be careful."

I visualized Sam sitting on the edge of my couch, leaning forward with his elbows resting on the top of his knees, his left hand in a fist holding his head, his right hand pressing his cell to his ear—while staring helplessly at the floor. "I'll fill you in on all the details," I said. "Love you. Give Watson a hug. Bye." I should have called Sam earlier, but I didn't have anything to tell him, except we found a dead girl.

I put my cell on vibrate and headed back to Sgt. Costa's office. The aroma of freshly-brewed coffee filled the air. "Smelling good in here," I said as I sat down in the chair on the guest side of the desk.

"All right, let's get started. Bernie called me late last night. He's on his way over here now, but in the meantime, I'll give you a brief synopsis of his findings. He figures our Jane Doe was between twenty and twenty-five years old. She appeared to be in good health. He figures she died sometime Friday afternoon. He's still running tests to determine an actual time of death. He also found that she was approximately three months pregnant."

I reached forward and set my coffee on the desk. I wasn't prepared for what Bubba had just told me. I leaned back in the chair, folded my arms across my chest, and took in a deep breath, instantly exhaling when my lungs couldn't hold any more. "Is he sure?" I asked. It was a foolish question. Bernie would never have said it if he wasn't absolutely positive.

It seemed like ten minutes, even though it was only about thirty seconds, before either one of us spoke.

"Do you think the teddy bear she was holding had any significant meaning?"

Sgt. Costa reached up and rubbed his eyes. "Sorry, I didn't get much sleep last night. The image of our Jane Doe kept re-appearing in my dreams. Questions streamed across my mind like an old fashioned movie marquee and I had no answers—none. But, to answer your question, I have no idea."

There was a soft knock on the window to Sgt. Costa's office. It was Bernie. He was holding a cup of coffee in one hand and a manila folder in the other. I got up to let him in and slid a chair from the corner over to the desk. "Good morning," I said. "Or rather, just morning."

Bernie acknowledged my greeting and settled himself in beside me. Sgt. Costa nodded as he took a mouthful of coffee.

Bernie looked troubled. "I'm sure Bubba filled you in on what I found."

"He did," I said. "And now it begins. We know approximately the when. We don't know the who. We don't know the why. We don't know the where. Now my question is: do we know the how?" I turned to Bernie for an answer.

"Yes and no," he said. "But before we get to the how, let's take a look at the where. He opened his folder, turned a couple of pages then stopped. "Bubba, take a look at this." He handed Sgt. Costa a page from the folder. "After you finish reading it, please give it to Casey." Bernie sat back in his chair and sipped his coffee until we both finished reading.

"When I examined her body, I found sand and sea grass in several areas." He must have sensed us looking at him because he stopped talking. "Don't look at me in that tone of voice." He smiled, trying to break the tension that had built-up in the room. "I know what you're going to say. Sand and Cape Cod go together like coffee and cream. That's true, but when you add a special sea grass to the mix, you come up with a more specific location."

"Now you've got me confused." I raised my eyes in a puzzling expression and tossed my hands out sideways.

"Bubba, do you remember the experiment the National Seashore Research Lab conducted about six or seven years ago over on the east side dunes, just as you round the corner across from Seaside Cottages?" Bernie waited for Bubba to search his think tank.

"I do. We had to post details there so nobody would trespass and contaminate the area. In fact, wasn't it some kind of medical experiment? Weren't they trying to grow a certain kind of sea grass that could be used somehow in cancer research?"

"I have no idea what you guys are talking about," I said.

"Well, I guess it was determined the soil and weather conditions in this particular area were ideal to produce this special grass." Bernie rocked in his chair, turned his head to one side, then with a deep sigh continued, "It was very interesting to read about and, if it had actually worked, it would have been instrumental in the development of a cure for that horrible disease." I could see the pain in Bernie's face. The memories of his wife reflected in his eyes.

Sgt. Costa stood up, came around from the back of his desk, and rested his hand on Bernie's shoulder. "Do you want to take a break?"

"No, I'll be okay. Actually, I'd like to continue." Bernie managed a smile to let us know he was ready.

"Casey, I'd like to assign Officer Maloney to work with you on this case. I don't know if he told you, but he comes from a long line of police officers. I've got a good feeling about him. With your direction and his desire to learn, I think we've got ourselves one hell of a detective in the making."

I shook my head in a positive motion to show Sarge I totally agreed. Besides, it would be fun working with a kid from the City.

"We'll need to get a team together to do a sweep of the location

Bernie is talking about. I'll call Truro PD first thing in the morning to see if they can spare a couple of guys to help. It's going to be very tedious, especially since we have no idea what we're looking for." Bubba stretched his neck up to look out his office window at the duty desk. "Does anybody, besides me, want another coffee?"

"I'll take one," I said.

"Bernie, how about you?" Bubba asked as he reached for his phone.

"I'm good. I already had four cups before I got here. Had to have something to keep me awake, since I was up most of the night."

"Officer Lambert, could you please bring two coffees. Yep, the same as last time. Thanks."

"Casey, I just assumed you'd be able to be here tomorrow morning. One of these days I'm going to get myself into trouble by making assumptions without asking." Sgt. Costa shrugged his shoulders.

"I'll call Chuck in the morning and explain everything to him. If I tell him we've got the exclusive, there won't be a problem. In fact, I know he'll give me the time to run with it as long as I check in with him periodically."

"Now that we've made some headway into the where, let's move on to the how." Bernie appeared anxious to share his theory with us.

"I checked for needle marks that could indicate a possible overdose. I didn't observe any. I checked for any noticeable trauma that could indicate some type of abuse, perhaps contributing to her death. Again, I didn't find any. Then there's always death by natural causes—you know, heart failure, aneurism etc. I've seen it before; somebody dies from natural causes and may be in the company of another person who can't accept the death. The other person tries to hide or conceal their loss in the fashion we found our Jane Doe. If you remember, she was in a very peaceful state. She wasn't tossed there. It appears she was gently placed beside the bed. There were no signs of a struggle inside the cottage, so I believe she died someplace else and was brought there. You both read the report on my findings, so you know she was approximately three months pregnant. It was possible her body couldn't accept the extra life feeding off her organs. Because of the time lapse between her death and the autopsy, I couldn't determine if this might be what happened."

"Are you telling us she died of natural causes?" Sgt. Costa asked. He knew the natural cause theory would make closing this case much easier, but judging from the look on Bernie's face, he wasn't going to get off that easy. "You believe she was murdered, don't you?"

"I do." Bernie's answer was short and to the point.

"Okay, if you think our Jane Doe was murdered, you haven't given us a clue as to how she died." I said.

"Let me finish," said Bernie. "I ran the regular series of toxicology tests all ME's use when trying to determine cause of death. They all came back one hundred percent negative. I almost recorded natural causes when I remembered a new tox test I was given a couple of months ago when I attended a seminar in Boston. From what I understand, it's still in the experimental stage. The president of the Board of Medical Examiners asked a couple of us old guys in the business to try it out if we had the opportunity. I tried to tell him it would be a waste of time and product to give me the kit. He disagreed."

Bernie had drawn me into his world. Not that I understood much of what he was saying, but the mystery he created gnawed at my brain. "What's this new test searching for?"

"It's supposed to detect any signs of a little known poison called Diotoxinal." Bernie hesitated. "That's the scientific name, of course. The common name is Baby Bomb."

Sgt. Costa shifted in his chair, tilted his head back and without moving anything but his eyes, made a sweeping observation of the ceiling. After a couple of seconds, he leaned forward on his elbows and directed his comments to both Bernie and me. "Baby Bomb might be very common to you, but to us, at least me, it's still foreign. We need to move ahead, so if you'll please give us something concrete we can sink our teeth into, I'd appreciate it."

"Anyway, I ran the test and it came back positive."

"Meaning, she had some of this Baby Bomb in her system?" I asked.

"Yes," Bernie replied. "This new drug of choice to abort pregnancy is not readily available to the general public. In fact, it's still so new that many doctors probably don't know anything about it. I say new, but new in the world of medicine could mean it was initially introduced ten years ago. As I said before, the test is still in the experimental stage and mostly because the drug itself is still undergoing testing. From what I understand, it's a very delicate mixture of chemicals. And, some of these chemicals could react with things as common as Vitamin C, causing a deadly reaction."

CHAPTER ELEVEN

My cell phone vibrated, breaking the silence that had crept into Bubba's office. I looked at the caller ID and saw Sam's name spelled out in bold green letters. "Hi," I said. "Hold on." I turned to look at Sarge and Bernie. "I've got to take this call, I'll be right back." I got up and stepped outside Bubba's office into the squad room.

"Okay, I'm back. I'm glad you called. I need a break. What a mess this case is." I could feel myself rambling and I'm sure Sam thought so too.

"You done, Sherlock?"

"Yeah, what's up?"

"I was just checking up on you. Are we still on for clams and rings tonight?"

I had forgotten that we had made plans, but didn't want Sam to know. "Well, of course we are. Did you think I'd forget?"

"Of course not." There was a hesitation, then a 'Snidely Whiplash' laugh.

"Okay, you caught me. Can't help it. You know my mind. I'm like Angela Lansbury when she gets involved with a murder way up there in Cabot Cove. In my case, my Sherlock instincts kick in."

"So, they've determined it is a homicide?"

"It sure is. You'll find this one very interesting. I find it not only interesting, but challenging."

"Listen, Casey, we need to talk about your involvement."

"We'll do that. And then I'll tell you how involved I'm going to get."

Sam let out a sigh. "Enough. Are we on for tonight or not?"

I looked at the clock on the wall over the duty desk. "It's two-thirty. I've got to find the girls, pick up my car at Marnie's house, then I'll meet you at my house around six o'clock. Sound good?"

"That's a plan. If something changes, give me a call."

"Sherlock signing out," I said and quickly pressed the end button before Sam could comment. I stood staring out the front window of the station. Sam had my best interests at heart, but I had to be my own person. If our relationship was going to go any further, he'd have to understand that. For now, I decided to leave it alone. I really do want, and more than that, need him near.

I shrugged my shoulders, took a deep breath and headed back to Sgt. Costa's office. "I think we've done as much as we can today. I'm going to find Annie and Marnie and head back up to the mid-Cape. We can get a fresh start tomorrow morning. I'll get here around 9:00. Is that okay with you, Sarge?"

"Yeah, I'll get ahold of Maloney and have him here too. I want him in on the ground floor." Sgt. Costa seemed puzzled.

"Sarge, you've got words and question marks swirling across your forehead. And none of it is making any sense. What going on?"

Bernie stood up and started toward the office door. "Bubba, I'm going to check out some more things tonight. If I have anything by tomorrow morning to add, I'll give you a call. There are a few more tests I want to run. If you need me, I'll be on my cell." He reached over and patted Sgt. Costa on the back and gave me a fatherly hug. "You take care of yourself, little lady. We'll talk soon." Without any more being said, Bernie headed across the lobby, waved to Officer Lambert as he walked past the duty desk, and headed out onto Shank Painter Road.

"Casey, I'm getting too old for this shit. It's starting to sink in more than I want it to. We have a young girl—a dead, young girl. We don't have any idea who she is or where she came from. She's somebody's daughter and . . . . " Sgt. Costa turned away. He lifted his hands to his face and wiped his eyes. After a brief moment, he composed himself. "This is the stuff I can never get used to."

I knew what he meant. Last summer, I'd gotten involved in the murder of a sixteen-year-old girl that was killed in a hit-and-run. It was a senseless killing of an innocent child. There's still nights when I wake up from a sound sleep and see her face looking back at me. This is one of the reasons Sam wants me to back off.

It was time for me to leave. Sgt. Costa needed to be alone and I needed to find the girls. We both needed a change of conversation and scenery. I walked over to Sarge, gave him a kiss on the cheek. "Please pass this on to the Mrs. See you in the morning."

Sgt. Costa walked me to the door. "Safe ride home."

I acknowledged with a nod of the head and off I went.

I had no idea where Annie and Marnie had ventured out to, but a quick call on the cell would take care of that. I hoped they had eaten some lunch because I didn't have time to stop. I was just checking my contacts for Annie's number, when my cell rang. "Well, hi," I said. "Great minds think alike. I was just about to call you guys. Where are you?"

"If you turn right and don't waiver off the beaten path, you'll bump into us."

I turned to see those two buffoons standing three buildings down, peeking around the corner, ready to pounce. I walked down to meet them. "Children must play." I rolled my eyes, then started to laugh. "I needed that! It's been a tough day so far." I went over and put my arms around their necks and pulled us together for a group hug. "Did you guys get lunch?"

"You're talking to me, remember." Annie folded her arms in front of her. "I knew you'd be tied up for hours so, yes, we had some lunch."

"Wc went to this neat little place down on the beach," said Marnie. "Annie, what was the name of that place?"

"Pinchers."

"Anyway, they had porch seating and hadn't closed it down for the season yet, so we sat outside, had lobster chowder in a warm crusty bread bowl and watched the locals flying kites along the shore. Can you imagine, it's October and seventy-two degrees out. What could be better?" Marnie threw her arms up in the air and spun around like a child.

I smiled. “Let’s go home.” We joined hands, walked down Shank Painter Road, crossed Bradford to Central, walked down Central until we came to Commercial, then turned left and headed toward the parking lot at MacMillan Pier.

“That was a hike,” said Annie as she leaned against the car trying to catch her breath.

“What you need is more exercise. In fact, we need to put that on our to-do list of winter activities,” I said.

“We could always mall-walk and kill two birds with one stone. Walking—shopping—walking—shopping. I think that has a good ring to it.” Marnie tried to keep a straight face. “Don’t you agree?”

CHAPTER TWELVE

There were a lot of cars trying to negotiate Commercial Street so we had to inch our way out into the intersection. Instead of following the parade of tourists, we cut across Commercial onto Ryder then took our first right onto Bradford Street. Eventually Bradford reconnected with Commercial. I wanted to ride out the shore road and go past the Seaside Cottages.

"Annie, would you please slow down when you ride by number three?" I asked.

Marnie rode shot-gun. Her head was turned toward the ocean. "The view from here is amazing. I wish I could remember it for its beauty and not something else."

There was silence until we passed number three. Then Annie spoke up, "So, Casey, are you going to fill us in on your meeting with Sgt. Costa and Bernie?"

"I'll tell you all we know—which isn't much."

Marnie turned sideways in her seat to give me her undivided attention.

"Our girl in the cottage is still labeled 'Jane Doe.' We have no clue who she is. Bernie is running some tests. I'm not sure which ones or what they're supposed to tell us. But as soon as he has results, he's going to be in touch. He did find out she was pregnant. But she either took, or was given, some kind of new drug to abort it—a drug not readily available on the market. It's still in the testing stage."

"Are they going to run DNA tests?" asked Annie. "You remember that the state police ran a whole mess of random DNA tests a few of years ago when Elaine Bradshaw was found murdered in her house. It's a long shot, but maybe they should check those."

“I remember that case well,” I said. “It was gruesome. She’d been dead for a few days before she was found. The smell stayed with me for weeks.”

“And you like this stuff?” Marnie grimaced.

“Of course not.” I shook my head and gave her the look. “I’m human—really I am. It’s part of my job. The part I don’t like. But it comes with the package. As far as those DNA tests go, I’m sure Bernie is already working on that.”

Annie glanced into her rearview mirror. “Well, what else?”

“Bernie seems to think she was murdered in the dunes and brought to number three. He found a piece of a specific species of sea-grass on her.”

“Explain, please,” said Marnie.

“Some years back there was an experiment performed in a small isolated section of the dunes. Actually the section is almost across the street from number three. Anyway, the scientists doing the testing couldn’t give unanimous thumbs up to the conclusions. So, they scrapped the whole thing. Bernie was very interested in it. It was supposed to be a break-through in cancer research.” I took a deep breath, then continued, “Bernie’s wife died of cancer.” I sat back in my seat and Marnie turned to face forward. “It was sad. He didn’t have any children so he’s pretty much alone,” I said.

“I’m going to pull into Dunkin’s. Does anybody want a coffee?” Annie asked trying to change the subject.

“An iced coffee sounds good,” said Marnie.

“I sure could use a French Vanilla. Let’s go inside, my treat,” I said.

The parking lot wasn’t crowded at all. “Everybody must be in town,” said Annie as she pulled into a space right in front of the door.

The two girls working behind the counter seemed glad to see us. When there are customers, the day goes by fast, but when it’s quiet, the day lasts forever. Annie and Marnie got some napkins and creamers and headed toward a table. I waited for our order, then carefully balanced the three cups and joined up with them.

"I'm coming back down tomorrow morning. Sarge is going to assign Maloney to the case. He seems to think he has a good head on his shoulders." I looked at the girls. They wanted me to tell them more, but there wasn't any more to tell.

"Do you have any idea what your next move is going to be?" asked Marnie.

I took a sip of my coffee. "Not really. We need to do some brainstorming. Hopefully, we can come up with avenues to pursue. We'll show a picture of Jane Doe to the town merchants. With any luck, somebody might recognize her. In the meantime, I'd like to start checking missing person reports and get some pictures to police departments throughout the state. Tonight I'll get my 3x5's started."

"Speaking of tonight," said Marnie, "are we doing anything?"

"I don't know about Casey, but I'm staying in. I've got a few things I have to do. Mike sent a report home with me. I told him I'd read it over the weekend and give him my opinion Monday morning."

"When Sam agreed to dog-sit for Watson, I told him I'd go out with him for clams and rings when I got home. In fact, he called earlier and asked me if we were still on." Actually, I missed him and was looking forward to the two of us being alone.

"Then I guess I'm having frozen pizza and a beer or two. I could always call my cousin." Marnie laughed. "Not! I'm afraid he'd say 'Sure, I'll be right down.' Since that whole ordeal with James last summer, he's become overly protective."

"You've got to imagine what he's going through. He considered James one of his best friends. He introduced you two. Now James is in jail, being tried for murder. It'll be hard for Barry during the trial. I'll be glad when the whole thing is over." Annie put her arm around Marnie.

I looked away. I could have been—almost was—his second victim. "Time to change the subject," I said.

We finished our coffee, waved to the girls behind the counter and headed back to Annie's car. With seat belts fastened, the radio tuned to soft rock and the windows slightly cracked, we started back down 6A.

A Patty Page song came on the radio –

If you're fond of sand dunes
And salt sea air ...
Quaint little villages
Here and there ...

As though on cue, the three of us started singing out loud.

"Cats howling would sound better. Good thing we don't sing for a living." I laughed then continued in my best performance voice.

"Hey, hi, Grumpy's. This is where it all started this morning," said Marnie as she turned and waved to nobody.

Without notice, Annie screamed, "Hold on," then slammed on the brakes and came to an abrupt stop. She instinctively reached her arm out in front of Marnie as though she was a child. When Annie realized they were safe, she pulled her arm back, held the steering wheel tight and leaned her head forward. Nobody could see it coming. Just around the bend was a barrage of blinking red and blue lights. "Whew," she said. "Another couple car lengths and we would have been part of that scene."

There were a couple ambulances, three police cars, and a fire truck. It must have happened within the last fifteen minutes or less because there wasn't a traffic back-up.

We weren't going anywhere fast, so I decided to get out and take a look. It was the newspaper reporter coming out in me. "I'll be right back," I said and quickly unlocked and opened the door. I recognized several of the cops on the scene. One, Officer Jack Harris, was off to the side. It appeared he was taking notes. He'd move his head one way, lean forward to get a better view, then go back to his writing.

From what I could see, a Toyota Highlander broadsided a Honda Odyssey—two big vehicles. It appeared all the passengers from those vehicles were outside and walking around. They all were looking behind one of the ambulances. I moved closer to Officer Harris. "I won't say good-afternoon, just 'hi' will suffice."

He didn't see me approach from the stopped vehicles. Without looking, he told me to stay clear of the scene.

"Jack, it's me, Casey Quinby."

He turned. "Casey, sorry. This is a sad one."

"It looks like all the passengers are okay."

"They are. Behind that ambulance is a bike. The kid looks like he's in his mid-teens. It appears he darted out of the parking lot over there," he said pointing to the Shell station behind us. "We figure he didn't see the Toyota coming around the corner in time to stop. It tried to swerve to avoid him, but the boy panicked and turned into its path. The Toyota hit him and then went into the side of the Honda. They're working on him now." Officer Harris rolled his shoulders and grabbed the back of his neck. "This has been a dangerous spot for as long as I can remember. It's going to take somebody getting killed here for the town to do anything about it."

"I'm with a couple of my friends in that white car over there. I think there's enough room for us to eke by and take that back road that goes behind the gas station. I can see this is going to be grid-locked for a while."

"Nice seeing you, Casey. Bad circumstances, but good to see you. You and Sam should come down to this neck of the woods and get together with me and the Mrs. for a couple of drinks and maybe dinner."

"Sounds good, I'll run it by him. Take care."

I scooted back to the car. "Bad accident," I said. "I think we can maneuver enough to get on the back road that runs around the gas station. It will be a little out of the way, but it beats sitting here."

"Annie, I'll direct you," I said. It took no less than twelve back and forth tiny moves to be able to clear the cars in front and in back of us. Once we opened a path, several of the cars behind us followed. We were finally on our way.

CHAPTER THIRTEEN

It was four-thirty when I pulled into my driveway beside Sam's car. I sat back, took a deep breath, and closed my eyes. I was tired. It had been a grueling day.

I jumped at the tapping on my window.

Sam was standing there, just smiling and tapping. He turned his hand in a circular motion, for me to open the window. "I heard your car pull in about five minutes ago. When I looked out, you appeared to be dozing." He bent forward, rested his forearms on the open window ledge and stuck his head in to give me a kiss. "You okay, Sherlock?"

"Yeah," I said. I caught myself gazing into his eyes. "If you move aside, I can get out; then you can give me a real kiss, and maybe a hug for good measure." I gave him a little wink.

He opened the door and made a sweeping motion with his arm for me to make a grand exit.

"Are you hungry?" Sam asked. "Or should I ask, are you too tired to go out?"

"Yes, I'm hungry and no, I'm not too tired to go out."

"Seafood Harry's is still open. I saw him the other day and he said he's not closing for the season until the end of October. The weather's been too good and so has business."

"I've just come off of a long ride. Let me hit the bathroom and we can get going."

"Go ahead. I'll grab your duffle bag and meet you inside."

Watson was waiting patiently for me. His tail was wagging a mile a minute when I opened the screen door. I patted my hands on my stomach for him to jump up. "This little guy is getting strong. He almost knocked me over." I said to Sam as he came in and shut the door. I got down on my knees and let Watson give me a loving lick.

"I've got an idea," said Sam. "I need to take Watson for a walk before we go. Why don't you do whatever, then the three of us can walk up to the beach. We won't walk the beach, just up and back. Should only take us a half hour."

"That sounds good to me."

Sam held the leash and I held Sam's other hand. *I think I could get used to this. All in good time—all in good time.*

It was five-thirty when we finally got on our way. There was really no reason to rush. We had nowhere special to go—except back to my house. "Those clams and rings are going to taste good. I think I'll have a white zin tonight instead of a beer." My mouth was salivating.

Seafood Harry's was surprisingly busy for a Sunday night so late in the season. I guess everybody had the same idea as we did. Only two more weeks, so we better take advantage of it.

Sam went to the counter to place our order and I headed for a table beside the windows looking out over the harbor. It was still light enough to see the array of boats moored at the marina, bobbing ever so slightly in the calm, protected waters of the inlet. Out on the horizon, I could see lights from the whale watch boat slowly approaching the docks.

I wondered if the whales had given their best performance today so the end of the season tourists could get their final 'oohs' and 'aahs' in before heading back to the mainland.

My thoughts were interrupted when I felt a hand on my shoulder. "Evening, Casey." It was Harry. "Haven't seen you lately. I was wondering how your friend is doing? I think her name was Marnie. That bastard, James. To think I used to call him a friend. He's no friend of mine."

"She's doing okay. It dealt a huge blow to her trust in people—especially men. And I can't say I blame her. She let her guard down and who knows what might have happened if he hadn't been stopped when he was."

"And you, Casey," said Harry, "You doing all right?"

This was the first time I had seen this side of Harry. He was usually the happy-go-lucky, Mr. Macho Man, who assumed every female he met wanted to jump in the sack with him.

"If Marnie needs a shoulder to lean on, be sure to tell her I'm here."

Good ol' Harry, I thought.

I looked around Harry to see where Sam was. Thank goodness, he was on his way to the table.

He put down the two drinks he was carrying and held out his hand to Harry. "Nice to see you, big guy. Got a good crowd here tonight. Did you ever consider staying open all year, or at least until the end of November?"

"I mulled it over. But it wouldn't give me much vacation time in Florida if I did that. Ya know, I gotta keep up the tan—for appearance sake, of course."

"Get out of here, will you." Sam laughed and motioned him to get lost.

I picked up my wine and proposed a toast, "to the good times—may they start now and never end." I reached over the table and clicked Sam's waiting glass, then smiled and took a drink.

Before I could take another sip, Sam held up his hand. "It's my turn. I have something to add." He held his glass, then reached over and took my empty hand. As we clicked our glasses, he said, "To us."

Those two little words shot through my body giving me goose bumps of joy. He hadn't said much, but he didn't have to. I understood.

We were drawn back into realty as the waitress set our food down on the table. "Two clam dinners, both with slaw and rings?" she asked.

"Yep, those are ours," Sam said as he slid one in front of me and pulled the other toward himself. "Dig in, Sherlock. You only get dessert if your finish your dinner."

After a couple of bites, I started up the conversation again. "Did you get done what you needed to do for the trial?"

"For the most part, I'm ready. I don't think this is going to be a long, drawn out process. The facts are pretty cut and dried. I probably shouldn't say that. Some of those defense lawyers make stuff up just to hear themselves talk. I swear they try to confuse the jurors. And, in some cases, they succeed." Sam took a drink of his beer. "I don't think that will happen this time. James wasn't as smart as he thought he was. Even though he didn't actually kill Becky, he thought he did. Your prodding and poking turned up the evidence that led to the real killer. He figured you were on to him and so he needed to stop you before you got to me with any more information. You didn't earn the name Sherlock from sitting home knitting mittens. Paranoia got the best of James and he lost it. He was his own worst enemy."

I wanted to forget last July. If Sam hadn't followed the bread crumbs I'd left as a trail, I wouldn't be here today. He found me unconscious in Mr. Parker's cellar. I was literally minutes away from knocking on St. Peter's door. Poor Mr. Parker wasn't as lucky. The only request I made of Sam was to get Mr. Parker's rocking chair—the one on his front porch—the one he sat in day in and day out, every minute of the day, observing everything from cars, to people, to sounds. I got it. Now, it sits on my back deck. Most days I make myself a cup of French Vanilla, settle into my chair, close my eyes and whisper a little prayer.

"Earth to Casey," said Sam. "A penny for your thoughts."

"I was thinking about Mr. Parker and his rocking chair," I said. "Every time I sit there, I can feel him looking down on me—watching me—trying to protect me. He didn't deserve to die the way he did."

"No, he didn't. But remember, ultimately it was his keen observations that opened that ever-so-slight crack in the case. He was truly a key player in bringing closure to Becky's tragic death."

Time to change the conversation. "Mangia, O'Brian," I said as I picked up a ring with my fingers and stabbed a clam with my fork. "Don't let your food get cold."

Sam slid his chair out from the table, "I'm getting another beer. Want a wine?"

"And you need to ask?" I said as he gave me a look, smiled and headed for the counter.

I looked out the window beside our table. Lights from some of the boats dotted the harbor and created reflective shadows across the water. *What a relaxing, beautiful sight*, I thought. *I wonder what it would be like to live on a boat. It could be the best of both worlds—dock on Cape Cod in the warm months and head for Florida to escape the winter cold.*

"What are you dreaming about now, Sherlock?"

"Oh, nothing," I said as I filled my mouth with food so I wouldn't have to add anything to my sentence. "Do you need to go over anything in James' case with me?" I asked.

"Not really, unless you have questions. I was with the District Attorney last Thursday and he told me he had everything he needed to proceed."

"The other day, Marnie told me she was going to sit in on the trial." I looked at Sam for a reaction.

"Do you think it's a good idea?" he asked.

"At first, I didn't. Then, I thought about it. James mentally hurt her pretty bad and I think she needs closure as much as I do. Of course, it's a different kind of closure, but just as important. Do you understand?"

"I suppose," he said with a sigh. "I suppose."

"I want to change the subject," I said.

Sam nodded in agreement. "I've got an idea. It's still early. When we leave here, let's go to Centerville and get an ice cream at the Corner Cone."

"You certainly have become a good boy turned bad. Fried food and now ice cream. I'm lovin' this guy sittin' across from me." I laughed and gently kicked him under the table.

CHAPTER FOURTEEN

We pulled into the parking lot at the Corner Cone. It was dark. The sign on the door read:

OCTOBER HOURS

FRIDAY, SATURDAY, AND SUNDAY

NOON 'TILL SEVEN

"Well, I guess that shoots the crap out of ice cream." Sam turned for my reaction.

"No it doesn't," I said. "We can go to Stop and Shop on Route 28, pick up a half-gallon and bring it home." *Wow, how permanent did that sound. It's my home and I made it sound like ours—a mere slip of the tongue. It did come out pretty easy though. Okay, enough of that.*

"Sounds like a plan. What kind do you want to get?"

Now he's even asking what kind I want. "Anything except peanut butter," I answered. "You make the choice."

"We should pick up a few more things too. I used all the orange juice, milk and cereal since there was only enough for one glass and one bowl."

"It would have lasted three days for me. Remember, my overnight was a spur of the moment thing and I didn't expect a house guest. By the way, are you planning on staying tonight?" I tilted my head, raised my eyebrows and looked at Sam for an answer.

"If you're a good girl, I just might. Besides, you haven't filled me in on your girls' weekend and your trip to P-town yet. And I'm sure you're just dying to do that." He winked, then proceeded to back the car out and head toward Route 28.

We found a parking spot in the first row at Stop and Shop, got out of the car and, like a *happy, little couple,* joined hands and walked into the store. Fifteen minutes later, we were back in the car with ice cream and enough food to get us through a couple of days. I looked at the bags in the back seat, then looked at Sam. "How long did you say you were staying?"

"It's not all for me, you know. I don't want my Sherlock and Watson to starve, now do I?"

Poor Watson, I thought. Sam and I have been gone for almost three hours. He must be ready for a walk—this time, just around the outside of the house and not down to the beach.

The driveway leading to my house was dark. "I meant to change that bulb last night," said Sam.

"I've changed it at least three times in the last couple of weeks. It keeps burning out. There must be something wrong with the fixture. One of these days I'll get somebody to look at it."

"I'm no electrician," said Sam as he handed me a couple of bags, "but, I'll make a mental note to check it in the morning. I don't like the idea of you coming home and not being able to see when you walk up the steps. You certainly don't need another fall." He leaned over and gave me a kiss on the cheek.

"I've been here for almost eight years and haven't crippled myself yet."

"The old bones get brittle with time." He scurried forward to avoid being hit with the ice cream bag.

Sam unlocked the door and had to coax Watson to one side so he could open it. "Hey there, little man, did you protect the homestead while we were away?"

Sam got down on the floor and rolled around, tossing his head back and forth, teasing Watson with one of his chewy toys. Sometimes I wonder if Sam got Watson for me or for him—probably a little of both.

I left the two of them playing on the living room floor and headed to the kitchen to put the groceries away. "Are you ready for your ice cream?" I asked.

"I'm taking my little man out for a walk. We'll be right back and we'll both be ready for a treat—ice cream that is."

"Aren't we funny tonight? Get going or I'll eat it all."

Sam hooked Watson to his leash. "Yeah, yeah, yeah," he said as the two of them dashed out the door.

My jeans were starting to feel confining. I figured I had just enough time to get them off and slip into a pair of Joe Boxers before my audience of two returned.

I walked out of my bedroom just as the front door opened.

"Look at my little quick change artist," said Sam. "I'd say you have had some experience doing this, but …."

"But is the last word you better say or the ME might be paying this address a visit."

"Only kidding, Sherlock. Let's have some dessert."

I was already in the kitchen before Sam finished his sentence. "Do you want any chocolate syrup on yours?"

"Sure, but just a little."

A couple minutes later, I emerged carrying a tray with two cereal bowl-size dishes and a small saucer of Breyers Cherry Vanilla ice cream. "Good choice," I said as I handed Sam one of the bowls and the saucer for Watson.

Sam had already pushed the 'all-on' button on the remote. We had five minutes to get comfy before a new episode of CSI came on. We both loved that show—one of our favorites. I didn't think I'd like it anymore when they replaced the Gil Grissom character, first with Marg Helgenberger, then, with Ted Danson. I couldn't imagine the bar manager on Cheers heading up the Crime Scene Investigation Unit in Las Vegas. I was wrong. Now, I can't wait to see him in action. I think I'm a little prejudiced, since he has a house on Martha's Vineyard and some of his mannerisms and expressions bring his character a little closer to home.

"I know the equipment they use to test the bits and pieces of evidence they've gathered are mostly props that don't really exist, but those high tech toys send waves of adrenalin throughout my body. Maybe one of these days, the real crime labs will catch up to the television technology. I hope I'm around to see it," said Sam.

We finished our ice cream and assumed the cuddle position for the rest of CSI. Of course, Ted got his man and both cases the department was working on ended with an arrest.

"Imagine if we could wrap up cases in an hour."

I tilted my head back and looked into Sam's eyes. "Only in Hollywood," I said. Normally, I'd stay up and watch Jay Leno. Tonight I was exhausted. It had been a long day and my thinker had shut off hours ago. If Sam hadn't been here, I might have skipped CSI—then again, maybe not. "I don't know about you, but I'm ready to hit the hay."

"I'll take Watson outside, then I'll be right behind you." Sam helped me up off the couch and clapped his hands to arouse Watson.

I shut off the lights, all except the table lamp outside the bedroom door. Sam could do that on his way in. I pulled my last clean night shirt from my middle dresser drawer. I remembered kidding earlier with Marnie about having to do laundry. Judging on how empty my drawers were, it really wasn't a joke. When I took my clothes off and slipped my night shirt on, I noticed Sam standing in the doorway watching me. "Do you like what you see?" I batted my eyelashes, then blew him a little kiss and walked down the hall to the bathroom. "Be right back," I said giving him a flirty little finger wave.

"You've got five minutes and I'm coming in." Sam folded his arms across his chest and resumed his position in the doorway.

I never washed my face and brushed my teeth so fast. Anything else was going to have to wait. After all, I was given only five minutes. Normal night bathroom time can take up to a half hour or more. There was a gentle tap on the door. "Go away," I said, then smiled. I opened the door to see Sam blocking my exit. I'm sure my eyes told the story. His navy blue and white plaid Nautica boxer shorts complimented his perfectly formed six-pack. Working out in the police department gym sure had paid off. He wrapped his arms around me, pulled me close, and whispered in my ear, "Meet you in the middle in five."

CHAPTER FIFTEEN

Boston

It was almost noontime. Katherine was about to put her research away for the day and head over to The Gallery, when a name flashed across the monitor. She had changed from researching the O'Ryan's to her adoptive mother's maiden name, Latham. The 1975 Dorchester City Directory she had been searching listed a Latham family living at 359 Hamilton Street. She determined it was her mother's family address. One of the names listed, besides her grandfather, grandmother and mother, was Emma. Her relationship to the head of household was recorded as niece and her age was listed as three. That made her eleven years younger than her mother.

"It was busy at the main desk, so I couldn't get back to give you a hand." Raji was standing behind her.

She was in deep thought. She heard him, but wasn't interested in answering.

He tapped her on the back of her head. "Hello, anybody home?" he said quietly.

"Oh, sorry, I guess I was so engrossed in what I was doing that I didn't realize it was you behind me." She wasn't ready to share her new find with anyone, so she closed out the site and changed the subject before he had a chance to read the monitor. "I didn't realize the time. Usually, you remind me I'm going to be late if I don't get a move on." She smiled. "So, now I really do have to get to The Gallery." She stood up, gathered her paperwork and slid it into her backpack.

"There you go again," said Raji, "carrying the weight of the world on your shoulders. I can at least help you until you get to the door."

"Thanks buddy. I'd appreciate it."

She was glad they were in a library and conversation was kept to a minimum.

When they got to the front door, Raji helped her slip her arms into the straps and hoisted the backpack up onto her shoulders. She kissed the tips of her fingers on her right hand and reached over to touch his cheek. "You're such a love. See you next Monday, if not before. Have a good one."

"You too," he said.

I hope The Gallery is quiet this afternoon. I need to work on my notes, she thought.

CHAPTER SIXTEEN

Boston

Katherine took her time getting to The Gallery. She was always early. Today was going to be different. Her thoughts were back at the library. Emma—if she was my mother's cousin . . .

"Hey, watch out!"

Katherine jumped back up on the sidewalk. She frantically looked around searching for the voice that had just snapped her mind back to real time.

A well-dressed, older gentleman reached out to steady her. "Are you okay?" he asked. "These pain-in-the-ass Boston drivers. They have no regard for lights, crosswalks, or pedestrians in general. Instead of making more roads or always widening existing ones, the city should invest in over-the-road walkways. But no, they'll wait until too many people are hurt or killed before they take any action." As quickly as he began his speech, he stopped.

"Thank you," was the only thing that came from Katherine's mouth. She was pretty shaken, but refused to display it, especially in front of a stranger.

"Do you have far to go?" he asked.

"No, I work around the corner on Newbury Street." She'd said enough, perhaps too much. "Again, thank you. Have a nice day."

"You're welcome," he said. "Watch where you're walking and you'll have a nice day, too."

He turned left, crossed the street and disappeared into the crowd that had emerged from the MTA exit ramp. Katherine continued to The Gallery.

It was her day to open. Every Monday, her boss, Mr. Grossman, went to lunch with a couple other shop owners. He usually made an appearance around three o'clock. She slid her backpack from her shoulders and fished in the side pocket for her key. As she glided it into the lock, she noticed the lights were on inside. There was a shadow of a person walking toward the door. Katherine pulled the key back and quickly moved away. The glare from the sun on the window created a smokescreen, bestowing a ghostly façade to the image quickly approaching the door. Just as she was about to turn and run to the Starbucks on the corner, the door opened and Mr. Grossman stepped out.

"Katherine, what's the matter?" The puzzled look on his face made her feel foolish.

"It's been one of those mornings you want to cancel and start over." She wasn't about to say anything about her find in the Dorchester City Directory. Mr. Grossman knew she was spending a lot of time at the library, but he thought she was researching painting techniques. Why would he think anything different? All she talked about when she was at work was her love of the artists that tastefully adorned The Gallery walls. "I was daydreaming and stepped off the curb, almost in front of a car that ran a red light. A man standing a few feet away from me yelled. Good thing he did, otherwise you'd be looking for another assistant."

"I put a pot of coffee on. Come on inside, sit down, and I'll get you a cup." Mr. Grossman stepped aside to let her pass.

"What are you doing here so early, anyway?" Katherine asked.

"Sidney and Charlie had things they needed to tend to. Sidney had to go to a closing on a re-finance for his house. Why he doesn't just take some money out of the mattress and eliminate a bill is far beyond me. And Charlie had a doctor's appointment. His wife was making him go. I don't know why and I didn't ask. She's crazy, you know."

"Since you're here and it's usually slow on Mondays, do you want to change some of the exhibits around?"

"Naw, my ambition up and left me this morning. Actually, it never appeared. I have some mail I've been avoiding, so I think I'll take a look. I know half of it is from new young artists trying to get a couple of spots in The Gallery."

"Mr. Grossman, that might not be a bad idea. We haven't put anything fresh up for a few months. Let's take a look at what they have to offer. Who knows, you might discover the 'new-world' Picasso and he or she could be from right here in Boston."

"Katherine, Katherine—you're such a dreamer. I wish I could share your optimism. The empty spaces are reserved for you. In fact, you promised me a painting next month. Have you been working on it?"

"Ah, yes and no. It's hard to paint at Peter's condo. We don't have a lot of room as it is and the light—well, it's not great. I miss my loft and being able to spread my paints out and express my inner feelings. My canvas was my field of flowers and my brushes were my magic wands that made them come alive. Someday, Mr. Grossman, someday." She knew she had the bubble-wrapped paintings at Peter's, but she didn't feel they were good enough to hang in The Gallery, so she never told Mr. Grossman about them.

"I've got an idea. Why don't you take the rest of the day off."

"It's only one-thirty." Katherine stood up and walked toward the wall where her paintings would one day hang. She turned to face her boss.

"Go ahead. Your day didn't start too good, maybe you can change it so it will end up much better."

"This is a surprise, and a very pleasant one at that. Thank you," she said as she reached for her backpack. "I'll see you tomorrow. And remember, take a look at those pictures."

"I will. I'll put the ones that seem interesting aside for you to look at. See you later." Mr. Grossman gave her a two finger salute and headed for the back room."

The bell on the door jingled as Katherine left. *I could go back to the library*, she thought, then decided she'd had enough library time for today. Peter wouldn't be home so she could take out her notes and try to put them in some kind of order. After all, he did say he was going to work with her over the weekend to see if they could come up with something concrete to pursue. If she had a little head start, it might help move things along.

She wasn't used to riding the MTA without the usual five o'clock crowd. It was comforting to be able to sit and relax a little before the conductor announced the approaching South Boston stop. Somebody had left a Boston Globe in the seat in front of her so she picked it up and flipped through until she found the movie section.

'The Odd Life of Timothy Green' or 'Hope Springs', no, thought Katherine. *Peter wanted to see 'The Amazing Spider-Man.'* It was still playing at AMC on Tremont Street. She knew he was going to call her around two-ish. Since he went in early, maybe he could leave work early. She folded the paper and tucked it into her backpack just in time to hear the conductor say, "Next stop—Brrrrroadway."

CHAPTER SEVENTEEN

Boston

At exactly two o'clock, Katherine's cell phone rang. She knew it would be Peter, but checked the caller ID anyway. "Hi," was the only thing that came out of her mouth.

"You okay?" he asked.

"Yeah, I got home early and was working on my notes. I didn't realize what time it was."

"Why are you home early?"

"Nothing's wrong. Mr. Grossman didn't go to lunch with his cronies today and I guess he thought I was a little frazzled, so he gave me the day off and with pay."

"Why did he think you were frazzled, as you put it?"

"The Boston traffic—I almost got hit by a car. We both weren't paying attention." She sighed, "It was nothing, really." Katherine sat down and opened the Globe to the movie section. *"Spider-Man"* is still playing at the AMC on Tremont Street. If you can come home early, we could go to the four-thirty show, then J.J.'s for supper."

"That sounds good to me. I'll clean up my desk and head out. I should be home in an hour."

"I'll be ready. Love you."

CHAPTER EIGHTEEN

I rolled over, eyes still closed, and reached out for Sam. Instead of an inviting, tender body my hand landed on a furry, warm Watson. He was all curled up and didn't even flinch as my hand came around and rested on the back of his neck. My senses were aroused with the sweet smell of French Vanilla coming from the kitchen. Next to Sam, my coffee makes my inners tingle.

I was still in bed when Sam peaked through the open door to see if I was awake. "Morning, sleeping beauty," he said as he came over and sat down beside me. He gently brushed my hair back from my face with his hand, leaned over, and gave me a kiss. "It's Monday morning—time to rise and shine."

"Do you have to be so cheery? Move, so I can get up."

"Coffee's ready whenever you are."

"Just let me brush my teeth and I'll be right there."

The image in the bathroom mirror wasn't pretty. My hair looked like a string mop that had dried up-side-down in some forgotten corner of a room. I smoothed it out as best I could, then, for the time being, pulled it back into a pony-tail.

"Are you ready? I'm putting the English muffins in the toaster."

I took a deep breath. I think I could handle this morning exchange every day, but I'm not sure about Sam. *Enough*, I thought. *Enjoy the moment*. I headed for the kitchen.

"I was going to set us up outside, but there was a little nip in the air so I decided not to. Watson's already had his breakfast and gone for a walk. So we can relax. Go sit down and I'll bring your coffee and muffin."

Sam was being overly nice this morning. I began to think he had an ulterior motive behind this special treatment.

"What are your plans for today?" he asked.

"Well, I have to go back to P-town and work out the nuts and bolts of operation identity. Before we can start putting this puzzle together, we need to find out who our Jane Doe is. I have a feeling this isn't going to be easy. We're going to canvas the area to see if anybody recognizes her. Before we start though, I want to send a sketch statewide over the wire to see if she pops up on anybody's missing persons list." I stopped just long enough to take a bite of my muffin and wash it down with some coffee. "With any luck, we'll get a hit."

"Do you need my help?"

"Let me get started first. I'm also going to talk to Bubba regarding an article for the Tribune. Of course, I'll run it by him before I send it to print. If our Jane Doe is local to the Cape, somebody outside of P-town might be able to give us some information. Since we have nothing at the moment to go on, any little hint we can investigate will be helpful."

Sam got up from the table and popped another K-cup into the Keurig. "You ready for another cup?"

I could hear the change in his voice. "Not yet," I said.

"Casey, you know I worry about you, don't you?" He turned to face me.

Ever since last summer when he almost lost me, he's been somewhat over-protective. "I promise you I won't go rogue and investigate anything on my own without letting you or someone know what I'm doing or where I'm going." I knew I was going to have a hard time keeping my word, but it was the only way I was going to get him off my back—at least for the time being.

"That's a promise I'm going to hold you to."

"I'll have that other coffee now."

He put another French Vanilla into the Keurig, reached over for my cup and pushed the brew button.

"Once I get things in some sort of order, I'd like Marnie to work with me on this one. I'm sure Mike won't object. I don't want to pull her into it, though, until I get a report from Bernie, the preliminary paperwork started and my story written. We need some direction, so if I can furnish that, we may be able to develop some sort of time-line and get answers." I looked over to Sam. "Am I making any sense or just rambling?"

"Sherlock, you do some of your best work when you ramble. You sometimes scare me though with that rambling of yours."

"I guess I'll take that as a vote of confidence." I smiled. "So what about you. Are you still working on your trial?"

"It's pretty much done. I'm having lunch at Finn's with Mike, then head on over to his office to review a few things. I feel we have a solid case. We're convinced the outcome will be favorable to the State."

I looked at the clock on the stove. "Yikes, it's almost 8:30. I wanted to be in P-town before 10:30. I told Bubba I'd give him a call, so he can have Maloney at the station when I get there."

Sam was leaning against the counter finishing his coffee. "How does pizza and beer sound tonight?"

"Only if it's pepperoni," I said offering a lip-smacking response.

"You're on. Call me when you're on your way home and I'll order it. Casey, one more thing—I need a hug." He reached out to me.

I melted in his arms. "Okay, okay. If this is a ploy to make me stay in Hyannisport rather than go to P-town, it's not working, Mr. Casanova." I did have to admit I was tempted.

I took my shower and made myself presentable. Jeans and a tee shirt were the designated dress of the day. I wrapped my hair in a knot and clipped it to the back of my head. It sure looked better than it did an hour ago. Before I left, I called Bubba to tell him I was on my way. He said he'd be waiting. I kissed Sam goodbye, told him I'd call him later and headed out the door.

I had just fastened my seat-belt and was starting to pull out of the drive-way, when Sam came running over to the car. He stood shaking his head.

“What,” I said as I put the window down.

“Do you think you might need this?” He asked waving my cell phone in front of him. “You’d forget your head if it wasn’t attached.”

“Thanks, buddy.” I smiled then proceeded to pull out onto the street. I gave him a wave as I drove away.

CHAPTER NINETEEN

Boston

It was six o'clock when Peter shuffled into the kitchen. Katherine was already sipping coffee and examining pieces of paper scattered over the entire top of the table. "Katherine, what in the world are you doing?" he asked in an up-toned angry voice. "For God sakes, it's only six o'clock," he said pointing to the digital clock on the stove.

"I know where the clock is. You don't need to show me. And, I know what time it is." She glared at him. "Keep your voice down before you wake the neighbors. I couldn't sleep, so rather than toss and turn, I got up, made myself a cup of coffee and began to look at my notes. I don't need to listen to your crap. And, I certainly don't need to listen to you yell at me. Why don't you just march yourself right back into the bedroom and go back to bed. Maybe, if you sleep a few more hours, you'll act like a human being."

Peter shook his head and walked to the bathroom.

Katherine tried to stop the tears, but it was too late. She didn't want Peter to know she'd been crying. She ran some cold water on a paper towel and dabbed her eyes, hoping they wouldn't swell. Lately everything seemed to trigger an emotional response.

Fifteen minutes later, Peter emerged from the bedroom in a pair of Red Sox Joe boxers and a matching navy blue tee shirt. "Remember when I got these?" he asked spinning around like a model.

"I do." Katherine smiled. "We went to the last game of the season a few years ago. You said you needed to get them so you could dream about the boys of summer all winter. It certainly didn't make them do any better." She walked over to Peter and put her arms around his neck. "Please hold me. I don't know what's wrong.

I just need you to try to understand me. You said you'd help me this weekend. Well, let's get an early start and maybe we can put most of it to bed."

"That would be great. I want my girl back." He gave her a kiss on the cheek. "How about some donuts? I'll run over to Manny's and grab us a dozen."

"I'll make a fresh pot of coffee. Don't forget my powdered lemon."

"I wouldn't dare." Peter grabbed his wallet and headed out the door.

CHAPTER TWENTY

Boston

Katherine tried to organize her notes in some type of a timeline. The information she got last Monday from the 1975 Dorchester City Directory revealed significant facts crucial to her family history. She finally felt she was making some headway. She was on the fence as to whether or not she was going to show Peter her mother's letters. "I need to be honest with him," she whispered to herself. Her backpack was leaning against the leg of the table so she reached down, took out the letters and set them beside the copy of the directory page. She went to the bedroom and took her adoptive birth certificate, her adoptive father and mother's birth certificates and both of their death certificates and laid them beside the letters.

"I'm back. Manny just put out some old fashioneds. They're still warm. I got me some of those and I got you a couple lemon filled." Peter put the box on the counter. He grabbed two dishes, a handful of napkins and two fresh coffee cups.

"I've already got a cup."

"Nope. We're starting fresh." He poured the coffee and carried it to the table. Then he put four donuts on another dish and set it down beside the cups. "These will give us some energy or at least a sugar high. We can talk while we eat."

Katherine nodded in agreement and sat down. "I've arranged my stuff in order. Last Monday when I went to the library, I researched the O'Ryan genealogy. I looked up my mother, Mary. I don't know if you knew her maiden name was Latham. It seems as though, Mary Latham is quite a popular name. I was about half way through the hits when I came across one in Dorchester. It referenced the 1975 Dorchester City Directory. I pulled it up on the screen and there she was—my Mary Latham. I know because it had my grandfather and grandmother's names on the record."

"Why didn't you tell me about this sooner?" Peter's heart skipped a beat. The birth certificate his friend had gotten for him really did belong to Katherine. Now he had to figure out how he was going to tell her about it.

"That's not all of it," said Katherine. She picked up the copy of the City Directory record. "Take a look at the section I highlighted." She handed it to him and waited for his reaction.

"Who is Emma?"

"It appears she's mother Mary's cousin."

"Do you have to call her mother Mary?"

"Yes, so that I can differentiate between my adoptive mother and my real mother." She took a deep breath and looked down. "And, I think I know who my real mother is—at least in name."

"I'll be right back. I've got something to show you."

She heard Peter open the closet door and as quickly as he opened it, he closed it. When he came back to the kitchen, he was carrying an envelope. He sat back down beside her. "Last June I asked a friend of mine who works at City Hall about sealed adoption birth certificates."

Katherine picked up her coffee with two hands and leaned back in her chair.

Peter felt her stare go right through him. "At first, he told me there was nothing he could do. Then a couple weeks later, he called me. He asked if we could meet for lunch. We went to Jack and Marion's on Boylston Street. After we ordered, he handed me this envelope." Peter's voice softened. "I didn't want to get your hopes up, so I didn't show it to you."

"What is it?" she asked.

"It's a copy of a birth certificate. I wasn't sure it was yours. I tried to find out more, but we got busy at work and I didn't have time. The name on the certificate is Emily Mae Latham and her date of birth is August 10, 1988."

Tears rolled down Katherine's cheeks. "When were you going to tell me?"

"I made a mistake. I should have shown you before. I just wasn't sure. You were already hurting and I didn't want to give you false hope if it wasn't yours." Peter's voice cracked. He cleared his throat and tried to speak, but nothing would come out.

Katherine wasn't sure what to do. A few minutes passed before she reached over, set her cup on the table and put her hands on the envelope.

Peter watched as she removed the folded paper from inside.

It was a birth certificate issued by the City of Boston. The child's name was recorded as Emily Mae Latham. The sex was female and the date of birth was August 10, 1988 at 7:15 am. The place of birth was Brigham and Women's Hospital on Francis Street in Boston. Katherine stopped reading. She laid the certificate down and slid her chair closer to Peter.

She rested her head on his shoulder. Her tear stained face paled against his navy blue tee-shirt. He put his arms around her. "Katherine, I'm sorry."

"I knew it was going to be hard, but it's what I wanted. I need to know so I can move on with my life—our life."

Peter wiped her cheeks and kissed her forehead.

She moved just enough to reach over and picked up the certificate. She closed her eyes, sucked her lips in and took a deep breath. "My mother's name is listed as Emma Latham and her address is 359 Hamilton Street, Dorchester. It's the same address as mother Mary." She again handed Peter the copy of the directory page. "My real mother was mother Mary's cousin. Emma was only fifteen years old when I was born."

There was one more critical piece of information staring at her. The space on the certificate beside father's name was filled in—Gregory Bradshaw—no address, just a name.

CHAPTER TWENTY-ONE

Bubba and Maloney were standing beside the front desk talking to the Duty Officer when I came through the doors. "Mornin' boys," I said, trying to mimic Jayne Mansfield.

Maloney laughed as Bubba said, "The only thing you and Jayne have in common is the blonde hair." Without waiting for a response, Bubba headed for the break room.

"I assume you've got a fresh pot of coffee brewing?" I asked as I fell into step beside him.

Maloney followed. "The Sarge must know you pretty good. He had me dump out the one left over from roll-call and told me to make sure the new one would still be perking when you walked in."

"Wise man," I whispered as I gave Maloney a wink.

Since there wasn't anybody in the break room, we sat down around the old-fashioned chrome and gray marble-swirled Formica table and began our morning meeting. I always felt ideas spawned in brainstorming sessions, like this, can sometimes be the most valuable.

"Bubba, first thing I'd like to do is canvas the area and show an artist's rendering of our Jane Doe to the locals. Did you have a sketch drawn up for us yet?"

"I'm way ahead of you. First thing this morning, I had Bill Butkus take some of Bernie's pictures and make a rendering. They worked together with regard to the eyes, hair and skin colors along with any facial identification marks. I think their combined efforts produced a sketch as close to reality as you're going to get. The finished product is on my desk. I've also got all the information that would appear on a missing person's poster ready to be merged with the picture. Hopefully, somebody will recognize this girl so we can be one step closer to solving at least one of the questions—the who."

"Did Bernie get the results back from her DNA test yet?" I asked.

"No, not yet. He's going to push Boston, but those guys are swamped."

"Sam has some friends in the Boston crime lab. He told me that if you need his help for anything, he's there for you."

Maloney leaned forward and put his coffee cup down in front of him. "Also, Sarge, my father is tight with some of those guys. I'm sure he'd call in a favor or two."

"Let Bernie do his thing first." Bubba slid his chair back, giving himself enough room to stand up. "Fill up your cups, if you want, and join me in my office." And with that said, he topped off his coffee and headed out of the break room.

Maloney turned to me and said, "I saw the sketch—really life-like. She was a beautiful girl, so if she's been in town for a while and has been out among the locals, somebody should recognize her."

"Normally I would agree with you, but since the weather has been so warm, the tourists have still been frequenting the area. If she was just another visitor this could be a problem. Before we go jumping to conclusions, though, let's get that poster ready and start pounding the pavement. Who knows, maybe we'll get lucky." I walked to the counter, filled my cup and held the pot up for Maloney.

"I'm done," he said as he washed his cup and set it in the strainer. "Let's get started."

We walked over to Bubba's office. He had all the information ready for us. I looked at Jane Doe's face. This was the first time I'd seen her with her eyes open. It was eerie. I felt her staring at me, asking why and trying to tell me who she was. I picked up her picture and held it gently with both hands. "We'll find out who you are and who did this to you," I said, forgetting I wasn't alone.

Both Sgt. Costa and Maloney looked at me, but didn't say a word.

"Bubba, do you have that computer program that automatically pops out a missing persons flyer when you key in the information and a picture?"

"We do. Are you okay with the information or do you want to add anything more?"

"At this point in time, I think this is all we have. If we find more, we'll revise It," I said nodding my head in approval.

Bubba handed everything to Maloney. "Why don't you make up a hundred copies. That way we can saturate the town. Casey, once we do this, you'll have to get your story into the paper. People around here know that something is going on, but aren't exactly sure what. They know that a body was found, but aren't sure if there was a murder or somebody died from natural causes. We haven't released anything official."

"I'll be right back." Maloney got up and headed to the back of the station.

"I'll call Chuck this afternoon to let him know I'm coming in with a story so he can give the production room permission to run it in the Wednesday edition. I'll write the story tonight and take it to the Tribune in the morning. My boss usually trusts my judgment and very rarely wants to see the copy before he gives it the okay. I'm very fortunate that way." I looked to Bubba for his approval. "As far as that trust—you're going to have to trust me too. I won't have time to show it to you before it goes to print. Are you okay with that?"

He leaned back in his chair and took a deep breath. "I've always trusted your abilities and this time is no different. Go ahead and do what you have to do. If I get any additional information from Bernie or anybody else that I think you need to know before you write your story, I'll give you a call."

"Fair enough," I said.

There was a knock on the door. Maloney opened it and handed Sgt. Costa a few of the flyers he had just run off.

"Great job. You two have your work cut out for you, so I suggest you get a move on. I'll see you in a couple of hours. Call me if you need anything."

Maloney slid the rest of the flyers into a manila envelope and out we went to strut the streets.

"I think it will go faster if we drive the squad car down to MacMillan Pier and head out from there." Maloney reached into his pants pocket for the keys. "I'll be right back to pick you up."

I nodded and quickly scooted to my car to retrieve a pad of paper and a couple of pens.

CHAPTER TWENTY-TWO

"It's been a while since I worked on a Jane or John Doe case. They can get frustrating. I find it hard for a person to lose their identity. In some cases, after we've found out their real name, we realize the loss of identity wasn't a mistake. In essence, the Jane or John wanted to get lost or hide for a while. And, then of course there are the situations where somebody else tried to conceal the 'who' by making sure Jane or John didn't have any identification on their person. Since it doesn't appear our Jane committed suicide, I'm assuming the person who put her in cottage number three stripped her of any tell-tale paperwork, etc." I looked at Maloney for a response.

"I'm sure you know this is my first Jane or John Doe case. I've only worked on one other murder investigation. While I was in Boston, my father had a case that needed a lot of leg work. He talked the Chief into letting me help. I never saw the actual murder scene, only the pictures. It was pretty gruesome. The biggest difference was that they knew who the assailant was. The guy was a piece of shit. I know I shouldn't say this, but he got what he deserved. He raped a seven year-old little girl, tortured an old lady and was the prime suspect in the disappearance of his girl-friend. The girlfriend was never found. Those were only a few of his shining moments. To call him a shiesty character would be kind."

"This line of work can take the rose color out of your glasses real fast—if you let it. It's a job. It can be very disturbing, but it can also be very rewarding and satisfying. If you're going to make it, you've got to accept the challenge and stay positive. A sprinkle of compassion doesn't hurt either. But, offer it wisely. Take my word for it, if you remember those things you'll be a good cop."

"Sarge was right about you. He told me to listen and follow directions. He said if I did that, I'd be learning from the best."

I wanted to smile. I guess I was wearing my wanna-be detective instincts on my sleeve. It made me feel good that Bubba had paid me a compliment usually reserved for a real cop. We pulled into the parking space on the Pier marked POLICE PARKING ONLY. I picked up the manila envelope and my briefcase and got out of the car. "If I remember correctly, when we came down Sunday there were more stores open if we take a right on Commercial."

"I know more of the restaurants are open in that direction. And, unless she had a place to cook, she'd need to eat somewhere." Maloney motioned for me to lead.

"I think we'll make better time if we don't zigzag. So, first stop, The Lobster Pot."

Since it was only ten-forty-five in the morning, the restaurant wasn't open yet for business. Maloney rapped on the door and within seconds Shawn answered and motioned for us to come in.

"Hi Casey."

"Morning," I said.

Hey, Maloney, what's up?"

"We've got ourselves a problem. I'm sure you heard a girl was found dead at Seaside Cottages last Saturday. Our problem is this—we don't know who she is." Maloney took a flyer from the envelope and handed it to Shawn.

He studied it, made several interesting facial gestures, rubbed his chin and said, "She doesn't look familiar. Sometimes I have young girls come in looking for work. Most of our employees are steady and dependable. We're fortunate. But, there's always a few that aren't—you know what I mean?" He flipped up his hands in a 'what can I say' motion. "Those come and go, so I'm always looking for few waitresses. But, this girl, I don't recall seeing her at all. I can show it around and see if anybody's seen her."

"That would help. Also, since you get a lot of locals, I'd like to post a flyer somewhere in the restaurant. If we're lucky, maybe somebody will recognize her face."

I took a roll of tape from my pocket to let him know we'd like to post it before we leave.

Shawn looked around. "Why don't you put it beside my menu over there." He pointed to a prime spot just inside the door. "Anything I can do to help."

I extended my hand to meet his. "Thank you. If you hear anything, please contact Officer Maloney." I moved to the spot Shawn had assigned to us and hung the flyer. "By the way, dinner Saturday was perfect. The girls can't wait to come back," I said. "And, Sam said to say hi."

Maloney said his goodbyes and we were out the door on our way to the next stop.

"First stop down. I'm sure we'll find most of the merchants willing to help. It's a close knit community. I like that. In Boston, nobody wants to get involved. Of course, there's no comparison—a huge city versus a quaint village."

Our next stop was a breakfast/lunch, tiny mom and pop business. 'One Eye Open' has been in operation for as long as I've been coming to P-town. Their little write-up by the door says they came over with the Pilgrims. Needless to say, some of the décor includes pictures depicting the Mayflower, John Smith and Pocahontas. The salt and pepper shakers are turkeys. And their everyday lunch special is a *Day After Sandwich.* On the menu, below the day after sandwich, the byline read, *Why wait for Thanksgiving ... don't we give thanks every day!*

"Maloney," came a booming voice from the kitchen door. "You and the lady want a little breakfast?" There were six people sitting at the tables and all heads turned in our direction.

We walked over to where Mr. Big Voice was standing. "Jimbo, I'd like you to meet Casey Quinby. We've got a situation in town and she's helping us out. She's a reporter for the Tribune, actually she's the head investigative reporter."

Jimbo quickly circled to face me. An inquisitive look overtook his smile.

I felt an interrogation in the making. *Brace yourself girl*, I thought.

"A situation, you say?" Jimbo laid his left arm across the top of his belly and rested his right elbow on it giving him a perfect perch to secure his chin in his cupped hand.

"Last Saturday, we found a body in cottage number three over at Seaside. It was a young girl. She didn't have any identification on her and nobody in this area has reported anyone missing. We don't think she's a local, but we're hoping somebody may have seen her and can help us so we can locate her family."

"Maloney, I think there's more than you're telling me." Jimbo stayed his stance. "Was this a murder or did she commit suicide?"

I could tell he wasn't going to let up. "At this point, Jimbo, we don't have all the facts. The ME is doing lots of testing and the results are still out. We're doing the leg work. If we could put a name to the face it sure would help." I knew he wanted to know more, but I had given him all he was going to get. "You can do us a tremendous favor though. We have flyers for you to look at." I reached over and took the one Maloney was holding. She may have come in to eat either with someone or by herself."

Jimbo had taken his glasses from his shirt pocket and was studying the picture of our Jane Doe. "I can't be absolutely positive, but I think she was here last week. I remember because I had never seen her before. She was a pretty young thing, dressed very—well, let's just say not in your typical P-town fashion. Maloney can tell you, I have a thing about knowing my customers. Some say that I'm nosey. I say I'm just being friendly."

"So, you are reasonably sure this girl was here last week."

"Yeah, in fact, a couple times. The other odd thing was that she was wearing the same clothes and they didn't look mussed or slept in."

"Since many of your customers are in here every day, they might have noticed her. With any luck, they might have also seen her around town," Maloney said, pulling another flyer from the envelope. "You keep that one for yourself and I'll post this one," Maloney said. "Casey, let me have the tape, I'll stick this up and you can say our goodbyes to Jimbo."

I wanted to slap the kid silly. He'd just passed Mr. Jimbo on to me to cut the conversation short and make our get-a-way out the front door. "Don't hesitate to call Maloney if you recall anything else," I said. "You've been very helpful. We'll keep you posted." I shook his hand and spun around to see Maloney holding the door open for me.

"Slick move," I said giving him the look. "You're catching on way too fast."

The smirk he gave me was one of a fifteen-year old boy who just found his soul mate in an older woman.

"Wipe that shit-eating grin off your face."

We laughed and continued up the street.

The next two storefronts were small shops that had closed for the season after the Labor Day tourists had left. As we passed a narrow alley that ran from Commercial to the water, I heard voices. They were muffled so I couldn't hear what they were actually saying. "Maloney, there's voices coming from down there." I pointed into the alley. "If they're street people, I think we should show Jane's picture to them."

Maloney took a flyer and we headed toward the inaudible conversation. I let Maloney lead the way. It doesn't hurt for vagrants, if that's what they were, to see a uniform first. I told Sam I'd play it safe. He'd be proud of me. Of course, this was an easy safe. But safe, none the less.

"Officer, what you want? We didn't do nothing. We just minding our own business. We kinda just hanging out here waiting for Mr. Jimbo to throw his garbage out. He knows we go back behind the building and pick it. We gotta eat ya know. Times ain't that good. We is in-between jobs."

"Listen guys, I'm not here to harass you. You haven't done anything wrong. But, I do need your help."

"You need our help? Bring it on, my man."

"We need you to study this flyer—look at it real good. In fact, let's step out into the light so you can get a better look." Maloney had turned on his stern voice.

We both stepped aside to let them pass, then we followed. They were a sorry sight in the alley, but in the sunlight it was evident they'd been working the streets for years and probably right here in P-town. I wouldn't be surprised if drugs had led to their downfall. The smell was a strong indication they hadn't bathed in forever and if they took their clothes off, they'd probably run away to look for a laundromat.

"Mr. Officer, I seen this girl walking by herself down the other end of Commercial. She looked sad. I asked her if I could help. I think I scared her. She looked at me like I was a ghost or something and ran away. Sometimes I have that effect on people."

"Do you remember when you saw her?" I asked knowing the answer would more than likely be clouded by the *deep purple haze* that surrounded this guy.

"I know exactly what day it was." He perked up; proud he could offer a concrete answer.

My eyes opened wide and I tilted my head sideways, trying to drag out a response with a look rather than words.

"It was last Wednesday. I know that because my SSI check was deposited in the bank on Tuesday and on Wednesday, I needed some money." He looked down. "I had to pay some bills."

Yeah, right, I thought. *I'm sure his biggest bill was to his drug dealer.*

Maloney reached into his pocket. "Take my card and this flyer. If you want to help this girl, show her picture to your friends. If you find out anything else, please give me a call."

By this time, I had tactfully put my hand over my mouth and nose trying not to breath in any of the air surrounding our witness. I watched him walk back to his buddy, who had already returned to the end of the alley. The light from the far end created two distinct silhouettes. One was holding a paper—I assumed it was our flyer and the other was slumped over presumably reading it. What a waste—two lives that didn't start out in this direction, but somewhere down the road took a wrong turn. They were certainly life members of the dead-end club.

"Do you think it would be okay if we taped flyers to the storefronts that are closed?" I asked. "You know the people around here far better than I do."

"I don't see that to be a problem at all," he said.

We backtracked to the two stores we had just passed and posted Jane's picture for the passersby to see.

"There were a bunch more stores open yesterday when we rode by. In fact, Annie was surprised they had stayed open so long after the season."

"Some of the people I've befriended since moving here told me that yesterday was their last day until April. A couple of them had their bags packed and as soon as they locked up, they were headed to Florida. What a life—Cape Cod in the summer and Florida in the winter." Maloney looked up at the beautiful blue sky dotted with puffy white cotton balls and took a deep breath. "But for me, I wouldn't have it any other way. I love New England."

"That makes two of us," I said nodding in agreement.

"We've covered about all we can on this side. If we cross and head back down Commercial, about half way, there's a small deli that serves great chowder. You up for it?"

"I could eat chowder every day," I said as we crossed the street.

There were a couple of rooming houses we hit before we stopped for lunch, but the owners didn't recognize our Jane Doe. The only Bed and Breakfast that was still open took a flyer to show the owners. The girl we spoke to there was just helping them out while they ran errands. She seemed to be about the same age as Jane and showed great concern. She asked if she could have a couple extra flyers to pass around to her friends and, of course, we gave them to her.

Maloney stopped in front of a little convenience store just before the deli. "You'll like this guy. He's much like Jimbo, in that he knows everybody and sees everything. If Jane came in, he'll remember her."

A little bell jingled as they opened the door. A man, short in stature and round in girth, came out from the back room. He smiled as he extended his hand—first to me, then to Maloney.

"Maloney, what brings you out for a stroll today with this beautiful young lady?" He eyed Maloney's uniform up and down. "I don't think this is a pleasure walk or you would have ditched the blues." His face got solemn and he stopped talking.

"You're observant. That's why we're hoping you can help us." Maloney handed Mr. C a flyer. "She's missing. Actually, she's dead. She was found in cottage number three over at Seaside."

Mr. C looked up from Jane's picture, studied my face and looked back down. "Is she a relative of yours?" he asked repeating the look up and down.

"No, no," said Maloney. "I'm sorry, I didn't introduce you. Please say hello to Casey Quinby."

Again, Mr. C held out his hand and shook mine. "I recognize that name." The look on his face indicated that his think tank was running through its boxes of stored information. "Of course, you're the reporter for the Cape Cod Tribune. Ah, yes, and the one who was instrumental in solving that murder case that happened last summer in Bourne."

I didn't have a chance to speak when he continued. Without turning away from me, he fanned his arm 180° to indicate the array of reading materials he offered for sale. "I carry the largest selection of newspapers around. We have visitors from so many states and countries both on and off season. They want to stay abreast of, not only the local news, but things that are happening country and world-wide. They don't want to fall behind, so they rely on me to keep them informed." He motioned to indicate the spot where the Tribune resided, sandwiched between the Boston Globe and The

New York Times. "Your paper is right there with the big boys. I read the Tribune first, then move to the others when I have time."

"I'm flattered to know I have a fan. And as a representative of the paper, may I say, thank you." I smiled and moved over beside Maloney to suggest it was his turn to speak.

"Our Jane Doe is just that because we don't know who she is. She was found with no identification. The picture on the flyer is an artist's rendition of photos taken at the ME's office. Bernie worked with Bill Butkus to create the most accurate portrayal of our victim."

"You say victim?" There was a question in Mr. C's voice. "Do you think there was foul play involved?"

I winced inside. Maloney may have leaked a little too much. "At this point in the investigation we have to consider everything. Tests have been taken, but the results are not in yet. Once we get those, we will be able to make a more definite determination as to the cause of death." I hoped my brief little spiel of double talk satisfied Mr. C's curiosity—at least for the time being.

Mr. C picked up the flyer Maloney had put on the counter. After a few moments he looked at us. "I can't be one hundred percent positive, but I'll give it ninety-five percent. This girl did come into my store last week. Let me think. I believe, no, I know she was alone. She bought some *pickie* food. Do you know what I mean? Chips and candy, and a couple of bottles of water—and a newspaper. I even remember which one. I remember this because she forgot it on the counter. She came rushing back and in a soft-spoken, sweet voice she asked if I had found it. It was still right where she left it. It was a Boston Globe."

"Mr. C would you be willing to pass out some of these flyers to your friends?" I asked. "It would be extremely helpful." Before I finished my sentence, Maloney had several flyers ready to hand over to him. Mr. C took them. "Thanks," I said.

"We've still got lots of ground to cover. We certainly do appreciate your help. Here's my card. If you hear anything else, please give me a call."

Mr. C took Maloney's card and looked at me. I figured he wanted a card from me too, so I reached in my pocket and handed him one.

"Thanks," he said. "See you later Maloney. I'll be in touch."

Once out the door Maloney patted his stomach. It was his way of saying 'time for lunch'. And I agreed.

CHAPTER TWENTY-THREE

"Chowder time," said Maloney, as he stopped in front of a dinky hole-in-the-wall two doors down from Mr. C's. He opened the door and motioned me in. "Let's sit at the little table next to the window. I'm getting a bowl and a piece of crusty bread. How about you?"

"Same," I said. The deli was small, but cute. The hanging lights were made from interesting old lobster buoys and the walls were draped with fishing nets cradling shells of all shapes and sizes. Behind the cash register was a rustic, grayish-colored frame housing what I assumed was the first dollar the owners rang in. Beside the dollar bill picture was a family photo. It looked like it dated back several generations. *The fisherman of P-town*, I thought. They were standing beside what seemed like a pretty big fishing boat. If those people could talk now I wonder what they'd say about their town. I was still in deep thought when Maloney came back to the table.

"They'll bring our food over when it's ready. You look like a Diet Coke kind of girl, so I ordered you one." He tilted his head sideways and shrugged his shoulders, then sat down in the chair across from me.

"You did good." I was curious to find out a little more about Maloney. "So, you got a girlfriend?"

"Getting a little personal, don't you think?" He folded his arms on the table in front of him and smiled.

"No, just curious. Actually, I'm being my nosey self, as Sam would say." I figured I better get that in so he didn't think I was making a move on him.

"When I applied for the job here, I'd just ended a four-year relationship with the girl I thought I was going to spend the rest of my life with. I suppose that was one reason I left the city. I wanted something entirely different." He shook his head and rolled his eyes. "And boy, that's what I got. I'm getting used to it now, but at first I wasn't sure I'd done the right thing. I still go home to visit. There're some things I miss, but all-in-all I'm convinced I made the right move. Have you ever been to Boston?"

"I've gone a couple of times with Sam. He goes on business and I tag along. Sometimes I can sit in on the seminars, but most of the time I hang around and take in the sights and sounds of the big city."

"Here comes Charlie with our chowder," said Maloney.

A ruddy-faced old man came out from behind the counter carrying a tray with two steaming bowls and a basket of bread. "Best chowder around these parts, little lady, and Ma bakes the bread fresh every morning." Charlie set our food down, smiled and waited until I took my first spoonful to see my reaction. "Was I right?" he asked.

"You know it. This is great! You can't beat homemade cooking." I gave both Charlie and Maloney a thumbs up, then dipped my spoon back in for a refill.

"Casey, I've got a question for you. Your friend Marnie, tell me a little about her." His eyes searched mine for a reaction.

"Marnie moved to the Cape last July from New York City. She had just graduated from law school and decided she wanted to get away from the Big Apple to pursue her career."

"From New York City to Cape Cod. Isn't that a little drastic? I mean a hundred and eighty degree change in lifestyle."

"Her father is an attorney in the City. She could have gone into his practice and probably become a partner. I guess deep down she'd had it with the fast pace of city life. Her cousin moved down here years ago. He's a Court Officer in Barnstable. He finally convinced her to visit and that's all she wrote. She took the Massachusetts Bar Exam and is waiting to hear whether or not she passed."

"Is she seeing anyone?"

"Well, Maloney, there's a little problem there. But, to answer your question, no she's not seeing anyone."

"What's the problem then?"

"Last summer she met a friend of her cousin's. He was also a Court Officer in Barnstable. His name is James. It seems that James had a lot of deep seeded problems that nobody knew about. I've known him for almost as long as I've lived on the Cape—eight years. And, I had no idea he was such a screwed-up person. He wined and dined her—made her feel welcome."

"Where is this leading?"

"Did you read about the hit-and-run in Bourne last July? And the death of the star witness in the investigation?"

"I did hear something about it. Is that the case Bubba was talking about when I first met you last Saturday?"

"Yep," I said. I took a deep breath and continued, "Without getting too much into it, James was involved in both. He would have claimed another victim if Sam hadn't stopped him."

"Would that victim have been you?"

"Bingo." I still shudder to think what might have happened to me if Sam hadn't come along when he did. "Anyway, back to Marnie. He didn't abuse her physically, but mentally her trust took a huge hit. So you're wondering if she's available. I'm not sure." I didn't want to answer any more questions, so it was time for me to change the subject. "Let's get back on track. Did you show Charlie a flyer?"

"I did, but he doesn't recognize her. He said he'd put one in his window."

"I wish we had something concrete to go on," I said. "The only possible clue we have is that Mr. C thinks she was in his store and bought a Boston Globe."

"Maybe Mr. C and his Boston Globe story will pan out." Maloney took another spoonful of chowder. "There are a few more stores and restaurants between here and MacMillan Pier that haven't closed for the season. We should be able to knock them off within a half hour. After that if we head south on Commercial and work the street the same way we did this morning, we should be done by three o'clock."

“Sounds like a plan to me. Let’s get going,” I said, thanking Charlie as I headed for the door.

Maloney was a little quiet as we started down the street. I hoped he didn’t start in again with more questions about Marnie.

For the next two hours we pounded the pavement. Maloney handed out flyers while I asked questions. Nothing.

We stopped in front of the Donut Hole Coffee Shop. The smell of freshly ground coffee escaping from the open door formed a finger beckoning me to come inside. “Maloney, I don’t know about you, but I could use a cup of coffee. A French Vanilla would sure hit the spot. In fact, it’s my treat.” I smiled and he nodded in agreement.

“Wow, would you look at those cookies,” I said as I perused the shelves guarded by a glass partition.

A young girl, who was in the process of bringing some freshly-baked oatmeal raisin delights from the kitchen to fill the trays, came over to where we were standing. “May I help you?” she asked in such a sweet, soft voice. It made me do a double take to see if she looked old enough to be working.

“I’d like a French Vanilla coffee, please,” I said, then looked toward Maloney for his order.

“I’ll just have a medium, black coffee, but I’d like one of those cookies you just put in the case.” He made a smacking sound with his lips.

“And how old are you?” I raised my eyebrows and smiled. “Better make that two,” I said to the girl behind the counter. “I’m certainly not going to sit here and watch him eat one without having one myself.”

The little counter girl wore a tag with the name Tessa engraved on it. Years ago when I worked at Friendly’s Ice Cream in Shrewsbury, I always felt more connected to someone when they took the time to read my name tag, then use it when they talked to me. “Tessa, what a beautiful name,” I said.

"Thank you. It was my grandmother's, then my mother's and now mine. Who knows, someday I might pass it along. If you go sit at a table I'll bring your order over to you in a minute."

The only other person in the shop was a lady sitting at a two-seater in the corner, drinking something and working on her computer. Again, we took a table by the window. "If a window table is available, I always take it," I said to Maloney. "That way I can look out into a little corner of the world and wonder what's going on across the street, behind the white cottage—like the one with the black shutters and hunter green door."

"You're weird." He made a face and leaned back in his chair.

"No, just nosey. That's what makes me a good reporter. And, I have to admit sometimes it gets me into trouble."

I turned to see Tessa walking slowly across the floor with our coffees. Instead of making two trips she was trying to balance a small paper plate on top of each cup. One tipped sideways and the plate and cookie fell off.

Maloney got up to help her. "I'll get that for you." He reached down and picked up the plate and broken pieces of cookie.

Tessa put the two coffees on the table and in an embarrassed, quiet voice said, "I'm sorry. The other girls have no trouble doing this. I'm just learning." She hustled back behind the counter to get another cookie.

"You did fine. By the time summer comes you'll be an old pro." I glanced over at Maloney. He'd already taken a bite of cookie and was washing it down with some coffee. "Can I please have one of the flyers?" I asked.

He reached into the manila envelope, pulled one out and handed it to me.

I looked around. No other customers had come in. "Tessa, could I please show you a picture. We're trying to identify this girl. Does she look the least bit familiar?" I sat back and waited for her to study the sketch.

Tessa pulled up a chair from the next table and sat down. "She does look familiar. I think this girl was in here last week. She was quiet and seemed kind of sad. She bought a coffee and went to the table where that lady is sitting. She had a newspaper. She was here for quite a while." Tessa leaned an elbow on the table then cradled her chin in her hand. "I remember that she had several refills. In fact, she asked to use the ladies room between two of them, then again before she left."

Maloney listened intently.

"There was something else," she said.

I could see the wheels turning in Tessa's head as she struggled to give us accurate information. "She asked me if I knew of any rooms for rent. I told her about Miss Daisy's rooming house a few blocks up the street. I wasn't sure if they had any vacancies, but it was a decent place. The person who owns it is a friend of the man who owns the Donut Hole. His name is Omar. My parents know him too. I've heard he's helped lots of kids who show up in town and don't have a place to stay."

I took my pad of paper from my briefcase, jotted down a few notes and listed a couple of key words I could use later when I write my story for the Tribune. This could be the first real bit of evidence in our effort to identify our Jane Doe.

"Tessa, you've been very helpful. If we give you a few flyers, would you ask if you can post one in the window and maybe pass the other two among your friends?"

"Of course I will. How can I get in touch if I hear anything or have any more information for you?" she asked.

Maloney handed her one of his cards. "I can be reached anytime through the police station. And Casey can be reached at the paper." He leaned over for one of my cards, then handed it to Tessa.

"Let me have that back for a second. Here's my cell phone number. No matter how insignificant you think something might be, please don't hesitate to call me. Also, if you remember anything else give me a call." I handed my card back to her.

She walked to the door with us. "I didn't ask you before, but is that girl okay?"

I contemplated dancing around the answer, but didn't think it would be fair to her. "No, Tessa, she isn't. She was found dead at Seaside Cottages last Saturday."

Tessa gasped and for a moment appeared frozen in time. She stood as still as a statue, allowing only her eyes to move cautiously around the room. "I. . .I. . .I didn't hear anything about it."

"Tonight I'm writing a story for the newspaper. It'll appear in the Wednesday edition."

Maloney caught my attention. "We need to get going. Remember Tessa, don't hesitate to call me if you need to talk," he said, nodding his head in hopes of obtaining a positive response.

"Yes sir, I will."

"You take care," I said and with that we were out the door.

"Before we make any more stops I think we should see if Omar is around. Miss Daisy's is a couple of blocks up the street. Cross your fingers, this could be our big break."

I agreed with Maloney.

CHAPTER TWENTY-FOUR

Miss Daisy's was a fitting name for the pink and green gingerbread style house situated in the middle of a yard framed by an antique white picket fence. The flowerbeds on either side of the walkway were home to at least four different colored daisies—not to mention the rose-colored, year-round wooden Shasta cutouts. The front door was painted the same antique white as the fence and the trim came from the paint can used to create the Shasta's. White lace curtains hung in the front-facing windows and old-fashioned roll-up shades were pulled half way down.

I almost wondered if this was a façade—like you see on a movie set. "Colorful doesn't even begin to describe this picture," I said without looking at Maloney.

Just as he reached for the knob, the door opened and a man, who introduced himself as Omar, invited us in. "Good afternoon," he said as he led us into the front sitting room. "A policeman in uniform hanging around outside my house isn't good for business." He tilted his head sideways and looked at Maloney for a response.

"Omar, you know me, Rusty Maloney. I was having dinner at the Lobster Pot with Sgt. Costa and his wife a few of months ago and you were at the table beside us. In fact, you and your friend, Freddy, joined us for an after-dinner drink. I'm the new kid on the block from Boston."

"Oh yeah, you're from the South End—same as Freddy. Oh God, he didn't shut-up for days. All he talked about was that Irish Bar. What the hell was the name?"

"JJ Foley's," Maloney said. "It's one of the best. Casey, one of these days I'll take you and your friends there. Remember those things we miss—well, that's a big one."

Maloney was just about to introduce Casey when Omar looked at her and said, "Let me introduce myself. I'm Omarald, but my friends call me Omar. And if you're hanging around this guy, you're my friend. So my friend, what can I do for you today?"

"Well, now let me introduce myself. I'm Casey Quinby, a reporter for the Tribune." At this point that was all the information I was going to offer.

Since he was directing his question to me, I took the envelope lying beside Maloney and pulled out one of the flyers. "We're trying to find anyone who may have seen or talked to this girl, probably within the last week. Tessa, at the Donut Hole, told us she thinks this is the girl she told about Miss Daisy's. We're hoping she's right."

Omar took the flyer from my hand and without hesitation said, "I rented this girl a room last Tuesday. She was very quiet. There was something about her, though. She appeared to be troubled. P-town is a haven for troubled kids trying to hide out for a while. People are very protective here. Sometimes that's not a bad thing."

My heart began to pound. "Can you give us her name?"

"Let me get my records." Omar turned and headed for what I presumed to be his office. The door was open and I could see bookshelves over-loaded with different sized books, some standing, others lying down. A big, dark mahogany desk was situated so that the person sitting behind it could see anyone walking in the hallway.

"Boy, the inside of this house certainly doesn't match the outside," I whispered so only Maloney could hear me.

Omar reappeared in the doorway. "You know, I haven't seen her since last Friday. I wasn't overly concerned because she was paid until the end of the month. I didn't figure she'd pay, then skip out. It's only been a couple of days. Maybe she decided to go back to where she came from to pick up some more clothes or something. She didn't come with much luggage. In fact, she only had one of those flowery duffle bags and an overstuffed backpack."

“Do you have a name?” Maloney asked.

“She registered as Emily Latham.”

Maloney asked the questions and I wrote.

“Do you know where she was from?”

“I don’t ask. I fancy myself a good judge of character. If I feel they might be a problem, I require them to fill out a rental form. When they hesitate, I tell them I’m full and to check back later. I never see them again. Emily was sweet. She was quiet. I figured her to be just fine.”

“Did you have much conversation with her?”

“No. She asked me about restaurants and where the closest grocery store was. I don’t allow cooking in the rooms, but they do have refrigerators. If they need to heat something up, they can use the kitchen. She also wanted to know where she could buy a newspaper. We all know Mr. C has every on or off Cape newspaper you’d desire, so I sent her there.” Omar stopped. “Am I missing something here?”

Maloney looked at me then, back toward Omar. “Emily, if that is her name, was found dead last Saturday in cottage number three at Seaside.”

“I didn’t hear anything about it.” He scowled. “There’s not much that misses these ears.”

“Until our conversation with you, she was listed as Jane Doe. You’ve furnished us with the first bit of information to help us determine her identity.”

Maloney was doing a great job. Bubba was right; the kid had a head on his shoulders. A little Sam in the making.

“It hasn’t been in the Tribune yet, but tonight I’ll be writing a story for the Wednesday edition. We didn’t have much to go on. Actually, we didn’t have anything but a dead body. There are still a lot of questions to be answered.” I hesitated, then continued, “Omar, you’ve been a tremendous help.” Since I didn’t know him, I had to be careful how I asked the next question. “Could you please keep our visit and conversation just between us for the time being?”

I looked directly at Omar and kept talking, "We believe the girl in cottage number three was murdered. If Emily Latham is our Jane Doe's real name, we don't want the person who did this to get panicky and leave the area. And, that brings up another question—is our suspect still around?"

Omar was sitting straight up, intently listening to what I was saying. The expression on his face was somewhere between perplexed and distraught. "P-town is, and has been my home for thirty years. We are a close-knit family. We've been very fortunate not to share the violence that dominates big cities like Boston and New York or even forty-eight miles away in Hyannis. When something like this happens in our community it affects everybody. Since this is surrounded by so much uncertainty, any leak would only cause apprehension and anxiety. You have my word. I won't discuss this with anyone." He leaned back in his chair, folded his arms and shook his head. The strong, reassuring look that greeted us when Omar first opened the door was gone.

"If you think of anything else, please give me a call." Maloney reached over and gave Omar a card. "You've been a great help. There is one other thing. Can we take a look at Emily's room?"

"Of course," Omar said as he stood and led us to the stairway. "Wait here, I have to get the key."

"Maloney, you got your gloves with you?" I asked.

"I do and I have a pair of throw-aways for you." He took a packet out of his pocket and handed it to me. "I have some evidence bags too."

"Be prepared," I snickered. "Isn't that the Boy Scout motto?"

"Good thinking—I was a member." He raised his eyebrows.

Omar walked toward us with a ring of keys dangling from his hand. He started up the stairs and motioned for us to follow.

The second floor was tastefully decorated in a nautical motif. I recognized some of the pictures hanging in the hallway. I stopped in front of the one of a Christmas tree made out of lobster traps. It was decorated with colorful buoys and bright red ribbons. Every

Christmas the locals would construct it on the little common in front of MacMillan Pier. It never ceases to amaze me how creative some people are. Ironically, beside the room that was occupied by Emily Latham, was a picture of the Provincetown landscape taken from the beach front at Seaside Cottages.

Omar opened the door and stepped aside so we could go in. He glanced around the room, but stayed in the hallway.

Nothing appeared to be out of place. The flowered duffle bag that Omar had mentioned earlier was on the chair in the corner, but there was no backpack. There was a brush, a couple of barrettes, and a Scunci twister on the bureau. A pad of paper and a pen were on the table.

We put on our gloves.

Maloney was headed for the bathroom, when I called him back. "Take a look at this." I pointed to the pad of paper. "She was apparently writing a letter or note to somebody named Peter." The words 'Dear Peter' were written on the top of the paper. "If you look closely, this was not the first thing penned on this pad. See the indentations? It goes all the way down to the bottom. She may have written something, then changed her mind, then decided the first draft was okay after all. Since the original one isn't here and it isn't in the waste basket, I'm assuming she took it with her. We know she didn't have it on her person when we found her, so either Emily mailed it or the person she met up with has it."

"I'm going to see if there's anything in the bathroom that may be of help."

"If her toothbrush is there, why don't you bag it for DNA." I took out my notebook and started writing. I listed everything that appeared to belong to Emily Latham. There wasn't much. "Hey, Maloney, hand me an evidence bag big enough to hold this pad."

"Here you go," he said as he stepped out of the bathroom.

I slipped the pad of paper and the pen into the evidence bag, peeled the self-seal strip off and secured the opening. "We can't take a chance of contaminating anything that could lead us to a positive identification of our Jane Doe." I caught a puzzled look on Maloney's face. "What's bothering you?"

"Omar identified our Jane Doe as Emily Latham."

"Yes, he did," I said. "And more than likely he's correct, but we need absolute proof of identity before we can change her name from Jane to Emily. We've got lots of items that Bernie can use to get DNA. Once he confirms the DNA found on these items matches Jane's DNA, we can hopefully narrow down our search."

We finished scouring Emily's room for any more clues that might lead us to who she was and where she came from.

"Omar, I need you to lock this door behind us and not let anybody in. I'll talk to Sgt. Costa and get back to you within the next couple of days," said Maloney.

"Of course, not a problem—anything I can do to help."

We stepped out into the hallway and watched as Omar locked the door. "Let me give you my cell phone number in case I'm not here and you need to get in. I don't go far."

He turned and started down the stairs. We followed.

"Be right back," he said and headed for his office. Not even a minute went by when he returned with a piece of paper in hand and gave it to Maloney.

"You've been extremely helpful," I said and extended my hand. "Thank you."

CHAPTER TWENTY-FIVE

Boston

Even though Katherine had finally found out who her birth mother was, she still harbored a feeling of emptiness. There was one more avenue she had to explore—Gregory Bradshaw—the man listed as her father. Since her mother was only fifteen when Katherine was born, the 'why' she was conceived probably was not the result of love. She didn't want to think about the alternatives. *Emma Latham,* she thought. *What a pretty name. I wonder what she was like.*

Peter insisted she use his computer to do her research. After all, he was now privy to everything. He had supplied the final bit of information she needed to complete her mission. He had also supplied her with a new twist. "I can order Ancestry.com for you."

"Why don't I continue to use the library, at least for a little while. Ancestry.com isn't cheap and I may not need it much longer. Besides, I'm going to check out the more recent city directories first. Maybe I can come up with something more current."

"Okay, but will you keep me up to date and let me know what you find?"

"I will and I won't go off on my own to check anything out. Deal?"

"I'll hold you to that," said Peter. "I've got an idea—since its Saturday, do you want to go into the city? We can work the library for a while, then get some lunch. Better idea, if we do the library for a couple hours, we can make it to Abe and Louie's before 3:30 and still be on the lunch menu. We'll make it a mini-celebration."

A smile formed on Katherine's face. "We haven't done Abe and Louie's for a long time. I can already taste their steak sandwich or maybe the lobster mac and cheese." She jumped up. "First in the bathroom." And she was off.

It was good to have Katherine back, thought Peter.

CHAPTER TWENTY-SIX

It was four o'clock when we left Miss Daisy's rooming house and headed to MacMillan Pier. "I have to make a call."

Maloney got behind the steering wheel. I walked to the back of the cruiser and hit number one on my cell.

Sam's voice was a welcoming change. "Hi," he said. "Where are you?"

"I'm still in P-town, but we're about to wrap things up for today. We're on our way back to the station. Bubba's probably waiting to talk to us. I'll give him the abbreviated version. If Maloney wants to stay and fill in the details, that's his choice. I'm ready to call it a day."

"Are we still on for pizza and beer?"

"Sounds good. Just remember that I have to write a story for the Tribune tonight, so after supper I won't be much company." I hesitated then said, "See you in about an hour and a half." I wanted to tell Sam I thought he should go home to his own place tonight. After all, he's got the trial starting tomorrow and he needs to be focused. I've got an hour and a half ride home. That'll give me plenty of time to plan my strategy. I'm not saying I don't like playing house, but sometimes I like my 'me-time' just as much.

I took a deep breath and looked out over the ocean. This case wasn't going to be easy. I could feel it. I opened the passenger side door and slid in. "Okay, let's get back to the station. I'll stay and talk to the Sarge for a little while, but I have to get home. I've got homework I have to do. My boss is expecting a story to be on his desk before ten o'clock tomorrow morning. I'll need a copy of the flyer picture. For the time being, we won't be able to use a name other than Jane Doe. Once we get a confirmed report from Bernie, I can do a follow-up. I'm hoping somebody recognizes the sketch."

"What about sending out a missing persons APB?" Maloney asked.

"I think that goes without saying. I'm sure Sarge will agree. In fact, he's probably waiting for us to come in so he can send it out to PDs both on and off Cape. That way they can make copies for the morning briefing. We need all the help we can get." I looked at Maloney. "You did a great job today. I just want you to know that," I said. "Sarge was right. You're going to make a great detective."

Maloney tilted his head and gave me a sideways look. "It helps to have a fantastic teacher."

"Don't make me blush," I said.

Sgt. Costa was sitting in his office. When he saw us, he beckoned us to come in and sit down. "I've got the missing persons poster ready to blast out. Is there anything I should add before I press the button?"

Maloney spoke up, "We have a possible identity, but can't divulge it to the public until Bernie gives us his stamp of approval. We think her name is Emily Latham, but for the time being she's still Jane Doe."

My student did just fine. I gave him a nod of approval. "Bubba, I've got to head to Hyannisport. I've got a story to write." I stood up, walked over to Sgt. Costa and gave him a hug. "Maloney can fill you in on all the details of the day. I'm sure the Sarge will find them very interesting. I think we made headway. You know how to get ahold of me if you need me, otherwise I'll give you a call tomorrow." I left Sgt. Costa's office, waved goodbye to the Duty Officer and headed toward the parking lot. My 'baby' was waiting for me. One good thing about my 2003 light green Mazda Spider convertible was, it stuck out in a parking lot—especially one full of dark blue or black and white vehicles.

I slipped into the soft cream-colored leather seats, snapped the seat belt into place and instinctively locked the doors. I was ready for the ride home—ready except for my cup of French Vanilla at Dunkin's. In about fifteen minutes that wouldn't be a problem. By the time this case is over, the Truro Dunkin Donuts will be offering me a job because I'm in there so often.

There wasn't any traffic to speak of, so my ride time should be cut down considerably. After a couple of welcome sips, I decided to check in with the girls. I turned down the tunes and hit number two on speed dial. Annie's phone went right to her message center. She must be in a meeting with Mike. "Hey girl, it's just me. I'm on my way home. Staying in tonight, so when you get settled give me a call." I figured Marnie was probably in the same meeting, but pushed number three anyway. I was right. The recorded voice on the other end said, "I'm either swimming, shopping, eating or working—so please leave a message and I'll get back to you as soon as possible." I left the same message on Marnie's message center as I did on Annie's. I really wanted to share my day with my two side-kicks. After all, they were there when Jane was discovered.

I turned the volume on the radio back up. The Beach Boys were singing *I Get Around.* My mind wandered back to last July when Annie got tickets for the Melody Tent and the three of us went to see The Beach Boys in concert. It was the first time I'd met Marnie. Imagine just four months later, you'd think we grew up together. Before I knew it, my coffee was gone and I was entering Yarmouth.

At the first traffic light, I hit number one to let Sam know I was close. He answered on the first ring—so not like him. "I'm hungry," he said. "I'll call in the order now. By the time I get to Jack's Lounge and back you should be home."

Short and sweet, I thought. I figured he had worked all day on his reports for tomorrow's trial and was stressed out. "See you then," I said and the phone went silent. I shrugged my shoulders and continued on my way.

Sam was right. We pulled into the driveway at the same time. He stopped to let me go in front of him. That was a good thing 'cause I didn't have to move my car later—when he left.

I got out of my car and waited for him to join me. Since he held a six-pack with one hand and the pizza with the other, he was at my mercy. I leaned in between them and gave him a kiss. "Smells good," I said as I turned to unlock the door. I let him go in before me so he could put the food down and give me a real kiss.

Watson's tail was wagging non-stop. I got down on my knees and wrapped my arms around him. "How's mama's little boy?" I pulled my head back and was greeted with warm, sloppy kisses.

Sam leaned against the door jamb with his arms crossed, just smiling as he watched the two of us. "He's been good company today," he said as he reached over for my hand to help me up. "But, I missed you."

I welcomed his hug and gentle kiss. I do love him. "It certainly was a busy day. We covered a lot of ground. And, now if we don't break out the pizza, it's going to get cold." I gave him a quick kiss and said, "I'll revisit that later."

"That's my girl, food before anything else."

"Where do you think all this energy comes from?" My new under-the-cabinet radio was already set to 101.1, the Wave, so I hit the on button. I looked at the radio, then at Sam. "This Beach Boy's song was playing when I left the Dunkin's in Truro." I started humming the tune to *I Get Around.*

"Don't quit your day job." He laughed. "Let's eat."

CHAPTER TWENTY-SEVEN

"I'm taking your advice and heading back to Bourne tonight. Although I have my notes and reports for tomorrow in order, I think I want to go over them one more time. Besides, you have to get your story done for tomorrow and I certainly don't want to be a distraction." He snickered. "If you know what I mean," he said as he moved his eyebrows up and down and pretended to twirl the ends of a handle-bar moustache. "Also Sherlock, I'm not going to bug you about the case. The only thing I want to say is be careful. After this week, if you need my help, I'll be there for you. Of course, if there's anything you need right away, don't hesitate to let me know."

"I might have you call your buddy at the crime lab in Boston. The last time P-town sent up DNA to be tested it took over a year. Do you remember that case?"

"I sure do. In my opinion, there was no excuse for it. I do know, however, they've got a lot of new equipment, so that should never happen again."

"If you go into the office in the morning before you head for the courthouse, check to see if you got a missing person's flyer. Sgt. Costa is probably sending them out as we speak. Our girl is still listed as Jane Doe until we get a positive DNA match. Before I go into it any further, let me get my notes together. I'm sure I'll have questions and since Detective Adams is away until next Sunday, I'm sure I'll need to brainstorm with you." I stuffed another bite of pizza into my mouth and washed it down with the couple of mouthfuls of beer left in my bottle. "Pizza, beer and Sam—what more could I ask for?" I turned to see Watson sitting patiently waiting for the last few scraps. “Looks like I better add Watson to that list.”

We laughed. Sam reached over and ruffled the fur on the boy’s head. Watson responded with a little yip and an enthusiastic tail wag.

After we picked up the kitchen, Sam said, “I’m going to head out. I’m not sure if I’ll make it into the office in the morning, but I’ll have Bill check on the flyer. I’m also not sure what time the judge will break for lunch, but when I do get a break I’ll let you know how things are going.” Sam’s duffle bag was packed and waiting just inside the bedroom door alongside his briefcase.

I was already piling my notes on the kitchen table when he re-appeared. “Thanks for supper,” I said.

He put down his stuff and gave me a huge bear hug and a kiss to last a couple of days. “A dinner fit for a princess.” He smiled. “Okay, enough of this. I’ll be on my way.” He headed for the door with Watson and me at his heels. “Watson, take good care of Sherlock.”

I waved as Sam pulled out of the driveway. Back inside, I leaned against the door. He’s a good man. There was one more thing I had to do before I started my tedious homework assignment. I headed toward my Keurig, slid my cup in the holder, popped in a K-cup of French Vanilla and hit the brew button. Within seconds, the aroma of fresh coffee filled the air. I took my cup, picked up my cell phone and headed for the back deck and my rocking chair.

At least ten minutes had passed when *The Entertainer* started to play on my cell phone. I checked the caller ID. It was Annie.

“How did it go today?” she asked. “I’m sorry I couldn’t take your call before, but we were in a meeting with Mike. Actually, we were in meetings most of the day. Marnie was with me.”

“I figured that when she didn’t answer her phone either.”

“Marnie and I were talking today. We need to do another girls’ night out. We can’t go to the Melody Tent, but we can have a nice dinner like we had at the Paddock. And, maybe, if there’s a good movie playing we could do that too."

"I'm all for dinner, but this P-town case is taking lots of my brain power, so my thinker might not enjoy a movie right now. I do want to run something by you though. One of these nights maybe we can get together and hash over this case. I'm sure you're going to get it real soon in the DA's office. I'd like to let you know what we've come up with, the evidence we've found and my thoughts on the whole situation."

"No problem. Let's set up dinner. Since Marnie doesn't know lots of places yet, we can decide where to go. If we go early enough, we can go back to either your house or Marnie's and do a bull session." Annie waited for an answer.

"What are you doing tomorrow night?"

"Nothing and I know Marnie isn't doing anything either. In fact, we were going to suggest Tuesday night."

"Now that we've got that settled, where do you want to go?" I asked.

"How about The Yarmouth House? I haven't been there since the Sheriff's fund raiser last June. Their Mussels Isabella appetizer in white wine with garlic and shallots and a touch of lime butter is out of this world. Can you tell I order it whenever I go there? I know all the ingredients."

"And, I love their calamari with the sliced cherry peppers. You're making my mouth water and we haven't even mentioned the entrees. I'm sure Marnie will enjoy this as much as she did The Paddock." I could already taste those little deep-fried pieces of squid.

"I'll give her a call, tell her I talked to you and figure out a time. Is six o'clock okay?" Annie asked.

"Perfect," I said.

"All right then, I won't call you back tonight, but I'll give you a call in the morning before we head for the courthouse."

"Bye," I said and hit the end button.

CHAPTER TWENTY-EIGHT

I've never had trouble writing a story, but for some reason this one was throwing me for a loop. My wastebasket was surrounded by crumpled up papers that didn't score two points on the toss and my jeans were starting to close in like a strait-jacket. I could recite my notes backwards and forwards and not come up with anything new. I'd been sitting far too long at the kitchen table in front of my computer with nothing but my thoughts. Watson had given up a long time ago and was curled up somewhere in the living room.

I wrapped my hands around the back of my neck and pulled forward trying to ease the tension. Maybe if I get comfy and pour myself a glass of white zin my thinker will start to produce something worthy of a front page story. It didn't take much to talk me into it.

My diagnosis was just what the editor ordered. The wine relaxed me and the loose, baggy clothes set me free—a perfect combination.

It was almost one a.m. when I finished. I read the article a couple more times, then sat for what seemed an eternity, sipping on what was left in my wine glass while staring at Jane's picture. "If you really are Emily, and I believe you are," I whispered, "I'll make sure your story is told."

I was brought back to reality when I heard Watson whining by the kitchen door. "I know buddy, it's late and mama hasn't paid much attention to you all night." I opened the door and let him out. He turned to see if I followed. I crossed my arms and shook my head. "Not tonight." The air had cooled considerably. It won't be long before old man winter shows his paled-out, ice blue face and releases gusts of blistery cold air. Watson must have felt the change too. Before I knew it, he was bounding up the stairs and back into the house. "Good boy," I said and rewarded him with a treat.

I put Jane to sleep. Now, it was our turn. I pulled down the covers, climbed in, gave Sam's pillow a kiss goodnight and pulled the covers back up. When Watson was thoroughly satisfied I was comfortable, he jumped up and settled in where Sam's feet would have been. The last thing I remember was setting the alarm.

CHAPTER TWENTY-NINE

"Yikes!" I yelled as I scrambled out of bed. I think I scared Watson. I don't think I've ever seen him move so fast. He was off the bed and out of any path I'd be taking. He's only been with me for three and a half months, but he can read me like a book. I must be an easy read. I checked the back of the alarm clock. It either rang and I shut it off or I thought I set it, but didn't. Whatever the case, I was running late.

I scurried to the bathroom, brushed my teeth and turned on the shower. A quick glance in the mirror produced a horrible image. *Why would Sam want to wake up to this—I certainly don't,* I thought. Some days a shower feels better than others. This was one of those feel good days. I needed a pick-me-up and those warm beads of H2O did the trick. I didn't have time to blow dry my hair, so I pulled it up in a pony tail—one of the perks of having long hair. Fortunately, I'd done a small load of laundry last night so, I had a clean pair of gray chino's and a purple and gray stripe long-sleeve jersey hanging in my closet. I didn't feel like wearing sneakers and it was a little cool for sandals, so I grabbed my moccasins from beside the bureau and was ready to go.

Watson was sitting patiently beside the pantry door. He knew where his food was and he wasn't going to let me leave before he got fed.

My cell phone rang as I was mixing some water with his Kibbles 'n Bits. The ID read Annie. I hit the on button and secured it between my ear and shoulder. "Mornin'," I said.

"We're getting ready to head over to the courthouse. Marnie's here with me. We're all set for tonight as far as dinner is concerned.

I'll call The Yarmouth House later to make a reservation for six o'clock. It shouldn't be busy, but you never know."

When I turned to put Watson's dish down, the phone popped out and went flying across the kitchen floor. "Hold on," I yelled. Within seconds, I had my phone back and had somewhat composed myself. "This hasn't been a great morning," I said. "It started when I screwed up the alarm. You know how that goes."

"I do," said Annie. "Have you given any thought to the bull session after dinner?"

"Let's see what time we get done and how we're feeling. I think all three of us are going to have a pretty hectic Wednesday. But who knows, we're kind of weird, we get rejuvenated talking this real life murder mystery lingo."

"If you think I'm going to admit you're right, you're crazy." Annie laughed.

"I'm running late. I've got to get my story to Chuck for a quick review, then take it to Bucky in production, so he can schedule it for Wednesday's Tribune. I'm not sure what I'm doing the rest of the day. I may be taking a quick trip to P-town, but I'm not sure. Give me a call when you have a free minute."

"Okay, will do."

I gathered my briefcase, patted Watson and headed out the door. I was at the end of my driveway when it occurred to me that I hadn't had my morning coffee. I suppose I could wait until I got to work, but sometimes, depending on who makes it, the Tribune's coffee could grow hair on an egg. If I swing by Dunkin's, I can pick up a dozen donuts as a peace offering for being late. Besides, a donut would sure taste good.

I got my French Vanilla and ordered a dozen donuts. Per my instructions, the girl behind the counter put eleven in the box and one in a bag. Inevitably, someone would have taken my sugar jelly before I had a chance to get to it. That could have triggered a murder at the Tribune. I pulled into the Tribune parking lot and decided it would be easier if I called Jamie and asked her to meet me at the door. That way I wouldn't have to negotiate how I was going to balance everything, open the door and get to the break-room without having an accident.

"Morning, Casey," Jamie said as she greeted me. "How goes it?" She held out her hands to take something.

"I'm great. It's seventy-six degrees and the sun is shining." I handed her the box of donuts. "Will you please take these to the break-room for me? Take one out for yourself first." I continued down the hall to my office. From where I was standing, I could see that Chuck's door was open. *Good, at least he's somewhere in the building,* I thought. I put my briefcase on my desk, opened it and took out my copy of the 'P-town Jane Doe' story. I sat down to read it one more time before I gave it to Chuck. I didn't even get through the first paragraph before my boss appeared in the doorway eating a donut and sipping a cup of coffee.

"Glad to see you could make it in today," Chuck said with a note of sarcasm in his voice.

"Sorry boss, no excuse, I overslept." I shrugged my shoulders and gave him my best winkled-nose face. "I've been burning the candle at both ends. This story was hard to write. It shouldn't have been, but there's something about it that tells me it's going to get complicated. It's a gut feeling."

"Your gut feelings have gotten you in trouble before. Remember, you're a reporter not a detective. I welcome your ability to dig in areas nobody else would even think of looking in. You possess a special sixth sense. You know that I appreciate what you write for the Tribune. And, the stories you end up with are far beyond the scope of a normal investigative reporter. But, you need to be careful. Someday it might catch up with you."

"I haven't got caught yet—close maybe—but I'm still around. It's my nature," I said, "you know that. I can't help it. Now you sound like Sam. He's been hovering over me ever since the incident last July."

"I suppose you don't listen to him either." Chuck smiled. "Finish whatever it is you're doing and head over to my office."

"Be right there, boss." I wasn't going to change anything so I didn't need to finish reading. I took my story, coffee, donut, and a pen and walked down the hallway to Chuck's office.

"You snagged the lemon filled. The white powder on your face is a dead giveaway." I laughed, handed him my story and sat down. "See what a good detective I am."

I watched as Chuck read and re-read my article, then laid it on his desk in front of him. He took a deep breath before he lifted his head to speak, "Casey, you've got a way with words. It's remarkable how you make them come alive—how you make them paint a picture." He got up from his desk, turned and walked to the window at the back of his office. He folded his arms and stood quietly staring out into the courtyard. Without changing his position, he said, "She obviously didn't live in Provincetown." He shrugged his shoulders. "Why do you think she was there?" He turned to look at me.

"I don't know. I feel there's a lot more to her story and I intend to find out what it is. Don't think I'm crazy, but she's the one who's going to tell me."

"I don't doubt you for one minute," he said. "As your boss I will tell you to do whatever you have to do in your investigation in order to finish your story. But, as your friend, I will tell you to be careful. I know how you step over the line with both feet flying before you think of what's happening on the other side. Granted, you usually uncover that special piece that slips so smoothly into the puzzle. Just remember, somebody out there doesn't want you to complete the picture. And, as you've experienced before, that somebody will try to stop you."

"I hear what you're saying. And, believe me, I don't want to go through the same ordeal I went through last July. I'll be careful and I'll keep in touch so you know where I am and what I'm doing." I waited for a reply.

"I'll hold you to that."

"As far as this piece of the story, it's good to go. I'll call Bucky and tell him you're on your way to production and I want it to run front page in tomorrow's paper."

"Thanks, boss. I won't cause you problems and I won't disappoint you."

"I know you won't. What's on the agenda today?" he asked.

"I'm going to call Sgt. Costa to find out if all the missing persons' APBs went out and if so, has he heard anything back yet. I know it's a long shot, but maybe we'll get lucky. That information will determine what I'm going to do this afternoon. And, hopefully, Bernie will get a verified match on the DNA sometime today. That will be the first confirmed clue as to her identity. At least the identity we ascertained in one of our interviews."

Chuck had a puzzled look on his face. "You've got a name?"

"She was recognized by the proprietor of Miss Daisy's—a rooming house in P-town. We don't know if she gave a fictitious name or if, in fact, that was her real name. So, yes we have a name." I leaned forward on Chuck's desk. "That's my first dilemma."

Chuck looked at his watch. "I've got a few things to do, then a lunch meeting with the Town Manager. Is there anything else you need me for?"

"Nope. I'll call you tomorrow. Have a good one and tell Jim I said 'hi'." I got up, gave a little nod and headed to production.

"Mornin'," I said as I walked across the floor to where Bucky was standing. "I just left the boss's office."

"I know," said Bucky as he reached out to take the folder I was carrying. "He called to tell me you were on your way. Another intense case, huh?"

"Yeah, you could call it that." I didn't want to get into a discussion with him. Bucky's a good guy. He's good at his job. His problem is that sometimes he runs his mouth. He figures that one day I'll break and fill him in on where I am in an investigation. Never happen. "Well, got to get back to work. Thanks." I patted him on the shoulder and quickly headed for the door.

I didn't need one, but I hit the break room to see if there were any donuts left. "No such luck," I whispered. There was coffee in the pot, but I assumed it was left over from the morning and I wasn't that desperate.

Jamie was still sitting behind her desk. "Are you going anywhere for lunch?" I asked.

"I'm going to get a salad at Subway and bring it back here," she said. "Do you want me to bring you something?"

"A salad sounds great. Let me get some money. I'll be right back." I took a twenty dollar bill from my wallet and brought it back to Jamie. "My treat. You get what you want and I'll have a small oriental chicken salad with sesame dressing. Could you please get me a pink lemonade too?"

"You staying in today?" she asked.

"I've got some calls to make and depending what I get for answers, I'll probably be here most of the day."

"Okay, just let me finish this memo and I'll call to order lunch."

"Thanks, I really appreciate it."

CHAPTER THIRTY

It had been a long time since I'd eaten lunch at my desk. It was a slow day, so there weren't a lot of people moving around in the corridor outside my office. I took my recipe box from my briefcase and began taking the cards out. I kept them in the order they were inside the box.

I had transferred most of my notes onto cards. Since I've been doing investigative work, I find it an easier method in creating a timeline of events. So far it's worked pretty well. I use two different colors. I wrote actual facts on white ones and questions still not answered on pink ones. Jane's case had almost an equal amount of each. Usually I numbered them in case they got mixed up, but this time was different.

There was a knock on my door. I motioned Jamie to come in.

"Here's your lunch and your change." She set my salad and lemonade down on the desk and handed me some coins wrapped in a few dollar bills. "Thanks again," she said.

I took a big bite of my salad and was eye-studying my cards when my cell rang. "Hello." There was no response. I glanced at the caller ID. It read *unknown*. "Hello." Nothing. *Must have been a wrong number*, I thought. I shrugged my shoulders and went back to my salad and cards. Not two minutes went by and my cell rang again. This time I looked at the caller ID before I answered. Annie's name appeared in the little window. "Hi," I said as I welcomed the sound of her voice.

"Did you try to call me a couple minutes ago?"

"Yeah, I did, but it went down before you answered. I was at the top of the stairs in Super Court. I forgot it's a dead zone."

"How come the caller ID read unknown?"

Annie laughed. "I had Michael's phone."

"Well, that was kind of creepy—no name and no answer." I was relieved there was a logical explanation. "How's the trial going? And, how's Marnie holding out?"

"The trial is going smoothly, just as planned. James is showing no emotion. He just looks at the table in front of him. He doesn't even turn to look at his lawyer when he speaks to him. It's pretty sad." Annie stopped abruptly, then continued, "You know what I mean."

"I do know," I said.

"This whole ordeal is hard on Marnie. She knew it would be, but she's tough. She'll be okay. She wanted me to tell you that she's looking forward to girls' night out tonight. Is six o'clock still okay with you?"

"Perfect. I'll meet you there. You know it's been a while since we've gotten together to solve the problems of the world." I laughed. "Later."

I thought about giving Bubba a call, but decided to wait until after I finished my lunch. Instead, I started to re-read the notes that referred to the interviews Maloney and I had conducted on Commercial Street yesterday. Most of them didn't offer any concrete information, but a couple of them did stand out. In my mind, the idea of Jane buying a Boston Globe indicated that she had some connection to Boston. What that connection might be, I have no idea, but I intend to find out.

I was reviewing the notes I took at Miss Daisy's when my cell rang. Again, the ID read unknown. I hesitated—maybe it was Annie again. "Hello," I said cautiously.

"Casey?" There was a pause. "It's Sgt. Costa."

"Hi, Bubba." I felt relieved. "I was just getting ready to call you. Did you get all the missing persons' APBs out yesterday?"

"We did, but haven't gotten any responses yet."

"What about Bernie, have you heard from him regarding the DNA test?"

"Yes, I have. At least we have one thing going for us. The DNA on our Jane Doe and the DNA we gathered at Miss Daisy's was a match. So, I'm officially changing our records from Jane Doe to Emily Latham."

"Bubba, the only problem we might have there is we're not sure if Emily Latham is her real name. Omar thought she looked honest and never asked her for identification when she rented the room."

"You've got a point there. I ran it through the system and came up with nothing, but that only means she doesn't have a record."

Sgt. Costa's voice was muffled. I imagined him with his elbow firmly planted on his desk, his chin resting in his hand and his fingers over his mouth as he studied the picture on the flyer and talked to me at the same time.

"Is Maloney around?" I asked.

"He went out to check a few more places to see if anybody had seen Emily. I expect him back within the hour. Is there something I can tell him or do you want him to give you a call?"

"When he gets back, give me a call and put me on speaker phone. I want to run something by the two of you," I said. "By the way, the Tribune is going to run a story tomorrow. Is that okay with you or do you need to read it first? At this point, I'm not going to change her name."

"I agree. Go ahead and print the story. I trust your judgment as to what the public should know. I'll call you as soon as Maloney gets back."

"Later," I said and hung up.

CHAPTER THIRTY-ONE

Boston

A hit on Ancestry.com provided Katherine with a date of birth and a date of death. Gregory Bradshaw was born in 1932 and died in 2009.

She stared at the computer screen. This man was old. How could he be her father? When she was born her mother was fifteen. He was fifty six. It seems that all hope of finding more about her real family was slipping away.

She'd come this far and wasn't ready to give up. Since Gregory Bradshaw died in 2009, something might show up if she Googled him. She had nothing to lose. Katherine pulled up Google.com and typed in his name. A tap of the enter button delivered five pages filled with articles related to him.

She clicked on the first one. It was a copy of his obituary. Her father was born in Cambridge, Massachusetts, the only child of Esther and Henry Bradshaw. He graduated from Harvard University and Harvard University Law School. *So, he was a lawyer,* thought Katherine.

The obit went on to list several organizations he had been a member of. It also touched on his life after retirement and how he split his time between Cambridge and Truro. The best of both worlds—a house in the city and a beach cottage on Cape Cod.

The article went on to list his wife, Carol, and a daughter, Elaine, who pre-deceased him in 2008.

Katherine closed her eyes and sat back in her chair. The words she'd just read scrolled across the back of her eye lids. Unconsciously, she folded her arms, rested them on the desk beside the computer and buried her face in them.

Raji's voice snapped her back to reality when he leaned down and whispered, "Are you all right?"

"I'm fine. I didn't get much sleep last night, so it must have caught up with me."

"I didn't see you leave and knew it was getting late, so I decided to check on you."

"If only I could win the lottery, I wouldn't have to worry about opening up somebody else's business."

"If you win the lottery, remember your best friend and take me with you. But, if I remember correctly, you don't play. That would make it a little difficult to win, don't you think?" he joked.

Katherine smirked. "You're right, as usual." She gathered up the stuff she was working on and slipped it into her backpack.

"Here, allow me." Raji put both straps over his right shoulder and waved his hand for her to walk in front of him.

"Thanks," she said when they got to the door. "See you next week."

"You too. Have a good one."

Hopefully, Mr. Grossman won't make an early appearance today. She wanted to take time to arrange her notes in some type of order, then tuck them safely away in an inside zipper pocket of her backpack. Peter never went through her backpack, but lately he'd been asking lots of questions. Until she could prove this Gregory Bradshaw was really her father, she wasn't going to share the information she had uncovered with Peter. Maybe out-of-sight might lead to out-of-mind. She'd answer his questions soon enough.

Mr. Grossman wasn't at The Gallery when Katherine unlocked the door and reached in to flip on the lights. It was a welcomed silence. She pulled the shades up enough to let some natural light in hoping to enhance the beauty of the pictures hanging so still on the stark white walls. A couple of the pictures needed to be straightened, but, all in all, The Gallery was ready to embrace the public.

The new information she had found in her search today

consumed her entire thought process. She had a couple of new leads—very important leads that led to questions. Would it be proper to try to get in touch with her father's widow? Did his wife know anything about Katherine or her mother? How would she even begin to approach this lady? And, what about the deceased daughter? If Katherine was correct and this Gregory Bradshaw was her father, then his daughter, Elaine, was her sister. Her mind was spinning. She needed to calm herself.

The bell on the front door jingled. Katherine closed her book of thoughts and what-ifs and got up to help the lady who stood admiring the new water color of the Boston Common that Mr. Grossman hung last week.

"It's lovely, don't you think?" Katherine's appreciation of art blossomed through. "We just hung this painting a few days ago. A young artist, Amy Whiteman, asked us if we'd feature a few of her paintings." Katherine had never met Amy, but the sincerity in her voice made her believable. She prided herself in knowing the various artists names in case situations like this arose. "Amy's artistry with water colors is truly magical. She makes the colors flow and the picture come alive. And her interpretation of the scene is different than any I've seen—it's inspiring."

"I agree," the lady said without taking her eyes off the painting. "I've never been in The Gallery before. I was having coffee at Starbucks, across the street, and decided to take a look."

"Since you've never been here before, why don't you take a look around and if you have any questions, I'll try to answer them for you."

"I appreciate that, but I like this one. Could you please wrap it up and I'll take it with me." She reached into her purse for her wallet. "Do you take American Express?"

"Yes, we do," I said as I carefully lifted the painting from the wall. "Why don't you have a seat while I get this packaged. It will only take a few minutes." *I wish it was one of mine*, thought

Katherine. It took less than ten minutes to secure the painting for transport. Katherine brought the package to her customer, ran her American Express card, had her sign the receipt, then helped her open the front door. "Thank-you. I hope you enjoy it in your home as much as we've enjoyed having it here in The Gallery."

Quite satisfied that she had sold a painting done by a new, young artist, she went to the back room to find something else to hang. Tucked in the corner was another water color. This one was of the North End. It was also painted by Amy Whiteman. She didn't remember these pieces coming in. Out of curiosity, she decided to ask Mr. Grossman who Amy was and why they weren't put out before. She got lucky this time. The customer hadn't asked her any questions about the artist—good thing because she didn't have any answers.

Katherine didn't hear the bell jingle or the door open. Mr. Grossman appeared in the back room just as she was lifting the painting out of the corner.

"What are you doing?" asked Mr. Grossman.

"I sold the Amy Whiteman painting you hung last week, so I was replacing it with another one. She's a remarkable artist. Have we had these here long?"

"No, I met this young lady a couple months ago, one Monday when I was having lunch with Sidney and Charlie. She was waiting tables. I don't know how the conversation came up, but she said she was a senior at Mass Art. After some idle chit-chat, I suggested she come by The Gallery with a few of her paintings." Mr. Grossman stood smiling as he reached over to take the picture Katherine was holding. "She's good—real good. Reminds me of you."

"I'm flattered."

"Well, flattery will get you nowhere. Get your brushes out and start painting." Mr. Grossman put Amy's painting down. He folded his arms in front of him and gave me a raised eyebrow look.

"I'll get started—soon. I promise."

"Promises . . . promises. It's three o'clock—get going so you don't miss your train. I'll see you tomorrow."

I picked up my stuff and hurried out the door. I didn't want Mr. Grossman to start again. "Bye."

CHAPTER THIRTY-TWO

Boston

Katherine was in such deep thought, that she almost missed her subway stop. She jumped up and managed to get between the doors before they slid shut.

It was three-forty-five when she got to the condo. Her mind was fighting her body—they simply weren't working in conjunction. She went inside, dropped her backpack on the floor and sat down on the couch. Peter had a dinner meeting tonight with one of his clients, so he wouldn't be home until late. Usually, Katherine didn't use his computer to look things up. This time was an exception. She knew she couldn't make it back to the library until next Monday and she needed answers before that.

She figured she'd check the Boston phone directory for a listing on Carol Bradshaw. Forget that—it was like trying to find a needle in a haystack. She decided to try whitepages.com on the computer. Bingo—several Carol Bradshaw's came up, but only one with the same address listed in the obituary. Katherine noted the address and the telephone number. She then tried Googling the daughter's name.

"Oh my God!" she screamed, then covered her mouth with her hands. She hoped nobody heard her. There were pages and pages of articles about Elaine Bradshaw.

She had been murdered. Tears rolled down Katherine's cheeks. She pulled up story after story recanting the brutal murder that took place in Provincetown in 2008.

Katherine and Peter had visited Cape Cod several times, but didn't go down as far as Provincetown. Once they stayed in Hyannis and then a couple of times in Dennisport.

Things were starting to get confusing. Maybe Peter was right. Maybe she should let things lie. But, she'd come so far. The only person left that could help her fill in the blanks was her father's widow.

Her thoughts were interrupted when her cell phone rang. It was Peter.

Her quick 'hi' was cut off when Peter asked, "Have you had supper yet?"

"No, I was getting ready to warm up a piece of pizza."

"Why don't you hold off? Our meeting just finished and our clients had to make a flight, so we won't be going out to dinner. I'm heading out the door as we speak. Do you want to go over to L Street Tavern for a burger and a beer?"

"I can handle that. I'll be ready when you get home."

"I'm at the T-station now. See you in a half hour."

Katherine wasn't ready to share her find with Peter. She had gathered so much information that she needed to arrange it in an orderly sequence before going any further. Once she got that done, then maybe she would sit down and go over it with him.

Her plan was to list all the names she'd come up with and their relationship to her. Obviously, there wasn't time to start it now, so she cleared the computer and put her stuff away.

Not five minutes later the door opened. Peter was right on time, he always was. He handed her his briefcase and headed toward the bathroom. "I'll be right out, then we can get going."

"Okay," she mumbled quietly. "Whatever."

Peter walked out of the bedroom still drying water from his hands. "Did you say something to me?"

"Nope."

He leaned over and gave her a kiss. "I'm hungry, let's get going," he said as he opened the door and gestured her out. "We didn't even stop for lunch. It's what they wanted. I hate these kiss-the-clients-ass meetings. Anyway, now I'm home and can put all that behind me."

"This is a pleasant surprise. I didn't want warmed up pizza anyway."

Katherine looked at Peter. He was studying her. "You feeling okay?"

"Yeah. Why do you ask?"

"You just look a little pale to me, that's all."

"Nothing's wrong. Mr. Grossman is hounding me to start painting again. He wants to hang something in The Gallery."

"Not a bad idea. You've got a few started. Why don't you work on them?"

"I'll pull out the watercolor of Abe & Louie's. I always liked that one. Problem is I just haven't been in the mood lately."

"We went there last Saturday. Didn't that spark any enthusiasm to complete the painting?" Peter put his hands on his hips and tried not to smile. "I get it," he said. "You had the steak sandwich Saturday and you want to go back for the lobster mac and cheese."

"You know, that might do the trick," Katherine said.

"Then it's a date. We'll write it on the calendar. But for tonight, it's good old L Street."

Ever since *Good Will Hunting* came out, the Tavern has customers every night. Monday's a little slower, but sometimes, even on a Monday, you have to wait for a seat. Two people were leaving the corner table beside the window. Nobody was waiting so they walked over and sat down. The waitress came over to wipe the table and get their drink order.

"Hi guys. Haven't seen you for a couple of weeks. Have you been away?"

"No, just busy," said Peter. "Works picking up and that's a good thing, but some nights we're just too tired to go out."

We're too tired, thought Katherine. She smiled. "I'll just have a Diet Coke, please."

"No beer tonight?" asked Peter.

"I don't think so. For some reason my stomach is a little iffy, so I'll stick to the coke."

“Okay.” Peter turned to the waitress. “I’ll have a Michelob light.”

“Thanks. I’ll get your drinks and be right back to take your order.”

Katherine was checking out the menu when Peter asked, “Do you know what you’re having?” He stopped for a moment, then continued, “I think I’ll have a blue cheese burger and curly fries. No, maybe I’ll get the onion rings.”

“You get the rings and I’ll get the fries, then we can share. I’m getting a cheddar burger on grilled sour dough bread.”

When the waitress came back with the drinks, Peter gave her their food order.

A couple of their neighbors were sitting at the bar. He went over to say ‘hi’, but Katherine stayed at the table and waved when they turned to acknowledge her. It must have been guys night out cause their girlfriends weren’t with them.

As usual the burgers were wonderful and done to perfection. There was a Patriot’s game on the television behind the bar. Everybody was in a great mood. The Pat’s were leading seventeen to nothing only four minutes into the game. They started the season with a good record. “We should try to go to a game before it gets too cold,” Peter said. “What do you think?”

“I’d like that. Does your buddy from the Court House still have an in to get good tickets?”

“I think so. I’ll give him a call tomorrow and ask. The most he can do is say no.” Peter reached over for some fries. He looked around. “Imagine this was a nothing place. Only the locals and students came here and just like in the movie, there were fights and words exchanged all the time. Now look at it. They’ve cleaned up their act and put themselves on the map. I think some people come here thinking they might see Ben Affleck or Matt Damon. And, who knows, they are in town every now and then. The ghosts of Ben and Matt will live in this place forever.”

“That’s like seeing Elvis at Graceland. Only difference, Elvis is dead," she said, then laughed.

"Do you want any dessert?"

"Not here. I'd like to get some ice cream from the corner store and take it home," Katherine said tilting her head to one side waiting for a response. "I've got a craving for some chocolate almond chip."

"Diet Coke and now a craving for ice cream. Are you keeping something from me?" Peter looked over his eyebrows at her.

"Very funny," she said.

The waitress came back with their check. Peter handed her thirty five dollars and told her to keep the change. "See you next time around." He waved to his friends, who were still sitting at the bar, then put his arm around Katherine and they headed for the door.

CHAPTER THIRTY-THREE

I had lost track of time. It was almost three o'clock. Sgt. Costa told me he'd give me a call when Maloney got back to the office. He should have been back by now. *I'll wait until three, then try calling them.* No sooner did that thought cross my mind when my cell phone rang.

"Hello," I said.

"Hi Casey, it's me. Maloney got in about ten minutes ago. I'm putting you on speaker phone." There was a click.

"Good afternoon." Maloney's voice appeared upbeat.

"Hi, to you too. Did you get any new information in your travels today?" I asked.

"Not much. Remember those two guys in the alley? I bumped into one of them—literally bumped into him. He was running out between the buildings and I was right there. I don't know what he was running from and I didn't ask. But, he told me he passed the flyer around and a couple of people saw Jane, I mean Emily, around town. He didn't add anything else, just that she had been seen. I took it with a grain of salt. It doesn't add anything to the case and I don't know if I really believe him."

"I hear you," I said. "Anything else?"

"No, just the curiosity factor now. Word got around that we were asking questions and people wanted to know what we knew."

"Sometimes I'm glad I'm not in a uniform. That way I can be a little inconspicuous, if you know what I mean." I could hear Bubba chuckle in the background. "You know, the eyes aren't always following me."

"That's a matter of opinion," said Bubba.

"Okay you guys, enough." I decided it was time to get serious. "Let's get back to the subject at hand. You both with me?"

"We're both here," came two voices from the other end.

"I was going over my notes. The thing that stood out the most to me was her purchase of the Boston Globe. Very rarely do I look at the Globe. How about you two?"

"I can't remember the last time I did," said Bubba. "It may have been three years ago when Elaine Bradshaw was murdered. And, then it was because I was curious as to how they covered it."

"I probably peruse one more than both of you, only because I came from there and still have ties to the old neighborhood."

"That's my point. I think she had some type of ties with Boston, or at least the Boston area."

"Hmm."

"Maloney, could you check with your father to see if they got the missing persons APB?"

"Casey, I'm one step ahead of you. I called him this morning and asked him if he'd check it out. He called about an hour ago and said they got it and they'll be distributing it tomorrow morning at roll call."

"Can you call him back and share my Boston Globe reasoning with him? Maybe he can call some of his cronies in other precincts and give them a heads up. I have a strong feeling about this Boston connection." I waited for an answer.

"No problem. I'll call as soon as we get off the phone. He's probably done for the day, but I'm sure he'll do it first thing in the morning."

"Great," I said. "I'm taking the night off. Marnie, Annie and I are having a very much needed girls' night out. I'll talk to you tomorrow."

Two goodbyes came from the other end, then the phone went dead.

I put my notes back together, slipped them into a couple manila folders and put them in my briefcase. Even though I planned on spending some time in the office tomorrow, I decided to take all my stuff home just in case I can't sleep; it will give me something to do.

After all, I had a room-mate Saturday and Sunday nights, last night I wrote my story, now tonight it's dinner with the girls, then home by myself.

I checked my watch. I had plenty of time to get home, take Watson for a walk, kick off the shoes and relax in Mr. P's rocking chair. I do some of my best thinking there.

CHAPTER THIRTY-FOUR

Watson was waiting patiently inside the door. "What a great little guy you are," I said patting him on the head. His tail was wagging a mile a minute. I'm sure he wondered where Sam was. For the last few days, he's had more company during the day than he's ever had. Dogs are pretty smart, though. He probably knows what's going on better than I do. Maybe, Sam even told him. I wouldn't put it past him.

We had time to walk to the beach. The tide was out and the water was calm. Soothing little ripples danced across the horizon. The blue water and the blue sky were separated by a fine line only an artist could paint.

I sat on the sea wall for a few minutes and watched Watson run back and forth chasing the sea gulls. They knew Watson couldn't catch them, so they'd swoop down and land just long enough for him to race over, then they'd take off again. If I didn't know better I'd say they were laughing as they flew away.

I clapped my hands and called for him to come join me. It was time to leave. I hooked up his leash. He took one last look at his playmates and we headed home.

My house phone was chirping when we went inside. "What," I said as I lifted the receiver.

"Just checking to see if you were home." Sam knew how much I hated that ring tone.

I've told him to change it back to a normal bell, but somehow he conveniently forgets. I think he likes to torture me.

"I am. We just got back from a beach run. Watson lost the race with the gulls again. It was fun watching, though." I took the receiver and headed out to the back deck to sit in Mr. P's rocker. "How did the trial go today?"

"Fortunately, as planned. I keep waiting for some surprises to spring up, but so far, nothing. Mike's done his homework, so things should be okay. I hope it wraps up by the end of the week." There was silence, then Sam spoke, "And, how about you?"

"Well, I have a hunch. I ran it by Sgt. Costa and Maloney earlier. I think our girl is from Boston or has Boston ties. You know Bubba sent the missing persons flyers out. I asked Maloney to call his father to see if they got theirs. They did and they talked about it at morning roll call." I didn't want to get into any more detail. "Hopefully, when I talk to you tomorrow night I might have something to pursue. Right now I'm just drawing straws."

"Casey, I know your straws. Remember, you promised me you wouldn't go rouge. Well, I'm holding you to it." Sam sighed.

"Don't worry, big guy, I'll behave. Marnie, Annie and I are going out tonight. You know—our famous girls' night out. You should be more worried about that, than a little murder case."

"Don't be a smart ass," said Sam in a semi-serious voice. "So, where are you ladies going?"

"Maybe I shouldn't tell you." I laughed. "We're going to the Yarmouth House. Marnie has never been there and Annie and I haven't been there for a long time. It will be fun. We talked about staying over at Marnie's, but with everything going on, we decided to keep that for another time."

"Have a great time. Don't have too many zins and I'll talk to you tomorrow."

"Yes, daddy," I said sarcastically and hung up.

Now it was getting late and I had to get a move on. Watson's sixth sense kicked in. I swear he can understand every word I say. Before I had a chance to get up from my chair, he was already standing in front of the door. "Okay, boy, you know I'm going out for a while tonight. You behave and keep an eye on the house. I won't be too late."

He tilted his head from one side to the other and looked at me with those eyes.

"No, baby, I can't take you with me. Not this time."

I hurried to the bathroom, took a quick shower, did the necessary fluff-and-buff stuff and headed for the closet. Since it might be a little cool in the restaurant, I decided to wear my new Liz burnt orange jersey and a pair of tan pants. Actually, the cool part didn't make a difference, I wanted to wear my new duds. It's not often I get dressed up, but tonight seemed like the right time. I forgot I bought an orange and brown plaid purse to match. If I can find my brown shoes, my outfit will be complete. Nobody else wears them, so I can't blame anyone else for misplacing them. I was about ready to give up, when I caught the toe of one peeking out at me from under the shoe rack. The other one wasn't far behind.

I brushed my hair, put on a little make-up and was ready to do the town or at least have dinner. "Not bad," I said as I passed the full length mirror in my bedroom. "Sam, eat your heart out," I said with a little chuckle in my voice.

When I got to the kitchen, Watson was standing in front of his snack cabinet waiting patiently for me to reward him. "Move aside. You've been such a good boy, I'm giving you a couple extras. Now, don't eat them all at once. Save a couple for later." I bent down and gave him a hug.

I made sure the back door was locked, grabbed my keys and my purse and headed out the front door. I was so looking forward to dinner with the girls.

I left early and there wasn't much traffic, so I got to the restaurant before Annie and Marnie. The parking lot was about three-quarters full. That was about right for a Tuesday night, off-season on Cape Cod. If this was July instead of October, there would be a line waiting to get in.

There were empty seats at the bar, so I made my way over.

"Hey, Casey, long time no see."

"Hi, Dave," I said. "It's been busy, but that's no excuse." He had been the bartender at the Yarmouth House as long as I could remember. There were a few others that worked with him when it was busy, but he was their main man.

"Heard about your ordeal last summer. That was unbelievable. I'm glad you're okay." There wasn't anybody waiting for a drink, so he could get in a little talk-time.

"Annie and our new friend, Marnie, are meeting me for dinner. We're introducing Marnie to the best places and the best bartenders on the Cape." I winked then batted my eyelashes at him.

Dave smiled. "I'd follow you two anywhere." A couple more people came around the corner and sat down a few seats away from me. "Before I get busy, can I get you a drink while you're waiting for the girls?"

"Yeah, that sounds good."

"The usual?" he said.

What a memory. My white zin with a side of ice appeared within seconds. "You're good!"

"I know. I never forget what a pretty lady drinks," he said and moved to the couple to take their order.

I hadn't taken two sips of my wine, when I heard Annie and Marnie giggling as they came around the corner.

"Are these seats taken?" Annie asked.

"Why, no my dear, you're welcome to them," I said trying to keep a straight face. It didn't work. I burst out laughing.

I stood up and we gave each other hugs.

"I so need this tonight." Annie made herself comfortable on the stool beside mine. "I'm sure we all need it."

Marnie took a deep breath. "Will you please introduce me to the bartender, so I can order a drink."

"No need, little lady, I'm Dave and you are?" He held out his hand.

"Marnie."

"Glad to make your acquaintance, Marnie. You're living dangerously—hanging out with these two." He smiled.

"I'm finding that out. But, it's a little too late, I can't seem to get away from them." Marnie turned to see our reaction. "In the meantime, I'll have a glass of merlot."

"And, let's see," Dave said as he looked at Annie, "you switch your drinks so many times, I'll have to take a guess. I'll go with a glass of chardonnay."

"Good job. I'll take that glass of chardonnay." Annie nodded. "A drink and a show."

"You girls will have to come around more often. I missed you. Teddy should be right back. He just went up to the office to take a call."

We weren't there more than ten minutes when the maître-d' came to tell us our table was ready. Our table was in the front of the restaurant near the water wheel. I think Dave talked to Mr. George and asked him to find us one there.

"Will you look at this," I said. "The best table in the house."

"First the Paddock and now the Yarmouth House. I think I'm sticking with you guys. I like your taste," Marnie said as she slipped into her chair. "Who does all the decorating?" Marnie seemed mesmerized. She wasn't paying any attention to our conversation. She was just looking all around.

"Teddy's wife, Angie, is the creative one. She does all the decorating herself. Isn't it amazing?" I said. "I've never been to their house, but I bet it's beautiful. They have two other restaurants—totally different from this one." I took a sip of wine. "Boy does this taste good. A couple of these should do the trick."

"I second that," said Annie.

We were chatting and perusing the menu when the waitress came to our table. "Hi Casey, I haven't seen you since last summer. How you doing?"

"I'm fine. You remember Annie," I said. "Let me introduce you to our friend, Marnie. She's an import from New York City. We're trying to convert her to a Cape-y." I looked at Marnie. "And I think we're doing a pretty good job."

"You're in good hands," she said as she readied to take our order. "Let me tell you about the specials. It's lobster night, so, of course, all the specials are lobster dishes. We have a two pound lobster stuffed with crabmeat and scallops. That's always yummy. Then we have a lobster, shrimp, and scallop casserole and last, we're offering a lobster scampi. The last one is new. I've served quite a few tonight and everybody seems to love it."

"You changed my mind," said Marnie. "I was going to have the shrimp scampi, but the lobster scampi is calling my name."

"You've got it. How about you girls?"

"I'm having my favorite, the veal marsala. I can look at the menu for an hour and I'd still not order anything else." My mouth was already watering. "But, could I please have penne instead of linguini?"

"Of course."

Annie closed her menu. "I think I'm with Marnie. I'm getting the lobster scampi special."

"Do you want to split an appetizer?" I asked. "With all this food, one is probably enough."

"Marnie, have you ever had mussels?"

I knew Annie was going to choose Mussels Isabella. I liked them too, so I didn't mind.

"No, but I have a feeling I'm going to have them tonight."

Annie turned to the waitress. "We'll get one order of Mussels Isabella and share it."

"Thanks, I'll get these right in for you. Does anyone need another drink?"

We looked at each other and almost in unison said, "Not right now."

"Here we are." I held up my glass to toast. "The meeting of the minds is called to order."

We clicked glasses and nodded in agreement.

Marnie rested her elbows on the table and leaned forward. "If it's okay with you guys, I'd rather not talk about the trial tonight."

"Fine with me," I said knowing that she must be hurting inside. "How about I fill you in on the P-town case?"

"I'm dying to hear what's going on," Annie said as she set her glass on the table.

"One big development is that we think we have a positive ID for our Jane Doe. She registered at Miss Daisy's rooming house on Commercial Street a week ago under the name of Emily Latham. That we know for a fact. If she gave her real name, we've uncovered a major clue. The next step is finding out where she's from."

"Do you have any idea at all?" Marnie asked.

"Nothing concrete. I have a hunch, though. Through the interviews Maloney and I conducted with the locals, meaning both business people and residents, we know she bought a Boston Globe at a little news store."

"Hmm," Annie thought for a moment, then said, "Who would buy a Boston paper in P-town unless they were connected in some way to Bean Town?"

"That was my thought exactly."

"Okay, so to back up a step. Yesterday Sgt. Costa sent out missing persons' APBs under the name Jane Doe to all Massachusetts police departments. Hopefully, they were picked up and distributed at morning roll calls."

"Have you heard from anybody yet? Marnie asked.

"No," I said. "But, remember when we first met Maloney, he told us he transferred to the P-town PD from the Boston PD. He was stationed at the South Boston precinct." I looked at the girls who were listening intently, then continued, "Well, his father is still at that precinct. Maloney was going to get in touch with him tonight or tomorrow morning. I asked Maloney to see if his father would be our Boston eyes until we confirm or rule out the Boston connection."

Annie had a puzzled look on her face. "I thought Sam had a lot of contacts in Boston. Have you asked for his help?"

"No, and I don't want either one of you to talk to him about our conversation." I wasn't smiling. They both knew I meant what I said. "I'll fill him in when, or if, it becomes necessary."

"You're treading on thin ice." Annie picked up her glass and took a sip.

The smell of mussels swimming in garlic butter and herbs penetrated our senses as our waitress set them down in the center of the table.

"Marnie, you do the honors." I handed her an appetizer plate. "You liked the escargot at the Paddock, I'm sure you're going to love these."

Annie and I each took a spoonful.

"Just as good as ever?" I turned to see Teddy standing behind me.

"You bet—just as good as ever," I said. "I'd like you to meet Marnie. She came for a visit last July and never left. You know the feeling."

"I do," Teddy said, putting his hand on Marnie's shoulder. "And you teamed up with these two? You're a glutton for punishment." He smiled. "No really, I can't think of two better friends to have. Enjoy your dinner and I'll talk to you before you leave."

"Back to our crime solving." I took a drink, then continued, "Tomorrow the Tribune is running a story. You'll find it vague and very generalized. I did it that way for a reason. It also still refers to the victim as Jane Doe. I didn't mention the fact that she was pregnant and that she was murdered some place other than in cottage number three. If our killer thinks we know too much, he or she, might disappear."

"That's if the killer reads the article."

"You're absolutely right Annie, but at this point we have to go on the assumption that whoever did this is watching and reading."

"I think I'm understanding this stuff better the more I hang around you two. And, of course, it doesn't hurt to work in the DA's office."

Marnie's eyes opened wide as she watched our waitress put our dinners on the table. "One of these is enough food to feed the three of us. I know what I'm having the next few nights for dinner."

"You certainly don't leave here hungry," our waitress said. "Can I get anyone another wine?"

"I'll take a white zin," I said.

Both Annie and Marnie followed my lead.

"This is out of this world. I thought the meal at the Paddock was wonderful, but this lobster scampi gives a whole new meaning to heavenly." Marnie stopped talking and concentrated on her dinner.

"I have to admit that I agree with Marnie," said Annie. "We've taken her to two of the best restaurants on the Cape. We're spoiling her."

Marnie managed to speak in between bites. "If that's what it is, then don't stop. I can get really used to this."

Two hours had passed, before we realized how long we'd been sitting, talking, and eating. It was nine o'clock. I looked up to see Teddy heading our way. "Would you girls like an after-dinner drink? Perhaps a white crème de menthe or a Bailey's on the rocks. They say it sooths the stomach." Before we had a chance to answer, Teddy had called the waitress over. "I've got to get back to the office. Sorry I couldn't spend more time with you. In this business, you never know what or who's going to pull you away." Teddy took a deep breath. "Marnie, it was nice meeting you. I hope to see you girls again soon."

"Thanks, Teddy," I said and stood to give him a hug. "Please say 'hi' to Angie for me."

"I will. Maybe next time you're here she'll be around. Take care."

We sipped our drinks and decided to do a sleep-over at Marnie's next weekend. "I'll ask Sam to watch Watson again, only this time maybe he'll take the boy to his house." I was afraid that he'd move back in for another week if he came to my house. If I had him underfoot, I wouldn't be able to study the P-town case the way I wanted to. Once I get everything in place, I'll run it by him, but until then I need to do this on my own.

The waitress brought the check. We added a healthy tip and divided it by three. It was well worth it.

I rubbed my stomach, as I reached over to pick up my to-go box. "I'm so full, I hope I don't fall asleep on the way home." I laughed.

There weren't many people left in the restaurant. A couple of regulars were sitting at the bar talking to Dave. I raised my hand to blow him a little air kiss, while Annie and Marnie just waved. The air had cooled off—probably a good thing. *If I crack the window a hair, it will help me stay alert*, I thought.

"Why don't you call me tomorrow when you get a break. That would be easier than me trying to reach you, especially if you're in the courtroom."

We did our usual group hug, then headed for our cars. Marnie rode with Annie, since they lived relatively close to each other.

The ride home seemed long. I guess I was just tired. I couldn't wait to get my jammies on and crawl under my puff with Watson at my feet. What more could I ask for—protection and a foot warmer rolled into one.

I almost overshot the turn into my driveway. "Wow, that was bad," I said out loud. "I must have been daydreaming." My yard was exceptionally dark. It was still daytime when I left, so I must have forgotten to turn on the outside light. Sam would have had a fit. But, I won't get the lecture tonight because he won't know. And, I don't intend to tell him.

It was comforting to have Watson waiting for me on the other side of the door—tail wagging and whimpering to let me know he missed me. I flipped on the kitchen light and automatically looked around to make sure we were alone. It was a habit that I couldn't break—Watson or no Watson.

Once I turned on the outside light, all the monsters I was sure were surrounding my house disappeared. Watson didn't want to be outside any more than I did, so he quickly went about his business and ran back in.

Normally, I'd watch a little TV before making love to my pillow, but tonight I didn't want anything except a rendezvous with the sandman.

CHAPTER THIRTY-FIVE

Boston

Tuesday morning came too quickly, Peter was already up and dressed for work when Katherine shuffled into the kitchen. "You're the early bird this morning." She walked to the Mr. Coffee and poured herself a cup. "Ummmm, this tastes good. I hope the caffeine kicks in real fast. I need a good pick-me-up. I don't know why I'm so groggy this morning."

"I can answer that for you. You tossed and turned all night."

"Meaning I kept you awake?" Katherine asked.

"Yea, something like that," he said. "I figured there was no need to lay in bed and look at the ceiling, so I got up and got ready for work. I'm heading out. I'll give you a call later." Peter picked up his briefcase, gave Katherine a quick kiss and was out the door before she had time to say anything else to him.

She shrugged her shoulders went to the toaster to make herself a couple pieces of toast before she showered. Since Peter was gone and she had an extra hour, she decided to take a fresh look at her notes. That was probably why she was so restless last night. There was more going on in her head than she could handle. She had to come to a decision—should she contact her father's widow and confront Carol Bradshaw with the barrage of questions that she was trying to find answers to? Or should she file everything away and continue trying to build a life with Peter?

Before she made a decision, she decided to put things in order to see if they made any sense. The information she'd found would determine if she would go on. Katherine pulled a notebook from her backpack and started to list the people she presumed to be members of her birth family. She started with her birth mother's name:

Emma Latham:
born: 1973 died: 1990 (presumed)
Gregory Bradshaw:
born: 1932 died: 2009
Carol Bradshaw: (Gregory's wife)
born: ???? died: still living
address: 2465 Belmont Street
Cambridge, Massachusetts
telephone: 617-842-9923
Elaine Bradshaw: (Gregory's daughter—my half-sister ??)
born: 1964 died: 2008 in Provincetown (murdered)

Katherine studied the information. It was pretty cut and dry. There was no doubt in her mind what she was going to do next.

She glanced at the clock. It was eight forty-five. If she hurried, she might make it to work on time. She took a quick shower, threw on a pair of new jeans and a jersey, stuffed everything in her backpack and ran out the door. Fortunately, she made it to the T-stop just as the subway train was pulling up. The twenty minute ride would give her a chance to compose herself before facing Mr. Grossman. Not that she didn't like the man—she did—but today she wasn't sure if she liked anyone.

Mr. Grossman wasn't at The Gallery when she arrived and nobody was waiting to rush the place when she opened the door. She didn't feel like making a pot of coffee, so when Mr. G showed up she'd suggest Starbucks. She'd offer to pay, but she knew he wouldn't let her. Then he'd hand her the money and she'd go across the street and get them both a hot mocha latte with whipped cream. It was a little ritual they went through every now and then.

Katherine walked around The Gallery to see if anything had changed. The other Amy Whitehead painting was still hanging where she had put it yesterday, but there was an empty space beside it. *Mr. G must have had a sale after I left*, she thought. For the life of her, she couldn't remember what had been hanging there.

The phone rang. "Good morning . . . The Gallery of Newbury Street . . . Katherine speaking."

"Morning Katherine." It was Mr. Grossman. He sounded like he had a frog in this throat.

"What's wrong with your voice?" she asked.

"I've either got a cold coming on or my allergies are starting to kick up. I didn't get much sleep last night. I'm taking the morning off, but I'll be in somewhere around one o'clock."

"No problem," I said staring out the window in the direction of Starbucks. "I'm going to lock the door for about ten minutes and run across the street to get a latte. Then I'll be good to go."

"Can you work on the inventory for me? I started it yesterday afternoon before I closed, but didn't get too far. It's on the right hand corner of my desk."

"Sure thing boss. You take it easy and I'll see you later."

"Thanks Katherine," he said.

First on her list was the latte. She put the phone on hold, grabbed some money from her backpack, locked the door and ran across the street. This time she made sure no cars were coming.

She had done the inventory many times before. It wasn't like they had thousands of pieces of candy to count. The sales slips for the month were attached and already tallied. She could finish it up in an hour.

It was eleven o'clock when she wrapped up the inventory. "Done," she said softly. She reached down and unbuckled her backpack. The notes she'd worked on earlier at home were in a folder in the front pocket. Katherine cleared the desk of Gallery stuff, took the folder out and started to go through her notes.

The list she had made was sitting on top staring at her. She obviously couldn't talk to Gregory Bradshaw or Elaine Bradshaw, but she could talk to Carol Bradshaw. Katherine was sure that if she explained everything to Carol there wouldn't be a problem. After all, Katherine was only trying to find her birth family. She wasn't trying to cause problems.

She lifted the phone and started to key in Carol's number, but hung it up before she pushed the last digit. Katherine wasn't sure if she could go through with it. She rested her elbows on the desk and cradled her head in her hands—gently rubbing her forehead. A heavy sigh broke the silence. She sank in the chair, leaned her head back and stared at the ceiling. It held no answers. There was nobody to tell her what to do. Nobody, except Peter, and she knew what he would say. If she was going to do this it had to be now.

The phone rang just as she was about to pick it up to call Carol. "Hello," she said.

"Yes, this is The Gallery. We're open until five o'clock today."

"You're welcome."

Let's try again, she thought. Katherine steadied herself, then dialed Carol's number.

"Hello," came a voice from the other end.

"Hi, is this Carol Bradshaw?"

"It is. Who am I speaking with?"

"My name is Katherine O'Ryan."

"If you're selling something, I'm not interested."

"I'm not selling anything. Please don't hang up."

There was a dead silence.

"I'm not quite sure where to start, but I need your help."

"That's pretty vague. You need my help? You better give me a good reason why I should keep talking to you."

"I don't know how to start. I was adopted right after I was born. My adoptive father died ten years ago in an automobile accident. My adoptive mother died last February. Just before she died, she told me I was adopted. Until then, I had no idea I was. That was all she said, but I found some letters in her personal belongings that indicated who my birth mother might be."

"How does this involve me?"

"Carol, this is hard to explain over the telephone. I believe we're related through Gregory Bradshaw. Do you think we could meet and I could show you what I've found?"

Carol didn't say anything for the better part of a minute. Actually, she didn't know what to say. "I don't know why I'm even talking to you," she finally said. Okay, I'll agree to meet with you, but at someplace like Starbucks or Panera. I want to get this over with. I'll be available tomorrow after one o'clock."

"I have to work in the morning, but I can meet you at the Starbucks on Newbury Street at one—if that's all right with you." Katherine's voice was starting to quiver.

"I know that Starbucks. I'll meet you there. This better be on the level or I'm going to call the authorities. Do you understand me?"

"It is and I do," said Katherine. "Thank you."

The voice on the other end was gone. Katherine's breathing became heavy. She felt sick to her stomach. Had she done the right thing? She slumped forward on the desk. "Stop second guessing yourself," she murmured. "You did what you had to do."

CHAPTER THIRTY-SIX

Boston

It was a normal Peter morning. He was in a hurry to get to work. This morning he didn't even make coffee. "I'm meeting a couple of the guys at the Dunkin's by the office this morning. I figured you could pick up a coffee or a latte at Starbucks." He leaned over and gave Katherine a kiss. "You don't mind, do you?"

"Of course not, I like Starbucks better anyway." She saw the look on his face. "I'm only kidding. Go ahead and have a jelly donut for me."

Katherine was relieved when Peter left. Now she could get herself ready for the meeting with Carol Bradshaw. Her stomach was a little queasy. *Probably nerves,* she thought.

Fortunately, Mr. Grossman said she could have the afternoon off. He told her to take the whole day, but she told him that wouldn't be necessary. She kidded him and said she'd take the other half another time.

Katherine decided to wear a pair of navy blue slacks, a white and navy striped shirt and a navy with white polka dot scarf. She looked in the mirror and nodded with approval. Since she hadn't taken anything out of her backpack, it was ready to go. She slipped on a pair of brown Grecian sandals and headed out the door.

CHAPTER THIRTY-SEVEN

Boston

The morning went by quickly. The anticipation was killing her. She had no idea what Carol Bradshaw looked like. She only had a voice and that wouldn't help. On the other hand, Carol didn't know what Katherine looked like either.

At twelve-fifteen, Mr. Grossman walked over to Katherine who was standing in the front window staring out to the street. "I thought you wanted the afternoon off," he said.

She looked at the clock above the back door. "I'm only fifteen minutes late. I'll be leaving shortly." She smiled and headed toward the office to get her backpack.

Mr. Grossman was straightening a painting when she returned. "I've been meaning to change this one. What do you think? It's been here for almost six months."

Katherine knew Mr. Grossman didn't like to be alone in The Gallery. Some days he didn't do much talking, but none-the-less, there was another body there if he had something to say. "I'm leaving now. Thanks and I'll see you in the morning. If you come in early enough I'll spring for the latte." She smiled and scooted out the door before he tried to start another conversation.

She wasn't sure if Mr. Grossman was watching her walk away, so she decided to walk up the street and around the corner—out of his sight. If she crossed the street a block down, he probably wouldn't see her walk back to Starbucks. Hopefully, there would be a table inside for them to sit and talk.

Katherine was a little early, but this way she could watch the people coming in and try to pick out Carol Bradshaw. For all she knew, Carol might already be inside doing the same thing. She opened the door and walked in. There didn't appear to be a single woman sitting alone, waiting for someone. The table in the far corner was available, so Katherine slipped her backpack off, set it down beside one of the chairs and sat herself down to wait for Carol.

Ten minutes passed before she saw, what appeared to be, a single woman came through the door. She didn't head for the counter. Instead, she stood to the side of the front window and looked around the coffee shop. Her eyes caught sight of Katherine sitting by herself, without any food or drink on the table. Katherine smiled and stood to acknowledge her. The woman walked toward the table.

She reached out. "Hello, I'm Katherine O'Ryan. Are you Carol Bradshaw?" Katherine waited for a response.

Nothing was said. The two shook hands.

Katherine motioned for the woman to sit down.

"Yes, I'm Carol Bradshaw."

"I was just going to get a cup of latte. Would you like something?"

Carol looked at Katherine, studying her every move. "I'll just have a Grande with three creams and one Splenda." She was very curt with her answer.

"I'll be right back." There were four people ahead of Katherine. She was glad. It gave her a few minutes to compose herself. Katherine placed the order and moved to the end of the counter to wait for them to deliver it. She glanced over at Carol, who sat very still, just staring at the table—showing no emotion what-so-ever.

"I have a latte and a Grande for Katherine," called the girl behind the counter.

"That's me," said Katherine. She took the drinks and headed back to the table.

"Thank you," said Carol.

"You're welcome."

A few minutes went by, then Carol asked, "What is it you're looking for?"

Katherine reached down and took the folder from her backpack.

"As I explained to you on the telephone, I'm trying to find out information on my birth family. Until last February, I didn't know I was adopted. As you can well imagine, it came as quite a shock. My mother was dying and she wanted me to know. There have been days I wish she hadn't told me. But she did. And, ever since then I've done nothing but wonder who I really am."

"You mentioned some letters you found in your mother's personal belongings that indicated who your birth mother might be. What does that have to do with me?" Carol gave Katherine a piercing look and said sarcastically, "I'm certainly not your mother."

"Carol, please hear me out." Katherine sighed. "This is not easy for me and it won't be easy for you to hear what I have to say. But, it has to be said. I'm hoping we can handle this in a civilized manner. I'm not out to hurt you and I hope you'll feel the same way towards me when I tell you the story."

Carol lifted her coffee and sat back in her chair. "I'm listening."

"My mother's name was Emma Latham. My birth name was Emily Mae Latham. Emma Latham was my adoptive mother's cousin." Katherine searched Carol's face for some emotion—anything—but there was nothing. "Emma was fifteen-years-old when I was born. She was a child herself."

Carol set her cup back on the table and leaned forward, this time showing interest in what Katherine was saying.

"I didn't tell you on the telephone, but somebody got a copy of my real birth certificate. That's how I found out my birth name. The birth certificate also listed a name in thc space reserved for father." Katherine looked straight at Carol. "The name recorded as my father was Gregory Bradshaw."

Carol sat straight up. "Are you crazy?"

Katherine looked around to see if anybody had noticed the change in Carol's voice. Fortunately, they were all engrossed in what they were doing and not paying any attention to the table in the corner.

"My deceased husband had one daughter and her name was ..."

"Elaine," Katherine butted in. "I know that she was murdered on Cape Cod in 2008."

"Where did you get this information?" Carol's voice had calmed to a whisper.

"From various sources." Katherine wasn't sure what to do or say next.

The two sat uncomfortably sipping on their drinks.

"You probably don't understand why I'm going to such trouble to find my birth family. My boyfriend would tend to agree with you. After all, I'm twenty-three years old and until seven months ago, I was content being Katherine O'Ryan." She reached up and put both hands over her face. She prayed she could hold back the tears. "I want nothing more than to know my heritage—to know what kind of a family half of me came from. If Gregory Bradshaw is my father, I think I have the right to know."

Carol's mind was working overtime. She wondered how much this girl knew about Gregory Bradshaw. Was this all a scam? Was Katherine role-playing—the innocent, illegitimate child trying to cash in on a very lucrative inheritance? Carol figured she had to go along with Katherine. If she didn't answer Katherine's questions, she probably would go somewhere else to find somebody who would. Carol determined it would be in her best interest to furnish bits of information to Katherine. First, she needed to gain Katherine's confidence. Once that was done, Carol could mold or twist the truth to fit her version of the Bradshaw story. If she was careful, her adaptation should satisfy Katherine.

"You sprung this on me. I understand you wanting to know. I suppose if I was in your shoes, I'd try to do the same thing. I commend you on your research. I'm just not sure how I can help. I wasn't in the Bradshaw picture in nineteen eighty-eight when you were born. I met Gregory in nineteen ninety-seven. You would have been nine-years-old. I was working as a representative for a medical supply house in Boston. He had a case that involved a drug we sold.

It was considered a controlled substance, therefore it was carefully documented as to who purchased it and when. After the case was over, he called and asked if we could meet for coffee. I thought he had some questions he needed answered, so I agreed to meet him. I knew he'd won the case, so I didn't think anything about it. He was much older than me, but there was something about him I liked. Coffee turned into cocktails, then dinner and the rest is history. We were married on June 16, 2001. This was my first marriage and his third. His first two wives died. Elaine was his daughter by his first wife."

"Did you know Elaine well?"

"Well enough. She didn't approve. I was born in nineteen-sixty-six and she was born in nineteen-sixty-four, so I was two years younger than her. She and her father would argue constantly about it, but there was nothing she could do. She was definately a very talented person. I don't know how much you know about her, but she was somewhat of an icon in the fashion industry. She lived a fast paced life on Beacon Hill and never married, but had lots of boyfriends and lots of money. One day, she got fed up with the fast life. We never understood what happened and she never offered an explanation. She up and left Boston and moved to Cape Cod. One of her cousins was selling a year-round cottage in Provincetown, so she bought it and moved within a month."

"Did you keep in touch with her after she moved?"

"She mellowed out a little, but we were never close. It was after Elaine's death that her father's health began to fail. He blamed himself for pushing her away. He would always say 'if only she stayed in Boston'." She watched as Katherine took everything in. Carol felt certain she had gained Katherine's confidence.

Katherine was overwhelmed with everything Carol was telling her. She picked up her cell phone to check the time. "We've been sitting here for almost two hours. There's so much more I'd like to talk to you about. Do you think we can meet again sometime soon?"

"We can. Are you available for lunch on Thursday?"

"I don't think that will be a problem. I'll check with my boss tomorrow. If you don't hear from me, it will be fine. Where do you want to go?

"That depends on you. Where do you work?" Carol asked.

Katherine wasn't sure if she should tell her about The Gallery, then decided it wouldn't be a problem. After all, they just exchanged very personal information—the name of her work place didn't seem to matter. "I work across the street at The Gallery," she said. "Any place around here would be fine."

"Do you know the deli a couple blocks up, around the corner? They have a great hot pastrami sandwich. How about I meet you there the same as today, one o'clock?"

"You mean Mac & Mary's?"

"That's the one."

"I'll be there. I've got to catch the three o'clock subway to Southie."

"Katherine, it was nice meeting you. I'll see you Thursday." Carol picked up her purse and as fast as she came in, she was gone.

Katherine took a deep breath. She couldn't believe this was happening. There were still unanswered questions, but she felt well on her way to getting them answered.

CHAPTER THIRTY-EIGHT

Boston

Peter hadn't been in the door two minutes when Katherine announced, "I have an incredible urge for Chinese food."

"What brought that on?"

"I have no idea, but do you want to go eat at China Gardens or get take out and bring it home?"

"We'll go there and eat." Peter was curious about Katherine's upbeat behavior. "Good day at The Gallery?" Peter asked.

"Yeah, you might say that." Katherine grabbed her purse and started for the door. "You coming?"

"By the way, you look very nice. Did you have something special going on today?" Peter stood eying her.

"No, what's with all the questions? I decided to wear some different clothes, that's all."

CHAPTER THIRTY-NINE

Boston

Wednesday, Katherine was back to her normal jeans and jersey attire. Peter left early again for work. She liked having some time to herself in the morning. Except for having a slight stomach ache, she felt good. Yesterday's meeting with Carol went great. She seemed like a nice person.

Katherine wanted to surprise Mr. Grossman so she left early. When he arrived at The Gallery, there was a slice of lemon pound cake and a mocha latte waiting for him. "I should let you have a few hours off more often," he said as he took a bite. "You're beaming from ear to ear. I take it you had a good afternoon. Maybe you can channel some of that enthusiasm into a painting."

"I just might do that. You never know." She shook her head and gently waved her finger at him.

"Since you brought it up," she said, "I'm going to lunch with a friend tomorrow. I'm meeting her at one o'clock at Mac & Mary's, just up the street. Is that okay?"

"I think I can count on one hand the total number of times you've left The Gallery for lunch and one of them was with me, so that doesn't count. Of course, it's okay." He smiled. "They have great hot pastrami sandwiches. It's even better if they melt some cheese on the top."

"I'll take that into consideration. Thanks."

CHAPTER FORTY

Boston

Katherine sat on the edge of her bed. Peter was still in the bathroom. "You going to be much longer?" she asked.

"I'm done. It's all yours," said Peter as he walked out of the bathroom and headed for the closet.

The butterflies were swirling around in her stomach again. Katherine was beginning to get concerned about these funny feelings she was having lately. She chocked them up to the release of built-up stress she'd been harboring for months. But, if her nerves had calmed down and the stress was starting to go away, why was she still experiencing uneasiness?

Maybe it was the Chinese food they had last night, she thought.

Once Peter left, she searched her closet for something to wear. She decided on a pair of tan slacks and a brown flower print shirt. "Wow," she said, standing in front of the mirror as she tried to zip her pants. "I know I haven't worn them for a while, but I didn't think I gained weight." She hung the tan ones back up and took out a pair of black ones. "These are a little tight, too, but I'm wearing them anyway." Katherine sat back down on the bed. It was as though somebody slapped her up side of the head—the uneasy stomach and the tight clothes. She fell down on her pillow and began to cry. "This can't be happening to me," she said burying her head. Things were starting to fall into place for her. She knew a baby wasn't in the cards for her and Peter—at least not now.

Her morning at The Gallery went by slowly.

Mr. Grossman came in at eleven. "I want to talk to you about something," he said and pulled up a chair for her to sit down beside his desk. "This is our slow season and my wife has been bugging me to take her on a cruise to the Caribbean. I've made excuses for years and I don't have any more to give her. So, I've been thinking. How would you like to have a week's vacation, too?"

She was taken aback by what Mr. G just said. "Of course, I'd like to take a week off, but . . ."

"But, nothing," said Mr. Grossman. "You're a valued employee and I want to give you a week off with pay. The thing is this," he rolled his eyes, "unbeknownst to me, my wife already booked the trip. It sails this Sunday from Miami. She and her girlfriend thought it would be wonderful if they made all the arrangements and surprised their husbands."

"I don't know what to say." Katherine didn't know how to react. "I know Peter can't get the time off on such short notice, but there are a few things I'd like to do, so this would certainly give me the time to do them." She sat back and smiled. "I don't know how to thank you."

"You want to thank me, then start a picture and finish it." He raised his eyebrows. Mr. Grossman looked at his watch. "Hey, don't you have a lunch date at one? It's ten till. You better get going."

"What would I do without you?" Katherine got up, walked over to Mr. G and gave him a kiss on the forehead. "See you in about an hour." With that, she grabbed her purse and ran out the door.

Carol was already at the deli and waved to her as I came through the door.

"Sorry I'm late. I was talking to my boss about a couple of things."

"I just got here myself." Carol reached down beside her chair, lifted up a bag and set it on the table. "I brought something for you to look at."

Katherine couldn't imagine what Carol had in the bag.

"Let's order first and I'll show you while we're waiting."

"Okay," Katherine said in a puzzled voice.

The waitress took their orders as Carol proceeded to remove the contents of the bag and set it between them on the table. "This is a photo album of Gregory Bradshaw and his daughter long before I came into the picture. I thought you might like to see it."

Katherine could feel her hand shaking as she reached over to open the album. The first page appeared to be a family photo. "Who are these people?" she asked.

"This is Gregory, his first wife and his daughter, Elaine. I think he said she was three in this picture. It wasn't long after this was taken, his wife died. He never told me what she died of. Actually, he never told me what either wife died of and I didn't ask." Carol had baited the hook on Tuesday and today she caught the fish.

Katherine was captivated by the man in the picture. She studied his face—his eyes. Could he see her? Did he ever think about her? Did he even know about her? These were questions she'd never have answers to. Then there was Carol. Carol was no blood relation to her, but if Gregory was her father, then Carol was her stepmother. She liked her and hoped Carol felt the same way.

"I have lots more pictures and memorabilia at home. Maybe you'd like to see it?"

Carol invited Katherine over to her house—the house she once shared with Gregory Bradshaw. "I'd love to." Katherine had been drawn into a living day-dream. How was she going to share this with Peter? For the time being, she decided not to. When she had some concrete proof that this Gregory Bradshaw was her birth father, then she'd tell Peter all about it. "My boss just informed me he is going to close The Gallery for a week. His wife surprised him with a cruise and they leave Sunday. So he gave me a week's vacation."

"Are you doing anything Sunday?" asked Carol.

"No, since I didn't know about this unexpected pleasure, I have nothing at all planned." Katherine thought about what she would say to Peter. "Actually, Sunday wouldn't be good, but how about Monday morning, say around ten o'clock?"

"Monday morning it is. If I'm not mistaken, you already have my address and phone number. But, I'll write down the T route for you. It's not hard. Give me a call a couple stops before and I'll meet you at the Harvard Station. Where will you get on?"

"At Broadway."

"That's the red line, so you won't have to change trains. The Harvard Station is about seven or eight stops inbound on the same line. Do you live in South Boston?"

"I do. I was raised there." Katherine hesitated about giving Carol any more information. For some reason, she felt comfortable with Carol, but there were a few things she needed to keep inside—at least for the time being.

Their sandwiches came. The rest of Katherine's lunch hour consisted of small talk about her job at The Gallery and her aspiring dreams of becoming a famous artist. She didn't say anything about Peter. "I'd better be getting back to work. Again, thank you for being so understanding. I had no idea what to expect the first day I called you."

Carol listened to Katherine intently. "I wasn't adopted, but my family life wasn't the greatest. So, I have a selfish motive for helping you."

Katherine wasn't sure what she was talking about. "I don't understand."

"Let's put it this way, you missed out on a family that could have given you lots of love and support. I had a family who didn't know the meaning of those words. So, if I can share some of my memories of Gregory Bradshaw with you, it will make us both happier." Carol hoped she hadn't laid the frosting on too thick. She knew Katherine wasn't going to stop searching, so if Carol could steer the direction of the search to benefit her, that's what she had to do. Who knows what might happen when Katherine finds out that Gregory Bradshaw left Carol with a considerable inheritance.

CHAPTER FORTY-ONE

Boston

When Katherine didn't feel well Friday morning, she decided to stop by the CVS on her way to work and pick up a pregnancy test. It would be better if she did it at work, than at home. If she was pregnant, it would definitely put a cog in the wheel of her relationship with Peter. He didn't even want to talk engagement, let alone marriage. And there was no way she was bringing a baby into this world without a mother and father who loved him or her. She would never put a child in the same situation she was in.

Mr. Grossman was already at The Gallery when Katherine got there. He had a mocha latte and a slice of lemon pound cake waiting for her. His was half eaten. "I couldn't wait, it smelled so good," he said as he picked up his cup and took a sip to clear his mouth of the cake he had just eaten. In front of him were about ten brochures, all spread out—some opened.

"What have you got there?" Katherine asked as she sat down beside his desk. "Oh, by the way, thanks for the goodies. You've spoiled me by introducing me to these Starbuck treats. Too many of these are going to make me fat." She jokingly shook a finger at him.

He laughed. "Somebody has to help me indulge in this sinful behavior. I've chosen you." He lifted a couple of the brochures from the desk and handed them to Katherine. "I picked these up yesterday on the way home. At first, I wasn't excited about going on this cruise. But, after looking at these, I can't wait."

He handed her the brochure of Key West, Florida. "This is the first stop on the cruise. "It's where Hemmingway lived. Did you know that? My wife told me she wants to take the tour of his house and also the Truman Little White House. I think those will be very interesting. Of course, I want to stop at Margaritaville and have a margarita and some nachos. She said she'd consider it. I know she'll go—she loves those nacho things."

"Have you looked at this St. Thomas brochure yet?" Katherine was eying the pictures of the stores along the main street. "They list several jewelry shops, each one boasting of great deals on diamonds."

"Yeah, I saw that. My wife had it on top, so she probably read the same thing you just did." Mr. Grossman rolled his eyes. "She'll come home with a new ring, I'm sure of that."

"It sounds like you're going to have a great time." Katherine excused herself. "I'll be right back. I want to see more." She took the CVS bag out of her backpack and walked to the bathroom off the back room. She knew he would still be at his desk reading about the places he was going to visit. It didn't take long. Her worst fear had come true. She was pregnant. She heard the phone ring, so she knew she had a few extra minutes to gather everything up, stuff it back in the box, then hide the box in her backpack.

Her boss was just getting off the phone when she re-entered his office. "That was the lady you sold the Amy Whitehead painting to. She wants to know if we have any more." Mr. G was beaming. Whenever he sells something created by an unknown, he feels like he's discovered the next Picasso. "She's coming down this afternoon." He looked over his glasses at Katherine. "That leaves two empty spaces—reserved for you."

"Okay, back to the brochures," she said without looking at him or making a comment.

It was a quarter-to-three when our Amy Whitehead fan came in. Mr. Grossman introduced himself, then turned the conversation over to me.

"I'm glad you enjoyed Amy's painting. She is a talented person. Let's go take a look at the other one of hers we have hanging." Katherine led the way.

Mr. Grossman stayed back, but observed Katherine at work. He stepped forward when he saw the customer nod in approval. He assumed she'd agreed to purchase the painting. "Can I wrap that up for you?" he asked.

"Yes please, I'll take it with me." She paid and headed for the door. The bell jingled as she walked out.

Mr. Grossman looked at his watch. "You've missed the three o'clock train. If you hurry, you can make the four o'clock one. I don't want you to get stuck in the rush hour mess."

"I'm fine. Remember, I'm going on vacation too, so I've got plenty of time to rest and stay out of the rush." She laughed.

"And paint," he added.

"Goodbye. Have a wonderful cruise. Take lots of pictures. I want to see you in that speedo!" she giggled. "See you when you get back." She went behind the desk and gave him a hug and kiss. "Don't forget the sun screen."

The last words she heard were, "Yes, mother."

CHAPTER FORTY-TWO

Boston

"It's Saturday, why are you up so early?" Katherine rolled over to see Peter slipping his legs into a pair of jeans.

"I forgot to tell you that some of the guys from work are getting together at the Common for a Frisbee match. We're meeting at Dunkin's at nine o'clock. Since it's almost eight-fifteen, I'm going to get a move on. They also said something about going over to the Black Rose Pub after. I don't know what time I'll be home."

"And you were going to tell me this, when?" Katherine sat straight up and stared at Peter.

"Why don't you work on one of your paintings?" he said without looking at her.

"Peter McCarthy, its times like this you infuriate me. Just go, get out of my sight!" she jumped up out of bed and went to the bathroom. No sooner had she closed the bathroom door, she heard the front door slam.

She was glad he left. Lately, he's been in his own little world anyway. Now she wouldn't have to sneak around trying to get things together to take to Carol's house on Monday. She decided to make a list of questions. If she didn't write them down, she knew she'd probably forget the most important ones.

She thought about going to Manny's to have a donut and coffee before she got started, then opted to stay home instead. A plain bowl of cereal would probably sit better in her stomach. Maybe later she'd head over to L Street and get a burger. When Peter goes out on one of his 'boy' dates, he usually doesn't get home until late. It was like he'd put her *birth family thing* right out of his mind. She didn't need him anyway. She had moved things along on her own.

And, now the baby news—this would cause their relationship to drift further apart. 'Boy dates' or baby diapers. Katherine stood with both hands out in front of her, palms facing up and bouncing them up and down like a scale. The 'boy dates' won out.

She pulled her stuff from her backpack and stacked it on the table beside her cereal bowl. The old information she had gathered from the library computers, she put on the back of the table. Her notes on her meetings with Carol were toward the front. The letters to mother Mary from Emma and the birth certificate that Peter's friend had gotten were in a pile in the middle. As she sat eating her cereal, she looked from one stack to another, then back to the first one, then to the second—making mental notes of what her next step was going to be.

When she finished eating, she put her dishes in the sink and headed for the bedroom to change into a pair of sweatpants and a jersey. In case somebody came to the door she wanted to look somewhat presentable.

The birth certificate caught her eye. She picked it up. Emma Latham and Gregory Bradshaw—what was their story? A young girl and a man forty-one years her elder. Was it rape? Or a young girl infatuated with a rich old man? Those questions will never be answered. The only two people who knew the truth were dead. Then there was Elaine Bradshaw. How much did she know? After all, she was nine years older than Emma. So that would make her twenty-four when Katherine was born. Now, Elaine's gone too.

There was something wrong. Katherine felt a pain of loneliness overtake her body. I never knew my birth parents. My baby is going to know at least one of its parents. She'd deal with Peter later.

Katherine got to thinking. Since Elaine Bradshaw had been murdered, the Provincetown police department must have taken DNA samples. Or maybe because they knew who she was they didn't have to. She had nothing else to go on though. She figured her best bet would be to go to Provincetown and find out what Elaine was like. She could probably go to the Clerk of Courts Office at the Superior Courthouse and read the case file on record. She knew they were available to the public. You couldn't take them out of the office, but most courthouses had an area where you could sit down and hand copy information or pay to photo copy reports.

If she found out DNA samples had been taken, then she would have to figure out how she could have hers done and have the two compared. This would confirm whether or not Elaine Bradshaw was her blood sister. And if she was, then Katherine would be entitled to at least half of the Gregory Bradshaw estate.

"Oh my God," said Katherine. "Did I just think all that stuff?" She sat back down, still clutching her birth certificate in her hands.

Katherine didn't tell Peter about the vacation time Mr. Grossman had given her and, at this point, she wasn't going to tell him. He'd go off to work on Monday and she'd go to Carol Bradshaw's house as planned. Katherine had a huge decision to make. She knew she needed some time away by herself.

Tuesday morning, after Peter left for work, she'd pack a travel bag, take the money she'd been saving out of the drawer, go to the P&B bus terminal and head for the Cape. She contemplated leaving him a note letting him know where she was going, but then thought better of it. She'd have her cell phone if she needed him. This was something she wanted to do on her own. She'd explain about the vacation time later. And, she knew Peter couldn't contact Mr. Grossman to ask him anything because he was going to be out of the country.

She was undecided whether or not to tell Carol about her plans to compare her DNA with Elaine Bradshaw's. She might mention her trip to Cape Cod, but nothing else. Although, she did toy with the idea of telling Carol that she was pregnant. If Katherine thought about being an heir to Gregory's estate, then she was sure Carol would come to the same conclusion. Carol had been nice to Katherine, but money can change a person and sometimes not for the better.

It was one o'clock when she realized she was getting hungry. She knew Peter wouldn't be home before her, so she left her stuff on the table and headed to L Street.

The fifteen minute walk to the L was invigorating. Fall was starting to creep in. Katherine took a deep breath. The air was clean and clear.

A couple more months and it will be a heavy jacket, gloves and a hat, she thought.

The L was quiet. After all, it was early in the day. The action usually began after six. She loved their mushroom, swiss burger—well done with a side of curly fries and a Diet Coke. Katherine liked sitting at the bar and listening to the tourists talk about Matt Damon and Ben Affleck as though they were going to walk through the door at any minute.

On the walk home she made a mental note of what she was going to pack to take to the Cape. For sure she was going to take a light jacket and a couple sweaters along with two pairs of jeans, a pair of kakis, four jerseys and a dress. She didn't know why the dress, but she was taking one anyway. And so she wouldn't feel alone, she decided her little one eyed teddy bear should go along for the ride. She remembered the day mother Mary sewed a little red heart over a hole in teddy's paw. Katherine tried to blink back the tears, but it was too late. A couple ran down her cheeks and dripped onto her shirt. She rubbed her eyes, took a deep breath and kept walking.

The tension that surrounded Katherine and Peter on Sunday was so thick; you could cut it with a knife. There were noticeable tones of anxiety in their conversations. Katherine began to feel very uncomfortable in Peter's condo, but she didn't have any place else to go. He didn't get home until almost eleven o'clock Saturday night and Sunday he spent most of the day in front of the television. He never once asked how she was doing with her research into her birth family. It was becoming quite obvious he didn't care anymore.

CHAPTER FORTY-THREE

Boston

Monday morning Katherine got up early and was showered and dressed before Peter. She made a pot of coffee, poured herself a cup and was sitting at the table waiting for him to come out. "Would you like some toast?" she asked.

Peter took his to-go mug from the shelf, put in a couple shots of cream and filled it with coffee. "No, I'm just going to take some coffee and head on out."

"How about tonight—want to go to JJ's for dinner?"

"I'm not sure what time I'll be home. Why don't you get yourself something at the market and I'll grab a sandwich."

"Peter, I think we need to talk." Katherine's voice was soft.

"Yeah, we will," he said and was out the door.

She felt hurt and alone.

Katherine didn't want to get stuck in the morning rush at the T-station, so she took her time gathering her stuff. It was nine o'clock when she headed out the door to go to Carol Bradshaw's.

CHAPTER FORTY-FOUR

Boston

"Good morning," came Carol's voice from the other end of the phone.

"Hi," said Katherine. "The train just stopped at Kendall Square, so I should be at Harvard shortly."

"If you come up the eastbound stairway and walk one block down Main Street, there are a couple of drop-off spaces. I'll meet you there. I have a red Mercedes, you can't miss it."

"The trains moving again. See you in a few."

Anxiety was the word of the day, thought Katherine.

She was anxious about her meeting with Carol. She was anxious about being in Gregory Bradshaw's house. She was anxious about any new information she might get. And, she was anxious about her situation with Peter.

"Harvard Square," bellowed the conductor's voice over the loud-speaker.

Most of the people on the train were getting off at this stop. A lot of them looked like students. She looked around and got her bearings. The eastbound stairs were to her right. She walked up the two flights, then followed the directions Carol had given her. She wasn't at the drop-off spaces more than a couple minutes, when a beautiful, shiny red Mercedes pulled up. The window went down and Carol said, "I'm here, come on in."

"I got stuck in a little traffic at the Square."

"That's okay, I just got here myself."

The two shared idle chit-chat on the ride to Carol's house. Carol had a mannerism that calmed Katherine. She sensed this, so was somewhat careful about what she said to her.

Carol made several turns, then pulled into a driveway that ran beside a stately red brick house with black wooden shutters and a muted red front door. "We're home," said Carol cheerfully.

We're home? thought Katherine. *This isn't my home, it's hers.*

She followed Carol into the house through a side door that brought them into the kitchen. The smell of freshly baked cookies filled the air. Katherine hadn't smelled that since mother Mary died. She closed her eyes and took in a big whiff of the distant memory. "It sure smells good in here." The words just came out.

"I baked this morning—thought we could use some energy to keep us going. Why don't you put your purse on the table and I'll show you around the house."

"I'd like that," Katherine said as she put her purse down beside one of the kitchen chairs. She didn't think it was right to put it on the table. Actually, she was afraid she might scratch the finish.

Carol gave her a first floor tour of the house ending up in the family-room. There was a beautiful fieldstone fireplace that was more than a decoration and a mantle full of pictures. Right in the middle, in the biggest frame, was a picture of Carol and, Katherine presumed, Gregory Bradshaw all decked out in a gown and tuxedo.

Carol watched as Katherine studied the picture, then said, "That was taken two years before Elaine died, when Gregory was still healthy and happy." She stared without emotion at the picture.

Katherine detected a new coolness in Carol's personality.

Carol must have realized it and not wanting to blow her cover quickly changed her demeanor. She went back to being warm, friendly and, most of all, welcoming. "Let's go back to the kitchen. I always find I do my best thinking there." Carol picked up a few photo albums that were on the coffee table as she walked by.

Katherine followed her into the kitchen. She couldn't help but think this whole scenario seemed like a set-up, but if she used it to her advantage without Carol realizing it, she may come out the victor.

"I dug out some old albums. I thought you'd like to take a look at those pictures rather than the ones of Gregory and me." Carol opened one of the books, then got up to put on a pot of coffee and plate up some cookies.

Katherine thumbed through the pages of old photos. They weren't interesting because they meant nothing to her. She couldn't conjure up any feelings for the old man that might be her birth father. She decided that she wanted to know more about Carol. "Did you go back to work after Gregory died?" she asked.

"No, I was left pretty comfortable, so I didn't have to."

"Don't you get bored?"

"Sometimes, but I've stayed in touch with a lot of the people I used to work with. We get together quite often for dinner or take off for a weekend—much like I used to do before I got married."

"Do they still work for the, what was it, medical supply place?"

"Most of them." Carol's expression changed. "Why do you ask?"

"Just curious, I guess." Katherine answered nonchalantly. "It's like when I lost my adoptive parents, I got lost in the shuffle. I didn't have a place to go back to, except with Peter, and lately it seems like I don't even have that."

"Why, what happened?"

"To tell you the truth, I don't know. Maybe my obsession with finding my birth family drove him away. He wanted me to be content just being with him. At first he said he'd help me, but when I started to put the pieces together he backed away."

"How much did you tell him?"

"Remember I told you he got a copy of my sealed birth certificate. Well, he saw my real mother's name and Gregory Bradshaw listed as my father. If you want to know the truth, I don't think he'd remember either one. It was like he put it completely out of his mind."

Carol took an inner sigh of relief. She didn't want anybody snooping into her business, especially her finances. Katherine was enough of a problem. She didn't need a nosey boyfriend helping her.

Katherine flipped through some more of the pictures—asking questions only to make Carol think she was interested. "Were any of these pictures taken on Cape Cod?"

Carol moved closer to Katherine. "If you go to the back of this album, I think most of these were taken at the Cape."

Katherine was more interested in the Cape pictures than the Boston ones.

While she was looking at those, Carol got up and said, "I'll be right back. One of my albums has some more recent Cape pictures. We visited Elaine several times after she left Boston and moved back to the Cape."

Katherine closed the album she was looking at when Carol came back into the room.

"Let me find the ones of Elaine," said Carol as she turned several pages, then came to a stop. "These were taken at Elaine's house and the next ones were taken in Provincetown." Carol slid the album over in front of Katherine.

"Is this the house she lived in when she was murdered?"

"It was. Gregory refused to look at these pictures after Elaine died. This is the first time I've taken them out in three years."

Again, Katherine noticed Carol's face was without emotion. She must have really hated Elaine.

"What did she do in Boston?"

"She was in the fashion industry. Elaine was a free-lance writer and worked with almost all the top designers in the area. They loved her. Sometimes she'd travel to New York to cover high society events, but she never wanted to live there."

"Did she stay in the fashion world after she moved?"

"No, she said she'd had enough and just wanted to withdraw to a life she once knew. Besides, she said something about starting a family. She didn't have a boyfriend or a male friend. She actually had lots of them. Her father would get disgusted with her. They'd argue and she'd tell him the apple didn't fall far from the tree. I think some of that was directed towards me. Actually, not I think it was—I know it was. She made it perfectly clear that she didn't approve of her father marrying me."

I closed the album I'd been looking at and moved it aside. "I hope I didn't stir up too many bad memories. You've given me lots to think about. All indications point to this Gregory Bradshaw as being my birth father. But I have to be sure. There's one more thing I have to do."

Carol's face wrinkled up and question marks danced across her forehead. "Is it anything I can help you with?" she asked.

"I don't think so. I'm going to take the bus to the Cape and see if I can find out more about Elaine's death." *Here goes,* she thought. "Since it was a murder, the Medical Examiner's Office may have taken her DNA to compare it with other samples found on evidence gathered at the crime scene. If that be the case, then I can give them a sample of my DNA. They'll be able compare the two and determine whether or not she is, or should I say was, my sister."

Uneasiness grabbed at Carol's insides. "Why don't you let me give you a ride? I don't mind and I'd like to know the results myself."

"This is something I have to do on my own. I've already checked the bus schedule and know there's one leaving tomorrow morning at nine-thirty. I plan on being on it. I'm going to go straight down to Provincetown. It's off-season, so I'm sure I'll be able to find a place to stay for a week or so. I'm going to do a little scouting before I tackle the DNA question. If I find something, I'll give you a call." Katherine picked up her coffee cup and took the last sip.

"Why don't you give me your cell phone number, in case I come across something in Gregory's files that might be of help to you."

Katherine hesitated, then decided maybe Carol was being sincere, so she proceeded to give her the number. "This has been very interesting. I'm sure we'll talk soon. Thank you for your time and most of all your help." Katherine stood up and lifted her purse from the floor onto the seat of the chair. If you think my purse is heavy, you should see my backpack. It might be a back breaker, but it holds my life in it. One of these days, I hope it gets lighter." She hesitated. "Besides, I'm going to have to cash it in for a diaper bag sometime in the not-so-distant future."

Carol stood up and looked at Katherine as though she had seen a ghost. "Are you telling me that you're pregnant?"

"I just found out. I wasn't going to say anything, but maybe now you'll understand why, more than ever, my birth family is important to me."

Carol's eyes opened wide. She shook her head and stared at the ceiling. "I guess I do."

"Can you please give me a ride back to the T-station?" Katherine asked.

"I'm sorry, of course I can. Let me get my purse." Carol's stone-like stance crumbled. She walked into the other room. Seconds later, she returned with her purse hanging from her shoulder and keys dangling from her finger.

It was a quiet ride to Harvard Square. Carol dropped Katherine off in the same spot she had picked her up. They waved goodbye as Carol pulled away.

CHAPTER FORTY-FIVE

Boston

Katherine had plenty of time before Peter normally got home to put some clothes aside. Tomorrow morning, she'd pack them in her duffle bag and head out.

Walking around the condo, something didn't feel right. As she walked by the kitchen table on her way to the refrigerator, she noticed an envelope. It had her name on it. It was in Peter's writing. He must have been home. It was sealed. She figured he wanted to make sure she read it. If she ripped open the seal, then he would know she had.

Katherine,

I've decided to stay at a friend's house for a few days. There're some things I need to sort out. And I need to do it on my own. I looked in your backpack—something I've never done before. I found the pregnancy kit and the test strip. I don't think I'm ready to be a father. I don't know where I'm going with this, but for both our sakes we need to figure it out.

Peter

Katherine was taken back. Her stomach filled with butterflies. She felt sick—and not baby sick. Did he know she was planning on leaving? How could he? She went to her backpack and pulled out a pad of paper and a pen and began to write.

Peter,

I've gone to Cape Cod to check out some leads I found regarding my birth family. I now know who my birth mother is, but I'm not one-hundred percent sure about my father. This trip should confirm that one way or the other. Please don't try to find me. This is something I need to do on my own. Our lives have drifted in different directions these past few months. What we had together was special, but things have changed and are about to change even more.

With my upcoming responsibility as a mother, I have to understand why my own mother gave me up. Unfortunately, you don't share the joy of having a child. My life has taken on new meaning. I have no ill feelings toward you, instead a part of me will always love you.

Please take care of yourself...

Katherine

She didn't bother putting her note in an envelope. She folded it, wrote Peter's name on the outside and put it in the middle of the table. She took the note he'd written and slid it into the inside pocket of her backpack.

There was no need to wait until morning to pack. She decided to get ready tonight, then she could get an early start. She remembered that the ride to Hyannis by car took a little over an hour, then to Provincetown she calculated another hour and a half. The bus made several stops along the way. If she added two hours, to be on the safe side, she should be in Provincetown by noontime. That would give her plenty of time to find a place to stay.

The bus was a half-hour out of the station when her cell phone rang. She checked the caller ID. “Hello,” she said in a quiet, somewhat reserved voice. “I’m fine,” she responded to the question the caller asked.

“No, I don’t want you to meet me in Hyannis. I have a few things I want to check out on my own.”

“Okay, but today is Tuesday—I should be able to get done what I want to do by Thursday. I’ll call you Thursday night and we’ll figure out someplace to meet Friday morning.”

She actually felt she was finally taking control of her life—and it felt good.

CHAPTER FORTY-SIX

I was just stepping out of the shower when my cell phone rang. If I didn't know better, I'd swear somebody's looking in my window and knows I'm in the shower. I don't look that good naked. I laughed. That would be spooky. Almost like something out of a Psycho movie. As long as Watson is the one who comes through the door and not Anthony Perkins, I'll be all right. I knew I wouldn't get to the phone before the caller went to ID, so I grabbed a towel, dried off, then went to the bedroom to check for either a missed call or a voice mail.

Someone had left a message. I looked at the clock. It was eight-thirty. The make-shift knot I had tied in my towel had come undone. When I leaned over to pick it up, the phone rang again. "Hello," I said struggling to resume my dignity.

It was Sam. "Good morning, Sherlock."

"Did you just call a few minutes ago?" I asked.

"No, that must have been your other secret admirer. I wanted to catch you before I went into the courtroom. I just finished reading your P-town murder story—good job. The picture is great—very clear. If somebody knows this girl, they'll certainly be able to identify her."

"Thanks, hopefully all the departments we circulated the flyer to will get it out to the public. I'm going to call Maloney to see if he's talked to his father yet this morning. You're going to like this kid. He's a little you." I laughed. "If that's possible."

"They're starting to go inside. I'll tell Annie and Marnie I talked to you and you're still amongst the living. Maybe they'll fill me in on the conversation from girls' night out."

"Maybe, they won't," I said.

"And maybe we can grab supper tonight? Anyway, I'll call you when we break for lunch."

Before I could get another word in, Sam had disconnected the call. I couldn't figure out if it was because he was in a hurry or he didn't want to hear my response to his supper date. Supper will be okay if I don't get caught up in P-town with Maloney and Sgt. Costa.

Since my missed call wasn't Sam, I figured I'd check it out. It was Maloney. Still standing in my bedroom with my re-wrapped towel, I dialed his number. "Sorry I missed your call," I said.

"I knew I'd hear back from you as soon as you looked at your phone. I heard from my father already this morning. He made sure everybody saw the flyer at morning roll call. In fact, he made enough copies so that everybody got one. He's going to make sure the rest of the shifts get some to hand out, too."

"Please, thank him for me."

"He also told me that he's going to take a couple of the guys he works with and canvas Southie. Everybody knows everybody in Southie. So if this girl has frequented any of the bars or restaurants, someone will recognize her. Maybe not know her name, but anything will be a start."

"Our Jane Doe, or Emily Latham, doesn't seem like a girl who collects toothbrushes. Judging from her appearance, she's quite the opposite. Although, in this day and age, you never know. Anyway, I hope they come up with something."

"When this settles down, maybe the 'girls' will join me and my dad for a real South Boston Irish pub tour."

"You're on," I said.

"Are you heading down this way today?" Maloney asked. "Sgt. Costa wants to know."

"Unless he gets some new information that I need to go over with you guys, I'll probably work from home. I might even go into the office for a while."

"I'll keep you posted," he said.

"Thanks—talk to you later."

Before I get any more calls, I better get dressed. I forgot Watson was lying down on the floor at the end of the bed and almost did a header. I think I scared him more than I scared myself. I took the last pair of clean jeans hanging in the closet and my favorite Mickey tee-shirt. The first order of the day, after my coffee, was to do laundry, otherwise tomorrow I'd be shit out of luck. Those are the perks of being able to work from home. I'm no housekeeper, but if I combine it with something I like, then I usually get stuff done.

I threw my clothes in the washer, made myself a French Vanilla, grabbed my briefcase and headed for the back deck. The outdoor thermometer read seventy-one degrees, no wind and not a cloud in the sky—a perfect fall day. I took my notes out of my briefcase and laid them on the table. Miss Daisy's kept creeping into my mind. I felt there was something more there—something we must have missed.

Omar said she had a flowery duffle bag and an over-stuffed backpack. We never did find the over-stuffed backpack. She must have taken it with her, but whoever murdered her didn't want it to be found. They obviously took it with them. I couldn't help thinking there was something in that backpack that would definitely link Emily to the person who killed her. Then there was the pad of paper that she had written a note or letter on to somebody named Peter.

I leaned back in my chair and, with my foot, pulled out the chair beside me to use as a foot rest. I closed my eyes and tried to imagine Emily—what she was like—what she did for a living—and most of all where she came from. She had a very innocent look about her. It didn't appear she'd been living a hard life—at least on the outside. We'll never know what was happening inside.

My thoughts were interrupted by the buzzer on the washing

machine. The first load was done. I put the clothes in the basket and went outside to hang them on the clothesline. I hadn't made my bed yet, so I decided to strip it, wash the sheets and hang them outside too. My mom always said you sleep better when your sheets are dried outside and the fresh smell gives you sweet dreams. *The things you remember.*

Watson's bark brought me back to reality. My cell phone was ringing—again. I had left it on the kitchen table so I ran to get it before the caller hung up. "Hi," I said without looking at my caller ID. It was Maloney.

"Casey, my father just called. He thinks he has something for us. The bartender at the L Street Tavern is pretty sure he recognizes her. He called her Katherine. There are too many names being associated with our Jane Doe. The question is—will the real Jane Doe please stand up?" Maloney hesitated. "Bad choice of words, I know, but we might actually have a creditable lead."

"That's exactly why I didn't change her name from Jane Doe to Emily Latham in my story for the Tribune. The L Street Tavern is where I went with Sam," I said.

"It's not far from where I used to live. My father and the two other guys with him are still canvasing the area. He said he'd get back with me later. I think we should take a ride to Boston tomorrow morning and do some checking for ourselves. Hopefully, we'll have a little more to go on." Maloney waited for my answer.

"I agree with you. The two departments working together should be able to come up with something we can work with. I want to find the bastard that killed our girl. I don't want this to become a cold case. The person who did this appears to be very cleaver. It was calculated and carried out in a very organized manner. Whoever did this has covered their tracks. I intend to uncover them and bring justice to this girl's memory." I was seething inside. "Is Sgt. Costa all right with us heading to Boston?"

"He said we've come to a brick wall down here and if my father thinks the person that identified our Jane Doe is on the level, we should make the trip. Since that's my neck of the woods, I'll drive, besides I'm taking an unmarked. How about I pick you up around eight-thirty?" asked Maloney. "You'll just have to give me directions to your house."

"Eight-thirty is fine. But, instead of you trying to find my house, I'll drive to the Cape Cod Mall and park in the row closest to Route 132, near the main entrance. I have a little green Madza. It stands out, so I'm sure you won't miss it."

"I've seen your car. It was parked in the police lot on Monday—remember?"

"Not thinking," I said. I heard what Maloney said, but some of it didn't sink in. I had a feeling we were going to have a problem with a name for Jane. I do believe her name is either Emily or Katherine. The challenge is going to be finding out which one. Hopefully, this bartender knows more about her and, after tomorrow, we'll know who she really is.

"Okay, I'll see you in the morning. If I talk to my father again, do you want me to give you a call?"

"Not unless it's really earth shattering. You can fill me in on the ride to Boston. Tonight I'll compile some questions we will need to get answers for. I'll run them by you so you can see where my thinking is headed. And, you may want to add things or have additional questions." That was my project for the night. "See you in the morning."

No sooner did I hang up, my cell rang again. "This phone hasn't stopped all day. I'll probably get hit with extra minutes."

"I'll take that as a 'hello'. How's my Sherlock doing?" It was Sam. I forgot he wanted to do supper. Probably, not a bad idea—I could run a few things by him and see what he thinks. Maybe he can give me a few suggestions.

"I'm hanging in there. Do you still want to get some supper tonight?"

"That's why I called. We're on a break, so I figured it was a good time to try to find you."

"Find me? Where did you think I'd be?"

"I have no idea and I don't even pretend to know—because most of the time I'm wrong."

"Smart ass." I pulled a chair out from the kitchen table and sat down. "I could go for some nachos and a couple of beers. Want to go to Sam Diego's?"

"Fine with me. Fortunately, I left a pair of jeans and a jersey at your house for just such an occasion. That way I don't have to go to Bourne then back to Hyannisport. It looks like we might wrap up a little early. The attorneys are getting ready for closing arguments, but they won't start them this afternoon. I'll come over when I finish here."

"I'm not going anywhere, so I'll be home. Tell the girls I'll talk to them later."

"They're calling us back in. See ya."

CHAPTER FORTY-SEVEN

I jotted down several questions on a pad of paper, then transferred them to my 3x5 cards. If I do an interview with my pad of paper in front of me, I have a tendency to doodle and by the time I'm finished, it takes me an extra hour to decipher what's what. Besides, I can have more than one file card for the same question. This way, I can record each person's answer to a particular question separately. When I start reviewing everything, I can move the cards around and group them by question or incident or person or place or description. I learned this eleven years ago when I was at the Police Academy.

I might as well get clothes ready for tomorrow. Knowing Sam, he won't leave any too early. I've even got a sneaking suspicion he plans on staying the night. If he does, I'll run my questions by him to see what he thinks. He'll probably have a few more to add. If he didn't have that trial going on, I have no doubt he'd suggest taking a ride to Boston with Maloney and me tomorrow.

I was just finishing up my laundry when I heard a car coming up my driveway. I looked at the clock on the microwave—it was five minutes after four. I looked out the window to see Sam already on his way to the door. Before he could knock, I opened it, stuck my face out, closed my eyes and puckered my lips.

"I hope your face never freezes like that."

He wrapped his arms around me and planted his lips gently on mine. "Welcome to Hyannisport," I said jokingly. I almost slipped as I welcomed him home.

He smiled. "Well, are you going to let me in?"

"I haven't figured that out yet."

He lifted me up and moved me to one side. "I don't know about you, but I need a beer," he said. "It's been a long day." He walked to the fridge and got one out for each of us. "Let me get this monkey suit off and slip on my jeans. I'll meet you on the deck."

It was comfortable having Sam around—at least on a part-time basis. Watson followed Sam into the bedroom. He sure knows who his master is. "Don't put any snacks out," came a voice from the other room. "I only had a cup of chowder for lunch, so we can go to Sam Diego's early. Of course, if that's okay with you."

I had grabbed a package of whole wheat and cheddar crackers and a cup of French Vanilla, so I was pretty hungry myself. "Sounds good to me," I called back.

There was no breeze, to speak of, when I went out onto the deck. I looked around. The leaves were still painted with a blend of reds, oranges and yellows. In another month, they'd be gone and my protective blanket of foliage would give way to open windows of opportunity for Jack Frost to lay a dusting of cold, uninvited snowflakes.

"Where in the world is Casey Quinby?"

I didn't even hear him come out. I must have been on another planet. "I'm right here, my darling, just waiting patiently for you to bless me with your presence."

"You are so full of it."

"I know that. That's why you love me." I laughed. "Would you still be around if I was normal?"

"You've got a point there," he said, nodding as he took a sip of beer.

"So how did the trial go today?"

"Like we figured. It should wrap up tomorrow or Friday morning at the latest. The evidence is cut and dry, so the jury might have a verdict by Friday afternoon." He took a deep breath. "I'll be glad when it's over. This one hit too close to home." He looked at me and raised his eyebrows. "Know what I mean?"

"Yeah, yeah, yeah," I said, then quickly changed the subject. "So, did Marnie and Annie reveal the stuff we discussed at girls' night out?"

"I could lie and tell you they did, then try to pry it out of you."

"You wouldn't get to first base."

"It would be fun to try." He sat back and resumed his beer drinking pose. "By the way, the girls are meeting us at Sam Diego's. I hope you don't mind."

"Of course not, that'll be fun. Too bad, Barry won't be joining us. I haven't seen him much since last July. He's stayed kind of low. Not at all like Barry. He might have been a pain-in-the-ass, but he was ours."

"I was going to surprise you, but Barry is coming too. He looked like he needed a night out with friends. This whole ordeal has torn him apart."

I put my stern face on and waved my finger. "You're a good man, Sam Summers, and don't let anybody tell you different." Then I laughed. "What time did you tell them?"

"Five-thirty—is that okay with you?"

"Perfect, I'm going just the way I am."

"Jeans and a Mickey t-shirt—I wouldn't know you any other way." Sam's face wrinkled up like he was in deep thought. "That's not quite true. I think I'd know you without anything on."

I crumpled up my napkin and threw it at him. The sun was reflecting off the face of Sam's watch so I couldn't read the time. "Should we be getting ready to leave?" I asked.

He turned his wrist to check. "Probably. We'll finish these beers and head on out."

"I'm going to get ready. Would you please give Watson his supper?"

"Sure. I'll be right behind you. I'm just going to veg out a little longer."

As much as Sam made jokes, I knew he was hurting inside. I was glad I didn't have to be at the courthouse to testify at James' trial. And, I think Sam was glad too. Finally, it was going to be over.

CHAPTER FORTY-EIGHT

We got to Sam Diego's before the girls and Barry so we decided to get a table in the back room. Sometimes it's a little quieter out there.

"I think I'll have a frozen margarita. I haven't had one for eons." I was just about to order, when I saw the crew walking through the front room. I stood up and waved my arms to catch their attention.

Annie and Marnie sat down and Barry walked around the table and gave me a hug. "I needed that," he said.

I gave him a kiss on the cheek. "It's really good to see you," I said. "You're looking good."

"Flattery will get you everywhere." He laughed and we sat down. "Sam, thanks for the invite. I appreciate it."

"Hello, ladies. I'm glad you guys came," said Sam. "It's like old times. We haven't been here for a long time. Let's order some drinks, then we can figure out the rest once the important part is done."

We called the waitress over. Annie and I ordered frozen margaritas, Marnie ordered a frozen strawberry daiquiri and the guys ordered beers.

"I read your article in the Tribune this morning. I hate the Jane and John Doe cases." Barry sighed. "So many of them go cold."

"If I can help it, this one will not turn into a cold case. The P-town officer I'm working with and I think we have a name. We're heading into Boston tomorrow to talk to a lead his father may have gotten for us."

"His father? Please explain," said Barry.

"I'm sorry. Maloney was on the Boston PD before transferring to P-town. He comes from a long line of Boston cops. They were all stationed in Southie. His father still works out of the South Boston precinct."

"Casey, what's with this Maloney. He transferred from Boston to P-town? Um. . . is there anything else you want to tell us about him?" Barry stopped talking and looked to me for a response.

"There nothing more to tell you, except that he's a man's man. Is that what you wanted to hear?" *In some ways, Barry will never change*, I thought.

"The P-town PD sent an APB to all Massachusetts Police Departments, along with a flyer with an artist's sketch. Maloney's father took more of an interest in it because it was his son's case. He canvased an area of South Boston and we have a possible identification."

"What made you concentrate on Boston?" Barry asked.

"We got a heads up from the local P-town newspaper store that our Jane Doe had purchased a Boston Globe there. The guy who owns the store had never seen her before. Why would somebody buy a Globe in October, unless they had an interest in Boston? So, we took it and ran with it."

Annie and Marnie sat and listened. I knew Sam was chomping at the bit to get involved, but figured he'd wait until we got home. Besides, I had already told him this stuff earlier. Barry was getting ready to ask another question when our waitress arrived with our drinks. Saved by the booze.

"We got to talking and didn't figure out what we're going to order." I looked at Sam. "What do you want?"

"Unless anybody wants something in particular, do you want to get stuff to share?"

We all nodded in agreement.

Sam turned to the waitress and said, "Can you please just give us a couple more minutes, then we'll be ready."

"I'll be right back," she said and headed back to the front dining room.

"All right. I'll start it with an order of nachos supremo with some extra guacamole and sour cream on the side," said Sam.

"How about a large order of habanero chicken wings?" Barry was already licking his chops at the mere thought of hot and spicy wings. "Is there anything else you girls would like?"

"What's a cheese crisp?" Marnie asked.

"Don't they have Mexican restaurants in New York?" I laughed. "Only kidding."

"Actually a cheese crisp would go good with the chicken wings," said Annie. "I think you'll like it."

The waitress came back to the table. "Do you know what you want? A mini-bus full of people just came in and I want to get your order into the kitchen before theirs."

Sam placed the order. "Before she leaves, does anybody, besides me, want another drink?"

Barry motioned he was ready, but Annie, Marnie and I decided to wait until the food came.

"I can't go with you tomorrow," said Marnie, "but after this week, if you go back up, can I tag along? I'm sure Mike will let me go."

"There probably will be another trip up and I don't see a problem with you coming with us. I'll have a better idea of the whole situation when we get home. I'll keep you informed. You'll be needing all this information for the DA's office when this case goes to trial. Of course, the official documents will come from the P-town PD."

I could smell the chicken wings as the waitress set down the tray on the next table. The habanero sauce must be hot tonight. She set the nachos right down in front of me. "Yum, I'm not waiting." I dug my fork into the mountain of tortilla chips, refried beans, tomatoes and jalapenos and slid a healthy serving onto my dish, then pushed the platter toward Annie and Marnie. "These are exceptionally good tonight," I said as I stuffed a bite into my mouth.

"I won't ask you to repeat that," said Sam pretending to move back from the table. "I'd probably end up wearing a mouthful of munched up nachos."

I shook my head indicating a positive response.

Barry's dining habits hadn't changed. At the rate he was scoffing down the chicken wings, we were going to have to get another order. I reached over and took one wing and a piece of cheese crisp. "This was a good idea I had to come here. We should do something like this a couple times a month."

I turned to look at Marnie. She was trying to wash down a bite of chicken wing with her strawberry daiquiri. "The next time we come here, I'm ordering regular wings. Wow, these are really, really hot."

Barry chimed in, "Wimp."

"Why don't we order one now. I know I'll have some," said Sam as he called the waitress over. "In amongst those orders you just put in for that big party, could you try to squeeze an order of regular chicken wings for us?"

"No problem."

"Thanks."

Barry took a break from the food chain. After gulping down a slug of beer, he folded his arms and rested them on the table. "Casey, how do you get so involved in police stuff? I mean, you're a reporter. Aren't you afraid you might get yourself mixed up in something you can't get out of?"

Sam didn't say a word. He just turned his head in my direction and waited to hear my answer.

"You do know I've got a degree in criminal justice and was one step away from completing the Police Academy—with top honors, I might add—don't you? It was my dream to be a detective. I would have been a damn good one, too."

Sam reached under the table and rested his hand on my knee.

"When I came to the Cape, I was fortunate to help several of the PD's research some cold cases. They didn't have the manpower or the time to delve into them. I was going to Four C's to get a degree in journalism, so aside from my studies, I had the time. I pride myself in helping them solve ten cases ranging from murder to rape to drug trafficking. I developed a good rapport with them, so now they call me when they can use some help." I watched Barry's facial expressions as I spoke. "I thought you knew all that."

"I knew some of it. I didn't mean to get you upset." Barry tried to look at me with puppy-dog eyes. "You're good at what you do, so I guess I wanted to know the whys. Now I know."

"The PD's call me their 'Kelly Girl' detective and that suits me just fine." I smiled. "Don't back up or you'll be wearing wings."

"Here Marnie, try these. They're not as hot." Sam handed her the platter.

We each had another drink and just sat and talked about goings on around town. Once the tourists go home, places like the Melody Tent and the Cape Playhouse close down, but there's plenty to do if you know where to look.

"I think we should call it a night, we've all got busy days tomorrow," said Sam. "I'll get the waitress."

"No need. Tonight is on me," said Barry.

Marnie moved over and leaned on her cousin's shoulder. "Thank you, but you don't need to do this."

"I know." He smiled. "But, I want to. I'm glad you all enjoyed it because it might not ever happen again."

Marnie fun-punched his arm then moved away so he wouldn't do it back.

I looked at a smiling Marnie, then back to Barry. "I can see you two when you were kids out some place with your parents. You're two peas in a pod."

"That we are—at least sometimes." Marnie scooted back to Barry and gave him a hug.

"Let's get going before we start swapping remember-when kids stories," said Annie as she slid her chair out and stood up. Besides, I've got to take these two home, so I'm on punishment for the next half-hour. "Sam, I'll see you tomorrow and Casey, I'll talk to you tomorrow."

We walked to the parking lot, said our goodbyes and Sam and I headed to his car.

"That was a fun night. I'm glad you suggested Sam Diego's."

"I was surprised when Barry picked up the tab. That was probably his way of saying thank you for lots of different things," I said. "I'm sure his trust was shattered and being able to rely on us means a lot to him."

"Change of subject."

"That's okay with me."

"Do you have anything you want to go over with me tonight before you go to Boston in the morning?" asked Sam. "It's only eight o'clock, so we've got plenty of time."

"First things first," I said. "You have a clean shirt hanging in the back-seat and your overnight bag is on the floor. Are you planning on staying the night?" I gave him the raised eyebrow look.

"Since you asked, I thought I might grace you with my presence." He grinned and reached for my hand.

"Watson will be happy!" I exclaimed.

CHAPTER FORTY-NINE

"I don't feel like having another beer. I'm going to make a cup of coffee. What about you?" I asked.

"I'll join you with coffee, but not that French Vanilla stuff."

"There's regular, there's even decaf. Remember, you were staying here for a while—you bought it."

"You're right. I did." Sam was leaning against the counter with his arms folded watching me tussle with Watson. "I'm going to get comfortable, then let's get started with your Boston stuff. Okay?"

"Yep, I'll get a snack for the little guy, then I'll be right behind you."

If I didn't know better, I'd swear Watson understood every word we said. He always seems happier when the three of us are together—like family. Actually, most of the time, I felt the same way.

"I thought you were coming in right behind me," Sam said.

"I was, but I got involved with the other man in my life." I rubbed Watson's head, winked at Sam and headed to my bedroom to get changed.

Sam stood, shaking his head as he looked from me to Watson, then back to me. "No problem, I'll make the coffee," he said as he headed for the cabinet to get a couple K-cups.

"There's some Oreo's in the other cabinet, if you'd like to put some on a plate," I called from the other room. He'd fuss about not being hungry, but those were Sam's favorite cookies, so I knew they'd be waiting for me when I returned.

He had lifted my briefcase onto the middle of the table, but left it closed awaiting my instructions. I respected him for that. The plate of cookies were off to one side and my coffee cup was positioned on my Keurig waiting for somebody to press the brew button.

"Before we get started, how about a hug and a kiss?"

I welcomed the suggestion and, without hesitation, encouraged Sam's embrace. It felt good—so good, that I could easily forget the cookies and coffee.

Sam could read my mind like a book. "We'll have plenty of time for this later. Let's get going, so we can finish at a reasonable hour."

I pulled my head back, looked into his eyes, gave him a little lip-kiss and smiled. He knew that was my 'oh, all right' answer.

Sam took care of the coffee, while I took my notes and 3x5 cards out of my briefcase and arranged them on the table. I felt confident that I was in control with the investigation, but any little bit he could add would be welcomed.

Sam took the time to read my notes. He knew the 3x5's had the same information on them, but in a different format, so he didn't bother to check them out. When he finished, he said, "Did you hear back from any other precincts in Boston? Actually, any police department in Massachusetts?

"No, not yet. I think we got such a quick response from South Boston because of Maloney's father."

"No doubt, that's the reason. Do you want me to call a few of my buddies from other Boston precincts? Since they already have the flyers, maybe they would expedite them. A couple of the guys owe me favors, so this will be a good time to call them in."

"That'll be great. Another possible face recognition will certainly help. Since the lead we have stems from a bartender, our Jane Doe may live in that area. In all probability, she works someplace else. And, maybe, she doesn't come from Southie. Maybe, she moved there. There's lots of maybes we need to get answers to." I looked at Sam. "I really don't want this to get buried in the cold case files."

"Sherlock, you're more diligent than a lot of 'real' police officers, detectives even. Just remember, Cape Cod is a lot different from Boston. You get a lot of privileges here that you won't get there."

"I thought of that. Having Maloney with me should eliminate the problem. Maloney knows it too, but I'll remind him that he's in charge. I'll brief him on the way up, so he doesn't look to me for answers to questions we may get asked."

"You'll be like Castle. He writes books and you write for a newspaper. He gets involved and gets caught up in things he shouldn't. You do the same thing, but he's an actor and you're not—remember that. His safety is covered in a script. Yours isn't. You write your own script and I want you around for a happy ending." Sam looked over his glasses. "Get what I mean, Sherlock?"

When I get the over-the-glasses look, I know he's serious and this wasn't the time to make a joke. "I understand perfectly."

"Do you have a couple extra flyers with you?" asked Sam.

"I do." I reached in my briefcase and pulled out a handful. "Maloney will be bringing more tomorrow, so you can take these."

"First thing in the morning, I'll give Jonny Columbo a call. I know he's working days, so he should be there. Besides I have his cell phone number if he's not. Sgt. Columbo works out of the Back Bay area. That covers part of Boylston and Beacon Streets and a large area in between. Then I'll call Fred Watson. I haven't talked to him for a while, but I'm sure he's still trying to run the Beacon Hill precinct. He's like a fixture there. He'd cuff himself to a holding cell before he'd take a transfer. He's quite the character. But, he's one who can dig up anything once he puts his mind to it." Sam got up from the table. "I'm going to have another cup of coffee. Want one?"

There were three Oreo's left on the plate. "I guess I'll need one to wash down another cookie." I puffed out my cheeks and looked wide-eyed at Sam, then started laughing. "If I keep up this eating, I'll need new clothes."

"What you need is to work out. We'll finish the cookies and

coffee and I'll be your coach."

I couldn't help but smile. If there was anyone I wanted to work out with, it was Sam.

CHAPTER FIFTY

Morning came much too quickly. I rolled over to give Sam a kiss, but he was already up. Once I got my head on straight, I could hear the water running in the shower. I knew he had to be at the courthouse by eight o'clock to meet with Michael and last night he said he wanted to make the Boston calls early, so I figured he would be up and out early. I turned to look at the clock. Early wasn't the word for it. It was only six-thirty. I was awake now, so I might as well get up and start getting ready myself.

It wasn't a jeans and t-shirt day, so I scoured my closet for my tan pants and chocolate brown button down. Since I don't wear them much, they were hung in the back. I remembered buying a scarf to go with the outfit. If it was anywhere, it had to be in the end table beside my bed. "Bingo," I said out loud.

"Bingo what," came Sam's voice from the bathroom.

He certainly doesn't miss a trick. He hears everything. "I found the scarf I was looking for on my first try. That's all." I just shook my head. "I've got some time. Want a coffee before you leave?"

"Yeah, that sounds good. Would you please put an English muffin in the toaster, too. I'll be right out."

I hadn't even taken the muffins from the package when Sam came through the doorway. "You certainly are the early bird today," I said as I pushed the lever down.

"I want to get those Boston calls started before they call us into the courtroom. Hopefully, I can catch both those guys I told you about last night. Otherwise, I'll have to leave a message for them to call me back. I'll keep my cell on vibrate. Since, the lawyers are doing closing arguments, I can leave the courtroom, if I have to."

The muffins popped up. I spread them with butter and handed them to Sam. "Want some jelly?" I asked.

"No, this is good."

I took our coffees from the counter to the table, then sat down with him.

"If you talk to them and they need more information, they can give me a call. As you know we don't have much more info, but let them ask. Hopefully, I will have more information after we check out our Boston lead."

Sam checked his watch, quickly ate the last bite and washed it down with his coffee. "Be careful going to Boston. I know Maloney is driving, so he should know where to go. Driving there and driving here is like trying to get around in two different worlds. Call me when you get a minute." Sam got up and moved toward the door. "If I don't hear from you by noontime, I'll give you a call."

He leaned over and gave me a kiss, patted Watson on the head, and went out the door. He was a man on a mission.

The Cape Cod Mall was less than a fifteen minute ride from my house, so I had plenty of time to get ready. Sam had tossed the Tribune in on his way out. I tried sitting down and scanning through it, but my mind was already in Boston. So, I decided to clean up the dishes, take my shower and get dressed.

CHAPTER FIFTY-ONE

It was eight-fifteen when I pulled into the Mall parking lot. Since it doesn't open until ten o'clock, there weren't many cars around. There was no way Maloney could miss me and my little green spider.

I had just laid my head back on the seat, when I heard a tapping on my window. It was Maloney. He was parked beside me. I didn't even hear him pull in. I put up one finger to indicate I'd be right with him. Everything I was taking was tucked neatly in my briefcase, so I didn't have to scramble to gather everything up. I got out, locked up my baby and slid into the seat beside Maloney.

"Nice new car," I said.

"Compliments of the Sarge."

"Are you ready for this—your first big gig. There's going to be a detective slot open when Adams retires. Sarge figures Adam's going to put his papers in sometime within the next six months. He's been taking vacation time and a lot of sick days. That's a dead giveaway retirement is lurking in the near future. I think you have a good chance of filling that slot. This case is a test."

"Did the Sarge tell you that?" asked Maloney. "Or are you painting your own picture of my future?"

"Do you think I'd fill your head with lots of false hopes?" I looked at him. He was young. This would be an opportunity of a lifetime. I would give anything to have it. "This is something I'd never kid about. Sarge thinks you have lots of potential and also thinks I can help you. That's why we're in this together."

"Sorry, Casey, I didn't mean to sound like a spoiled kid." He glanced in my direction. "Are we okay?"

“Of course we are. I probably would have said the same thing if I was in your position. Just remember, I want to help you.”

“I will.”

“Okay, then let’s get started.” We were already on Route 6 heading off Cape. “We might as well get this out of the way before we get into Boston traffic.” My briefcase was on the floor resting against my leg. I had to unfasten my seat belt in order to lean down far enough to get my set of cards from the bottom of the case. Before I got it hooked back again the annoying beep, beep, beep, reminded me I wasn’t in compliance with the seat belt law. “Hold your horses,” I said and snapped the buckle into place. “When we’re at L Street Tavern, I’ll use a pad of paper to write down the answers we get, then later I’ll transfer them to my 3x5’s. I like this method, it helps me keep organized. And, I can find what I’m looking for much easier than shuffling through papers.”

“I think I’m going to like this class,” Maloney said. “Sorry, I forgot to bring an apple for the teacher.”

“Are you finished?” I asked. “This is scary—you remind me of a little Sam.” My smirk was enough to let him know it was time to get serious. “The first thing we’ll do is get our bartenders name. It’s a good habit to always get the name first. That way there’s no mistaking who said what. A misidentified quote can change the outcome of a case. It doesn’t happen often, but if you write down the name of the person you’re interviewing, then it will never happen to you. Next, we’ll show him the flyer of our Jane Doe.”

“He’s already seen it. Obviously, it’s the same one my father showed him.”

“It is. But, since you’re the investigating officer, you need to have the witness—in this case the bartender – confirm the identification. Again, record his response.” I glanced at Maloney. “I know this sounds like Investigations 101. You went through the police academy, just like I did. So, you’ve probably heard this all before, but I have a feeling there’s a lot more to this case than meets the eye, so a review of basics for both of us is a good idea.”

"Will you jump in if I miss something?"

"Of course I will. The bartender did give your father a name." I flipped through my cards. "Here it is. He only had a first name—Katherine . Like I said before, she didn't appear to be a barfly, so maybe this bartender could think a little harder and come up with the name of a possible companion—be it male or female. And, if we get a positive answer, then maybe he can give us a last name, if not for her, for the companion. Right now, there are a lot of ifs. We need to eliminate some of them. This may create a whole new set of questions—making the ones I compiled obsolete. Well, maybe not entirely obsolete, but incomplete. That's when we'll have to wing it. What we can do, though, is have some other questions ready based on additional information the bartender might furnish. For example—if he knows a companion's first name and not a last name and knows approximately when they were in there last, does he remember if either one of them paid with a credit card? If so, we'll need him to look back in his transactions to try and match something up. That's a long shot, but maybe we could get lucky."

"Southie is a pretty tight knit community and L Street Tavern is mostly frequented by locals. So, if the bartender recognized our Jane, then he should be able to give us more. And, if by chance, he doesn't have more—somebody in that bar will. I guarantee it."

"Before we jump to any conclusions about what he knows and what he doesn't, let's go over a few more things." I was flipping through my cards when my cell phone rang. It was Sam. "Good morning," I said. "I didn't expect to hear from you so early."

"I wanted you to know I got ahold of both of my Boston contacts and they're more than happy to assist in whatever they can do. They're going to get copies of the flyer and post them in some strategic locations. As far as doing a sweeping canvas, they said the same thing as I did. It would be virtually impossible, but they'll personally hit a few high spots. They're going to have post offices, in their respective areas, hang some around the lobby. And, they're going to deliver a stack to the local libraries to be hung in spots most frequented by library goers."

"Thanks, buddy." I shook my head as I let out a deep sigh. "You're the best."

"I won't forget you said that." Sam laughed. "I'll get back to you as soon as I hear from anyone. By the way, say 'hi' to Maloney for me. And, tell him I wish him luck working with the great Sherlock Quinby."

I didn't even answer him, I just pressed the end button.

"That was Sam, if you didn't figure it out. He said to say 'hi'. A couple of his buddies in precincts other than Southie are doing him a favor by distributing flyers and checking in with some well-populated high spots that are frequented mostly by locals."

"I think I'm learning from the best and I'm not being sarcastic—I mean it."

"We just passed a sign saying there was a Dunkins at the next exit. I could use a coffee. Do you mind if we stop?" I asked. I was craving a French vanilla, but more than that I had to use the bathroom.

"No problem," he said easing over into the right lane. "I could use one too. I'm sure they've got some at the station, but it's probably crap like we have—that is unless you're there. The Sarge always pulls out the good stuff and makes a fresh pot just before you're due to arrive. You've got that guy wrapped around your baby finger."

I smiled. "Free help, he's got to do something to entice me." We pulled into the lot. Maloney insisted on buying. I left him in the line while I hit the ladies room. He was standing by the door when I came out.

"Do you want any sugar or that sweetener stuff?"

"Nope, I'm good to go," I said taking my coffee from him. "Thanks, the next one's on me."

We got back into the car, took a couple sips of coffee and headed out to the highway. For some reason, I had a good feeling about how the day was going to go. Call it woman's intuition or whatever you want to, but so far things were moving right along. I knew we were getting closer to Boston because the traffic was starting to get heavy. We had missed the morning rush hour, but it's never clear sailing into the City. I only know this from the time I came here with Sam. Other than that, I stay on the other side of the bridge.

"Where do we get off?" I asked.

"Exit fifteen," he said. "It should say Morrissey Boulevard/ JFK Library. The exit ramp leads right into Morrissey. Ironically, the Boston Globe building is right down the street." He tapped his fingers on the steering wheel. "If it wasn't for them, we might not be pursuing this lead."

"Are we meeting your father first or going directly to L Street?"

"The Tavern probably isn't open yet. There should be somebody there, I'd say around ten thirty, so I figured we'd stop at the precinct first."

"Sounds like a plan to me."

"He said he might go with us to talk to the bartender. Sometimes these neighborhood guys are not as cooperative with outsiders as they are with one of their own."

Maloney was on his home turf. His level of confidence seemed to accelerate. I was glad to see that, especially since he was about to have a big moment in front of his father. He was covering a case usually handled by a veteran detective.

I snapped back to reality when Maloney swerved into the right lane and flew down the exit ramp. "Yikes, if you ever decide to leave the police department, you could drive a car in the Indy 500. I'd give you a personal reference. I think I left my stomach back on Route 3."

He laughed. "You should ride with me through rush hour traffic. And, the best part is, I've never had an accident."

"There's always a first time," I said as I gave him the look. My 3x5's were all over the passenger floor and that's where they were going to stay until we got to the precinct.

It wasn't ten minutes later when we pulled up in front of a two story brick building. "This looks fairly new," I said.

"They built it somewhere around 1997. My father transferred here when it first opened and has been here ever since. My grandfather did his last two years here. I'd say, most of the guys assigned to Southie are from the area or close to it." Maloney shut the cruiser off and started to get out of the car.

"Hey," I said unbuckling my seat belt. "I've got a mess to clean up over here, remember? Maybe you could come over and give me a hand."

He leaned into the car and clapped.

"If I could reach you, they'd probably change me with assault." I had put my briefcase on the sidewalk and was making sure I'd gotten all the cards.

"Sorry, Casey, I was only kidding."

"I know you were. Guess maybe I'm just a little tense. I'm hoping we're going to be successful this morning with the interview." I slipped my cards into one of the pockets on the outside of the briefcase. "Okay, let's get this show on the road." I grabbed my case and turned to follow Maloney into the precinct.

In the lobby there were benches and some chairs along the walls, a huge clock, cameras mounted on the ceiling in each corner and a showcase, I assumed was plexiglass, displaying memorabilia and citations for accommodation. There wasn't a desk or an open doorway. There were doors, without windows. The doors were cold, hard steel with tamper-proof locks, that I presumed were locked up tighter than a bull's ass. There wasn't a duty desk or an officer anywhere to be seen. The receptionist was behind a well-protected bullet-proof cage with a microphone type of apparatus to communicate with visitors.

Maloney didn't hesitate. He walked over to the caged-in welcoming committee of one. "Good morning, Mary Ann, how's it going?"

She looked up. "Maloney, what in the world brings you back to this neck of the woods?" she said in an excited, up-toned voice.

Before he could answer, she threw another question in his direction. "Did your father know you were coming? Because if he did, he's in trouble for not telling me. I would have baked you a batch of brownies with the fudge frosting you like."

I stood beside the cage with a shit-kicking grin on my face. She was old enough to be his mother.

"You come on in here. I'll call for Big M." The door beside the cage buzzed and I followed Maloney through.

"Mary Ann," he said, "I'd like to introduce you to Casey Quinby. She's the head investigative reporter for the Cape Cod Tribune. She sometimes works with the Provincetown PD on cases."

"Are you two working on a case now?" Her face became stern.

"Ah, saved by the dad – again, I might add." A uniformed officer entered the front office from a back hallway and reached out his hand to me. "Casey Quinby, I assume. Glad to finally meet you. I'm Rusty's father. My friends call me Big M."

Maloney shook his head. "Always one step ahead of me. Can we go someplace to talk?" He turned toward Mary Ann. "See you later."

She stood with her hands on her hips and nodded. "You bet you will."

I smiled and bid her good day, then followed the two Maloney's into the hallway Big M had just come out of.

CHAPTER FIFTY-TWO

"Casey, have a seat," Big M said as he motioned me to sit down in one of the chairs in front of his desk. Maloney sat in the other one. "I'm sure Maloney told you about the bartender at L Street. He said he works every day during the week from ten-thirty to seven, but to be on the safe side I'll give him a call before we head on over. By the way, do either of you want a coffee—it's fresh." He turned to his son and winked.

"I caught that." I smiled. "My reputation precedes me." I turned to Maloney. "Did you let your father in on my police department coffee secret?"

"You mean the one where Sgt. Costa makes a fresh pot minutes before you arrive? I can't let another PD show us up." Big M laughed.

"In that case, yes, I'd love a cup—Thanks."

Big M got up and without saying anything more, walked out of his office and around the corner, to what I assumed, was the break room.

"He likes you—I can tell. I think he had a lengthy conversation with the Sarge. I don't know that for sure, but judging from his easiness with you, I think he did."

I could tell that Maloney was relaxed and for this I was glad. As quick as Big M left his office, he was back with three cups of steaming hot coffee. "I forgot to ask if you want cream?"

"No, this is just the way I like it," I said. "Again, thanks."

"I'm sure Maloney told you that a couple of my guys from the precinct were going to do some additional canvasing. They went out yesterday afternoon and checked with some businesses that they felt our Jane Doe might have visited—like a small corner grocery store, a mom and pop convenience store, a donut shop and a dry-cleaners. They got an id at the donut shop—not a name, but a face recognition. The corner grocery store said she frequented their business a lot, most times with a male companion. Both businesses said the visits were on the week-ends, indicating both parties must work during the week."

I felt more confident we definitely were going to get something we could run with.

"After we leave L Street, we can head over and talk to them ourselves."

Maloney appeared to be in deep thought. "Maybe we should check JJ's. We know our Jane Doe is in her early twenties, so I'm assuming her friend is probably close to the same age. And, actually, we don't know if her companion is just a friend or a boyfriend or maybe even a husband. Besides, by the time we get over to JJ's, it will be time for lunch."

"What bothers me is the fact that this companion hasn't reported her missing—not to us or any other Boston precinct. I checked before you got here. I know I'm jumping ahead, but he could be involved in her disappearance and ultimate death." Big M has been in this business a long time and when a seasoned cop senses something, it should be looked at closely. "Just keep that in the back of your mind as we check these leads out."

Big M checked his watch, then picked up the phone and dialed the L Street Tavern. "Morning, is Charlie Bean there?" There was a hesitation. "Yes, I'll wait." He covered the mouthpiece on the hand-set. "They said he was in the stock-room getting a keg. I could either wait or call back in about five minutes. You heard my answer."

About two minutes went by before there was any more conversation between Big M and the person on the other end of the phone.

"Hi, Charlie," Big M said, "This is Officer Thomas Maloney from the South Boston precinct. You spoke to a couple of our officers yesterday regarding a missing person. I believe they told you somebody else from the department would be over to talk to you some more about it."

I don't exactly know what was said on the other end, but Big M said, "Yes, we do need to talk to you this morning. I assure you it won't take long. We'll be over in about twenty minutes, please make yourself available. And, we may need to talk to a few of the other employees." He threw his hand up and spread his fingers in a motion of disgust. "Thank you," he said and hung up. "There was a day when you called on an establishment, like L Street, they'd be more than happy to help. Now, it's like pulling teeth. The respect level stinks." Big M shook his head and sighed. "But, when they have trouble with a patron, they expect us to appear at the snap of a finger." Big M called Mary Ann and told her he'd be out of the office for a couple of hours.

I hadn't taken any of my notes from my briefcase, so it was ready to travel. We got up and again I followed the Maloney's out of Big M's office, through the squad room and out the back door to the parking lot. Maloney told me to ride in the front, but I said I'd be perfectly comfortable in the back.

CHAPTER FIFTY-THREE

The L Street Tavern was practically around the corner from the precinct. We were there in less than ten minutes and that included parking time. Since it was early, there was a space in front. When I got out of the car, I noticed a sign on the edge of the sidewalk. It reminded any would-be-parkers that a permit is required to occupy the space. But, since we were in a cruiser, the permit was a mute issue.

"I'll take another flyer in, along with my 3x5's," I said.

"Your what?" asked Big M.

"She'll tell you later," said Maloney as he held the door and suggested I follow his father inside.

Big M walked up to the bar. He showed his badge to the person standing there. "Is Charlie available?" he asked.

"I'm Charlie. Are you the officer I spoke to a little while ago?"

"Yes, I'm Officer Thomas Maloney." He reached out to shake Charlie's hand. "This is Casey Quinby and, my son, Officer Rusty Maloney. They are here from Cape Cod. The missing person was found dead in Provincetown." He took one of my flyers and handed it to Charlie. "Take another look. You told my officers her name was Katherine. Are you sure?"

"I'm positive. I don't know her last name, though," he said without taking his eyes off the flyer. "The officers who came in the other day didn't tell me she was dead." He came out from behind the bar and sat down at one of the tables. We sat down with him. "Let me think for a minute." He took a deep breath, then continued, "She rarely came in here alone—most of the time she was with her boyfriend. Actually, I think they lived together." He leaned his elbow on the table and rested his chin in his hand. Her boyfriend's name is Peter. I'm almost positive he was here last week. He sat with some of the guys at the bar. She wasn't with him." He looked at Big M. "Was she murdered?"

Maloney answered, "That's what it appears. We're investigating all aspects. That's why we need your help. Anything you can tell us is important. We'll decide what is relevant and what isn't."

"I'll do my best. She seemed like a nice person. She was always quiet—never caused any problems—never buddied up with the guys at the bar. If she came in by herself, it was during the day and she sat at a table, had lunch, then left. It didn't happen often."

"The boyfriend—do you have a name other than Peter?" Maloney asked.

"No, I just know his first name is Peter. I don't know too much about him. Again, not a trouble maker—stayed to himself. Sometimes he'd come in to watch a ballgame with the guys. I don't think he hung around with them other than here. I think they were just bar buddies. If you know what I mean."

"I do know," said Maloney. "Do you remember how he paid?"

"Wow, that's a tall order." Charlie leaned back in the chair and scratched his head. "Most of the time, I think he paid by credit card. She didn't. She paid cash."

Maloney thought for a moment, then asked, "Is there any way you'd be able to check your charge card receipts?"

I looked at Big M. He hadn't said a word. He let his son do all the talking. I could see how proud he was of him. I imagine he didn't like it when Maloney left Boston to take the P-town job.

"Yeah, I think so. Let me get last week's receipts from the office. I'll bring them out here 'cause there isn't much room back there. It'll only take me a minute." Charlie was already on his way to the office before anyone could say anything.

"This could be a huge break for us," said Maloney. "It's a long shot. But, I've always been a gambler and my bet is on Charlie coming through with a name. Do I have any takers?"

"It kind of sounds like Charlie liked our Jane Doe a little. He became a much more caring person when we told him she was murdered," I said.

"It's the Southie thing. We have a bond. If one of ours is hurt, then we rally to see whoever did it is punished," Big M said. "The problem is sometimes the bond doesn't include the police department. But it looks like, in this case, Charlie is going to help us, that is, if he can."

The door to the back room opened and Charlie came out carrying a box of papers. "These are last week's credit card receipts. Why don't we move to a bigger table." Charlie pointed to the far corner of the bar. "This way, not only will we have more room to go through these, but if anybody comes in they won't bother us."

For such a small place, I was amazed at the number of credit card receipts in the box. "Let's divide these up and get started." I had already reached in and grabbed a stack.

"Usually, we put the number of people in the party in the upper left hand corner. I'm not sure why, but we've done it for years—ever since I've been here."

"And, how long have you been here?" I asked.

"I worked here when I was in college, then left for a couple of years. Mr. O'Toole, the guy who owns the place, asked me if I'd come back as the manager. He made me an offer I couldn't refuse—so here I am. That was seven years ago. So, it's been nine years in all."

I had gone through about twenty slips, when I came across one with the first name Peter. The last name was Mattero. I looked at Maloney. "I thought this was the Irish end of town. I've got a slip here for Peter Mattero."

"The Peter you're looking for definitely isn't Italian. Ever since the Tavern was in the movie, 'Good Will Hunting', we host a lot more outsiders—if you know what I mean."

"I think I get the drift," I said. "I'm in the minority right now. Well, I'm actually half Irish. My mother's grandmother came from

Ireland, so I guess that makes me a mini-member of the clan." I laughed.

Maloney looked up. "Here's another Peter slip—last name, Martin."

"Put that one aside. Once we go through all these, I can look at the date and the number of people served. To stop for each one will only slow the process down."

"I agree," Big M said without stopping his search.

It took us about fifteen minutes to find all the slips charged by a person with the first name of Peter. There were twenty-two in all. The rest of them we put back in the box. Charlie took it off the table and set it on the floor beside him. "Let me take a look," he said. Maloney straightened out the piles and handed them to Charlie.

He checked each one very carefully—putting each slip in one of three piles.

"What's with the piles?" Maloney asked.

"This pile is for the definitely not's." Charlie pointed to his left. "The other two piles are for degrees of maybe. Before I put the definitely not's back in the box, let me look at them one more time." He picked them up and carefully studied them again. "Your Peter is not one of these. I know all but two personally." He turned and dropped them in box. Charlie picked up the pile directly in front of him. "I think I know who these three are", he said and handed them to Maloney. "They only come in once in a while. This next guy usually brings business associates in for lunch. He likes to tell the 'Good Will Hunting' story. Charlie stopped, got up from the table and asked, "I'm going to get a Coke. Would anyone else like anything?"

"I'll have a Diet Coke, please, "I said.

Maloney said, "I'll have the same."

And Big M asked, "Is the coffee fresh?"

"Yes sir, it is."

"Then I'll have a cup," he said.

"I'll be right back." Charlie left and headed for the kitchen.

I turned to Big M. “Well, what do you think?”

“I think Charlie is on the level. I have a feeling we’ll leave here today with probably a couple of names to check out.”

Maloney jumped in. “Who knows, he still has one more pile to go through. He may come up with ‘the’ Peter we’re looking for.” He stopped talking when he saw Charlie coming from the kitchen with Big M’s coffee.

“You need cream or sugar?”

“Black is good,” Big M said as he took a sip. “Good coffee.”

“Now that the big guy is happy, I’ll get our drinks.” Charlie snickered and headed for the bar. After he set the rest of the drinks on the table, he said, “Let me get back to these receipts. The lunch crowd will start meandering in soon. Sometimes it can get crazy since I’m the only bartender on. Without hesitation, he picked up the last pile and started looking through the slips. About half way through he stopped. “This is your Peter. I distinctly remember when he was here last week. He was sitting at the bar and a friend of his came in. The friend didn’t call him Peter, he called him McCarthy. They were sitting in the middle of the bar, so I was pretty much in front of them the whole time they were here. His friend called him McCarthy several times.” Charlie handed the receipt to Maloney. “Yep, I’m ninety-nine percent sure he’s your guy.”

Maloney took the receipt. “Charlie, please take another look at our flyer. You called her Katherine, right?” Maloney looked at Charlie for an answer.

“I did call her Katherine. I’m sure that’s her first name. And yes, she’s the girl usually with Peter McCarthy, but not last week. He was alone.”

“You said she’s the girl usually with Peter McCarthy. Does that mean he brings other girls here?” Big M asked.

“No, he’s either with her or alone.” Charlie nodded his head.

I had been flipping through the remaining receipts while Charlie was talking. I stopped abruptly when I came to another Peter McCarthy receipt. “Look here, another receipt for our Peter.”

Charlie reached over to take it from me. “And, this indicates he was a party of one, just like the other receipt.” Charlie pointed to the number one in the right hand corner.

“I know this is a long-shot, but do you, by any chance, know his address?” Maloney asked.

“I don’t. Although, I don’t think it’s too far away, cause he walks here. Most of our customers are locals. The parking is almost non-existent and what there is requires a residential permit.”

Big M rested his elbows on the table and leaned forward. “Charlie, would you mind if we took these receipts? I’ll see that you get them back.”

“Let me take a copy. You can have the originals, but I’d like to have something as a record for the books.” Charlie stood up and held out his hand for the receipts. “Be right back.”

Big M, Maloney and I got up to wait for him. People were starting to come in. That was our cue to leave.

“If you have any more information, please give me a call.” Big M handed Charlie a card. He put his cell phone number on the back. It’s easier to reach me if you call my cell.”

Maloney reached out to Charlie. “Thanks, you’ve been very helpful.”

“If there’s anything else I can do, you know where to find me.” Charlie shrugged his shoulders and bid us a good day as we left L Street.

CHAPTER FIFTY-FOUR

"What do you say we grab some lunch at JJ's? That's another hang-out for locals. I don't think my officers have been there yet. So we'll kill two birds with one stone. No pun intended." Big M rolled his eyes and headed for the cruiser.

"I'm real happy with the information Charlie gave us. When we get back to the station, we'll look up this Peter McCarthy. If we're lucky, he'll be in the telephone book. If not, we'll use some of my father's resources to get an address. This is the first big break we've had. Actually, it's the first any break we've had." Maloney beamed. "With any luck, we'll get a back-up confirmation from the staff at JJ's."

I smiled. "Am I detecting a little bit of home-sickness?"

"When you're from Southie, you always carry some home in your heart. Am I sorry I left the department here to go to P-town? Absolutely not. I came from a family of Southie police officers, but I've got a new family now and I'm lovin' it."

"Know what, Maloney, I believe you. Now, let's get going—I'm hungry." I opened the cruiser door and got in.

JJ's is a sports bar—very tastefully decorated with Boston sports memorabilia. Big M looked around and headed toward a table off to the side near the waitress station. There were seats at the bar, but because technically we were working, it wouldn't be a good idea to sit there. Since it was lunch-time, it was pretty busy. Big M knew the waitress who came over to our table.

"Good afternoon, Molly," he said. "Got any good specials today or do I have to talk to that boss of yours?"

"You're in luck, Big M." She smiled and slid three menus and a Monday's special sheet down in front of us. "They had corned beef and cabbage yesterday. The corned beef sandwiches are wicked good. I had one before I started work. It comes with coleslaw and pub fries. I'll sneak a piece of cheese on it, if you want." She batted her eyelashes at him.

"We've got to stop meeting this way. My son might get the wrong idea and go home and tell his mom." Big M cocked his head in the direction of Maloney.

"You kidding me," she said. "Mrs. Maloney would be glad to get rid of you." She smiled. "How about some drinks?"

Maloney and I ordered Diet Cokes and Big M got a ginger ale.

"I'll be right back to get your orders."

"If Molly says the corned beef sandwich is good—it's great. I usually put a little creamy horse radish on it along with the spicy mustard."

I wrinkled my face to mimic a painful expression. "Do they serve a double order of Tums with that combination?" I asked. "I'm going to try one, minus the creamy stuff."

"Make that three. I've had their corned beef sandwiches many times. You can't beat them—corned beef is to Southie, like lobster is to P-town."

Molly came back and took their order. "Hey, Molly, before you leave, take a look at this picture."

She picked up the flyer and walked to the waitress station. The light was better there. I could see her studying it. Then she returned to our table. "You know, Big M, she looks familiar. I'm sure I've seen her in here—not for a while though. I don't know her name. I think she came in with a guy, but we see so many people every day." She scrutinized the flyer again. Molly looked at the bar. "Why don't you ask Denny? He has a photographic memory. If she ever sat at the bar, he'll remember her." "He's not real busy. Now would be a good time."

"Thanks, I'll do that," said Big M.

Molly left to put our order in and Big M headed over to the bar.

"Do you want to go up there with your father? I'll wait here and you can fill me in when you come back."

Before Maloney could get up from his chair, Big M was back and Denny was with him. Denny pulled out the fourth chair and sat down.

Big M introduced us to Denny. I'm going to turn the questioning over to my son. It's his case.

"I saw Big M show you the flyer of our Jane Doe, so I'm assuming you might have something to share with us or you wouldn't have left the bar, especially during the lunch crowd."

"You're right. I know this girl. Her name is Katherine. She's a nice girl—very quiet, pretty too. She never came in by herself. She was always with a guy. I don't know his last name, but his first name is Peter. And, I believe they live together—somewhere in the neighborhood." He looked at me. "By the neighborhood, I mean Southie." Denny looked at the flyer again. "Wait a minute," he said. "Should I be saying she was a nice girl?"

"I'm afraid so," I said. "She was the victim of a homicide."

"Where?" he asked.

"Provincetown," said Maloney.

"Where's her boyfriend?" Denny was noticeably shaken.

"That's what we need to find out. We just need to talk to him." Big M felt bad for Denny. "We appreciate your input. Believe me, it was helpful." Big M folded up the flyer and slid it into his pocket and at the same time pulled out one of his cards. "Here's my card. If you see this Peter, please give me a call. Don't say anything to him, let us handle that."

"I will," said Denny. "I've got to get back to work. Will you please keep me posted? "

Big M nodded. "When we have something, I'll stop by."

Denny stood up, took a deep breath and headed back to the bar.

No sooner did Denny leave than Molly came out of the kitchen with our sandwiches.

CHAPTER FIFTY-FIVE

It was a quiet ride back to the station. I think we all were running scenarios through our heads. That's a good thing. Once we're inside, we can sit down and share our thoughts. Big M led the way. Maloney and I took the same seats we had occupied earlier.

Big M picked up the phone, "Mary-Ann we're back. Can you do me a favor?" He cupped his hand over the receiver and made a drinking motion with the other. Both of us nodded and silently mouthed cream, no sugar. "Can you bring three coffees—two with cream and one black." He smiled as though she could see him. "Thanks."

Big M reached down in his bottom desk drawer and brought out a Boston Phone Directory and a City Directory. "We'll try these first."

"My mother would have loved to have one of those books when I was little. She was always trying to find enough magazines for me to sit on so I could reach my food. Whenever she got them high enough, she'd sit me on top. I had to sit perfectly still and only move to eat, otherwise one of the magazines would go one way and I'd go the other." I stared off into nowhere. "The things that trigger memories."

He handed Maloney the City Directory and slid the phone book in my direction. "I'll use the computer while you guys try the old fashion method. You know—let your fingers do the walking." He laughed at his own rather lame statement.

Mary-Ann knocked on the door and Big M waved her in. "I liked it better when you had to come through the front door. With this new back door stuff, I never know who's in or out." She rolled her eyes and set the coffee on the desk.

"Thanks," I said and went back to my phone book reading.

It must have been at least ten minutes before anybody spoke. "McCarthy sure is a popular name. I've found a few P. McCarthy's, but either the age doesn't fit or it's a female." Maloney finished his coffee. "Anybody else having any luck?"

If I didn't know any better, I'd say Big M was playing a video game on his computer. I detected a slight smile on his face as he hit the mouse to advance a page.

"Not yet," I said.

Big M stopped smiling and moved his hand off the mouse. "Casey, have you looked in Metro South yet?"

"No," I replied. "Let me flip to that section." I turned to the section printed on light green pages. The title across the top of the page was Metro South. "Got it," I said as I hurried to find the listings for McCarthy. "Here we go." I counted the listings for Peter McCarthy. "There's twenty-four listings."

"Maloney slide on over closer to Casey to take a look at the streets." Big M looked at me. "He should be able to recognize the streets that are located in Southie."

"Do you have a highlighter?" Maloney asked his father.

Big M opened his top draw, shuffled a few papers around and handed Maloney a yellow highlighter.

"I think we're going to have a few Peter's that need to be checked out."

I watched as Maloney concentrated on the listings. It only took a couple of minutes. "I've got five possible Peter McCarthy's."

"Give me the street addresses," said Big M.

Maloney read off the five addresses.

"From those five, I've isolated three." Big M did something on his computer, then printed out whatever it was he was working on. I could hear the printer spitting out several pieces of paper.

Big M got up from his desk and walked over to the table in the back of his office. The printer had just finished the last page. He took them all from the tray and put them into a manila folder. "Let's take a ride. It's time to find Peter."

When Big M was ready to move, everybody better be ready. I was learning that real fast. Again we were like a mini-entourage—Big M, me and Maloney—heading for the back door. This time he didn't even stop to check out with Mary-Ann.

I wasn't about to ask, but once inside the cruiser, Maloney did, "Where are we going?"

Big M handed him the folder. "I've narrowed our initial search to these three."

I leaned up and looked over the front seat. "Maloney, move to the right so I can see what you're looking at." Big M meant business. It was a print-out from the Registry of Motor Vehicles. We had a picture of three Peter McCarthys and their personal information.

"We're heading back to L Street and JJ's to show these pictures to Charlie and Denny. If they recognize one of them, then we're going scouting. Hopefully, they will and it will be the same person."

For the first time there was silence. Big M moved quickly—passing cars and weaving down streets I'd find difficult to maneuver on a normal day. Before I knew it, we were in front of L Street Tavern. He pulled in front of the door and the three of us got out and walked inside. Charlie was still behind the bar.

Big M walked over to him and handed him the folder. "Charlie, I need you to take a look at these pictures and let me know if you recognize any of them."

Charlie opened the folder and laid them out on the bar. Without hesitation, he picked up the middle one. "This is the Peter McCarthy I know. He's the one who came in with your victim."

"Are you sure?" Maloney asked.

Charlie looked again. "I'm positive."

Big M gathered up the pictures and put them back in the folder. "You've been very helpful. I appreciate it." He turned and motioned us toward the door. "Thanks, I'll catch you later."

We got in the car and headed toward JJ's. Not one word was said until we pulled into their parking lot. "I think we'll be paying our Peter a visit real soon," Big M said as he headed up the stairs and into the restaurant.

I looked around, but didn't see Denny. Big M headed to the bar and we followed. "Is Denny still around?" he asked the kid behind the bar.

"Yeah, he's in the kitchen. I'll go get him."

No sooner did the kid close the kitchen door, it opened and Denny came out. "You caught me having lunch," he said wiping his mouth. "What can I do for you?"

Big M took the three pictures from his folder and laid them out on one of the tables in the same order as he'd done at L Street. "Recognize anybody?"

"Sure do," said Denny. "The guy in the middle—he's your Peter."

Again Big M asked, "Are you sure?"

"Absolutely, there is no doubt in my mind," said Denny.

"Thanks. I may need to take a statement later."

We headed back to the cruiser. Big M was good. If Maloney turns out half as good as his father, he'll make a hell of a detective. Bubba's instincts were right on. I only wish I was the one in training. Big M used the front of the cruiser as a desk. He laid the pictures out again in the same order.

"All right." He picked up the middle picture—the same one identified by both Charlie and Denny. "We're going to pay Peter McCarthy a visit. Let's see. It's only three o'clock, so if he works he might not be home. At least we can see where he lives and check out his immediate surroundings. Sometimes you can pick up some personality traits by where a person lives. If my memory is correct—this area was three family houses made into condos. When they were three family houses, everybody knew everybody. There were no secrets. But, times have changed and Southie is now a 'hip' place to live—or so I am told. I've always thought it was 'hip'. The condo people are mostly strangers and wouldn't know their neighbors if they bumped into them. I bet if we showed this picture around nobody would know him." Big M shook his head. "Now the girl—they might have seen her around. The guys—you know what I mean."

CHAPTER FIFTY-SIX

"Before we head on over, I need to make a call," I said. "I'll be right back." I walked a couple parking spaces away and called Sam. He answered on the second ring. "Wow, that's the fastest you've ever answered."

"Don't be a ball buster. Is everything all right?" he asked. "Are you still in Boston?"

"Are we playing twenty questions?" I laughed. "Yeah, we're still here. We think we've found our Jane Doe's other half. Maloney's father, Big M, has lived in Southie all his life and his family before him. He could draw a map of the area blindfolded and tell you where everybody lived and what they usually ate for supper on any given night." I switched my cell to my other ear and continued, "I don't know what time I'll be home. Do you think you could check in on Watson. I left him with enough food and water to get him through the day, but I'm sure he'd like to see you."

"There's nothing going on tonight, so I just might stay over at your house. I've got to go, I can see the Court Officer heading in my direction. Call me when you leave Boston."

"Will do," I said as I turned to walk back to where Maloney and his father were standing. "Had to check in with the home front."

While I was talking to Sam, Big M called one of his connections at City Hall to check the current city directory and the voting records for the names of the residents at the East Third Street address listed for Peter McCarthy. "Casey, I think we've got something. My buddy at City Hall said the records show two names in the McCarthy condo—Peter and a girl named Katherine O'Ryan."

My heart began to race. Now we had an identity or at least I think we did. After all, we thought we had an identity from Omar and that was Emily, not Katherine. "That's a positive move forward," I said.

Big M noticed my puzzled look. "What questions are you mulling around in your pretty little head?" he asked. "You can't merge a newspaper reporter and an investigator together without stirring up a pot of doubt that could lead to uncertainties—some warranted and some not. It's written all over your face."

"I never could play a good game of poker," I said trying to lighten the moment. "One of my questions is identity. Now that we know our Jane Doe goes by Katherine O'Ryan, where does Emily Latham fit in?"

"Who? asked Big M.

"Emily Latham is the name she gave to the owner of the rooming house in P-town where she rented a room."

"Okay, now I understand the clouds surrounding your head." He smiled as he opened the cruiser door for me. "Let's clear up Katherine first, then we'll move on to Emily."

"Sounds like a plan to me," I said.

Maloney agreed.

The East Third Street address was only a few blocks away. Big M pulled in front in a space marked for residents. I assumed there were unused spaces because most people would still be at work. And, from what Maloney said, a lot of residents in this area don't have cars at their building. They keep them in a garage and only use them weekends, if that.

Our little army of three, with Big M in the lead, walked up to the front door and, as if in formation, all three of us turned in unison to check out the mailboxes. Peter McCarthy and Katherine O'Ryan's names were listed on the middle box. If that was an indication of which unit they lived in, I figured they were on the second floor. Maloney pushed the corresponding doorbell and we backed up to wait for a reply.

To our surprise, a voice came over the speaker. "Can I help you?"

"Yes, my name is Officer Thomas Maloney with the Boston Police Department. We need to ask you a few questions—would you please let us in."

Without hesitation, the buzzer sounded and the door lock clicked allowing us to enter. I could see Big M slowly move his right hand inside his jacket. I know he was wearing a shoulder holster because I saw it at the station and he didn't take it off when he put his jacket on. I stepped back, not knowing what to expect, and let Big M and Maloney go in front of me. The door to the second floor condo was open and a young man was standing part way out in the hallway waiting for us. Big M had his badge in his left hand so that he could immediately confirm his identity.

"I'm Officer Thomas Maloney from the Boston Police Department," Big M said then turned to introduce us. "This is Officer Rusty Maloney from the Provincetown Police Department and Casey Quinby, an investigator working with the P-town PD. Are you Peter McCarthy?"

I liked the way I'd been introduced.

The second floor occupant answered, "Yes, that's my name. What's this all about?"

"We've got some questions we'd like to ask you. May we come in?" Big M asked.

Peter went back inside and motioned us to follow. "Please have a seat," he said.

We did and Big M started the questions with, "Do you know a Katherine O'Ryan?"

"I do," said Peter.

"Does or did she live here?"

"She did until a week ago. We had some problems and she decided to move out. I'm not sure exactly where she is, but I think she's somewhere on Cape Cod. Anyway, I know she didn't go to work yesterday because her boss, Mr. Grossman, called to see if she was all right." I told him I hadn't seen her for a week. He must have assumed I had been out of town on a business trip because he didn't pursue the subject." Peter's face was expressionless. "Mr. Grossman didn't seem too concerned—said he closed the store last week and gave her a vacation. He kind of chuckled, then said maybe she decided to do some painting after all. He told me he's been saving two prime spots in The Gallery for her works. He asked if I'd give him a call as soon as I heard from her. I told him I would." Peter had withdrawn into another dimension. Finally he took a deep breath, raised his eyebrows and shook his head. "I didn't know what was happening and I still don't."

Big M wasn't sure where Peter came up with the Cape Cod connection. He decided to wait before asking. *First things first*, he thought.

Maloney took Katherine's picture out of the envelope he was carrying and handed it to Peter. "Do you recognize this person?" he asked.

"Of course I do, it's Katherine." Peter stood up and looked at each one of us then froze. "What's going on here?" His voice became cold and his demeanor firm. "Where's Katherine? Has something happened to her?"

"I'm afraid so," said Big M. "She was found murdered in P-town last Saturday."

Peter turned away from us. He appeared visibly shaken. He walked over to the kitchen counter, rested his hands on the edge and dropped his head. I could hear him sniffing in an effort to hold back tears.

I took out my pad of paper in anticipation of taking notes. I sensed that Big M was ready to ask some questions.

"When was the last time you saw her?" Big M asked Peter.

"It was last Monday morning before I left for work. I came home early and she wasn't here. I left her a note to tell her I was going to stay at a friend's house for a few days. I needed time away to think. When I came home Friday, she was gone. I don't know when she left. Like I said, the last time I saw or talked to her was Monday morning."

Big M stood up. "I'm going to need to know the name of your employer and where you were last week."

"You don't think I had anything to do with this, do you?" Peter was back on his feet staring at Big M.

"It's routine."

"I don't care what you call it. I told you I didn't have anything to do with it. Why would I hurt her? I loved her." Peter's voice was elevated.

"Well, if that's the case, then you can answer my questions. Now, I'll ask you again, I want to know where you were last week—from Monday, the last time you say you saw Katherine, until the time we knocked on your door." Big M meant business and Peter knew it.

I moved over to the kitchen table so I could write as Peter answered.

"Like I said, I last saw her Monday. I left at the usual time to go to work and I assumed Katherine did the same. We were having problems. She wanted to talk and I brushed her off. After I got to work, I felt bad. I couldn't concentrate, so I came home. She wasn't here. I had no reason to think she wasn't at work until I saw her backpack in the bedroom. She never leaves her backpack home. I don't know what made me do it, but I looked in it. I found an open pregnancy test in the bottom. The test strip showed positive. I was upset even more. Now, I really didn't want to talk, so I left her a note. I told her I was going to stay at a friend's house for a few days to think—that I didn't know if I was ready to be a father. And, I left."

Big M's expression didn't change. "So you basically walked out on her."

"I'm not proud of what I did, but I didn't kill her," Peter said in a low, whispery voice.

"Do you know if she got your note?" Maloney asked.

"She did because she wrote one back. That's how I knew she went to the Cape. She said she needed to be alone. The note said she had to go there to check something out—something about finding her real father. She found out last February that she was adopted and since then she's been trying to find her birth parents. It's been driving me crazy. That's all she thought about. I told her she should be satisfied knowing she was raised by two people who loved her, but that wasn't enough. She said something about finding leads that might help her identify her birth father." Peter sat down and stared at the floor. "The note—it's in my dresser drawer. I'll get it for you." He moved toward the bedroom. Maloney followed and stood in the doorway while Peter retrieved a crumpled-up piece of paper from the top drawer. He walked back to the living room and handed it to Big M. "Did you know she was pregnant?" Peter asked.

"Yes, they discovered that in the autopsy," Maloney said.

I made a side note to myself. I was curious as to why Peter didn't use Katherine's name—instead he referred to her as 'she' most of the time. Also, unless I missed it, he never asked how she died. I tried to follow his facial lingo and came up empty. I didn't detect much remorse or regret at having lost Katherine especially at the hands of another person and not by natural causes. This whole scenario bothered me.

Big M wasted no time in his next request of Peter. "We'll need a list of names that can confirm your whereabouts from last Monday until today. That includes the person or persons you stayed with last week, people at your place of employment, or anyone you associated with during that period of time."

"I told you that I had nothing to do with her death." Peter stated emphatically and slammed his hands down on the arms of his chair.

"Here's the reality of the situation." Big M was losing his patience with Peter. "We can do this here or we can take you down to the station and you can answer the same questions there." Big M gave Peter a minute to answer.

"This whole situation has taken me by surprise. I have nothing to hide. I'll answer your questions here." Peter took a deep breath and began to give Big M a list of people who could vouch for his whereabouts.

"We'll need telephone numbers and, if you have them, addresses," Maloney said.

Peter took out his cell phone and as Big M gave him a name, he looked up the phone number and read it off to me. I could feel Sam sitting on my shoulder like a guardian angel saying *be careful you're in the big City. It's not the same as the Cape.* Then on my other shoulder was my Sherlock image saying *this is what you've always wanted—go ahead—play the role of detective.*

"Casey, are you getting this all down." I snapped back into reality and read what I had written back to him.

"Why aren't you at work today?" Maloney asked Peter.

"Actually, I had some vacation time coming, so I took a few days off." Peter's stare penetrated the floor.

"What days did you take off, Mr. McCarthy?" Maloney glanced at me to make sure I caught what was being said. "And, what did you do those days, since you already told us you didn't come back to the condo until Friday?" Maloney's eyes were now fixed on Peter.

Nobody spoke.

Big M broke the silence. "Did I mention that Katherine was murdered on Friday?"

Peter tensed up. "I came back Friday and didn't leave until Saturday afternoon."

Maloney picked up where his father left off. "Do you have a name and number of somebody we can verify that with, Mr. McCarthy? Somebody who saw you come in Friday and not leave until Saturday? Maybe you had a visitor or talked to a neighbor?"

"You'll just have to take my word for it." The tension came back into his voice and markedly blocked any little sense of remorse he might have previously displayed.

That was the last straw for Big M. He stood and instructed Peter to do the same. "Mr. McCarthy, I believe you'll get a memory jolt if we finish this interview at the station."

"Are you arresting me?" Peter raised his voice several octaves and started to move closer to Big M.

"Stop right there. We can do this very peacefully or we can cuff you. It's your choice." Big M removed his cuffs from his belt.

Peter chose to ignore Big M's instructions and continued to move toward him.

Maloney stepped in and, in a fit of anger, Peter tried to push him away.

That's all Big M needed. He quickly restrained Peter, spun him around, pushed him against the wall and cuffed him. "Mr. Peter McCarthy, you're under arrest for assault on a police officer. You have the right to remain silent when questioned. Anything you say or do may be used against you in a court of law. You have the right to consult an attorney before speaking to the police and to have an attorney present during questioning now or in the future. If you cannot afford an attorney, one will be appointed for you before any questioning, if you wish. If you decide to answer any questions now, without an attorney present, you will still have the right to stop answering at any time until you talk to an attorney. Knowing and understanding your rights as I have explained them to you, are you willing to answer my questions without an attorney present?"

Peter didn't answer. He just stood like a statue—staring at the floor.

Maloney took hold of Peter's arm and escorted him down the stairs to the waiting cruiser. Big M and I followed.

I watched as Big M put Peter in the back seat. Maloney slid in beside him. I rode in the front. Big M radioed the station to let them know we were on the way in with a prisoner and that he needed an officer to meet him at the back door.

I didn't turn around, but Peter was now labeled a prisoner. I tried to imagine what was running through his mind, if anything at all. I had questions, but they would have to wait. I needed to gather my notes and thoughts together and reproduce them on 3x5's. I was glad Sam was going to be at the house tonight. I wanted, no I needed, to run all this by him.

CHAPTER FIFTY-SEVEN

It was almost five o'clock when we got back to the station and moved Peter into one of the interrogation rooms. Big M and Maloney went into the room and I stood outside watching through the one way glass. I flipped the wall mic on so I could hear their conversation. Because he was at the station on an assault charge, Peter remained handcuffed.

Big M folded his arms and leaned against the wall closest to the door. He had stepped back in the questioning process. Maloney was seated in a chair across from Peter. Maloney rested his arms on the table, joined his hands together and moved forward to face Peter. He sat slumped down in his chair staring at his shadow that appeared as a placemat in front of him. It was a sad scene.

Did he kill her in a fit of rage, I thought, *or perhaps in an act of desperation*. He didn't seem like a violent person, although he did confront Big M and push Maloney. Was it an automatic reflex because he felt cornered—threatened?

Maloney asked the same questions Big M had asked Peter back at the condo. And Peter, pretty much, gave the same answers. After almost a half-hour, Maloney palmed the edge of the table and pushed himself back in his chair. He stood up and walked over beside Peter. "I'm going to ask you one more time. Where did you go Friday after you left your condo?"

Peter was limp, his hands cradled in his lap.

"I'm going to give you five minutes to think about it. When I come back I'll expect an answer." Maloney nodded to his father and they both headed for the door. The two emerged from the interrogation room and joined me in front of the window.

"What do you think?" I asked.

"I think he'll have something to say when we go back in," said Big M. "So far, I'd say, it doesn't look good for him. Personally, I think he's hiding something. If you've been on the job as many years as I have, you have a sixth sense that comes into play when you're conducting an interrogation." Big M shrugged his shoulders. "It's not always right, but more times than not, it is."

Maloney walked over to the soda vending machine in the hallway behind us, dropped in six quarters and pushed the Aquafina water button. "I'm sure Peter could use some right about now."

The time limit was up so Big M and Maloney headed back into the room. Peter looked up. His eyes were red and troubled. Maloney opened the bottle of water and set it in front of him. Before they got started, Maloney switched the cuff position. Now he was cuffed in front. It was a little awkward, but Peter managed to take a few mouthfuls before setting it back on the table.

Big M resumed his position against the wall and Maloney sat on the edge of the table looking down at Peter. The positions taken by the two officers transmitted an atmosphere of authority and control.

"Peter, now that you've had time to think, I'll ask you again." Maloney didn't take his eyes off him. "Where did you go Friday after you left your condo?"

Peter inhaled like it was his last then very quietly said, "I drove to Cape Cod."

It's a good thing nobody could see the expression on my face. I didn't expect that answer at all.

Maloney pulled his chair out and sat down. "Did you talk to or meet up with Katherine?"

"No," said Peter. "I had no idea where she was. She never said. When I got to Hyannis, I called her, but there was no answer. My call went to voice mail and I left a message. I told her I was on the Cape and wanted to talk. I asked her to please call me back." He reached up with his hands and wiped the tears that had begun to roll down his cheeks. "I told her I was sorry. I told her that I loved her." He looked at Big M, then back to Maloney. "Please believe me, I didn't kill her."

"When did you head back to Southie?" Maloney asked.

"I decided to stay overnight."

"Did you get a motel room?"

"No, I slept in my car," said Peter. By this time he was visibly shaking.

Maloney looked toward his father. Big M nodded, then Maloney stood up and faced Peter. "This afternoon we brought you in for assault on a police officer. At this time, that charge remains open." All Maloney's academy training and his father's 'war' stories overtook his mind. Maloney hesitated then added, "Peter McCarthy, you're under arrest for the murder of Katherine O'Ryan."

Peter's eyes got big. A painful look of despair covered his face. He was petrified. Maloney went on to read him his Miranda rights for the murder offense and Big M buzzed the duty desk for two officers to take Peter to a holding cell.

I watched as Peter was led away. Big M and Maloney walked out behind him.

"Now the work begins," I said.

"We'll head back to the Cape tonight," said Maloney. "I'd rather you're not in the car when we transport him back to P-town. Tomorrow, I'll get one of the officers to ride back up with me to get McCarthy."

"I'll be perfectly fine if you want to take him back tonight."

"Actually, I'd like to talk to you about a few things on the case and we couldn't do that if he was with us. While I'm gone tomorrow maybe you can check some stuff out for me. I'll have to write an official report for Sgt. Costa, but in the mean time you can fill him in on what happened today." Maloney waited for my reply.

"I suppose you're right."

CHAPTER FIFTY-EIGHT

It was six-fifteen when we pulled out of the parking lot of the South Boston precinct. I was glad Maloney knew the back roads to get us to Route 3 South—otherwise we'd be stuck in traffic for I don't know how long. It had been a tiring day. I didn't want to admit it, but I was ready to get home.

My cell phone rang. I checked the caller ID. It was Marnie. "Hey, girl," I said in my best put-on up-beat voice. "What are you doing?"

"Cut the act. The question is—what are you doing? she asked. "I called your house and got Sam. He said he was waiting to hear from you. Well, I wasn't going to wait, so I called and guess what, you answered."

"I know, I know. I should have called earlier, but let me tell you, we haven't had five minutes to ourselves all day. I gave Sam a quick call, but I couldn't give him any details and right now I can't give you any either." I leaned back against the head rest. If I closed my eyes, I'd probably sleep until we got to Hyannis. "Hang tight, I'll give you a call when I get home. Maloney picked me up at the Cape Cod Mall this morning, so he'll have to drop me there to get my car. I should be home by eight o'clock. I'm going to call Sam and have him get a pizza." I could taste the spicy bite of the pepperoni as I spoke. "I'll call you then."

"Okay," said Marnie. "By the way, tell Maloney I said 'hi'."

I laughed. "I think he heard you. Cell phones in small spaces aren't very private."

He was smiling. "Tell her I said the same."

I slid my cell back into my purse. "So, what do you think?" I turned toward Maloney. "This case seems to be almost cut and dry, yet I have questions that have to be answered before I can delete the word almost. I'm going to work with Sam tonight to see if he comes up with the same concerns I have. I know you're going to be getting back to P-town late, but I'm sure you'll sit down and go over some things before you try to get some sleep. Take a pad of paper and jot down thoughts and questions that run through your mind. During the next few days, you'll probably scratch half of them out, add new ones and ponder the remaining ones. It's those remaining ones you'll need to work on and get answers to."

"Now I know why Sgt. Costa told me to listen to what you say because I was learning from the best." He smiled as he maneuvered his way into the Route 3 traffic.

"If you talk to your father tonight could you ask him if he can get a search warrant for Peter's condo? I think you'll be able to answer some questions or concerns after you do a thorough search. A lot of Katherine's stuff is still there. She may have squirrelled things in between clothing, in shoes, or in old pocketbooks. And, I have a feeling that Peter hasn't disturbed any of her things, so you may find something important. What you have to remember is that what might not seem important to you could be very important to the case. I'd bag anything you have the slightest reason to believe might be pertinent—better safe than sorry." I stopped talking and looked sideways out the passenger window. I imagined most of our fellow travelers were on their way home. There was no way I could make this trek day in and day out for an eight hour a day job. Between the travel time to and from the Cape it would make for an eleven hour day. Not my cup of tea.

"Casey, did you ever think of becoming a private investigator?" Maloney asked.

"I've toyed with the idea. It's not an easy field to get into," I said. "And, there's a lot of competition. I've been kind of lucky.

I've developed a great relationship with most of the Cape Police Departments. Working with them on cases is like the best of both worlds. I have a job at the Tribune where I get a weekly pay check and, on the other hand, I work with the PD's using my investigative skills to help solve cases." I shrugged. "Casey Quinby, Private Investigator—it sounds good—maybe someday."

"I'm sure you wouldn't have any trouble hanging that shingle." Maloney swerved to avoid a BMW that decided he could fit in-between the half car length between us and the Ford 150 in front of us. "What an asshole. I feel like flipping on the siren and pulling him over."

"Relax, big guy. It's not worth getting your blood pressure up. Besides, Dorothy, we're not in P-town anymore." I chuckled.

"Let's change the subject," said Maloney. "When this is all said and done, do you think Marnie would go to dinner with me if you and Sam came too?"

"I can't speak for her, but I think she might consider it. She's a good kid. She got caught up in a bad experience when she first moved down here last June. But, that's over now and I think she's ready to move on. I will say, though, take it slow."

"Thanks, sis." Maloney grinned.

When I saw the sign—Sagamore Bridge, five miles—I knew we were almost home.

CHAPTER FIFTY-NINE

The smell of pizza and Watson barking greeted me at the door. Give me pizza and beer and rub my back and I'll follow you anywhere. Luckily only one person knew that. And, boy, could Sam give a dynamite backrub. He knew just what to do and when to do it. The table was set and Sam was taking two beers from the refrigerator.

"I even made frosties," he said, "two for each of us. I figured you'd have more than one."

"I might even have more than two." I dropped my briefcase and purse on the floor next to the couch. Watson was waiting patiently for me to tussle with him. I got down on all fours and exchanged banter with the boy for a few minutes. "We can resume this later, I'm hungry. It's been quite a day," I said as I settled down in front of my place setting. I took a welcomed sip of beer. "You don't know how good this tastes."

Sam gave Watson some treats and joined me at the table. "So, how was the Boston scene?"

"I'll take Cape Cod any day. First of all, I couldn't stand the commute. There's no easy way to get in and out. Second, the atmosphere is different. Maybe it's because most of the people walking around are not from the City. I have to say that Southie is different from Boston proper. The majority of the residents in Southie either grew up there, or are related to somebody who did. Maloney's father, Big M, probably crawled around the streets when he was a baby. He knew where to go, when to go, how to go and who to talk to. I was impressed."

"I told you Boston was not a town to reckon with. It's a real fun place to visit and play tourist, but I wouldn't want to be a cop there." Sam stopped to take a bite of pizza.

"I agree." I took another piece of pizza. "We picked up the boyfriend and brought him to the station. He swears he didn't kill her." I looked at the expression on Sam's face. "You don't have to say it. I know they all say they didn't do it. You'll be happy to know I didn't play Castle. I stayed outside the interrogation room and just watched through the one-way glass. Maloney and his father asked the questions. Actually, Maloney did most of the asking." I got up from my chair and went over to the couch to retrieve my briefcase. "He did a good job. The boyfriend, Peter, admitted he drove to the Cape last Friday—the day Katherine was killed. He said he wasn't able to contact her, but left a message on her cell phone. He also said he stayed overnight—not at a motel, but rather in his car. There's nobody to confirm his story. And, of course, that's not good enough."

Sam stood up. "Do you want another beer?" he asked.

"And another frostie," I said. "Beer tastes so much better in a frosted mug."

"Where is he now?" Sam questioned.

"They're holding him in the South Boston precinct. Maloney is going to go back up tomorrow."

Sam put his beer down on the table. "You're not going back tomorrow, are you?"

"No, I'm going to organize my notes and make a set of 3x5's. I've got some questions. After supper, I'll run them by you."

"I think best when I'm eating. I know you're chomping at the bit to get this show on the road. So, go ahead and ask away."

"Here are my concerns. Peter talks about a backpack. She must have taken it with her because it wasn't in the apartment. That was one of my reasons for getting a search warrant. He says he called her cell phone. When we found her she had nothing, let alone a cell phone. He talked about a lot of paperwork—some was the research she'd been doing at the library. The only thing in the room she rented were some clothes—no paperwork at all. He also mentioned a copy of her real birth certificate. Apparently she had figured out her real mother's name, but had no idea who her birth father was until she saw this birth certificate. It listed a father's name. Most times they don't do that. They only list the mother's name, but she hit pay dirt. The space beside father was filled in. Peter said the name was Gregory Bradshaw."

"Stop right there," Sam said. "Does the name Gregory Bradshaw mean anything to you?

"It does sound somewhat familiar, but I don't know why." I gave Sam a puzzled look.

"Remember the murder in P-town a few years ago. The girl's name was Elaine Bradshaw. The Bradshaw family owns or did own a sizable amount of property on lower Cape. Since I'm on Upper Cape I didn't get too involved. I do remember some of the particulars though. There was something about the DNA. My buddy in Boston got swamped with a whole mess of DNA samples they wanted tested. It took a long time. I know Mike Sullivan wasn't real happy with the fact it was going to take longer than usual. People were blaming the DA's office when it wasn't his fault at all. I think it took almost a year to get all the results."

"Tomorrow morning I'll give Bernie a call and ask him to run Katherine's DNA against the state's DNA bank. The results could prove to be very interesting." My mind was working overtime. I was glad Sam was staying over. I'd probably run scenarios all night if he wasn't here.

There was a lull in the action. I got up to clear off the table. Watson walked to the door and looked back longingly at Sam. "Ok, buddy,we'll take a little walk around the house."

I smiled. My big man and little guy make me very happy.

"I've got an idea," I said when they came back in. "There are some brownies in the fridge. I'll make us some coffee and we can sit outside on the deck. I can't believe its October. It feels like the beginning of September. But then I've always said I like the fall on Cape Cod the best."

"Fine with me," said Sam. "I'll get the coffee—you get the goodies. Do you want French Vanilla?"

"Of course, what other kind is there?"

CHAPTER SIXTY

"Oh what a night ... late October and I feel the heat ...what a very special time for me ... as I remember what a night," I sang as I stumbled into the bathroom trying to forget it was morning.

"First of all, don't quit your day job. I think I've told you that before." Sam shook his head and laughed. "And second, your word memory is a little off."

"Well, at least they can't sue me for plagiarism, now can they?" I always tried to have an answer for Sam. Problem is, he usually has a reply. One of these days I'll come out on top.

Sam had been up for at least an hour. He was already shaved, showered, and dressed ready to take Watson for a walk before breakfast. I knew he had to be at the courthouse before nine o'clock, so I decided to just wash my face and brush my teeth so I could spend more time with him before he left. I planned on working from the house today. That is unless my boss had something pressing for me to do. And, I was quite sure he didn't. After Sam leaves I'll check in and let him know where I am on the story.

I had two bowls of Kashi granola and the carton of milk already on the table when my guys got back. The brew button was blinking, signaling the water was hot. "Ready for your coffee?"

"Just let me wash my hands and I'll be right there," he said.

Watson sat between us—first looking at me, then at Sam. "Okay, I know. You want your breakfast, too." I poured some dry Kibbles and Bits into his dish and added a little warm water. His tail wagged like it was going to fly off. I just love the little guy.

Sam walked over and gave me a hug. "You're a good mommy." He chuckled.

"As long as I don't have to change diapers, I'll do just fine." I kissed him, took his hand and led him to the table. "Your breakfast is served. I want you to note how healthy it is. Coffee is on the way." I did a little curtsey, like a maid might do, then got Sam his coffee.

"What are you planning on doing today?" he asked.

"I'll call the office and give Bubba a call, but I think I'm going to work from home."

"Why don't you try using the laptop I got you a couple months ago? I bet the only time it's been out of the box is when I showed it to you. I set up the wireless, so you have no excuse. And, as much as you don't want to admit it, I know you know how to use it."

"It's too early to stomp all over your face. Now, shut-up and eat." I shoved a spoonful of cereal into his mouth.

This Kashi stuff was pretty good. Not as good as my gooey jelly donuts, but good. "Maloney asked if I thought Marnie would go out to dinner with him if you and I went with them. I said I thought she would. I'll broach the subject to her as soon as this Katherine O'Ryan case settles down."

"Speaking of food—do you want to meet me for lunch in the Village today? The judge has been breaking around twelve o'clock every day. We can go to Finn's if you'd like." Sam sipped his coffee waiting for my response.

"Sure. Why don't I get there a little early and get a table. If there's going to be more than just you and me, let me know so I can plan accordingly."

"Do you want me to ask Marnie and Annie?"

"That would be nice. I haven't seen the girls for a couple of days. I'm not going to mention the Maloney and Marnie date though." I hesitated. "Okay, unless I hear from you I'll plan on just the two of us."

Sam looked at his watch. "I've got to get going." He took his last mouthful of coffee, leaned over and patted Watson, who was lying beside his chair, then stood up.

I walked him to the door and like a dutiful little 'wife', gave him a kiss and watched him mosey to his car. *Wife*, yikes, what was I thinking.

Before I got started on my gumshoe stuff, I decided to take a shower and get dressed. I know me and if I didn't do it now, I'd still be sitting in Joe Boxers five minutes before I had to leave to meet Sam. After all my fluff and puff stuff was done, I cleared off the kitchen table and converted it into my *desk for the day*. I emptied my briefcase, but before I got into the *sorting stuff out mood*, I made myself another cup of joe. Fresh from the push of a button—what more could I ask for. Mr. Keurig, you're my hero. I took out a stack of 3x5's, my notes and two new pens—one blue and one red.

I decided to call Sgt. Costa to fill him in on my findings and to see if Maloney had left for Boston yet.

Bubba answered the phone, "Provincetown Police Department, Sgt. Costa speaking. How may I help you?"

So formal, I thought. "Morning, Bubba. It's only me—wanted to touch base with you before I got started on my notes. Did Maloney already leave for Boston?" I asked.

"Hi Casey, I figured I'd hear from you this morning." Bubba sounded down. "To answer your question, yes he already left for Boston. He took Fortuna with him. They left real early. I think they were out of here by six o'clock. Maloney figured they'd miss most of the rush hour traffic if they got an early start." Bubba took a deep breath. "I wouldn't do that commute for love nor money. Anyway, he set it up with Fortuna last night. I like Maloney. He's a smart kid and a real asset to the Department."

"I totally agree," I said. "Did you get to talk much to him?"

"No, not much. He told me you were going to call and give me a run down and that he'd meet with me when he got back. He indicated that you had a productive day."

"That we did. I'm working from home today. I find I can put

things together much better when there's nobody around. So, if you need me, you know where to find me." I had the feeling Bubba wanted me to drive to P-town, but not today, that just wasn't going to happen. "I need to do some internet research. The only time I'm venturing out is to meet Sam for lunch over in the Village."

"Say 'hi' to him for me," said Bubba. "When this is all said and done, let's get together—you and Sam and me and the Mrs."

"That's a date," I replied. "I'll give you a call sometime this afternoon. Just one more thing—take it easy, we'll figure this mess out."

"I know we will. Talk to you later," Sgt. Costa said, then hung up the phone.

Since I wasn't going into the office, and I needed to look some stuff up on the internet, I had no choice but to take out my new laptop and put it to the test. I told Sam I couldn't use a laptop because I couldn't get used to the pad where you had to slide your fingers to move the cursor. The man with all the answers got me a detached keyboard and a novelty mouse that looked like newsprint. He knew my next objection would be hooking up all the wires to make the thing work, so he got everything wireless. Just a little plug in the side made everything work like a desktop. After a short adjustment period, I decided my new toy wasn't half bad.

I went to Google and typed in the name Emily Latham. As I expected, nothing came up, then I Googled Katherine O'Ryan. This time it came up with the usual sites like instantpeoplefinder.com, intelius.com and a whole bunch of other ones that provide nothing more than an address unless you pay. The last address listed on those particular sites was Peter's condo in South Boston. I figured I wasn't going to get much information from them anyway.

The next name I typed in the Google search box was Gregory Bradshaw. Bingo in the front row. Not only were there the useless sites I had found for Katherine giving me addresses, there were a mess of articles and his obituary. *So he was dead*, I thought.

I pulled up the first article. It was a story about the murder of

Elaine Bradshaw in 2008. It listed Gregory Bradshaw of Cambridge and P-town as her father. Every article was pretty much the same. The details were cut and dry. At this point, I was more interested in Gregory rather than Elaine, so I went back and opened his obituary. He was born in 1932 and died in 2009. He was seventy-seven years old when he died. That made him fifty-six years old when Katherine was born. He was old enough to be her grandfather. And, according to the obituary, he was married to his third wife. It notes that his first wife predeceased him in 1990 and his second in 1994. So, when Katherine was born he was, in fact, married. *This is starting to come together*, I thought. His third wife is listed as Carol Bradshaw. I wonder if I can find an address for her. The obit says he was living in Cambridge at the time of his death. Maybe she still lives there.

I decided to check one more thing. I had a name and a city, so I opened whitepages.com and plugged in Carol Bradshaw and Cambridge, Massachusetts. There it was staring me it the face—an address. Carol Bradshaw lived at 2465 Belmont Street, Cambridge, Massachusetts. It even listed her telephone number—617-842-9923.

I leaned back in my chair, folded my arms across my chest and just stared at my computer screen. Should I or shouldn't I. My intelligent shoulder buddy said to call Bubba with the information or maybe run it by Sam at lunchtime. My inquisitive shoulder buddy said to give her a call. I looked at the clock. It was only eleven-thirteen. I had plenty of time before I was to meet Sam. This was a clear-cut case of defiance on my part. I promised Sam I wouldn't go rogue again in my investigations, but what harm would it do to talk to Carol Bradshaw. Besides, for all I know, she might not even want to talk to me. I had hesitated making the call a little too long. Now, it was time to get going.

CHAPTER SIXTY-ONE

There wasn't any traffic so I made good time. Since I didn't get a call from Sam, I assumed Marnie and Annie weren't coming. I parked behind Finn's and went in the back door. There was a table for two open next to the fireplace so I took it. No sooner had I sat down and my cell phone rang. Sam's number popped up on the screen. "Hi," I said. "I'm at the restaurant. I got us a table by the fireplace."

"Do you think you can find a table for four? I forgot to call you. Marnie and Annie are coming with me."

"And how long did you know that?" I asked.

"I forgot to ask them, so it's my fault not theirs."

"You're in luck. It's not crowded. I'll tell Alyson I need a bigger table. Are you on your way over?"

"We'll be leaving in about five minutes."

"Okay, see you then."

I moved to a table for four and ordered a Diet Coke. I knew what I was having. The Tuesday special is a lobster salad sandwich on Portuguese sweet bread. It comes with one side, so I get french fries. My three cohorts arrived the same time my Diet Coke did. "Hi," I said as they approached the table.

"I'll be glad when this trial is over," said Marnie. "From the looks of it, I think the lawyers will give their closing arguments tomorrow morning."

"And, I can't imagine the jury will need much time to deliberate," Annie added.

Sam just nodded. He looked at my Diet Coke then at me. "Did you already order?"

"No, of course not. I was thirsty so I ordered my drink. But remember today is Tuesday and they have the lobster salad sandwich special. That's what I'm getting."

Sam smiled. "That's what you always get. Sometimes you're so predictable." He raised his eyebrows. "And sometimes I have no idea what direction you're heading in."

"Very funny," I said. "I'll put money on it that you'll order the same thing I did. And how do I know that? Because you always do. So who's predictable now?"

Annie looked at Marnie, then at Sam and me. "Isn't love wonderful." She tilted her head sideways and batted her eyelashes.

"Alyson's on her way over. Do you guys know what you want?" I asked.

We all ended up ordering the special.

"Have you thrown your laptop across the room yet?" Sam laughed. He looked at Annie and Marnie. "I left her this morning with her new laptop."

"As a matter of fact, we're now the best of friends. I'll leave it at that for now." I didn't want to expound on what I meant. I certainly didn't want to tell them what I was looking up. If I did that, I know Sam would figure out what I was up to. "I just want to tell you that I still rely on my 3x5's. Of course, I might get some of the information I write on them from the computer, but for organizational and storage purposes, my 3x5's can't be beat."

Alyson came over to ask us if we wanted anything else. Nobody did.

"It's time to get back to the rat race." Sam stood up and we all followed. "We might get out early today depending where the attorneys are at. If they end their questioning any time after three o'clock, I think they'll call for a recess until tomorrow morning. I'll give you a call later to let you know what's happening."

"I'll be home working." I turned toward the girls. "When your case is done and my P-town case is done, we need some quiet time."

"I agree," said Marnie. "Maybe we can go to New York City and do some Christmas shopping. I'll have to check, but there's one weekend before Christmas when the Governor eliminates the sales tax. It's been a tradition for years. I used to get up early and hit the streets for literally eight hours. My hands would hurt from carrying bags. Trouble was most of the stuff was for me instead of presents for my family and friends."

"Sounds like a plan to me," said Annie.

"A weekend in New York and shopping—you can't ask for anything more." I smiled.

Sam was thoroughly bored with the conversation.

I patted him on the butt and gave him a quick kiss on the cheek. "I'll see you later," I said as I tried to produce a seductive wink.

They went out the front door and I headed to the back parking lot.

All the way home I contemplated what I would say if I made the call to Carol Bradshaw. I had to be professional, yet demonstrate a touch of compassion—not much, just enough to gain her trust. The word trust might be a little strong, but ultimately that's what I needed to do.

My stuff was still where I left it on the kitchen table. I had no reason to believe it wouldn't be. I made myself a cup of coffee and sat down to ponder the situation. I don't like talking about a case with somebody I haven't met. That's why door knocking was more my style than phone talking. Sometimes I think you can read more into a person's personality when you watch their mannerisms and demeanor, especially when they're answering your questions. When you're communicating over a stretched out wire the person on the other end could be sweating like a pig or blink-lying or staggering because they're half in the bag. All these scenarios could indicate some kind of guilt or cover-up. Sam always says I had a vivid imagination. If he knew what I was thinking now, he'd probably handcuff me to the bed until I displayed some signs of normalcy.

Just a little phone call. What harm could that be? I thought.

It was just after three o'clock when I picked up the phone and dialed the telephone number I had gotten from whitepages.com for Carol Bradshaw of Cambridge. The phone rang four times before a woman's voice said, "Hello."

"Carol Bradshaw?" I asked.

"Yes, who's calling?"

"My name is Casey Quinby. I'm a reporter for the Cape Cod Tribune. At the present time I'm working with the Provincetown Police Department regarding a homicide." I hesitated to see if she was going to hang up or join in the conversation.

"I'm not quite sure why you're calling me," she said.

"Before we go any further, were you married to the late Gregory Bradshaw?" I waited.

"I was. He died in 2009." Carol's response was quick—almost too quick.

"Well, Mrs. Bradshaw, your late husband's name has come up in this investigation."

"Is this a current case?" she asked.

"It is," I answered.

"Then how's that possible. He's been dead for two years."

"We have a suspect, but I have questions." Then I dropped the bombshell. "I really don't want to talk about this over the phone. Do you think I could drive up to Boston and meet with you?"

The silence seemed to last an hour when it was really only a couple of minutes. "I suppose it would be okay." Her answer was short.

"Since I'm not at all familiar with Boston, where do you suggest we meet? I was hoping for a place that would be real easy for me to get to.

Maybe it was my imagination, but Carol Bradshaw's voice suddenly gave the impression that she wanted to meet with me. I thought this was strange, but what the heck I was the one who initiated the whole idea of a get-together and she was going to accommodate me. "Are you free tomorrow afternoon, say about two o'clock?" I figured I could get down to P-town, talk to Bubba and see Peter before I headed off Cape. My meeting with Carol shouldn't take any longer than an hour or an hour and a half so I should be able to make it home by five-thirty. Sam would never know I was gone. If I got something worthwhile from my interview, I'd discuss it with him. But, if nothing came of it, I'd keep it my little secret.

"Two o'clock will be fine. Why don't you come to my house. That way you don't have to negotiate parking. Do you have the address?"

"I do, but let me run it by you to make sure it's right—2465 Belmont Street." I recited the information I had obtained from whitepages.com.

"That's it," she said. "When you get close, give me a call and I'll make sure you're on track."

"Thanks. I'll see you then." I hung up and replayed in my mind what had just transpired. Later I'd make up a list of questions to ask Carol. If Sam was coming over after court, I had to make sure all tell-tale signs of the telephone conversation to Cambridge were out of sight. He definately wouldn't approve of my impending road trip.

I fastened the clip on my briefcase and moved it to the corner beside the couch. I figured I still had a little time before Sam showed up, so I decide to give Bubba a call. I wasn't going to tell him about the Cambridge road trip either. I just wanted to make sure it was okay for me to meet with him first thing in the morning and also to talk to Peter McCarthy.

The duty desk officer answered the phone, "Provincetown Police Department, Officer Longo speaking, how may I direct your call?"

"This is Casey Quinby, I'd like to talk to Sgt. Costa, please."

"Please hold."

"Casey, what going on? I thought you'd call before this," was his greeting.

"I've been researching and trying to put two and two together. If it's okay with you, I'd like to take a ride down to P-town early tomorrow morning to meet with you, then with Peter McCarthy." I waited for a response.

"I'll be here. Do you want Finnigan here too?" he asked.

"That might not be a bad idea. Is eight o'clock okay with you?"

"I'm looking forward to it. "We're at somewhat of a standstill. Maybe a bull session will jar something loose."

"Then eight o'clock it is. See you then." I said and hung up.

Just in time. No sooner had I hung up with Bubba, I heard Sam's car pull into the driveway. Watson beat me to the door. Before Sam could get out of his car, we were like church greeters waiting to welcome him home. He leaned over to give me a kiss then bent down and gave Watson a fatherly rub on his head.

"How goes it?" I asked as we walked toward the house. "Did the lawyers finish up?"

"They did, thank goodness. Tomorrow they're going to be giving closing arguments. I'll be glad when it's over and I can get back to real work. Fortunately, Bourne's been quiet—usually it is this time of year."

"I've got an idea. Let's get a drink and sit out on the deck. It's a great place to mull over and solve the problems of the world—or at least of Cape Cod." I headed for the refrigerator to get a beer for Sam and my bottle of white zin. This was the perfect way to end a trying day and begin a meaningful evening.

Sam changed into a pair of jeans and his new Tom Brady tee shirt then joined me on the deck. On his way out he grabbed a handful of treats and a bowl of fresh water for Watson. "If we're going to have a drink, so is my buddy."

We laughed as Watson started slurping as soon as Sam set his bowl down.

"We're raising a lush," I said.

Sam glanced in Watson's direction, "If it's only water, we're doing okay. It doesn't appear you slaved over a hot stove all afternoon, so I'm guessing you want to go somewhere for supper."

I nodded. “You are so observant.”

“Do you feel like Italian?” Sam asked. “We could go to DiParma’s. It’s Tuesday night, I think Ben’s working. I bumped into him the other day at Dunkins and he wondered why he hadn’t seen us for a while.”

“I’m fine with that. I could go for some Mussel Bianco and an Antipasto Misto. Will you split them with me?” I smiled. “And, of course, another glass of my famous pink stuff with a side of ice.”

“That’s okay, but I’d like to get an order of Baked Stuffed Manicotti, too. What we don’t eat tonight you can have tomorrow.”

I gave Sam a puzzling look.

“Tomorrow after Court, I’m going to head home. I haven’t been there for a while and I should check in to make sure everything is all right.”

Every once in a while we need to take a break in our relationship. I didn’t want to let him know this was a good time to take a breather, so I put on a little pouty face and said, “If you must.”

We finished our drinks and headed out for supper.

CHAPTER SIXTY-TWO

I was up before Sam. It was one of those nights. I just couldn't sleep. I actually felt guilty that I hadn't told him I was going to ride to Boston to meet with Carol Bradshaw. I know he wouldn't approve and we'd end up in an argument. It's better to leave some things unsaid. Besides, I plan on being home early enough so that I won't draw any unnecessary attention to my whereabouts.

"You out there Sherlock?" came Sam's voice from the bedroom.

"If it's not me, you're in trouble," I said. I walked over to the bedroom door and stuck my head in. Sam was so inviting—sprawled across half of the bed. I knew I had an early morning planned, so I quickly turned and headed back to the kitchen. Next thing I know, Sam is standing in the doorway leaning against the door jamb.

"Did I just get the old brush-off?" he asked.

"I think so." I laughed. "I've got to get going. I'm supposed to be in P-town somewhere around eight o'clock. I know it's only six, but by the time I shower and get dressed, it'll be time for me to go. I'm not even going to stop for breakfast. I'll grab a coffee and donut on the way."

"And this early meeting in P-town—does that mean you've got something else planned for the afternoon?"

I walked by him and into my closet. I didn't want to make eye contact. I knew if I did, Sam would read me like a book and hound me as to my afternoon plans. "Nothing in particular planned. I want to talk to Bubba and to Peter McCarthy. After that, I want to sort through my stuff to see if I'm missing something. I might call Bernie while I'm down Cape to see if he's found anything else of interest." I really hadn't lied. I was going to do all that. I just didn't offer the *rest of the story*.

"One more time—I'll remind you—one more time. You're a reporter and not a detective or a private investigator. Don't wander into spaces you're not supposed to be in. You have a tendency to pry open the wrong barrel and after the bats fly out you drop in. Do you get my drift?"

Not wanting to get into an in-depth discussion about the fact that I'm a big girl, I ignored his lecture and headed to the bathroom and a cool eye-opening shower.

Sam was still in the kitchen when I emerged from the bedroom—dressed and ready to go. It was six-forty-five. "I'm already running behind schedule, so I'm going to get going." I grabbed my briefcase, purse, and car keys and headed for the door. "I'll give you a call when I leave P-town." I gave him a kiss, patted Watson on the head and scurried out the door.

The traffic was light so I didn't anticipate arriving much after eight o'clock. I was about half way there when a light bulb went off in my head. I was sure it wasn't too early to call Bernie. He's up at the crack of dawn. That's the fisherman in him. I tried to scan my contacts while negotiating the road. Not a good idea. An unplanned slight turn of the wheel almost sent me into the soft shoulder. There was a turn-off around the next bend, so I pulled in to make my call.

The phone only rang twice when Bernie answered. "Morning, Casey," he said.

"Do you always check your caller ID before answering?" I asked.

"You bet I do. In my line of work, you never know who might crawl out of their casket and try to contact me."

"Really, Bernie, so early in the morning." I shook my head. "Back to business, I have a request. Could you run Katherine's DNA against the state's DNA bank?"

"Of course I can, but what's with that?"

"I have a hunch and if I'm right it will jump right up and hit you in the face."

“Now you’ve peaked my curiosity. I’ll get that underway as soon as our call is finished,” he said. “When I hear anything, one way or the other, I’ll give you a call.”

“I’ll be with Sgt. Costa and Officer Maloney until about eleven o’clock, then I’ll be on the road,” I said as I pulled back onto Route 6. “I’ll talk to you later.”

I knew there was a Dunkin’s a few miles down the road, so I decided to stop and get a dozen for the boys. Of course, I’d let them know the jelly in the corner was for me. I figured Bubba was waiting until I got there to put on a fresh pot of joe, but my French vanilla was calling. Besides, I’m not a one cup girl so Bubba’s coffee won’t go to waste.

CHAPTER SIXTY-THREE

I slowed down when I rode by cottage number three. I imagined Katherine in the window trying to cry out—trying to tell me who did this to her. I was determined to find out. There was virtually no traffic on Commercial Street. I'd never been down to P-town this early in the morning. It sure was quiet—peaceful. Mr. C was outside his store bringing in stacks of papers the delivery service had dropped off long before the sun came up. I gave a little toot and waved. He waved back, but I don't think he knew it was me. I continued down Commercial to Central then across Bradford to the Police Station on Shank Painter Road. I could have stayed on the highway and come in directly on Shank Painter, but I felt like taking the scenic route through town.

Bubba was waiting for me. His smile widened when he saw the orange and white box from Dunkin's. "Can I help you carry something," he asked.

I handled him my precious cargo and followed him to the break room. I had left my Dunkin's coffee in the car. I didn't want Sgt. Costa to think I didn't appreciate his fresh coffee offering.

As we walked past the duty desk, Sarge asked the Officer to radio Maloney to meet us in the break room. Sarge poured us a cup of coffee, I took my jelly donut, he took a chocolate frosted and we sat down to start the meeting.

I was just about to ask Sarge what he thought of Peter McCarthy when Maloney walked in.

"Morning Casey. Did you bring these tasty little morsels?" he asked. "Hey, Sarge we should have her come to a meeting at least once a week." He got himself a coffee, took a donut and sat down at the table.

"I was just going to ask Sarge his impression of Peter McCarthy."

"I talked to him. I don't know. He's a hard one to read. I have to admit he doesn't appear to be a killer. But then, that doesn't mean he isn't one. I've got somebody eyeballing him. I wouldn't want him to do anything stupid."

"You don't think he'd try to commit suicide, do you?" I asked.

"Like I said, there's something that doesn't fit—if you know what I mean."

"He didn't say one word during the trip from Boston. He sat very still in one spot and stared at the back of the seat."

"Did you get that search warrant?" I waited for Maloney to respond.

"Yes, and we searched his condo. I did what you said—looked in Katherine's drawers, under the bed, in the closet—any place where something could be concealed. It didn't appear there was anything she was trying to hide."

"Did you find her backpack or any paperwork about the adoption?" I sat back in the chair and folded my arms. "Did you find her cell phone?"

"Nothing," said Maloney.

"Was your father able to check out Peter's alibis for his whereabouts, all except Friday and Saturday when he claimed to be in his car on the Cape?" I looked at Maloney.

"He did and they all checked out." Maloney took another donut. "Anybody want some more coffee?"

We both handed him our cups. "I'll have a little cream, please."

"Sarge, you want yours black, right?"

"Yep," he said. "Thanks." Sarge looked up, " Maloney do you have any ideas?"

"Why isn't he asking for a lawyer?" Maloney asked.

"He hasn't lawyered-up?" I asked.

"He hasn't talked, so I guess he's feeling that right now he doesn't need one. I'm sure he'll change his mind real quick before he gets to court." Maloney shrugged his shoulders.

"Maybe we should change our line of thinking. What if he's telling the truth? He has nobody who can confirm his story, but on the other hand he has nobody who can say he's lying." I leaned forward on the table and folded my hands together. "It's a possibility."

"I think the key to solving this case rests with Katherine." Maloney and I looked at Sarge. "By that I mean, we have to find her backpack. I'm afraid it holds the information we're going to need to solve this homicide."

"Sarge, would you mind if I talked to Peter? You can watch from the one-way glass, but I'd like to be alone in the room with him. He knows I'm not a police officer, so maybe he'll open up more to me than he has to you guys." I waited for his approval. "It's worth a try."

"Okay, but we're going to be watching just in case he snaps and you need us."

"Fair enough," I said. "Let's go." I glanced at the wall clock over the duty desk as we walked to the back of the station. It was nine-thirty. Sarge and I headed to the interrogation room and Maloney went to the holding cell to get Peter. Sarge stayed outside and I went in.

Maloney escorted Peter into the interrogation room and sat him across the table from me, then joined Sarge behind the one way glass.

"Good morning, Peter," I said. I felt like I was talking to an expressionless, broken mannequin that had been thrown out in the dumpster. "My name is Casey Quinby. Do you remember meeting me last Monday at your condo in Boston?" I asked the question slowly and carefully, much like a first grade teacher would ask a shy new student. There was no reply. "I'm here to try to help you. But, I can't do anything unless you help me first." I knew the guys were watching and listening to what was going on between Peter and me. So far, everything was between me and me. "I understand you didn't ask for a lawyer, so if you don't want to answer any of my questions you don't have to." I wanted to kick him under the table to see if he was actually alive. "Look," I said, "since you apparently have nobody else to help you, why don't you give me a try? You've got nothing to lose and maybe something to gain." I decided the next move would have to be his. My babbling to a zombie was just taking up valuable time.

The room was quiet. "Okay," I said. "It's not in my nature to beg, so since you've decided to ignore my offer to help, I'll be on my way. I've got more important things to do than sit and babysit an insolent child." This was my last means of trying to break the ice and engage in a meaningful conversation with him. I stood up, picked up my paper and pen and slowly started for the door.

"Casey—is it okay if I call you Casey?" Peter said in a small distant voice.

"Of course it is," I answered.

"I'm scared. I don't know what to do, who to turn to or who to trust. Katherine was my best friend, along with my lover. I didn't kill her. Please believe me—please help me." There were tears coming from his eyes.

There was a box of tissues on the window sill of the one-way glass. I got them and gave them to him, then sat back down. "There's a lot of puzzle pieces missing from this case. I need you to help me find them." I looked him square in the eyes. "I believe you didn't kill Katherine." I imaged the reactions of Sarge and Maloney at my last statement. Sarge would have to trust me on this one and Maloney didn't know me enough to pass judgment. Sam would tell me I'm overstepping my authority—and I was, but I felt it had to be done. I had a gut feeling and I always followed my gut. "I know you've answered these questions before, but I'm going to ask some of them again. Okay?" I asked.

"I'll answer as best I can." Peter moved his cuffed hands to the top of the table and was leaning forward on his forearms.

"We need to find her backpack and her cell phone. From what I understand, you said she carries her life in her backpack."

"Everything she thought was important was in it. I told her she was going to hurt her back if she didn't leave some of the stuff at home, but she insisted she had strong shoulders. I was surprised to see it on the bed the day I came home from work early. If she knew I'd be home before her, she never would have left it unattended. I don't know what made me look inside, but I did. That's when I found the pregnancy test suggesting a positive result. I don't know how long ago she'd taken the test, but it was the first time I knew about it."

From a man of few words to a man of many, I thought. Apparently, I had gained his trust.

"The cell phone is going to be a key factor in her whereabouts when you tried to call her. It will also tell us where you made the call from. You told us you were in Hyannis. We'll be able to confirm that and get an exact time you made the call."

Peter nodded, but didn't add anything else.

"Does she have any friends she would have confided in?" I asked.

"I know she talked to her boss a lot. Whether or not she confessed any of her inner most secrets or just everyday stuff, I don't know. I think I told the officers that she worked for The Gallery on Newbury Street. Her boss's name was Mr. Grossman. He must wonder what's going on. He called me and asked if I knew where Katherine was. He thought she must have taken some time to go to the Cape to paint. He said he'd given her a week's vacation because he closed the store to go on a cruise. The problem was, the week was over and she didn't show up for work—didn't even call. That wasn't like her." Peter shook his head. "I didn't know anything about it. I could have taken time off myself and we could have gone to the Cape together and worked things out." Peter's head dropped down in front of him. "I blame myself for this whole thing, but I didn't kill her."

"Take a breather," I said. "I'll be right back." I got up and headed out the door to talk to Sgt. Costa and Maloney. "Is there anything else you want me to ask Peter at this time? I believe I've made a breakthrough. Now it's our job to find the two most important items that may either make or break this case."

"Maloney and Fortuna searched his condo inside and out. So, we know they aren't there." Sgt. Costa rubbed his chin, "Why don't you two go back over to Miss Daisy's and take another look around. I know Omar has kept that door locked since you were there last."

"If it's okay with you, I'm going to head back to Hyannis. There are a few things I want to research." I looked at Maloney. "Maybe you can take Fortuna with you. He's familiar with what's going on, so he'll know what to look for."

"Are you going to share the subject of your afternoon research project with us?" Sgt. Costa asked.

"It might be nothing. I'll let you know as soon as I have or haven't got anything new." This was when I was glad I wasn't employed by the Police Department. It gives me the freedom to pursue avenues on my own without having to get permission from a long chain of command. I was my own chain of command. "Let me go back in for a couple of minutes, then I'll be on my way."

Bubba reluctantly agreed to my plan. "Maloney, you wait here for Casey to finish, then both of you meet me back in my office. I'll send Fortuna to take Peter back to the holding cell."

Peter was sitting in the same position that I'd left him in ten minutes before. "I need you to do some heavy thinking. Something that might not seem significant to you might be important to us. I'll see that you get a pad of paper and something to write with before I leave. I'm going to head out to do some research on my own. I should be back sometime tomorrow, if not, Sunday for sure." I walked over and patted him on the back. "If there's something to find, we'll find it. Later," I said as I walked out the door to meet Maloney.

It was ten-forty-two according to the digital clock on Sgt. Costa's desk when Maloney and I walked in. Sgt. Costa was sitting behind his desk writing something on a yellow sticky note. He stopped and put it in his top drawer when he saw us.

I spoke up, "Sarge, I'm going to head out. Like I said, I've got some things I want to do. I told Peter I'd see him either tomorrow or Sunday morning. You know how to get hold of me if you need to." I put my notes and pen back into my briefcase and slipped my purse strap around my neck. "Oh, by the way, please give Peter some paper and something to write with. Thanks," I said and with a quick wave, headed to the front door.

"She runs rogue. If she didn't get things done, I'd immediately nip that in the bud. For some reason, she can turn over stones that we only trip over. She'd be such an asset as a teacher at the academy—maybe someday she'll consider it," said Sgt. Costa.

"I'm going to get Fortuna and head over to Miss Daisy's. I'll check in when we get back," said Maloney.

CHAPTER SIXTY-FOUR

Even though it was October and the sun wasn't nearly as strong as it is in July, the inside of my car was warm and stuffy. The police department parking lot didn't offer any shady spaces to park my baby. I tossed my briefcase and purse onto the passenger seat and slid into the driver's side ready to start my jaunt to Boston.

I was almost to the Hyannis line, when I noticed my gas gauge was resting on empty. I pulled off at exit six and filled up at the station beside Dunkin's. A large French vanilla iced coffee would be the perfect companion for the ride to Cambridge. I didn't feel like going in so I went around the back and ordered at the drive-through. Before I left the parking lot, I retrieved my GPS from the seat pocket behind me, fed Carol Bradshaw's address information to the mini-computer and sat back to listen to the obnoxious female voice tell me to take a right onto the ramp leading to Route 6. "Yeah, yeah," I said out loud mimicking her every word. I wanted a GPS that I could program the voice of a suave, sexy male telling me where to go. Hmmm—maybe Sam would get me one for Christmas. With my luck, he'd have his voice programed into it and only give me directions to two places—work and home. I guess I better be satisfied with the obnoxious female.

The traffic going off Cape was light—typical for this time of year and this time of day. The hour or so ride to Cambridge should give me enough time to figure out questions to ask Carol. To be truthful, I didn't know exactly what line of questioning I should take. I wonder if she knew about Katherine. Why would she. Carol wasn't in the picture when Katherine was born. Gregory was married to his first wife. What a bastard he was. This whole trip might prove to be a waste of time, but at least it would satisfy my curiosity. Sam says, in my case, it isn't curiosity—it's being plain nosey. He could be right, but I'd never admit it to him. Anyway, he'll never know, at least until this case is over, that I went to Cambridge by myself and didn't tell anybody I was going. If he finds out, there will be no ice cream for me tonight. Oh well, I probably should start a diet anyway.

The questions just wouldn't come. I decided to wing it. I was pretty good at that. Once I meet a person, I can usually tune in to their personality and mold my interview around it. A barrage of questions can sometimes turn a person off, then it becomes a guessing game as to what's real and what's made up. This ride to Boston is too long for me to listen to some rich bitch concoct a fairy tale just to try to pacify me.

I know Katherine was researching her birth family and I know she had a copy of her real birth certificate. I also know that Gregory Bradshaw's name was listed as her father on that certificate. I wonder if Carol found something in her dead husband's belongings that could link him to Katherine. After all, he was a lawyer. He must have had boxes of legal paperwork—either his own or clients. That got me to thinking. *If there was a father's name listed on the birth certificate, would he have to sign off on an adoption?* If so, then there could very well be legal papers in his, now Carol's, possession giving permission for the O'Ryans to adopt Katherine back in 1988.

If Gregory's only known child was deceased—and she was—that meant all his money, property, and investments went to his only next of kin—his wife. Carol had to be sitting real pretty. Then along came Katherine—his unknown illegitimate daughter. I wonder if Carol knew that Katherine was pregnant. That would really cause problems. Her cushy, comfortable, undemanding life style certainly would suffer an unsympathetic blow.

This meeting was going to be interesting. I wish I had come up with these scenarios before I left the Cape. I would have taken someone with me. It was too late to turn back now. Sam and the girls are probably still at the courthouse. When I get off the highway, I'll call Sam's cell and leave him a message to call me. I don't dare tell him where I am. I know I'm in for a long, heated lecture as it is, so why give him time to prepare.

The obnoxious female voice that kept me company from Hyannisport to Cambridge spoke up to let me know we'd be taking a right exit off the highway in three point five miles. I hope she knew what she was talking about because I had no idea where to go. GPS's are great as long as there hasn't been major construction or changes to one-way streets. I had only sworn five times when I finally made the turn onto Massachusetts Avenue. Obnoxious female told me we'd be entering Cambridge in three miles. From there, the directions to Carol's house were pretty easy.

Before I got to the Belmont Street address, I pulled over and made my call to Sam. Just as I suspected, his cell went directly to voice mail. "Hi, it's me—just wanted to check in. I'm following up on some leads. Give me a call when you get free." I put my cell back into my purse and continued to my destination.

2456 Belmont Street was a well-kept red brick house with black wooden shutters and a muted red front door. The neighborhood of beautifully maintained homes boasted of money. I had relied on my GPS to get me to her address, so I didn't do a call-ahead. I pulled my little green spider into the driveway and parked beside a beautiful red Mercedes. I took a deep breath, picked up my briefcase and purse and got out of the car. I was going to bring my briefcase in with me, but decided to put it in the trunk instead. I instinctively locked my car, walked around to the front door and rang the bell.

Since there was a peep hole in the door for identification purposes, I imagined Carol Bradshaw's eyeball leaning up against it trying to size me up. Nobody answered the door. I rang the bell again, and this time followed it up with a knock. The door opened.

I offered the woman standing in front of me my hand. "Hi," I said. "My name is Casey Quinby. Are you Carol Bradshaw?"

"I am," she said. "I thought you were going to call me when you were close."

“I was, but my GPS seemed to be working okay, so I decided to let her do her job.” She still hadn’t let me in. “Would it be okay if I come in?”

“Of course, please come in,” she said and stepped aside. “I’m sorry. I guess I’m just so confused that I’m not thinking straight. Have a seat.”

I looked at her, trying to determine if she was genuine or a bit-actress looking for a job. At this point, I was going to tread on eggshells until I felt certain one way or the other.

“As I told you over the phone, I’m helping the Provincetown PD investigate a homicide. A young girl by the name of Katherine O’Ryan was murdered. Whoever it was that murdered her striped her of all identification and left her in a cottage that was closed up for the winter. We have reason to believe your deceased husband was her birth father because his name appears on her original birth certificate.” I finished my intro and stopped talking.

Carol Bradshaw sat on the edge of her chair. She appeared nervous—looking around and biting the inside of her cheek. “I’m sure there is more than one Gregory Bradshaw,” she said.

“You’re undoubtedly correct. There is probably more than one.” I changed the words, but repeated what she had just said. “But, for some reason she believed the Gregory Bradshaw that had ties to Cape Cod was the one she was looking for.”

“His ties to the Cape ended a long time ago. We hardly ever ventured over the bridge. We vacationed mostly in the Caribbean, in Europe, or took cruises.”

“If I’m correct—and I think I am—his daughter, Elaine, lived in Provincetown. I know you can confirm that for me.” I looked at Carol, but didn’t get a response. “According to Katherine’s boyfriend, Peter, she’s been doing a lot of research to find her birth family. My theory is that she read the same obituary I did—the one that listed Elaine Bradshaw as Gregory Bradshaw’s daughter. I’m positive you know the one I’m talking about.” I was sure Carol was ready to escort me to the door, but she didn’t. “Usually in a murder, they take DNA. When I get back to the Cape I'm going to ask the ME on the lower Cape if he'd check it out for me. If Elaine Bradshaw's DNA and Katherine O'Ryan's DNA match, then they were half-sisters."

"You've taken me by surprise." Carol shrugged her shoulders and rolled her neck. "I'm going to put a pot of coffee on. Will you have a cup with me?" she asked.

I studied Carol—will the real Carol Bradshaw please stand up. "I'd like that," I said. I looked around the living room. It was beautiful. The ceilings must have been fourteen feet tall with bold crown molding framing the entire room. There was a fireplace painted in the same off-white tone as the trim and the wainscoting. The walls above the wainscoting were a couple of shades lighter than navy and were home to a half dozen gold colored sconces. She didn't have heavy drapes, instead white custom made sheers, pulled back with blue rope, hung long enough to puddle on the floor. The furniture looked like it came from Ethan Allen.

I was starting to admire the accent pieces, when Carol came back in carrying a tray with two cups of coffee, cream, sugar, and a plate of cookies. She handed me a napkin and offered the plate of cookies. "I baked these this morning. They're an old family recipe that got handed down from my great-grandmother. I hope you like chocolate."

I took a cookie and set it on the napkin. The coffee is what I really wanted.

"Gregory's office is upstairs. One whole side of it is packed with boxes. I never opened them because I never had any reason to. He was meticulous though, so I think every one of them is labeled as to its contents. They all came from his office, so some of them probably have to do with clients. I'm sure the others are files regarding his personal affairs. He kept everything. He was so detail oriented. It drove me crazy."

I had made up my mind. I was now talking to the actress. I had to be careful not to believe everything she said. Of course, if there were boxes of personal papers, maybe I could find something that might help in the case. I suppose it was worth a try. That was, of course, if she was going to let me look through them. “The coffee’s great,” I said.

She could see I had already drunk most of mine. “Let me have your cup and I’ll get you more. I made a full pot.”

I was getting short of words so I figured the best thing to do was to just come out and ask her about the boxes of papers in the upstairs office. When she came back from the kitchen with my coffee, I asked, “Do you think I could take a look at some of those boxes? If they’re all marked, then it shouldn’t take long. Besides, you’ve already been very helpful to me and I’ve got to get back on the road before the City of Boston realizes it’s five o’clock.” She hadn’t told me anything I didn’t already know. What I did get from our talk was that she was hiding something. I would have to figure that out on my own, because I knew she had no intention of telling me what it was.

“Why don’t you bring your coffee upstairs and we’ll check out those boxes together.”

She was up off her chair and part way to the stairs, when I said, “Okay.” I followed her past what I presumed was a guest bedroom, then past what I was sure was the master bedroom. It was huge. I slowed as I walked by. The bed was to the right and to the left was a sitting area bigger than my whole living room. It was bright and tastefully done in shades of rose and green. She must have had it redone after Gregory died. I can’t imagine a man being comfortable cradled in that much pink.

The office was at the end of the hallway. The door was closed—actually, it was locked. “Wait here. I’ll get the key. It won’t take me but a minute—it’s in my nightstand.”

I watched her walk back to the pink bedroom. I took a sip of my coffee. I hadn’t checked my watch, but it seemed like five minutes had passed before she emerged and rejoined me at the end of the hall.

"The key wasn't where I thought I put it," she said. "But, I checked a couple other places and, *voila*, I found it." She held it up with her finger and thumb and shook it gently back and forth.

This was starting to feel bizarre. Now I was glad I had called Sam and left him a message to call me. Problem is, I didn't tell him where I was and what I was doing.

Carol unlocked the door and we both went in. She wasn't kidding when she said half the room was filled with boxes. That was probably why she kept the door locked. It certainly didn't reflect the ambiance of the rest of the house. She set her coffee down on the desk. I moved over beside her and did the same, then we walked over to the boxes and began reading the notations Gregory had made on each one of them. The first group we looked at were definitely client files. Carol walked back to the desk to retrieve her coffee. I continued to study the boxes.

Almost half way through, I came to a box labeled personal property holdings and the one on top of it read Elaine's legal dealings. I turned to Carol. "Do you think I could take a look in these two?" I pointed to the two boxes directly in front of me.

"Why don't we take them over to the desk. It would be easier than bending down trying to flip through folders. Also, if you needed to spread the contents of one of them out, the desk would be a more practical place to do it."

I agreed and we proceeded to move the two boxes. She directed me to sit behind the desk in Gregory's chair and she pulled one up from the corner of the room. I took a few folders from the box marked Elaine's legal dealings and laid them on the desk.

Carol sat and watched. I was just starting to read a copy of the Provincetown property transfer of ownership paperwork, when Carol asked if I wanted another cup of coffee.

"Thanks, but I'll finish what I have," I said and reached for my cup. I was on the second or third folder when I finished my coffee. I detected a bitter taste, but didn't think much of it.

I looked at Carol. She was watching my every move. I went to stand up, but couldn't. I quickly sat back down and tried to take a deep breath. I was afraid of falling forward onto the desk, so I tried to brace myself.

CHAPTER SIXTY-FIVE

"Casey, I'm returning your call. Where are you?" Sam waited a few seconds." If you can hear me, I suggest you answer your cell." Sam shook his head and returned his cell phone to its carrier just as Marnie was coming out of the courtroom. "Marnie, have you talked with Casey today?" he asked.

"I was about to ask you the same question," she said. "I was just going to give her a call."

"Don't bother," said Sam. "She left me a voice mail telling me to call her when I was free. Well, I'm free and apparently Casey isn't, so I left her the same message she left me."

"What was she up to today?"

"She told me she was going to P-town to talk to Sgt. Costa and Officer Maloney. She was also going to try to get ahold of Bernie Montalvo, the lower Cape ME. She wanted to ask him something about DNA." Sam raised his eyebrows, shook his head and looked off into the distance. "She scares me when she starts her *what if* thinking. When you're working from facts, things might take a little longer, but the path you take to find the truth is a lot safer. And, if I find out she's gone someplace unaccompanied, I'm going to personally take her to work every morning and handcuff her to her desk—then pick her up and handcuff her to the bed."

Marnie crossed her arms and leaned her face forward. "Being a little kinky, aren't we?"

"You know what I mean," said Sam. "The girl is stubborn and doesn't listen to reason. Tell me you don't agree."

"You're right, but you aren't going to change her, so don't even try." Marnie turned to watch the people leaving the courtroom. "When you hear from her, please tell her to give me a call."

"I will." Sam smiled. "Thanks for listening to my rambling. I know I probably sound like an overbearing father." He gave Marnie a wave and headed down the stairs and out the door.

Before he pulled out of the parking lot he decided to give Sgt. Costa a call. The P-town duty officer answered and Sam asked for the Sargent. "Hi, Sgt. Costa, this is Detective Sam Summers with the Bourne PD."

"Sam, hi, how are doing?" he asked. "I haven't talked to you in eons. You caught me on my way out the door. I'm going to put you on hold for a second so I can get back to my office."

"Okay," Sgt. Costa said. "What can I do for you?"

"I'm calling about Casey. She told me she was heading down to see you and Officer Maloney this morning." Sam paused then continued, "I've been trying to reach her, but she's not answering her cell. Could you tell me what time she left P-town?"

"Let me see. She left about eleven o'clock this morning. We did what we had to do and went over a bunch of questions we had about the murder, then she left. She said she had some things she wanted to check out and that she'd give me a call tomorrow." Sgt. Costa stopped abruptly and asked, "She's okay isn't she?"

"I'm sure she is. And, I know she'd be furious if she found out I called you, so can we keep this between us?" Sam waited.

"No problem. I'm on my way home, but don't hesitate to call if you need me."

"Thanks, I won't." Sam disconnected the call and started his car. He decided to use Watson as an excuse and headed toward Hyannisport. If she wasn't home, he would take care of Watson then leave. He'd done that many times, so if she came home while he was there it wouldn't be any big deal. And, if she came home after he left, she'd just thank him for looking in on the little guy. She didn't have to know he was keeping tabs on her, even though the girl did need babysitting.

Casey's car wasn't in the yard when he pulled in. He didn't expect it to be. He went about his chores, turned on the outside light and headed home to Bourne.

CHAPTER SIXTY-SIX

Oh my God, my head hurts, I thought. *What happened to me? Where the hell am I?* It was really dark. I couldn't see anything. And, it was really quiet. I couldn't hear anything. I felt around my immediate area. It seemed I was sitting on some type of wood floor. I ran my fingernails on the top of the wood—first one way and then the other. My fingernails would hesitate about every three inches or so when I went one way and didn't hesitate at all when I went the other way. It was hardwood flooring. I slowly and carefully moved my hands out to my sides. My right hand stopped, but my left hand kept going. I ran my right hand up the wall from the point where it had stopped to as far as I could reach without standing up. It was a door. I moved my hand from side to side trying to find a doorknob. There it was—on the right side. I tried to slowly turn the knob, but it wouldn't move. It was locked. I reached out with my left hand. The tickling movement of a piece of cloth scared me. I was in a closet. I was locked in a closet.

I sat real still trying to hear movement on the other side of the door. All of a sudden there was a click and a thin strip of light appeared under the door. Somebody was in the room. I was sure it was Carol. I decided not to call out. There was no doubt in my mind she drugged me and put me in here. I know if I begged her to release me it wouldn't happen. Besides, it's not in my nature to beg. She had played the actress and I sort of fell for it. That's what got me into this predicament in the first place. Now it's my turn to audition for the part.

If she opens the door I can make believe I'm still knocked-out and when she lets her guard down I can charge her. Since I hadn't tried to stand up, I wasn't sure if whatever she had put in my coffee had zapped me of my strength. I didn't have the luxury of finding out. Slow, quiet footsteps were getting closer. Plan B was to play a limp biscuit. For once I'm not going to be impulsive. I'll let her play her little game. Once I get my bearings, I'll figure out my next move.

The footsteps stopped. Outside the door there were two dark spots interrupting the strip of light. Carol was listening on the other side. I waited quietly—my heart was pounding. I heard something hit the doorknob. It must have been the back of her ring. Again, there was nothing. I realized the performance of my lifetime was about to begin. I was sure one hand was getting ready to twist the knob immediately after the other hand turned the key. I was right.

I resumed the position I was in when I came too. I wanted to look up and see her reaction. I wanted to look into her eyes. And, most of all, I wanted to know if she had a gun.

The door opened slowly. A cool draft penetrated my space. I stayed perfectly still, only moving my eyes trying to determine her exact location. She didn't say a word. Then, without warning she reversed her steps and left—locking the door behind her. I wanted to yell, *Yeah, I'm still here bitch,* but knew if I did that I'd probably never see the light of day again.

My idea to play possum bought me some time. I wish I knew what she had in store for me. I was quite certain she wouldn't keep me here too long. After all, I'm sure Sam will wonder where I am. If only I had confided in him. I promised him I wouldn't go off on my own again—and I did. I didn't tell the girls or Bubba or Maloney. And then there's Watson, I wish he could pick up the phone, call Sam and tell him that he was hungry because I didn't come home to feed him.

I don't know how much time passed until I heard familiar footsteps heading to my girl cave. This time they were louder. She was using them as a wake-up call. There was no hesitation when she got to the door. Within seconds, she inserted the key and opened the door as wide as it would go.

She backed up. "Casey, I know you can hear me," she said as she gave me a sharp jab with the toe of her shoe. "I'm going to give you some instructions and you will follow them."

I didn't like the tone of her voice. It was as if she was a stranger, somebody I had never talked to before, staring down at me.

"I hear you," I said. "What do you think you're doing?" I asked without looking up.

"You're not in a position to ask any questions. In fact, you're not in a position to do anything except what you're told to do. If I ask you a question, I expect you to answer. Do you understand?"

I didn't say a word.

She kicked me again. "Do you understand?"

I nodded. "Yes," I said.

"Now, I want you to stand up very slowly. Don't make any quick moves." Her tone was stern and direct. "I have a gun—it's pointed at you—and I'm not afraid to use it."

My worst fear had come true. Hand-to-hand I might have a chance, but I can't compete with the barrel of a gun. I slowly tried to stand up. My bad leg was cramped and hurting, but I wasn't about to let Carol know that. Once on my feet, I looked into the room where she was standing. She displayed no emotion. She stood in the center of the room with her arms extended forward clenching the butt of a gun that was aimed right at me. The worst part was that it appeared she knew how to use it.

"We're going to head down to the kitchen. Any attempt to defy my commands could prove fatal." She pointed the gun in the direction of the hallway door. "Now move it," she said.

I hadn't seen a clock yet, but it was dark out so whatever she gave me put me out for hours. *There must be a clock in the kitchen,* I thought. *I need to know the time.* The lighting in the hallway, down the stairs and through the foyer was dim—eerie. The kitchen door was closed, but there was a bright light crawling out under it.

Carol instructed me to open the door, go in, then close it.

I did. One of the kitchen chairs was pulled out and a bottle of water was on the table in front of it.

She instructed me to sit down, then moved around to the other side of the table. Carol stayed standing and never changed her target. The gun's barrel was still aimed at the center of my chest. "I got you a water. You must be thirsty," she said.

"I'm okay, thank you," I said.

"I think you're thirsty and you should take a drink." She waved the gun in the direction of the water. "Drink," she said.

She had clearly spiked my coffee earlier and I was sure she had done the same thing to the water. I took a deep breath, unscrewed the cap from the bottle and started to drink. I expected to lose consciousness within minutes, but I didn't. I couldn't figure out what Carol was up to and it bothered me. She looked at her purse that was hanging on the chair in front of her. In a split second she had transferred the gun to one hand, slipped her purse over her shoulder then resumed the two handed grip.

"We need to take a walk outside to your car." She gestured toward the back door.

I wavered a bit, but knew she meant business, so I did what I was told. We went outside, but I didn't see my car in the driveway where I had parked it earlier in the day.

"The door on the side of the garage is unlocked. Open it and go inside. Your car is in there."

I was starting to feel a little light-headed. I had to keep myself from passing out.

Carol freed one of her hands, dug into her jeans pocket and pulled out a set of car keys. They were mine. She tossed them to me. "Open the trunk," she said.

I froze. "Why are you doing this?" I asked.

"No questions—remember." She waved the gun at me. "Get in," she said.

I had no choice but to do what she said. I climbed into the trunk and curled up in a fetal position. My body went limp. I felt like a rag doll. *It was the water*, I thought. I could hear noises and Carol's voice, but I couldn't move.

Carol reached into her purse and took out a pair of handcuffs. She set the gun down on a shelf behind her. I watched as she unlocked them. She reached in, grabbed my right wrist and slapped the cuff on, then repeated the process on my left one. Beside the gun was a coiled up length of rope. She proceeded to tie my ankles together. I could feel the burn of the rope as she pulled it as tight as she could.

Carol left the trunk area. I tried to muster up some strength, but it wasn't going to happen. I heard her open the driver's side door and drag something out onto the floor. Before I knew it, she was stuffing things in beside me.

"You should have minded your own business. This girl, Katherine or Emily, whoever you know her as, was trying to invade my world. I paid my dues. I lived with that old bastard for a lot of years. When his daughter, Elaine, died—I didn't care. There was no love lost between us. She figured I was a gold digger. Maybe she was right—I did and still do like the good life. Before Gregory died, he told me of his affair. He said that the affair produced a child—a girl, but that she had been adopted by her mother's family, so there was nothing to worry about. He had no idea who she was or where she was. I never thought twice about it until I got a call from a girl claiming to be Gregory's daughter. I befriended the little bitch and led her to believe I would help her. She had already done a lot of research and was going to check one more thing that would definitely prove her birth father was my late husband." Carol took a deep breath, then leaned into the trunk and pushed my shoulder to see if I was still listening. "I called her last Thursday night and we made arrangements to meet last Friday morning in Provincetown. I picked her up and we took a walk on the dunes. She was clinging to a beat-up teddy bear—like a child clungs to a security blanket. She told me of her plan to contact the Medical Examiner to have her DNA checked against Elaine Bradshaw's DNA. I knew what the result would be and I couldn't let that happen."

I could see Carol glaring at me. It was hard, but without talking, I had to let her know I was listening. I moaned and moved my legs ever so slightly, so as not to cause her alarm.

She continued, "A few years ago, I thought I was pregnant. It wasn't Gregory's baby. A friend of mine who worked at a lab that was testing a new abortion drug got me a sample. I was supposed to take it for two weeks. After the second day, I lost the baby so I stopped. I hid the rest of the drug until last Friday when I saw the perfect opportunity to use it again—this time on Katherine. I only meant to abort her pregnancy, not to kill her. We made it to the car before she started to get logy. I wasn't about to bring her back to P-town. I remembered seeing a whole lot of small closed-up cottages along the shore road. I pulled in beside one of them to check it out. They were locked, but a quick swipe with a credit card eliminated that problem. I managed to get her inside. She wasn't breathing. I dragged her over to the space between the bed and the window. She looked so innocent. For a moment, I actually felt bad. She had dropped the teddy bear outside the car when she got out. I saw it there, so I went back to the car, got it and wrapped Katherine's arms around it. She looked so peaceful. I did what I had to do."

Carol stopped talking. A reflection of a light breezed by the open door that we had used to come into the garage. She slowly walked over to it, looked out, then closed it. It must have been a renegade beam from a passing car.

"I gave you the same drug and enough of it to shut you up—just like Katherine," she said just before she slammed down the truck.

CHAPTER SIXTY-SEVEN

Sam watched the six o'clock news while he finished eating the Big Mac, large fries and chocolate shake he'd picked up on the way home. He didn't feel comfortable not knowing where Casey was or what she was up to. He tried calling her land line. When the answering machine clicked on, he left a message for her to call him as soon as she got home. He waited another ten minutes, then called her cell phone. It went directly to voice mail. *That meant she hadn't picked up her calls for a while,* he thought.

He tried to busy himself to make the time go by, but nothing kept his mind off Casey. It was eight o'clock. Wheel of Fortune had just finished. He switched from channel four to ESPN. The announcers were running down the highlights of last week's football games and adding their comments about the upcoming Sunday afternoon ones. The Pats and Broncos were the Sunday night game. As much as he wanted to, he couldn't concentrate on what they were saying. He picked up his cell and called Marnie. "Hi it's me," Sam said.

"What's up?"

"Have you talked to Casey lately—by lately, I mean within the last four or five hours?"

"No. I thought she was going to stay home tonight and work on the P-town case. I know she was looking up stuff on her computer, but we really hadn't talked a lot about it. She's been so busy that we haven't had the time." Marnie waited for Sam to respond.

"I know she went to P-town this morning, but she left there before noon," he said.

"Have you talked to Officer Maloney?" asked Marnie.

"No—only to Sgt. Costa and he didn't have a clue where she was headed." Sam took a deep breath. "I'm going to drive down to Hyannisport. I'll plan on staying the night. If you hear from her, will you give me a call right away."

"I will and vise-versa," Marnie said.

Nothing else was said and both phones went dead.

When Sam pulled down Casey's driveway, he noticed the porch light was still on. He knew she wasn't home. She may have come home and left, but at that moment she wasn't there. Her porch light was always a dead giveaway as to whether or not she was home. The door was still locked. That was a good sign. And, Watson was waiting patiently inside—tail wagging and head bobbing with excitement at Sam's arrival.

He flipped on the kitchen light. "Hey, boy, where's your mamma?" he asked. "I sure wish you could talk." He patted Watson on the head, got him some fresh water and gave him a few extra treats. Sam walked over to the kitchen table. Casey's laptop was still open and her notes were scattered in piles around it. Whatever she was researching peaked her curiosity enough for her to leave what she was doing in search of concrete proof to substantiate what she found.

Sam powered up her laptop. It opened to mapquest.com showing detailed directions from the Cape to 2465 Belmont Street in Cambridge. Sam planted his elbows on the table, folded his hands as if in prayer and rested his chin on top of them. He stared at the screen. It wasn't telling him anything. He sat back in his chair and took a deep breath. *I have to think like Casey,* he thought. *Cambridge—why Cambridge?*

A copy of a newspaper clipping that was laying on top of the pile to the left of the laptop caught his eye. It was an obituary. He reached over and picked it up. It wasn't current, it was dated 2009. It was for a Gregory Bradshaw. Bradshaw—as in Elaine Bradshaw? It listed his residence at the time of his death as Cambridge. *She didn't—she wouldn't.*

The digital clock on the microwave displayed nine-forty-one in a bright neon orange. Sam took out his cell, checked his contacts for Jonny Colombo's home number and hit the green call button. Jonny answered on the second ring. "Sam, what's up?" he asked. "I saw your name on the ID."

"I've got a favor to ask you. There's a house in Cambridge I need you to check out," Sam said rather quickly.

"Sure, I'll do it first thing in the morning. What's the address?"

"No, Jonny, I need you to do it tonight. Do you think you can do this for me?" Sam sounded worried.

"Yeah, sure, but what's going on?" Jonny paused to wait for Sam's answer.

"It's a long story, but I have a feeling that a friend of mine is in trouble. Actually, it's my girlfriend, Casey Quinby. She's working on that Jane Doe murder case with the Provincetown Police Department and I think she found a lead and went to investigate it by herself." Sam stopped to take a breath. "That's it in a nutshell," he said. "I've been trying to get ahold of her. She doesn't answer her cell and she's not home. I'm at her house now." Sam went to the kitchen table and sat down in front of Casey's laptop.

"What makes you think she's in Cambridge?"

"When I got here her laptop was on the kitchen table, so I decided to check the last site she was viewing. She never got out of it, so when I moved the mouse her laptop opened to mapquest.com. She had gotten directions from her house in Hyannisport to the Cambridge address."

"Okay, give me the address," Jonny said as he fumbled to find a piece of paper and a pen. "I'm going to put you on speaker, so I can write the information down." He pushed the speaker phone button and set his phone down on the counter. "Go ahead," he said.

"It's 2465 Belmont Street. The resident is listed as a Carol Bradshaw. Casey drove her own car up. She has a 2003 light green Mazda Spider convertible. She's not at all familiar with Boston, so I know she wouldn't drive around the streets during the day let alone at night."

"If I remember correctly, that's a pretty ritzy section of town. Since I didn't take a cruiser home, I'm going to give the Cambridge PD a call and have them send an officer to meet me. It would be just my luck some neighbor would see a strange car combing the neighborhood and call it in. I've got a buddy that works nights. I'll give him a call. What was the name of the resident?" Jonny asked.

"Carol Bradshaw," Sam said. "She's the rich widow of Gregory Bradshaw. It was his daughter who was murdered in P-town a few years ago. That's not the case, but it's related. I'll fill you in later."

"Let me get going and I'll get back to you as soon as I check it out. Don't worry, if she's there we'll find her." Jonny hung up.

Sam got up and went to the fridge for a beer, then to the pantry for a bag of chips. He sat back down at the kitchen table and began to read Casey's notes. From her first conversation with Peter, she knew there was a father's name listed on Katherine's real birth certificate. Casey knew it was Gregory Bradshaw. She knew Katherine had done extensive research on the computer and had come up with enough information to undoubtedly link her to Gregory's dead daughter, Elaine. No matter how many times he read Casey's notes, the facts weren't going to change. Casey drove to Cambridge armed with enough information to implicate Carol Bradshaw in Katherine's death.

Sam moved to the couch and clicked on the television. CSI was flashing a snippet of next week's show. The eleven o'clock news on NBC was about to start. Watson jumped up and curled up beside him. "She'll be okay buddy," he said as they waited for a phone call from Jonny.

CHAPTER SIXTY-EIGHT

An hour seemed like eternity. Finally, Sam's cell rang. *Please be Casey*, he thought. Instead it was Jonny. Sam answered, "What did you find out? Was her car there?"

"Whoa, Sammy, her car wasn't there. There was a red Mercedes parked beside the house in front of one of the doors of a two car garage," Jonny said.

"Were you able to look inside the garage?" Sam asked.

"I was and there weren't any other vehicles in there either. If she'd been at the house earlier, she was gone when we got there." Jonny sighed. "The lights in the house were on, so I decided to see if anyone would answer the door. I rang the bell and knocked several times, but nobody came."

"Is the Cambridge Officer still with you?" Sam was trying to figure out his next move.

"He is. We stopped at a late-night Dunkin Donuts on Eliot Street down by Harvard. I wanted to talk to you before I went home in case you wanted me to do something else while I was in the area."

"I do, but I don't know what. I have Casey's plate number. I think I'm going to call in a missing persons alert. Believe me when I tell you this is not like her." Sam got quiet. "Jonny, I don't have a good feeling about this."

"Sam, you're too far away to go crazy on me. Tell me what you want us to do and we'll do it."

"Are there any parking garages around that are open to the public at night? Or are there any malls with hidden parking spaces? I'm sure if her car was sitting by itself in the middle of a big parking lot security would check it. I don't think many of them allow overnight parking. As far as the street parking, isn't most of it by resident permit only?"

"Because of such a large student population around here, security or campus police and the Cambridge Police are always checking anything that appears out of place. Let me have Officer Brady call the precinct to see if they've received any calls about an abandoned car. He can also have his Communication Officer put something out over the radio to alert the patrol cars in the area to be on the look-out for her car. If he puts it on a certain frequency, the college security and the campus police will be party to the same information." Jonny's voice was starting to reflect a note of concern. "Sam, give me her plate number."

"It's MA plate CQ 007."

"Why don't you let me check things out on my end first before you put out the missing persons alert," Jonny said. "I'll get back to you within the hour. There're a few more avenues I want to check out." He hesitated, then continued, "Sam, are you okay with that?"

"I guess I'll have to be. I'll let you do your thing, but call me as soon as you know or don't know something. Okay?" Sam felt helpless.

"I will. Meanwhile, if you think of anything else call me right away." Jonny didn't wait for Sam to answer. He hung up and immediately asked Officer Brady to make the call to the precinct. Jonny knew Sam was a seasoned detective and he also knew he wouldn't send another cop on a wild goose chase. He felt Sam's concern and was going to do everything he could to find Casey—if she was in the area.

CHAPTER SIXTY-NINE

"Hey Brady, I know the precinct put out a call over the radio regarding Casey's car, but I'd like to do some scouting on our own. Let's take a ride around Harvard Square. Some of those bars and restaurants are open late, so if her car is there it might blend in with the rest of the cars and the patrol might not see it." Jonny shook his head. "Although, Sam said it was a light green Mazda Spider. You might think it would stand out and somebody would notice it. There's also a parking garage nearby. We should take a ride through there too. But, before we do that, I'd like to ride by the Bradshaw house again." Jonny picked up his coffee and headed toward the door. "I'm curious why somebody would leave a bunch of lights on in their house and go out."

"You don't know whether she was out or not. I know she didn't answer the door, but that doesn't mean she wasn't home," Brady said as he unlocked the cruiser and climbed in.

"You're right, but I'd still like to check it out." Jonny fastened his seat belt and suggested Brady head back to 2465 Belmont Street.

"No problem, Sarge, you're the boss," Brady said as he took a left onto Mount Auburn then another left onto JFK Street. In less than ten minutes, Brady made another turn on Belmont Street.

"Brady, slow down, shut the lights off and pull over to the curb. I believe there's a woman getting out of a Yellow Cab in front of the Bradshaw house." Jonny unfastened his seat belt and moved up close to the windshield. "We need the number of that cab and the numbers on his license plate. He'll have to drive past us, so as soon as he starts to pull away, put on your lights so I can see the plate."

“I’ll get the numbers—you be ready to write,” Brady said as he focused on the approaching cab. “It’s cab number 259 and the plate number is ABA650.” Brady turned toward Jonny. “Did you get it?”

“I did. Good job,” Jonny said. “Let’s pay Mrs. Bradshaw a visit.”

Brady rolled his eyes and pulled up in front of 2465 Belmont Street.

“Watch the master at work.” Jonny smiled.

As he had done earlier, Jonny rang the doorbell and knocked on the door. This time the door opened only as far as the security chain allowed.

“I’m Sgt. Columbo of the Boston Police Department. This is Officer Brady of the Cambridge Police Department. Are you Carol Bradshaw?” Jonny asked, at the same time showing her his official identification.

She closed the door, undid the chain, then open the door all the way. “Yes, I am Carol Bradshaw. What seems to be the problem Sargent?” she asked. “I just got home. I’ve been out most of the night, so if something has happened in the neighborhood, I know nothing about it.”

“We understand you may have had a visitor earlier in the day. Her name is Casey Quinby.” Jonny didn’t take his eyes off Carol.

“No. I don’t know anybody by that name. Why would she be coming to my house?” Carol shifted her stance from one side to the other.

“She’s investigating a case and your name and address came up.” Jonny kept his questions and statements brief. He didn’t want to give her extra time to make up answers.

“I can’t imagine why. What kind of case is it?” Carol crossed her arms and shrugged her shoulders.

“I’m not at liberty to discuss it. Where were you tonight?”

“I was down at the Square. I had a little dinner, then a couple of drinks.”

“Were you with anybody?”

“Why the questions?” Carol’s behavior was noticeably changing.

"Just routine," Jonny said. "Were you with anybody?"

"No, I didn't feel like cooking or staying home, so I went out by myself."

"What was the name of the restaurant?"

"It was the Grafton Street Pub and Grill."

"Do you always take a cab when you go out?"

"I do, if I know I'm going to have cocktails. Now, if you're finished, it's late and I'd like to go to bed." Carol closed the door with Jonny still standing on the landing.

Sgt. Columbo and Officer Brady gave each other the look, then headed back to the cruiser.

"We need to talk to the cabbie that just dropped her off. I'll have communications give the Yellow Cab dispatcher a call. Where do you want to meet him?" Officer Brady asked.

"Do they have a field office somewhere around the college?" Jonny scratched his head. "No, wait, why don't we meet the cabbie at the Dunkin's we just left. If our Mrs. Bradshaw is telling the truth, we can head over to the restaurant and talk to the hostess or the bartender." Jonny looked at Officer Brady. "I don't think time is on our side."

"Let's get going. I'll call in on the way," Officer Brady said.

CHAPTER SEVENTY

The Yellow Cab pulled up to the Dunkin's on Eliot Street the same time Officer Brady and Sgt. Columbo did. They stopped him before he went in. "Hi, I'm Officer Brady from the Cambridge PD. I believe your dispatcher told you to meet us here."

"He did. He say you want to know 'bout lady I drop off on 2465 Belmont 'bout ten minute ago."

"That's right. We want to know where you picked her up," Jonny said.

"I pick her up at JFK and Mount Auburn. I think she drinking. She throw something in a bag behind big tree beside bench." The cabbie just stood waiting for more questions.

"Have you ever seen her before?" Jonny asked.

"Oh sure, I pick her up at her house and bring her home lots of times. She go to restaurant on Massachusetts call Grafton Street Pub and Grill."

"Thanks, you've been a great help." Brady reached into his pocket and pulled out a ten dollar bill. "Here, get yourself a cup of coffee and a donut."

It was time to pay Carol Bradshaw another visit, but before they did, they checked out the cabbie's story about the bag. Sure enough, there was a bag with an empty Grey Goose vodka bottle inside. Just in case, Brady slipped it into an evidence bag and put it in the truck.

Officer Brady and Sgt. Columbo pulled up in front of 2465 Belmont Street. The inside lights were still on. They headed up the front walk the same way they had done twenty-five minutes ago and resumed the same positions on the landing, then Sgt. Columbo rang the bell and knocked on the door.

The door opened.

"Carol Bradshaw, we need you to come with us," Jonny said as she tried to close the door. "I wouldn't suggest that." He stuck his foot between the door and the jamb.

"What's your problem?" Carol asked. She was noticeably unsteady on her feet. "I'm going to file charges against you two for harassment if you don't go and leave me alone. This is a quiet, respectable neighborhood. We don't expect you cops to be nosing around here when you should be out finding criminals." She was clearly babbling.

"You can say all you want down at the station. Now, let's go," Jonny said as he reached forward to assist her.

"Leave me alone and get off my property."

"I guess this isn't going to be easy," Jonny said to Brady.

"I think you're right Sarge." He stepped to the left of Jonny and took hold of Carol's arm. It didn't take much to get her down to the landing and turn her around so Sgt. Columbo could cuff her.

"We're taking you to the station for questioning in the disappearance of Casey Quinby." Officer Brady escorted her to his cruiser and Jonny helped him get her in.

"I want my attorney," Carol yelled. "You have no right to do this to me." She kicked the backseat. "Do you hear me?"

Jonny slid and locked the window that divided the front and back seats. "When we get to the station, a coffee might do her good. Maybe if she sits and stews for a while, her memory will return. After we drop her off, we'll head back down to the corner of JFK and Mount Auburn Streets where the cabbie picked her up. Can you call and have a couple of patrol cars head to the Square. Tell them we have reason to believe Casey Quinby's car is somewhere on or around those streets. They should have the description and plate number already. We should be there within thirty minutes." Jonny looked at his watch. He took his cell phone out and called Sam.

"Jonny, have you found her?" Sam's voice was frantic.

"No, Sam, but we might have a lead. I've got a couple cars on the way to Harvard Square to search a particular area. We've picked up Carol Bradshaw and are taking her to the station for questioning. She's had plenty to drink, so we're going to leave her in the holding room for a while. I want to go down to the Square myself and help in the search." Jonny stopped as Brady pulled into the station. "Sam, we're at the station. I'll get back to you as soon as I can."

"Thanks, Jonny. I can leave now if you need me to come up there."

"Let me follow-up on this first, then we'll make a decision." Jonny hit the end button. He knew there wasn't anything he could tell Sam.

Officer Brady ushered Carol Bradshaw into the station and handed her over to the assisting officer. "Take her to a holding room. Get her some coffee. You can change her cuffs to the front, but don't take them completely off. She's a wacko. We're going back to the Square to meet with Officer Coty and Officer Simon. They're checking out a few spots before we get there," Officer Brady said. "If you need me, I'll have my radio on."

They headed out the door to Brady's waiting cruiser and radioed Coty and Simon to meet them at Dunkin's on Eliot Street in five minutes.

Brady brought his laptop into Dunkin's and pulled up a map of Harvard Square. Jonny led the discussion. The cabbie said he picked her up here on the corner of JFK and Mount Auburn. Officer Coty, why don't you check out the area west of Mount Auburn, between Dunster and JFK. Officer Simon, take the area east of Mount Auburn, between Dunster and JFK. Bradshaw said she had dinner at the Grafton Street Pub and Grill on Massachusetts Ave. Officer Brady and I are going to run down there and ask them if she was there tonight. I don't think she was. After that, we'll come back and take the other side of JFK to include Winthrop and Brattle Streets. We'll meet back here in a half hour unless one of us finds something. Give me a call right away if you do.

Jonny and Brady had just turned the corner onto Brattle Street, when Officer Cody's voice came over Brady's radio. "Sargent, I think you better come over to South Street near Dunster. I'll park my cruiser in front of the driveway and wait for you. The driveway goes in beside the building and turns to the right. It ends in a very small parking lot. There are only two cars there. One is a dark blue Impala and the other is a light green Mazda spider convertible—license plate number CQ 007.

Without hesitation Brady flipped the switches to turn on the wig-wags and lights. They weren't far from the South Street location, but he didn't want any traffic to block their route. Within minutes, Sgt. Columbo and Officer Brady bolted out of the cruiser. All four officers ran down the narrow driveway and took a right into the darkest corner of the small parking lot where Casey's car was parked.

"Don't touch anything without gloves," yelled Sgt. Columbo. He stuck his hand under the door handle and pulled, fully expecting it to be locked. It opened. The interior light came on. The car was empty—all except for a set of keys dangling from the ignition.

"Sarge, you need to come here." Brady was standing behind the car. "There's a strap hanging out of the trunk. Do you want me to pop it?"

"I can open it with one of these keys faster than you can get the jimmy from the cruiser. I'll need your flashlight though. Officer Coty already had his flashlight focused on the trunk lock. The first key didn't fit, but the second one fit and turned—it popped open.

"Call for an ambulance," Columbo shouted. "Casey, can you hear me? Casey, its Sgt. Columbo. She's unconscious. She's got a pulse, but it's very weak. Tell them to hurry. Her hands are handcuffed and her ankles are tied. Brady, give me your cuff key then get those ropes off her ankles." Jonny's cell started ringing.

"Sarge, do you want me to get that for you?" asked Officer Simon. "No, I'll check it later."

"I hear the ambulance," said Jonny. "Coty and Simon, make sure they have a clear path to pull in."

“Hey guys, over here,” yelled Brady as he motioned them to the back of Casey’s car. “We didn’t know the extent of her injuries, so all we did was remove the cuffs and ropes. We didn’t want to move her.” Jonny and Brady stepped back to let the EMTs through to do their job.

I felt myself being lifted out of the trunk and being laid on a gurney, but I was unable to move. I didn’t even have the strength to open my eyes. I tried to make a sound, but my mouth was stuck shut. I sensed myself drifting a. . . .

Jonny was sure he heard a groan. “Casey, can you hear me?” he said. “You’re going to be okay. I’m Sam’s friend from the Boston Police Department.” Her eyes were closed and she didn’t move. “Casey, hang in there. They’re going to take you to Mass General. I’ll be right behind them.”

The EMTs secured Casey in the back of the ambulance, pulled out onto South Street then screamed down Dunster to Mass Avenue. Johnny and Brady followed.

Jonny remembered that he’d gotten a call while they were tending to Casey. He pulled his cell from his pocket and pressed the contact button to see who the caller was. It was Sam. Before Jonny called Sam back, he called the Bourne State Police Barracks. There was no way he was going to let Sam make the drive to Boston himself. After a brief conversation with the night commander, Jonny hung up and called Sam.

“Sammy, it’s me. We have her. She’s going to be okay. She’s unconscious, but her vital signs are good.” Jonny didn’t want to alarm Sam with the weak pulse. “She’s being transported to Mass General as we speak. We just hit the Longfellow Bridge, so we’ll be pulling into the hospital parking lot momentarily.”

“Does it appear that she was drugged?” Sam asked as he grabbed his keys and started for the door.

“Could be. That might be why she was like a limp biscuit,” Jonny said. “Listen Sam, I’ve made arrangements for you to be transported to the hospital. There is no way you’re driving up here by yourself. I called the Bourne Barracks. A State Trooper will be waiting for you in the parking lot. He'll bring you to Mass General. Come to the main entrance on Fruit Street and I'll meet you there."

"Thanks, Jonny. I'll see you shortly." Sam's voice cracked. He couldn't talk anymore. He rubbed one hand over his face to wipe the tears from his cheeks, while he tried to steer with the other.

CHAPTER SEVENTY-ONE

Jonny was waiting in the lobby when Sam came through the door. The State Trooper was behind him.

"Thanks," Sam said to the Trooper. "I'll be fine. If we need a ride back to the Cape, I'll give you a call. Please tell Commander Lewis I'll be in touch."

Sam turned to Jonny, "Have you seen her since she got here?" he asked.

"No, she's still in emergency. They said they'd let me know as soon as I could talk to her," Jonny rested his hand on Sam's shoulder. "Why don't we wait in the ER lobby?" He pointed to a door in the back of the room. "No need to walk all the way around the building," he said. "Follow me."

"I'll fill you in on what's happened while we're waiting to see Casey."

Sam didn't say a word until they got to the ER. Jonny could tell he was emotionally drained.

He went up to the window to let the nurse know he was back. "Sammy, why don't we sit over in the corner.

"Carol Bradshaw is being held at the station. I'll be heading back there to charge her with the attempted murder of Casey. There were some interesting items in the trunk with her. We found a backpack, two purses—I'm assuming one was Casey's—and a briefcase. I'm also assuming it was hers. We're going to check them for contents and have them run for fingerprints."

"Since I'm almost positive she was involved in the murder in

Provincetown, I'd like to have Sgt. Costa and Officer Maloney of the P-town PD come up to check the contents with you." Sam was sitting on the edge of his chair trying to stay calm. "I know they get into the station around six-thirty, so I'll give them a call then. I have no doubt they'll leave to come up as soon as we hang up."

The ER doors beside the nurse's station opened and a man with a white lab coat walked toward them. "I'm Doctor Shipman," he said holding out his hand first to Sam, then to Jonny.

"I'm Sgt. Columbo from the Boston Police Department and this is Detective Summers from the Bourne PD."

"You've got one very lucky lady back there. She's awake, but very weak. I believe she was given some kind of drug. What—I don't know. We'll have to do some tests, but I'm sure she's going to be fine. I'm going to keep her overnight. I'll see how she's doing and decide whether she can go home tomorrow or should stay one more night."

"Can we go back to see her now?" Sam asked.

"Yes—follow me."

Sam and Jonny followed Doctor Shipman past at least ten ER cubbies. "Here she is," he said and moved aside to let Sam in. *She looked so helpless just lying there, hooked up to all sorts of machines*, thought Sam. He walked over beside the bed.

I felt him take my hand, then lean down and give me a gentle kiss on the cheek.

"Sherlock, can you hear me?" he whispered in my ear.

I tried to tighten my finger around his. "Sam, I'm so sorry," I said in a faint, little voice. He brushed my hair back and kissed me again.

"Watson misses you." He smiled and shook his head. "But not as much as I do."

"Detective Summers, we've got a room ready for Casey. We're going to immobilize the machines and move her up to 3492 in the East Wing. It's a private room with a recliner. You're welcome to stay the night."

"I think I will," said Sam. "Jonny, I know you have to go back to the station. I appreciate all you did for Casey. If it wasn't for you, she wouldn't be here. I'll give you a call tomorrow when I know what's going on." Sam gave Jonny a hug.

"What are friends for," he said, then thanked the Doctor and headed out to the ER parking lot where Brady was waiting.

CHAPTER SEVENTY-TWO

I felt like somebody hit me with a hundred pound weight. I knew I was in the hospital, but the 'why' is still a little fuzzy. I didn't feel like moving anything but my head. I looked one way and watched the nurses as they passed by my door, then I turned the other way only to see Sam curled up on the recliner sound asleep.

I must have dozed because the round, black and white, mini school clock beside the thirteen-inch ceiling suspended television read seven-thirty and the last time I looked at it, it was six-fifteen. I was just about to call over to Sam, when a young, round-faced black girl came in carrying two trays.

"Good morning," she said. "Sorry, if I woke you, but I've got two breakfasts—one for you and one for your guest." She set one on my bed table and the other one on the end table beside Sam. "I'll be back in a little while to see if you need anything else."

She was gone before I could try to return at least some of the cheeriness she tried to bestow on me.

I looked at Sam. I caught him trying to close his eyes—pretending he was still asleep. Then I got the smile and finally a laugh. He stood up, draped a hand towel over his arm and announced, "Breakfast is served."

"Nothing like an unplanned breakfast-in-bed to start the day," I said, and gave him my best smile. I knew I was in for a lecture, but maybe he'd wait until after we ate.

The fuzziness was starting to clear-up. The why still lingered, but I felt I was more in control than I had been a couple hours ago.

Sam planted his hands on his hips and put his 'I'm-not-kidding-look' on his face. "Sherlock, I hope these powdered scrambled eggs, well-done bacon, cold toast, warm orange juice and cup of cold English Breakfast tea, act as a reminder of what can happen when you step out of your boots and run barefoot over glass. Do you get my drift?" Sam raised his eyebrows and braced himself for a comeback.

I had none. He was right. I made him a promise, I broke it and for the second time in less than a year, he literally saved my ass. "I feel pretty good. Will I be able to go home today?" I asked, praying that the answer was yes.

"We have to wait for the doctor to come by. It's his call." Sam put the food dome back over his dish. "I've got some calls to make." He sat down beside me, took my hand, then leaned over and gave me a hug and kiss. "Here's your TV remote. Give yourself some company for a few." Sam took his cell from his pocket and headed out the door.

He could have made his calls from my room, I thought.

"Hi Sarge," said Sam. "Just want to give you an update. Our little Miss Super Sleuth went out on her own again and almost got herself killed. Her sixth sense kicked in and she was dead on. It's a long story." She's a damn good detective—better detective than a reporter. Problem is, she doesn't know her boundaries." Sam let out a sigh.

"Is that a sigh of relief, I hope." Sarge was up from his desk ready to summon Maloney to his office. "Main thing is—she's okay."

"Yeah, she is. Carol Bradshaw is being held at the Cambridge PD. Since Casey seems to be doing okay, I'm going to assume the doctor will release her probably somewhere around noon. By the way, she's at Mass General. I'll call my buddy on the Boston PD and have him pick us up and give us a ride home."

"Sam, we have to come up there anyway. It's only a little after eight. We can be there by ten-thirty. Why don't you let us drive two cars up. We'll meet you at the hospital. All of us can head on over to the Cambridge PD. Casey can make her report, Maloney and I'll transport Bradshaw back to the Cape and you can take the other cruiser."

"That would work. I'm sure Casey's car is going to be tied up for a while." Sam laughed. "Maybe it will slow her down a little."

"Here's Maloney now," said Bubba. "We're on our way."

Sam didn't even have time to say thanks.

CHAPTER SEVENTY-THREE

I only closed my eyes for a second, or so I thought. I must have fallen asleep. The next thing I knew it was eleven o'clock. I could hear familiar voices outside my door. "Hey, who's out there? Anybody I know?" I asked. A hand came around the door jamb holding a large Dunkin Donut coffee cup. Even though I couldn't smell it, I knew it was a cup of French Vanilla. "Maloney are you attached to that hand?"

"You bet I am." Maloney, Bubba and Sam walked in and surrounded me. Maloney handed me my coffee and a DVD of *Good Will Hunting.*

"Ah," I said as I took a sip. "The best medicine—right here." I nodded and took another drink. "You guys know me too well. That's scary."

"You can say that again," said Bubba. "What did you think you were doing—coming up here by yourself?"

I ignored him and held up the DVD. "Is this supposed to have a hidden meaning?" I asked.

"I want it to serve as a constant reminder of your sole trip to Boston that was almost your last." Maloney crossed his arms and just shook his head. "I could have given you a DVD of *The Departed.*"

"Very funny. Can we go over this later?" I asked. "I'm just glad to see all three of you."

"And, we're glad to see you, too," Maloney said. "I told you I'd show you girls around Boston. You didn't have to try to do it on your own."

“Speaking of girls—Sam, did you call Annie and Marnie?”

“I did and if you think you had to face the music with me, just wait until you get home. They’re going to hit you with a whole symphony. Actually, Marnie stayed at your house last night, so Watson would have company.”

“Saved by the doc,” I said as Dr. Shipman made a welcomed appearance.

“Morning Casey. It looks like you’re doing okay. I’ve checked all your tests and everything came back negative, so I guess you’re free to go.”

“I feel like I’m being released from jail, into the hands of the parole board.” I smirked and gave each one of the guys my puppy dog look. “Doc, please tell them not to be too hard on me. I could suffer a relapse. Right?” I thanked the doctor and told the guys to get out of my room so I could get dressed. I stopped at the nurse’s station, signed release papers and the ‘mod squad’ headed out to the parking lot.

Bubba turned to Sam and handed him a set of keys for the extra cruiser. “We’ll meet you at the Cambridge PD.”

“Come on Sherlock. You need to make a report and then we’re heading home.” Sam opened the cruiser door, waited until I was securely fastened in, then closed it and walked around to the driver’s side.

We got to the station and were on our way to meet Officer Brady, when out of the corner of my eye, I saw a handcuffed Carol Bradshaw being taken out of an investigation room and led down a corridor to where I assumed the holding cells were. I froze. Sam didn’t say a word. He just put his arm around me and pulled me close to him.

“It’s over,” I said. “Peter will never know the love he lost. Katherine O’Ryan died last Friday and Emily Mae Latham was born.”

EPILOGUE

"Are you almost ready?" Sam was standing in the kitchen looking at his watch. "I've already walked Watson, fixed his Kibbles and Bits and filled his water bowl and you're still in the bathroom."

I opened the bathroom door and gave him the look. "We aren't meeting Marnie, Annie and her friend, Wayne, until nine-thirty. It will only take us twenty minutes to get to Marnie's house, so cool it," I said. "I'm ready. I just have to pull my hair back and put my sneakers on."

Sam was leaning over the kitchen table reading the morning paper when I walked in. "Since we didn't have any breakfast, do you want to grab something at Dunkins?" he asked.

"I could handle that," I said as I grabbed my jacket and purse. Watson gave me the sad eyes, so I put everything down on the table and gave him a hug. "He's one of the best things to come into my life this year."

Sam bent down and put one arm around me and the other around Watson. "If only he could talk, then my mission to infiltrate your world would be complete." He laughed.

"Today is going to be a little hard for me. It was exactly a month ago that Marnie, Annie, and I ventured down to P-town for a day of shopping, eating and doing whatever we wanted to do."

"The big difference is, this time I'm going with you and the girls. And, we're going to do all of those things, then meet Maloney, Bubba and his wife at the Lobster Pot." He smiled and kissed me on the cheek. "I'm really looking forward to it. What time a the reservations for?" Sam asked.

"Bubba said he made them for six o'clock. Hopefully, we'll be able to grab a cup of chowder at Charlie's deli before dinner. It's unbelievably good."

****

Three weeks had passed since my episode with Carol Bradshaw. I was fortunate the drug she gave to Emily didn't have the same lethal effect on me. Carol was taken into custody and booked for the murder of Emily Mae Latham and the attempted murder of yours truly. This one was too close for comfort.

Peter had been transported to the Barnstable Country House of Correction from the P-town PD to await a court appearance to charge him with Emily's death. It never happened and he was released two days after he'd been booked. I stopped to see him before he left for Boston. It will take a long time before he gets his life back together. He thanked me for believing he wasn't guilty. At the time, I really wasn't sure if he was or wasn't, but I did have some reasonable doubt. It's always that reasonable doubt that gets me in trouble.

A couple of good things came out of this mess. One was Marnie and Maloney are somewhat of an item. And, the other is Sam's got me thinking about a career change. Keep in mind, I'm only thinking.

What I do know is—my next involvement with one of the Cape Cod Police Departments will be to work on a cold case. At least that's my direction for now, but then who knows what the future will bring….

Made in the USA
Charleston, SC
02 October 2013